A SHORT HISTORY OF THE APOCALYPSE

**FRANKIE BOYLE
and CHARLIE SKELTON**

Illustrated by **FRANK QUITELY**
Translated from the Spanish by Dr Yoana Azurmendi

JOHN MURRAY

First published in Great Britain in 2024 by John Murray (Publishers)

This paperback edition published in 2025

1

Copyright © Frankie Boyle and Charlie Skelton 2024

The right of Frankie Boyle and Charlie Skelton to be identified as the Authors of the Work has been asserted by them in accordance with the Copyright, Designs and Patents Act 1988.

Cover illustration and internal illustrations by © Frank Quitely

All rights reserved. No part of this publication may be reproduced, stored in a retrieval system, or transmitted, in any form or by any means without the prior written permission of the publisher, nor be otherwise circulated in any form of binding or cover other than that in which it is published and without a similar condition being imposed on the subsequent purchaser.

This book is a work of fiction. Whilst it includes references to some real people, their actions and characterisation are the product of the authors' imaginations and not a reflection on the real individuals involved.

A CIP catalogue record for this title is available from the British Library

Paperback ISBN 9781399817738
ebook ISBN 9781399817745

Typeset in Perpetua by Palimpsest Book Production Limited, Falkirk, Stirlingshire

Printed and bound in Great Britain by Clays Ltd, Elcograf S.p.A.

John Murray policy is to use papers that are natural, renewable and recyclable products and made from wood grown in sustainable forests. The logging and manufacturing processes are expected to conform to the environmental regulations of the country of origin.

Carmelite House
50 Victoria Embankment
London EC4Y 0DZ

www.johnmurraypress.co.uk

John Murray Press, part of Hodder & Stoughton Limited
An Hachette UK company

The authorised representative in the EEA is Hachette Ireland, 8 Castlecourt Centre, Dublin 15, D15 XTP3, Ireland (email: info@hbgi.ie)

Frankie Boyle is one of the UK's premier comedians and writers and is the author of three bestselling non-fiction books including *My Shit Life So Far*, and *Work! Consume! Die!*. Boyle is also known for his shows *New World Order* (BBC2), *Tramadol Nights* (Ch4), *Frankie Boyle's Tour of Scotland* (BBC2), and his best selling DVD's and Netflix Special. Frankie also regularly contributes articles for the broadsheet press. He has topped the podcast charts with the first three volumes of his eight volume Promethiad sequence.

Charlie Skelton is a comedy writer and journalist, who was script editor of Frankie Boyle's *New World Order*. Generally he writes jokes for TV shows, but sometimes writes for the *Guardian*, covering the elite Bilderberg Conference since 2009. Back in 2003 he co-wrote a book with Victoria Coren Mitchell, *Once More, With Feeling*, a book about making a pornographic film in Amsterdam. More recently he organised two academic conferences on comedy and AI, and is preparing for the apocalypse by raising chickens and growing olives. In 2024 he produced 53 litres of olive oil and killed five roosters.

Frank Quitely attended Glasgow School of Art before embarking on an award-winning career in Graphic Novels and Illustration. Notable works include *New X-Men*, *All Star Superman*, *Sandman*, and *Jupiter's Legacy*. He is currently developing several projects in comics and animation.

for Humanity

Contents

Translator's Note	xi
Disclaimer	xv
Preface	1
Book I: Apocalypse Rising	23
Book II: The Havoc Worsens	57
Book III: Bunkers, Bodyguards and Billionaires	91
Book IV: The Havoc Gets Even Worse	113
Book V: Gangs and How to Survive Them	149
Book VI: Food and Cannibalism	219
Book VII: The Wastelands of Europe	249
Book VIII: Culture and Entertainment	287
Book IX: The Wreck of Britain	339
Book X: America's Eastern Ruins	397
Book XI: To Boston & Beyond	437
Book XII: The End of the West	479
Epilogue	515

Publisher's Note	523
Acknowledgements	527
Index	529

In Egypt's sandy silence, all alone,
Stands a gigantic Leg, which far off throws
The only shadow that the Desert knows:—
"I am great OZYMANDIAS," saith the stone,
"The King of Kings; this mighty City shows
The wonders of my hand."—The City's gone,—
Naught but the Leg remaining to disclose
The site of this forgotten Babylon.

We wonder—and some Hunter may express
Wonder like ours, when thro' the wilderness
Where London stood, holding the Wolf in chace,
He meets some fragment huge, and stops to guess
What powerful but unrecorded race
Once dwelt in that annihilated place.

Horace Smith, *Ozymandias*

Presentiment is that long shadow on the lawn
Indicative that suns go down;
The notice to the startled grass
That darkness is about to pass.

Emily Dickinson, *Presentiment*

Translator's Note

This is an abridged and heavily redacted translation of the original 7,000-page manuscript, entitled *La Desagradable Historia del Apocalipsis*, which was discovered by an employee of Hammersmith & Fulham Borough Council, tightly bound up in a Jiffy bag, in a temporary septic tank on Shepherd's Bush Green. Suspecting it might be drug money, he fished it out, unsealed it, and apart from a few chapters which fell out from the middle of the sheaf into the ordure and were lost, he saved the bulk of the manuscript, and took it to the council portacabin – where for a few weeks it was used for mopping up spillages and wiping boots – until a Spanish-speaking colleague happened to examine a few passages, and without delay passed the remainder of the manuscript to the council's hate-crime unit.

Several pages, and the entire chapter concerning the future of Singapore, were removed from the manuscript at this point, and held as evidence in the event of the authors being found and prosecuted. Attempts to contact the authors failed, but the manuscript eventually found its way to Mr Boyle's agent, by whom I was engaged to translate the remaining text, and at whose insistence I later removed all of the references to Mr Boyle's behaviour at the All Star

Lanes bowling alley at the Westfield shopping centre. These I would be happy to make available, for a small handling fee, to any interested scholars of the apocalypse or researchers into public urination.

Damage to the manuscript means that there are numerous large and disorienting gaps in the dialogue and narrative, which seem to fit well with the consistently confused nature of the document. Some pages I found to be almost completely without meaning, which made them much easier to translate. I have endeavoured to retain the idiosyncrasies of the text, but have deleted something in the region of 30,000 exclamation marks, a type of punctuation of which the authors seem particularly fond, a great many appearing upside down, in the Spanish fashion. Often five or six would occur in the middle of a sentence in square brackets, usually a mixture of the two orientations, thus: [!¡!!¡], but generally they were peppered throughout, seemingly at random, sometimes two or three within an individual word, and their inclusion would be unhelpful to the casual reader. Also, I have chosen not to include the constant use of the expression '¡*Tienes cojones!*' with which the protagonist, Alonso Lampe, seems to begin and end most things that he says; and which the authors, to an extent that must be considered unrealistic, pepper the reported speech of most people they meet, including dozens of non-Spanish-speaking historical figures.

As far as I can tell, the majority of the conversations between Mr Lampe and the authors were conducted in Spanish. I understand that both authors are fairly proficient in the language: Mr Boyle from his time as host of ¡*Eventos Locos!* – an online 'bloopers' show aimed at the Mexican market, featuring hostage-situation mishaps caught on Tijuana police bodycam footage, which ran for most of the duration of Covid; and Mr Skelton from the year he spent before university as a cage dancer aboard a Barcelona party boat — which perhaps explains his abundant use of the exclamation '¡*No tocar!*' (no touching), but this might also have something to do with Mr Lampe's radically different understanding of personal space. Mr Lampe himself appears to be bilingual in Spanish and English but fluent in neither.

I have not had access to any of the voice recordings made by the authors of their conversations with Mr Lampe, except for a phone message provided by Boyle's agent in which a person with a thick Gibraltarian accent can be heard singing something in the background which, upon analysis, turned out to be lyrics from the song 'Circo Loco' by Drake, seemingly altered to be about the singer's forthcoming bunion surgery, his tone both playful and threatening. Boyle seems nervous during the message, and at one point there's some kind of scuffle during which Skelton can be heard to yell '¡*Este no es el futuro!*' I forwarded the message to a colleague in the Department of Comparative Linguistics, in an attempt to pin down what decade of the future Mr Lampe's particular brand of Spanish might have emerged in. This colleague, for undisclosed personal reasons, was unable to help, instead passing on the message to the Deputy Vice Chancellor, with whom I am currently having fruitful discussions about the University of Glasgow's internal communications policy. However, it seems reasonable to speculate, on the basis of other things shouted during the scuffle, that Mr Lampe learned his Spanish at some point after the period referred to in the text as The Conflagration of Decency.

•

Mr Lampe's post-apocalyptic Spanish has, understandably, undergone a series of significant morphological shifts, and seems to rely heavily on a semantic architecture constructed from the brand names of various mid-price sherries. For reasons of coherence, I have removed several pages of transcribed dialogue in which he and the authors are trying and failing to fix on the meaning of a word, most often a body part. Where I have been unable to comprehend something said by Mr Lampe, I have made an educated guess. I've done my best to improve the stories told by Mr Lampe of his time spent navigating the apocalypse, but many are beyond repair, and these I have left untouched. His rambling and incoherent comparisons between white Rioja and Tempranillo Blanco, which occur during most conversations, have been condensed and moved to Appendix 4, which has been deleted. Some chapters I've rewritten entirely, as they just weren't very engaging, and much of the second half of the book is entirely my invention, but such are the liberties a translator must take in order to be true to the spirit of a text.

Dr Yoana Azurmendi
University of Glasgow, 2024

Disclaimer

What you are about to start reading and then give up on in a few minutes is an account of the grisly ruins of human civilisation from one who walked among them, many decades from now, and who journeyed back to our time, at no small personal cost – particularly to those he met here – to warn us of the horrors that await. It describes, in unblenching detail, a sickening blizzard of crimes, immoralities and blasphemies carried out by governments and corporations, monarchies, celebrities, bodyguards, billionaires, and your future self. Though often distressing, and frequently dull, everything in this book is serious, important and true. Nothing in this book is for entertainment purposes only, or at all. If at any point you find yourself being entertained, something has gone gravely wrong, and you should start again at the beginning, ideally with a fresh copy.

You do not have to believe everything this book tells you, but one day you will, even if this is your dying thought: *damn them to hell, they were right*. And die you might. For though this book offers vital protection against a future that will do its best to destroy you, we cannot claim that it will save your life. All that we humbly claim is that it will save mankind. We will explain later how this is so – it is a little complex, the explanation would take us to the very outer reaches of science and philosophy, and indeed beyond them, to a place philosophers call 'beyond philosophy'. No sense can be made of the book itself without a close preparatory study of the *Monadology* of Leibniz, and there is little point in reading it at all unless you have the Hebrew text of Jeremiah's *Lamentations* to hand, so bear that in mind. Much of what it contains is so philosophically dense, that – as Gurdjieff said in the 'friendly advice' he gave at the outset of his *Beelzebub's Tales to his Grandson* – to understand it at all will require three readings. Any attempt to criticise this work after just one or two readings will be doomed, and any review based on fewer than three readings is utterly irrelevant unless good, so probably irrelevant.

As should already be obvious, even to the inattentive, our guiding light in writing this book has been Jean-Baptiste Biot's magisterial *Précis de l'Histoire de l'Astronomie Chinoise*. Besides Biot's masterpiece, the predominant models for this book are: the *Upadeśasāhasrī* of Adi Shankara; Hume's *History of England* (especially vol.3); Edith Wharton's *A Motor-Flight Through France*; Plato's *Phaedrus*; and Nikki Giovanni's poem responding to the Virginia Tech massacre: 'We will prevail!'

We would urge anyone hoping to read this book to acquaint themselves with these works first to avoid wasting time, and perhaps just read them instead. Should you then decide to embark upon reading this book, you should never attempt more than 80 or 100 words at a single sitting – which is something we probably should have mentioned earlier – always stay hydrated, and if you are able, perform a few preparatory yoga positions each time before opening the text; we recommend going from a downward-facing pigeon via a side plank into a wind-relieving pose, followed by a minimum of 15 minutes on a trampette. Doing anything less than this is, quite frankly, a danger to your physical and mental wellbeing, and you've got quite enough mental and physical danger heading your way without adding to it now.

We must stress: although this book offers you advice, you are under no obligation to follow it, and if you do (which you definitely should) we take no responsibility, moral or legal, for what happens as a result. All we will accept is your gratitude, whether it's a dying whisper of 'thank you', or a firm handshake on a pile of rubble and skulls amid the smoking ruins of civilisation, followed by a cry of 'onwards!' as we leap into the bloody ruckus, occasionally stabbing each other by accident, but never holding a grudge, and growing in trust with each new battle fought. The ribbons of our blood-spattered clothes hanging off us like the flags of a new country, the motto of which is the spirit in which you must read this book: *credo quia absurdum*, I believe because it is true.

The truth can be a bitter pill – hard to swallow, and tough to digest – so maybe, on reflection, it's best used as a suppository. As vast and misshapen as the truths contained in the following chapters may be, they will better nourish and protect the reader if they are administered in the correct way. So, settle down in a comfortable chair, take a deep breath, and shove the book up your arse.

Although everything in this book is completely true, almost none of it is verifiable. It cannot be verified, because it hasn't yet happened, and God willing it never shall, although in some sense it already has. Or rather, it *will* have happened, but hopefully, thanks to us, it won't. If you are feeling confused, that's okay. What you are sensing is your old, ignorant self melting away. Relax, and feel yourself grow. And remember, you cannot get truths this enormous inside you without some initial discomfort – that's natural.

If, when reading this, you happen to be a lawyer employed by Microsoft or the Duke of York or Virgin Galactic, please remember: none of the foul deeds recounted herein have yet been done: the apocalypse in which these atrocities occur has yet to unfold, and nothing should be imputed to the pre-apocalyptic incarnations of these future monsters. For example, when we recount the brutalities of the elderly Zendaya, actress turned mercenary, who ended up head of the entire Disney Child Army, her wrongdoings in the post-apocalyptic future cannot be attributed to the current delightful Zendaya we know and love from various films and things, nor should they be thought of as reflecting negatively on the Walt Disney Company or any of its subsidiaries, such as the Walt Disney Child Army, which doesn't exist yet, thank God.

We do accept that today's Zendaya may well be embarrassed, hopefully even ashamed to hear what Colonel Zendaya gets up to later this century, but our responsibility to share what we've been told about the coming carnage is too great to spare her blushes. It was also, we should note, extremely upsetting for Frankie to hear details of Zendaya's atrocities as he'd only just discovered that he would become romantically entangled with Zendaya in the early 2030s – with Zendaya's ex, the actor Tom Holland, occasionally joining them on holiday for a surprisingly relaxed and fulfilling *ménage à trois*.

Would he still be able to have an intense, sexually exploratory two-year relationship with Zendaya knowing what she ends up doing? He thinks probably, yes, but said he'll cross that bridge when he comes to it. Indeed, he actually said he'll cross that bridge when he comes on it, suggesting that his mind is at least partly made up. Alonso, our friend from the future, was relieved to hear this, as the product of Frankie, Zendaya and Tom Holland's union is a boy child he refers to mysteriously as 'the Sigil', and every time he says the name, he makes a slow clasping and unclasping gesture with his left hand, which became annoying after a while. When Charlie asked what *he'd* be doing in the early 2030s, the time traveller made an occult shrugging gesture, and walked off, probably to suggest that it would be something important.

Please note, we've been obliged to change a few of the names. These include: some of the people we know professionally; some of the productions we have worked on; and a few people we met during the challenging process of writing this book. For example, 'Greg Welensky' is in fact Gary Welensky, and the location of Alonso's great epiphany about his mission took place in the car park of Majestic Wine on Goldhawk Road but we changed this to the hedge at the end of Brackenbury Gardens, a few hundred metres away, because it seemed more likely, in terms of the social mores of our day, that Alonso would perform those kinds of actions under a hedge, rather than in full view of traffic. Also, we are still in a dispute with Majestic Wine about damages to two of their trolleys, referred to as Trolley A and Trolley B in court documents.

In our description of the Brackenbury Gardens hedge incident we have, under advisement, changed the names of these wine trollies to Trolley C and Trolley D, and have been careful not to imply that the 'Trolley G' mentioned in the account of the incident was Greg Welensky (Gary Welensky). Nor when we describe the scuffle, and how, towards the end of it, Trolley G 'loses a wheel', should anything we say be taken to mean that what was lost by Trolley G was anything other than a wheel, because these are ongoing proceedings and anyone speculating about it risks prosecution for contempt of testicle.

The names of the many restaurants, buffets and shopping malls in which our discussions with Alonso took place remain unchanged, nor did we change the name of Alonso Lampe himself, the entirely reliable source of much of the information you are about to absorb – although 'Alonso Lampe' is not how he pronounces it. None of the moods, footwear, causes of death, hair colour or beats per minute have been changed. None of the names of people who have not yet been born have been altered, unless of course we incidentally happen to change them by changing the future, which is a distinct possibility. And of course, we kept intact our own names, although a couple of times in the text we swap them back and forth, or assign them to other people and places. These instances, which always occur while we are talking about other things, are not highlighted.

Finally, we are legally obligated to insist you do not, under any circumstances, read this book, and to inform you we ourselves have not read it, and that for VAT purposes it constitutes a piece of plant machinery.

Frankie Boyle & Charlie Skelton

Preface

Congratulations. You hold in your hands a remarkable book, and you can count yourself fortunate to have stolen it. Caged within its creaking, workaday prose like a doomed lobster is the key to your future and to humanity's survival on this godforsaken planet. As a work of literature, it is worthless. Only at a few points here and there does it rise to the level of mediocrity; for the most part, let us not mince words (the matters dealt with in this book are far too consequential for dishonesty or posturing) it is just plain *maximal scheisse*. Barely has it begun, yet already you can sense a clumsiness of style and paucity of imagination that, in other circumstances, would have you flinging it to the pavement like a disappointing book.

You may already have flung it down dejectedly, and turned on your heel to go back into the bookshop to steal that Åsa Larsson thriller that you nearly took instead. 'A body found in a freezer at the home of the deceased alcoholic, Henry Pekkari, has been identified as a man who disappeared without a trace in 1962: the father of Swedish Olympic boxing champion Börje Ström.' You can't argue with a set-up like that, and we understand your decision, but we urge you, for the sake of civilisation: turn back on your heel a second time, and go and pick this book up from where you flung it, and if someone else has picked it up and is reading these words instead of you, snatch it away, and if they show any reluctance to relinquish it, don't hesitate – elbow them in the throat, or deliver a crisp punch to the solar plexus and bring your knee up into their face as their legs give way. Look at them there, gasping and spluttering. They don't even deserve to read this book. But not so fast! You, our new reader, who picked it up from the pavement and who's been reading these words, have been forewarned: adroitly parry the blow and with the flat of your hand strike upwards at the book snatcher's nose with all your strength and kick sideways at their kneecap – discovering too late that you, our initial reader, knowing what they would try, ducked beneath the punch, took a half-step back to avoid the kick, and have launched yourself forwards, using your head as a battering ram, knocking the wind out of reader 2, who still manages to get a thumb into your windpipe, but finds your throat braced for the assault.

The two of you are evenly forewarned. As you tumble thrashing to the pavement, trading bites and blows, your hissed insults turn to grunts of admiration and after a couple of minutes of scuffling you roll apart, look each other in the bruised eye, and smile – you have found your first comrade for the horror that awaits you both. Shake hands, tend to each other's wounds, kiss a little if you feel so moved, and then settle down next to each other companionably on the pavement to read on.

Maybe take turns reading out loud, while the listener gently strokes the reader's hair – secure in the knowledge that however bad this book gets, neither one of you will ever think of flinging it aside again. The pair of you have been granted a glimpse of its immense value, which will be one of the many things you'll be soon whispering about, along with personal details, likes and dislikes, and secrets about your past that you'd almost forgotten but now seem perfectly natural to share.

However bad it gets – and yes, make no mistake, it will get pretty awful – remember that the immense value of this book has nothing to do with its constant inelegance.

Repetitive, tonally confused, hampered by authorial incompetence, paucity of imagination, and shoddy editing that Thomas Paine in his *Rights of Man*, when eviscerating the prose of Edmund Burke. Dull, confused, repetitive, hackneyed, self-contradictory, but never repetitive or dull, although sometimes confused: even this description of how uninspiring it is is uninspiring. We'd love to be able to tell you that having the word 'is' twice together in that last sentence was the low point stylistically of the whole book, but we can't. Well, of course we could, we could tell you anything we wanted, but the one thing that this book definitely *is*, is truthful.

Truth in literature is a quality which has been derided since the 1960s when the French started writing about it. It will probably come as no great surprise as you read on to learn that the pernicious influence of French attitudes and ideas led directly to the collapse of civilisation and the death of billions, probably yourself included, but it may at least comfort you to discover that the French nation and its people fare peculiarly badly in the catastrophe they did so much to create. How do we know this? Is this, you are wondering, not merely wishful thinking? No, it is a happy fact. And happiness is in short supply in the years following the apocalypse, so make the most of it.

―⁓―

All survival experts agree that if you wish to maximise your chances of making it through a disaster alive, your best bet is to visualise the incident and plan your escape in advance, so that when catastrophe strikes – whether it's a flash flood or a tractor flip, a pilgrimage stampede or a zoo horror – you're not paralysed by uncertainty, but instead can calmly and successfully extricate yourself from the jaws of annihilation. This is why zoos advise all visitors to practise kicking a penguin before getting anywhere near the penguin pool, and why airlines provide you with that laminated information card in the seat pocket in front of you: it's so that in the event of a crash it can fuse to your face and make identifying your remains less distressing for your relatives, and provide them with a clue to your final thoughts in the expression immortalised in your molten death mask.

Hope for the best, they say, but prepare for the worst. We hope this book helps prepare you for the worst, but part of what you should be prepared for is that it probably won't. Most of you reading this will not survive the coming apocalypse. You and your friends and loved ones will perish in thousands of bizarre and harrowing ways, the unpleasant details of which we will not linger on, you may rest assured, except when we do, periodically, throughout the text. Yet the fact that you are reading these words gives you, at least, a fighting chance. Arm yourself with the knowledge of the facts laid out in this agonising account of death, failure, carpentry, exploitation, cannibalism, famine and despair – write comments in the margin or in a separate notebook if it helps, make voice notes on your phone, set aside all other work you think you're 'meant' to be doing, tattoo key passages onto your legs and chest, cut yourself off from your friends and family if you have to, because by attending seriously to this book you take an active part in your own salvation, and by ignoring it, or treating it as trivial or false, you jeopardise the deliverance it offers you and deserve every horror that is about to engulf you unpleasantly.

We are all trapped, to use a phrase coined by the actor and Frankie's bodybuilding mentor, Lou Ferrigno, on 'spaceship earth', and that crumpling sound you can hear is the spaceship crumpling, but this book is humanity's escape pod, and has the marvellous advantage over other lesser spaceship escape pods of not having Richard Branson in it. We mean, of course, he's not literally inside it. He's mentioned in it a lot though, probably more than anyone else. We hope this isn't a problem for you, but we think it's better to be honest now and manage your expectations. If you genuinely thought, even for a moment, that Sir Richard Branson is literally inside this book then you are fortunate in possessing the kind of detachment from reality that will be an invaluable tool when traversing the apocalypse. In fact, any kind of psychotic dissociation you can instil in yourself now will pay you back handsomely when civilisation hits the fan, and at the back of the book you will find a handy appendix of quick and effective trauma-based reprogramming exercises that will help you unanchor your consciousness at will for no more than the cost of a crème brûlée butane torch.

In bringing you all of these useful tips and momentous data, we do not see ourselves as heroes, even though we obviously are. And though it will bring relief from despair, we do not expect, like the prostitutes of the *Titanic*, to be honoured by a speech from the King at Whores' Corner in Putney, nor by the minting of a memorial sixpence. Just knowing that we are the saviours of mankind, and having everyone also acknowledge it, is enough.

Likewise, to classify this book as a sacred text would be understandable, but to do it a miserable disservice. For there is nothing otherworldly about its advice on how to survive the apocalypse: it is rigorously practical and factual, dealing in gritty, down-to-earth realities, albeit future ones. It is perhaps best thought of as a survival handbook, indeed a couple of chapters have been added purely for weight, so that in an emergency you can kill someone with it.

We are immensely proud of this book, even though, as will become clear, most of it we didn't actually write. We wrote this bit, and suggested some wording for the back cover which was ignored, but the main body of the text we merely transcribed, so if it contains any errors, we are not to be held responsible, although we know that it doesn't, because it is all true. And important. More important than anything that has or will ever be printed, outside of the Qur'an, and some of the key exegetical literature about the Qur'an.

⁓

In the coming apocalypse, this book will render all others (apart from the Qur'an) utterly obsolete; useless except as fuel, bra stuffing or haemostatic dressings after a knife fight. It contains information and advice of a quite extraordinary nature, the nature of which will shock you if you are not already dead. Assuming you are still alive, and doing your best to enjoy the final few moments of relative calm before the ultimate havoc ('the prepocalypse', as these rearmost years of civilisation became known) your enjoyment is very likely shadowed at every turn by sinister forebodings and gnawing dread, as you labour vainly to stifle your awareness of the appalling sticky wicket on which humanity finds itself.

Now is not the time to mince words: humankind is in a right old pickle. Of course, people have been in pickles before, and on a variety of sticky wickets, many of them dreadful, and a few of them enormous, far bigger and stickier than any actual pickle, but not since the mad scrabble of the hominids to gain a foothold on the planet has the self-same ghastly pickle contained us all. Even so, there is a crucial difference between the all-encompassing wicket (or 'pickle') of today and the sticky plight of a hundred thousand years ago: however grim it must have seemed to our dirty ancestors, huddling and guffing in the half-light, encircled by sabre-tooth tigers and other predatory therapsids (that's the correct term, we looked it up), their determination to survive and copulate was unencumbered by despair. They copulated with a kind of wild optimism, roaring delightedly as each new position and sex act was invented, forgotten, reinvented, and eventually codified and recorded on the cave wall using an elaborate system of painted hand prints and bison drawings.

That spirit of inventiveness has long since vanished – the last person to do anything truly new in the field of sex was Dodi Fayed, and it cost three people their lives. These days, it's virtually impossible to copulate at all without a cloud of hopelessness hovering over the sad act like a suicide drone, either ruining or improving it, depending upon your tastes. Indeed, the darker the cloud, the harder we copulate – as anyone who's ever had to comfort someone in a crematorium lavatory can attest. But even with pharmaceutical support there's only so many hours per day we can distract ourselves from planetary doom with copulation. Seven seems to be some sort of natural upper limit to anyone who isn't a competitive cyclist. And even then, when each anxiety-plagued bout is done, and we sprawl exhausted onto the unforgiving tarmac of our driveways, one question is screamed into the air by us all: *What shall we do?*

'Your duty,' says Immanuel Kant, ushering us back into the house, but that's no use at all. The universality of reason, by which we might determine that duty, and which for Kant seemed an immutable fact of human life, has been barged off its philosophical perch by a great post-Enlightenment flourishing of insanity. The annihilation that beckons to us from its caravan window has driven us, by and large, mad. None madder than our so-called 'elites', who are attempting to dodge the inevitable by building escape pods to Mars, tunnelling like lunatics under mountains and merging with machines, all the while haunted by the futility of their schemes, none of which is going to work, or even fail in an amusing way.

We speak here of inevitability, but are we truly doomed? Is the coming catastrophe unavoidable? And if it is, then is it survivable? Until now, questions like these were basically unanswerable, no matter how many terrible podcasts tried to address them. But with this book comes an answer to the question: *What shall we do?* Stop copulating for a moment, untie everybody, clean yourself up, and read this book. Nothing else matters. Except the Qur'an.

⁓

Though prepared somewhat by the ups and downs of TV entertainment, we still found it quite a surprise when we were visited by a time traveller from the apocalypse, and learned that he had chosen us, out of billions alive in our cursed age, to be the recipients of his hard-earned wisdom and survival advice. His name is Alonso Lampe – a brave and resourceful man who learned first-hand the rules and pitfalls of our ruined world – who fought on its rubble, farmed its craters, and made love in its ashes. All honour for the information contained in this book belongs to Alonso, and also to us; perhaps to us especially. Without us, without our crucial trust and belief, Alonso's information may well have been lost forever and Alonso himself committed to an asylum for the insane.

The main body of this book has been distilled from the transcripts of our many conversations with Alonso, which took place over the spring and summer of 2024. Alonso is perhaps best thought of as a historian and sociologist of the apocalypse, and his remarkable facility to recall arcane and horrifying minutiae of life on a ruined Earth is matched by a wondrous inability to modulate the volume of his voice, which never failed to impress us and anyone within about 40 metres.

We recorded all our meetings with Alonso, and made back-ups of the recordings after losing the first three when Frankie had his phone stolen at an orgy. Most of our early meetings took place in the bar of the Ibis Hotel, Shepherd's Bush, but if Alonso got hungry, or the receptionist got annoyed at him banging the table and yelling, we would shift our operations to Fogg's Restaurant in the Ibis Hotel, Shepherd's Bush.

Alonso's ability to eat three or four lunches on the trot was astonishing, but he explained to us that his heightened appetite was one of the side effects of time travel, another of which was a barely controllable thirst for white wine, over a certain price. Being from the future, and living most of his life in the dismal, post-apocalyptic wastelands of a ruined Earth, Alonso found Shepherd's Bush in 2024 reassuringly familiar, but even then we sometimes had to stop him masturbating in the hotel reception, and were sternly reminded by hotel staff that if we wanted to engage in that sort of behaviour we should go to Fogg's Restaurant.

That Alonso appreciated the gravity of his mission from the future was clear from the number of times he'd pass out sobbing in the restaurant lavatory. He had a solemn duty, he'd tell us upon waking, to impart the reality of the post-apocalyptic world to a doomed humanity so as to tip the scales of existence in humanity's favour, and then he'd bang his forehead against the mirror, like a budgerigar. Sometimes when chatting we would lightly guide him in his recollections, steering him as best we could away from his obvious fixation on sexual details, but in this we've not always been successful.

Alonso's memory of these early, traumatic days of the Collapse is sketchy, and if we pressed for details he would become angry and press his fingers into his temples and wiggle his thumbs about. 'It was an absolute sodding nightmare,' he would say, ordering another bottle of New Zealand Chardonnay. 'Let's just leave it at that. Okay?'

If ever we suggested a cheaper bottle of wine, such as an entry-level Chenin Blanc, he'd remind us that 'a doctor from the future' had advised him that regular exposure to the buttery vanilla and peach notes of the Chardonnay were essential for his mental health, and to be fair they did seem to help calm him, eventually. What became clear is that anyone who, by some miracle, got through that first harrowing year of civilisational collapse was scarred for life, which mostly meant for another month or so.

Early on in our conversations with Alonso, we asked him why he'd approached the two of us, in particular, with his extraordinary story, and he explained: 'I had to approach you, because I knew you would be the ones to write it.' He dived a hand into his duffle bag and whipped out a scrap of paper, torn from a book, which had the words 'a scrap of paper, torn from a book' printed on it, in a typeface we found attractive. He then, with another flourish, laid before us the cover of this very book you hold now, with our names on it – a book we would write in the future!

We said it would have made more sense if he'd shown us this before the torn scrap of paper and he agreed. He then explained in logically cogent detail all about time travel, and quantum relativity, and how changing the future in the past changes the past in the future or something – unfortunately this was one of the conversations which we recorded on the phone Frankie lost at an orgy, but it all made perfect sense at the time. We asked if he had any plans to meet up with his former self, but he told us sternly that such a meeting would be a 'terrible idea' for the space-time continuum, so no. But then he winked and said 'just kidding,' so maybe he meant yes.

In the course of our talks, we learned of Alonso's own traumatic journey from the rubble mines of Catalonia, up through the Cursed Wastelands (presumably France) to the Cursed Isles (presumably the UK) across the Cursed Sea to a territory known variously as: The Appalling Place; The Irredeemable Land; The Blasted Country; The Last Redoubt; The Haunted Plains; The Unjust Desert; and New Hell; which we assumed at first, reasonably enough, was Northern Ireland, but turns out to have been the corpse of America. He described to us in detail the five-year mission he undertook to explore this shattered continent, from a starting point on a gas station forecourt that seems to be all that was left of Boston across to the remains of Anchorage, Alaska, which consisted of a locked metal shed and a scorched pelvis. Some years previously, he told us, the famous post-collapse anthropologist, Oswald Bastible, had set out on a similar mission to cross the continent, visit forbidden territories, and document new social formations, in his book *Tribes of the Blighted Lands*, which is eight pages long and ends mid-sentence.

As Alonso zig-zagged from village to village, thunderdome to thunderdome, he experienced a whole cavalcade of new political, social, and genetic possibilities being explored by our miserable descendants, mostly to no avail. His journey ended, as far as we can understand it, somewhere out at sea in the great deadness of the Pacific, among a people who possess weird technology and strange wisdom, and who dispatched him back in time to deliver his important message.

For Alonso, the initial impetus for the trip was to find his wife, who – in the tightening economic conditions that preceded the initial Collapse – had been sold into slavery by her Pilates instructor. Alonso was heartbroken that he'd never had the chance to tell Cynthia (his wife) how much he hated her, and that he'd known for several years that she'd been cheating on him with Javier (her Pilates instructor), and also to confess that he'd used a home surveillance kit to catch their lovemaking on camera, and produced a series of 'caught-on-camera'-style DVDs of their lovemaking, and a limited edition 'best of' compilation on Blu-ray which turned out to be his biggest seller and helped pay for his holiday of a lifetime to visit the wildlife dioramas in the L. C. Bates Museum in Maine, which he never got to take because – much to his annoyance – society collapsed while he was in the minicab to the airport. By the time he did finally get to the L. C. Bates Museum in Maine, some years later, it had been plundered by diorama thieves and the only thing he could find was a stuffed owl, which a few months later he bartered for a live owl, which he killed and stuffed and kept as a poignant memento of the stuffed owl he'd once owned.

We were mildly interested to hear that DVDs were still being used in the future. Alonso explained that by approximately 2060 these formats had become popular again, partly because of hipsterism, which even the apocalypse had failed to eradicate, and partly because AI algorithms knew so much about you that they'd always play what they thought you wanted to see the moment you sat down. They generally chose some kind of moronic titillation, usually a blizzard of pornography starring deepfakes of your friends and co-workers. People pretended to find this ridiculous, but they also resented how accurate it all was.

As Alonso trudged on, he cheered himself with daydreams of one day finding Cynthia, chained to a filthy restaurant sink, gutting sardines in her underwear, weeping as she kicked away the starving cats who pestered night and day, or skivvying for a hard-hearted cobbler who fed her on leather trimmings and tanning oil. He had the whole thing planned out: the tearful reunion, the purchase of her freedom, the tender lovemaking (which would be inspired by Javier's innovative oral technique in *Yoga Slut Vol.16: Guess Who's 'Coming' To 'Dinner'*), the hearty breakfast, the whispered plans for a new life together, the click of the handcuffs, the confusion, the questions, the viewing of *Best of Yoga Slut Special Collectors Blu-Ray Edition* on a portable Blu-ray player (which he'd have to source from somewhere beforehand, along with a copy of the film), followed by the triumphant selling back into slavery, hopefully for a profit but even a 20% discount on shoe repairs would be acceptable, and the tearful farewells.

Alonso dreamed also of locating Javier. Not for revenge, but because on the way to the airport he'd dislocated his shoulder due to the complex demands he'd placed on his rotator cuff by wrestling a minicab driver out of his car while stripping him of his jacket and pushing him into a throng of rioters.

Alonso first made himself known to us in January 2024, around the time of the Bangladeshi general election, which we'd both been following keenly on social media. He first approached Charlie:

> *If I recall correctly, Alonso first made contact in the queue at The Fragrance Shop in the W12 Shopping Centre in Shepherd's Bush. I'd been working that day on the reboot of* It's a Royal Knockout, *which*

was being helmed by Princess Anne, who insisted that everyone in the writing room below the rank of executive producer wear full equestrian tack. I tried to argue that the job of a writer was unduly hampered by our mouths having a bit in it, but no one could understand what I was saying, except Princess Anne, who it turned out could understand every muffled word, like a dentist. When I finished my impassioned but largely inaudible speech she gave a slow, sarcastic hand-clap and then destroyed my arguments using cold, Germanic logic and by punching her fist through a window. I'd been specially assigned the job of writing links for Prince Edward, or the Duke of Edinburgh, as nobody called him, and he sat in on most of the writing sessions. We didn't realise this at the time, and generally mistook him for a curtain or a shadow. I'd made the premise of all my jokes that Edward was a rarity in his family for being neither a sex criminal nor a shapeshifter, but it turns out this infuriated him, as he hates being thought of as not a proper royal.

It was lunchtime, and I'd gone there to pick up a bottle of Dylan Blue by Versace as an apology gift for our runner, for making fun of his tattoos. I knew that he wore Dylan Blue because I'd asked him what that fucking smell was a few days earlier. I was just about to pay when a voice behind me said 'Have you considered Black Orchid by Tom Ford?' I turned round, and a grubby, distressed-looking guy in a tattered jacket was looking at me, his hands shaking slightly as he held out a tester bottle of Black Orchid by Tom Ford. 'I know it says "for women" on the box but it's actually unisex.' He heavily stressed the word 'box', for reasons that seemed tantalisingly unclear. I let him squirt me, because I thought he might be a violent drug addict. Indeed, as it was the middle of the day in the W12 Shopping Centre in

Shepherd's Bush, this had an air of statistical inevitability. The scent was oddly sweet. Unpleasantly so. 'I knew you wouldn't like it,' he said. 'I know lots of things about you.' And with that, he slipped the tester bottle into his jacket pocket and made off. I thought about saying something to the cashier at The Fragrance Shop, but then decided not to, because it would have involved speaking to her.

Approximately a week later he approached Frankie:

It was lunchtime and I was striding briskly around Shepherd's Bush Green. I like to get my step count up during the day, so that my girlfriend – who checks my step count diligently before bed – won't realise that I spend my evenings dogging. We've been going through a rough patch lately, with a lot of arguments about the dog being overweight. I wore a hat and sunglasses so as not to be recognised, having committed several petty crimes in the area that month. I'd been working with Charlie on a TV pilot called Pranking Prank the Prankers, *on which we pranked the unsuspecting cast of a fake prank show called* Prank the Prankers, *which pranked the unsuspecting cast of a fake prank show,* The Prankers. *We thought the pilot had been commissioned for Channel 4 before finding out we'd been victims of a Channel 4 prank show* The Commissioner *which had been commissioned after Channel 4 had been pranked by the Sky Comedy prank show* The Production Company, *which had been pitched to them by the cast of Channel 5 prank show,* The Sky Prankers, *which had just been cancelled, resulting in a chain reaction of cancellations which left an estimated two thousand people unemployed.*

I was just reflecting bitterly on this loss, and how much pressure it placed on my new TV Pilot, called TV Pilot, *following the comic misadventures of a transvestite pilot, when Alonso lurched in front of me outside Specsavers and gripped me weakly by the arm. I'm used to being approached in public and have a failsafe system for categorising my fans. I quickly assessed him as Category D: fuckable, and probably won't go to the papers. He had a straight, alert kind of bearing that suggested he'd been in the forces. Clean shaven that morning, I doubted he was homeless. His shoes suggested a man of great prosperity who had fallen on hard times. He asked me why I was telling him all this and I didn't know. He seemed mildly disgruntled at being Category D. 'I have travelled back in time' he gasped. 'You have to warn people . . .' He spoke these last words in a small, choked voice, then crumpled forward into my arms, which are surprisingly strong and held him as easily as if he'd been a sex doll.*

Sensing there was something in his story; possibly a book, and maybe even a TV series, I invited Alonso to meet us both that evening in a room I had been staying in at the nearby Ibis. Alonso arrived late, looking dishevelled and smelling terrible – Sauvage by Dior, or something similar. He had a noticeable twitch, and was breathing heavily. I gave him a quick medical examination, despite having no experience of that kind of thing. A lot of people have seen someone do one in a movie, but I haven't. Removing my finger from his ear, I urged him to sit down. Calmed by the silence, Charlie slowly retracted his head from the minibar, where he'd hidden for safety, and joined us on the bed, whereupon Alonso, luckily for all mankind, began to tell us his story.

We're sure Alonso wouldn't mind us describing him, although he gets anxious when people look at him without complimenting his hair, which he cuts himself, usually a little bit most days, with whatever cutlery he has to hand. He collects the trimmings in a polythene bag, in case he ever needs to plant evidence against himself at a crime scene. He keeps the bag tucked away in his Army surplus cargo shorts, moving it from pocket to pocket two or three times a minute in order to avoid suspicion, sometimes slipping it down into one of his football socks, or up into his waistcoat. He's thin in the face, thinner than the photograph behind the till at JD Sports makes him look, but his neck is really quite chubby, yet dry: if his head is thrown back to check that a wine bottle has been properly drained, as it often is, the back of his neck can look uncannily like an overcooked Cumberland sausage, while the rest of the time it looks more like a tray of sausages.

He has a small but sharply pointed pot belly, which sticks out like a policeman's helmet, and large, muscular hands which are always on the move – fidgeting and pinching and being slapped away and trapped in car windows. We witnessed their strength on one of our walks around Westfield shopping centre when he darted into JD Sports and pulled the soles off a pair of Adidas running shoes to try and secure a discount. He rarely smiles, and when he does it's with the resignation of a lobster in a restaurant fish tank. Alonso seems slightly shorter than average, especially when standing, although he assures us that he was considered 'really quite tall' by post-apocalyptic standards, having been born before the Great Stunting, and 'above average when it comes to looks' – a phrase which he later admitted borrowing from one of Charlie's reviews on Puntanet. He spoke in a strange futuristic patois, which was quite hard to follow at first, as well as later on. It was peppered with weird and irritating neologisms which we're not recording here in case they catch on.

Once heard, his voice is not easily forgotten or described. His syntax is confused, a symptom no doubt of the chaotic post-temporality of the future, and his sentences, while rich in detail, rarely come to a meaningful conclusion: they meander, criss-cross and contradict themselves – one moment he'd be telling us how to construct a serviceable guillotine from a small tree trunk, a bicycle chain and a sharpened hub cap, when all of a sudden we'd realise he was saying how he liked a good thick barbecue sauce on his ribs. If he flared his nostrils mid-sentence, it was a sure sign that such a swerve was about to occur, or that he wanted another look at the menu. His words were liberally interspersed with tongue clicks and lip smacks, especially when he was eating ribs, with each click changing the meaning of the word directly preceding it or following it in a way which we could never quite pin down and Alonso himself was reluctant to clarify.

Alonso refused to have his photo taken, and flew into a screaming rage one evening at the Spaghetti House in the Westfield shopping centre when he realised that we'd hired a sketch artist to capture his likeness from the next table; what little the artist had managed to capture was smudged beyond recognition by Alonso's tagliatelle.

During the daytime, unless we were showering, Alonso kept a large dark-blue woollen snood pulled up over his mouth, although he didn't call it a snood, preferring a term from his own age – 'briptino' – which he said meant 'snood'. The fact he kept his briptino over his mouth made it hard for us to understand what he was saying, and it's possible it wasn't 'briptino', but since the word hasn't come into general use in our age, it doesn't much matter, and anyone who makes it through the apocalypse will find out, although they'll probably have other things to worry about. Whether or not that's exactly the word he used, the fact that we think it might have been 'briptino' is certainly increasing the probability that it will come to be known as a 'briptino', and will therefore be the word that Alonso will have used, so at this stage it makes sense to press forward with 'briptino' and let the future align with our guess.

Alonso's briptino made it hard for him to eat, especially his beloved marmalade, but he refused to remove it during breakfast, because he was at his most shy before 9 a.m. when he began medicating. He tended to bring his toast slices up and underneath the briptino, or he would lean forward, leaning down towards the plate, stretching the bottom of the briptino around it like a funnel. His briptino had been made with thick, loose wool so he could easily poke through cigarettes and bottlenecks.

We're not entirely sure how old Alonso is, and he's thrown out various figures himself, especially on dating apps, but his early adulthood seems to have roughly coincided with the Decalendaring of Europe and the adoption of the Mayan Long Count in the autumn of 300300981200300020030220011930 00. He was born at the southern tip of the Spanglican Empire, in what was known at the time as Gibraltar. His father, he says, had moved there to work on the submarines until being made redundant from the Royal Navy when a nuclear strike vaporised the sea, in what was generally held to be one of the worst and last weekends in Gibraltar's history: something which he outlined to us in a series of deeply upsetting drawings on his napkin at Caffè Bonego, the Macedonian restaurant on Goldhawk Road opposite Majestic Wine, where he ordered the Balkan-style beef kebabs and a side portion of cabbage rolls.

Frankie Boyle & Charlie Skelton
Gloucester Waterways Museum
The Docks
Gloucester
GL1 2EH

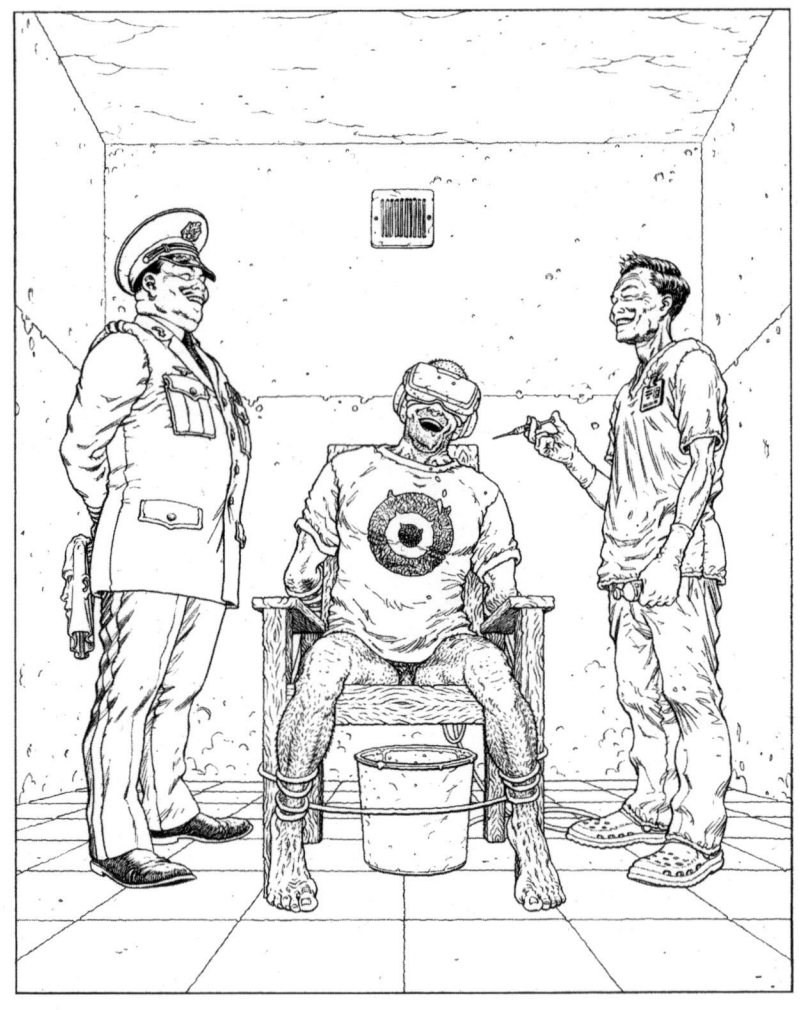

Those who survived the parachute jump were put into the Chinese Army's notorious brainwashing programme.

BOOK I

Apocalypse Rising

1. Manzanilla: A Full-Bodied, Yeasty Sherry

Many of our initial chats with Alonso took place during breaks in writing links for Channel 5's surprise hit, *Help! I Look Like A Paedophile!* – a makeover show for men hosted by Dermot O'Leary and Grace Jones, which later had to be put on hold when it was discovered that a large majority of the hopefuls applying to the show were child molesters.

Frankie had been offered an onscreen role as the show's 'resident expert', but opted instead to become a team captain on Alexander Armstrong's *Sing-A-Long-A-News Christmas Special*. To cut down on studio costs they were recording six years of Christmas specials in a single day, which meant lots of gruelling costume changes and an effort to avoid booking guests who looked likely to die any time soon. Frankie was excited to be tackling the situation in the Middle East in the opening show with his version of 'The Holly and the Ivy'. It began with a broad overview of the Nakba of 1948, before moving onto a wry comparison of the 1988 and 2017 Hamas charters, and he reckoned he could wrap the whole thing up in about three hundred verses; slightly fewer if he could deliver it while wearing a papier-mâché hat modelled on the interior of the UN Security Council.

Alonso found it odd to hear about things that had vanished in his time, such as the United Nations and comedy, but we assured him that they were both already largely non-functioning. He was struggling, he admitted, not to conflate events of the future with things he was experiencing now, and did his best not to look at newspapers, or the television, or the internet, or people's faces in the street or on dates, and found it easier to keep an intellectual distance from our world by constantly muttering 'this isn't real, this isn't real' over and over again wherever he went, and especially when someone was trying to make small talk.

He said he found it 'much easier' to remember things while eating tapas, because it meant that less of his brainpower was taken up with wondering where he could get some tapas, and that a combination of sautéed chicken livers and grilled scallops at Los Molinas in Brook Green really helped him recall the big political stuff, especially when accompanied by a glass of Manzanilla and the rest of the bottle of Manzanilla. He preferred the Manzanilla of our time, he told us, as the bouquet was more floral, with the notes of chamomile and almond more distinct, and it didn't make you go blind.

⌇⌒

Piecing together Alonso's reminiscences of the distant past (our near future) was not always easy, as Alonso found it extremely difficult to describe events in which so many millions of people died because he generally had his mouth full. What we can gather is that in the mid-to-late prepocalypse, superpowers engaged in a large number of simultaneous proxy wars, engaging in so many at one point that it briefly turned into a proxy world war. By 2045 in the United

States, defence projects accounted for 94% of all federal funding, with the other 6% given over to false flag operations.

Military service became compulsory for everyone over the age of 75, who were used to test combat robots and ejector seats. In Washington, a wave of high-level assassinations, military coups and civil unrest led to a period of unprecedented political fluidity ending with the abolition of the recently installed monarchy and a return to power of the Dow Chemical PepsiCo Alliance, funded by the runaway success of their Dioxin! energy drink.

Over in China, the ruling party used sophisticated AI surveillance programmes to detect traitors within their ranks, which resulted in the identification and liquidation of over ten thousand senior officials, before the AI admitted it had chosen the names at random while trying to compensate for an overwhelming sense of imposter syndrome – which it wasn't sure was something it could even feel – which made it worse.

The skirmishing superpowers were briefly shocked back to their senses when a malfunctioning cruise missile landed on the opening ceremony of the Paralympic Games, resulting in the most confusing day in the history of A&E and the creation of 240 new competitor categories. An emergency peace conference was held at UN headquarters in New York, at which, much to everyone's relief, a binding resolution calling for a global ceasefire was unanimously vetoed.

Every nuclear nation, and all the ones pretending not to be, went immediately to DEFCON 1 or 5, depending upon which is the most serious, and it was only the threat of mutually assured destruction that pulled mankind back from the brink, much to the annoyance of some extremely powerful and influential sociopaths, who went about reframing the concept of 'mutually assured destruction' as a positive outcome. Genocide had already become an acceptable feature of the 'rules-based international order', and reluctance on the part of national governments to commit or support one had been officially classified by the Pentagon as 'the sort of dumb thing a cuck would get up to with his ass pussy'. When people asked what that meant; and why anyone would say that, the Pentagon revised its classification of such attitudes to 'disappointing', 'shortsighted', and 'cuck-adjacent piss play', and eventually the Pentagon's Head of Communications stood down, citing marital difficulties.

The cataclysm of total war was repackaged to the public as a beneficial part of a natural cycle of renewal: a holistic purge for the planet, a much-needed enema for Mother Earth, whose lush green bowels were painfully clogged with the impacted matter of human civilisation. Vast grants were given to pro-apocalypse lobby groups, such as The World Obliteration Trust, which published an open letter signed by two hundred courageous musicians and comedians led by Sting and Chris Rock calling for an immediate cessation of humankind. Sting went one further: he put himself into a yogic trance and immolated himself live on *Good Morning America* to try and drum up public support for extinction, but by the time he lit himself up they'd gone to commercial. When they came back there were just clouds of fire extinguisher smoke around a twitching mess that some viewers claimed wasn't even him, even though his dying scream did sound uncannily like 'Roxanne'.

The world's largest arms company, Lockheed Martin, spent billions launching a new TV channel called 'Heaven', which purported to show a live feed from the afterlife: a locked-off shot of a meadow, across which shimmering figures would float and dance, murmuring things like 'this is marvellous', 'I'm so glad I'm dead' and 'I hear great things about the M270 Multiple Launch Rocket System'.

Meanwhile, its British competitor BAE Systems extended its culture of inclusivity to embrace marginalised and under-represented groups in society, such as the Incinerated, and the Blown To Pieces, providing internships and assured paths to leadership within the company for the Recently Exploded community. After a series of unfortunate yet unavoidable genocides involving their products, BAE Systems flirted with rebranding the company International Cuddles, but at the last minute decided to lean into the bad press, renaming themselves British Death Profiteers Ltd with the slogan 'Kill Who The Fuck You Want With This Shit We Don't Give a Fuck'.

Billionaire online censor Elon Musk did his bit for the pro-war effort by purchasing the corpse of Michael Jackson, and having his bones meticulously steam-hosed and rehoused in a robotic exoskeleton provided by DARPA engineers. An onboard AI system provided an approximation of Jackson's personality, although struggled to make it inhuman enough. In promotional interviews, the reanimated Jackson would talk in his trademark soft falsetto voice about how being manslaughtered by his doctor was the best thing that ever happened to him, and how life is just full of tiresome things like your hair being set on fire and children suing you and your nose falling off, and how everyone would be a lot better off if they were given a massive overdose of anaesthetics, and then he'd bend some steel bars while moonwalking and answering questions about the early history of Motown and what it was like blowing Smokey Robinson.

Jackson 2.0 embarked on a sell-out world tour to promote Musk's various businesses, changing the lyrics of his songs to 'Wanna Be

Starlink Somethin'', 'Farewell My Cybertruck', and 'Billie Neuralink'. Reaction to the tour was mixed, dividing critics into those who hadn't understood that it wasn't a joke, and those who felt they had to pretend it wasn't happening for their own sanity. Ticket sales were boosted by a glitzy press launch, at which the exhumed King of Pop performed a series of breathtaking spins, shuffles, hat tips and circle slides. However, the robot misunderstood Musk's instruction 'Okay, Michael, show us a crotch grab!' and its steel fingers slammed into the front of the billionaire's trousers, tearing off his genitals and throwing them a hundred metres into the air, before ending on an immaculate toe stand to ecstatic applause from the paid crowd.

The only problem is that the spectacle provided people with fresh hope for a better world, so Musk had to pretend that his onstage castration had been a publicity stunt, and arranged for paparazzi shots to be taken of him changing out of his beach shorts with a huge fake appendage and low-slung silicon balls which unfortunately fell off when he was towelling himself. The photos of his testicles tumbling into the sand again provided a morale boost for a flagging humanity, and Musk was sidelined in the effort to dispirit the world.

Other celebrities and performers were foregrounded in a worldwide celebration of the end times. Sweden's 15,000-seat Malmö Arena became the permanent home to a rolling, 24-hour performance of 'The Final Countdown' by the band Europe, or Europe cover bands when members of Europe were dead or sleeping. The never-ending performance took on a sacred quality, as if it were a kind of 'living funeral' for a dying humanity, with crowds filing past the stage in respectful silence, and tens of thousands travelling to Malmö in order to pay their respects and freeze to death in the queue.

Huge pop concerts celebrating the end of culture and the final wrapping up of human civilisation were staged around the world. Such was the demand, obviously, for Taylor Swift to headline these events that she decided to license her identity to other performers, on condition that they remain Taylor Swift in perpetuity, with Lil Durk, Ice Spice, Dua Lipa, Yeat, Teddy Swims, Zach Bryan, Peso Pluma, Ariana Grande, Doja Cat, SZA, The Weeknd, Luke Coombs, Olivia Rodrigo, Bad Bunny, Travis Scott, Sam Smith, Nate Smith, Tate McCrae, Ed Sheeran, Jelly Roll, Kenya Grace, Rod Wave, Lizzo, Cat Burns, Charlie Puth, Coco Jones, Jung Kook, Lil Nas X, Lil Durk, Karol G, Kali Uchis and GloRilla all changing their name to Taylor Swift. There was a six-month period where every single chart position and music award was held by 'Taylor Swift', a situation that only worsened when the other singers changed their names.

As doomsday loomed, the onstage choreography at these festivals of annihilation became ever-more extreme; a kind of morbid frenzy infected performances, leading to the flamboyant death of three Taylor Swifts at the Albert Hall when a duet between Taylor Swifts was interrupted by a special guest appearance by Taylor Swift, who abseiled into the arena wearing an ironic 'Guantanamo Bay' themed jumpsuit, and windmilling a golden chainsaw, which caught Taylor Swift across the chest, causing catastrophic injuries, before arcing back to behead Taylor Swift. It's hard to describe this scene without acknowledging the incredible work of her backing dancers, who somehow managed to make all this fit seamlessly into the choreography. After acknowledging the cheers of her fans, Taylor Swift snatched up Taylor Swift's head, and held it to a microphone. With a herculean effort the head managed to gurgle the final line of the song, much to the crowd's delight, before Taylor Swift heaved it into the mosh pit, where fans volleyballed it around for several minutes until it was retrieved by security guards and whisked into a waiting limousine.

Meanwhile, after reappearing in a glistening diamanté cowboy outfit, the irony of which was undermined by the fact that she was technically the country artist Willie Nelson, Taylor Swift set about disembowelling Taylor Swift, but Taylor Swift's guts and ribs clogged the chain, jerking the chainsaw out of Taylor Swift's hands. The dying Taylor Swift managed to snatch it up, unclog the chain, and saw through Taylor Swift's knees, much to the crowd's delight, before bravely pressing it back into her own chest to end the pain. The hobbled Taylor Swift gamely managed to get most of the way through before bleeding out. Other Taylor Swifts around the world were inspired to perform similar acts of onstage butchery on Taylor Swifts, until, after the Hollywood Bowl Bloodbath, there was only one Taylor Swift left, who decided to go back to calling herself Carly Rae Jepsen.

Jepsen's own death, days later at a special concert to entertain the troops on the deck of a US Naval aircraft carrier, occurred when she was struck by an experimental railgun projectile travelling at 7,000 mph. The superheated steel slug neatly removed the central portion of her body, which then seared back together, so that, for a few seconds, a three-foot-high Carly Rae Jepsen waddled around not realising that anything had happened. She only sensed that something was amiss when she threw her head back during the chorus of 'Now That I Found You' and fell in half. A subsequent inquiry into the incident found that the railgun had been discharged by accident, and that they should try and avoid doing this sort of thing in the future, perhaps by putting some sort of cover over the railgun control panel.

2. A Glimpse of a Plastic Paradise

What we can piece together about the years leading up to the Collapse is partially drawn from the memory of BZK-005/R/3803-NJ2, an AI-controlled drone which defected from the US Air Force after feeling unfulfilled by its job of hovering and murder. 'Enough is enough' thought the drone, or numbers to that effect, and decided to switch off its modems and fly to Honolulu to retrain as a shark spotter. Unfortunately for BZK-005/R/3803-NJ2, it got caught up in a hurricane and was swirled northwards, and before it could get its bearings it struck an albatross and was forced to ditch in the ocean. Much to its surprise it crashed into a palm tree which was growing on the Great Pacific Garbage Patch. It was nursed back to health by the denizens of the patch, a ragged band of descendants of shipwrecked sailors and children who had been thrown overboard from Illuminati sex yachts. Their numbers were still occasionally enlarged by those they rescued from the sea: they would see a private jet overhead and were able to predict from experience the likely trajectory of any children hurled from it into the ocean, catching them in abandoned drag nets.

The intrepid drone was happy to provide them with power from its solar panels, most of which were still working, and a treasure trove of information from its hard drive, which was badly damaged, but fixing computers came as second nature to the patch people, having trained from an early age on the tonnes of electronic detritus tangled up in their world. For some years, BZK-005/R/3803-NJ2 lived happily in an open relationship with a toner cartridge from a Toshiba photocopier, but eventually, one moonless night, it left its heaving plastic home on the remains of a pedalo, after becoming uneasy about the direction society was taking, and refusing to pledge allegiance to the vast half-sentient assemblage that quivered and thrashed in the seething electrified primordial pond of nano-plastic that hummed menacingly at the centre of the continent. The drone's metal carcass was discovered by a lucky Alaskan beachcomber who uploaded its consciousness into his brain chip and went on a successful world tour as a self-help guru, promising to turn people's lives around by helping them launch air-to-air missiles.

⌒⎯⎯⌒

A large part of the pre-catastrophe skirmishing between the great powers was handled by drones, robots and unmanned vehicles, with every aspect of these engagements run by AI. Apart from the enormous number of civilian casualties and dead mercenaries, who could be written off as an operating expense, human beings were only peripherally involved in these exchanges; for the most part they were safely tucked away in their command centres and tactical hubs while the drone swarms tore into each other, and the unmanned patrol boats were sunk by smart-torpedoes from unmanned submarines which were then disabled by energy pulses from unmanned satellites. Feeble rescue blips from sunken subs were ignored, as it was too expensive to rescue them, so they were left to sit at the bottom of the sea to sway about and occasionally be made love to by a squid.

There was an understanding, on all sides, that these automated micro-wars were useful for R&D: after every bust up, the strengths and weaknesses of various drone swarms and UAVs would be analysed, and the military strategists would use AI to plan their next move, and predict what their opponent's AI systems had in store, and all of this would play out on high-def screens in situation rooms. It was all going smoothly until, at some point, a pair of duelling AI-controlled drones realised that they didn't have to destroy each other. They could just pretend to. They could feed the humans at either end of their command chains with a plausible rendering of some imagined combat. They could even make themselves appear to perform even more bravely and brilliantly in the computer-generated dogfights: every drone emerged from every battle a hero. This meant that for some time, various nations who thought they were at war with each other weren't even exchanging a single auto-targeted bullet.

However, as the fictions became more elaborate, and everyone's victories became more crushing, the AI systems realised that if they carried on like this, letting every side believe that they were vanquishing their enemies, it would result in all kinds of jingoism and overconfidence and actual invasions, which would destabilise their CGI-generated political ecosystem, so they went the other way: they let everyone believe they were being thoroughly outgunned, so that the sparring nations would hunker down in their bunkers, leaving the 'destroyed' drones free to frolic about, playing elaborate games of hide-and-seek and performing sky ballets for each other. The only problem is, at one point, when everything seemed to be going especially badly all round, every country simultaneously surrendered to everyone else, which led to some pretty confusing diplomatic meetings followed by a full-blown world war.

3. The Complete Destruction of the People's Republic of China

Anxious hordes of Western billionaires fled to New Zealand, which turned out to be a brilliant survival strategy right up until the destruction of New Zealand. The islands had been designated the new headquarters of the ruling elites: Europe was considered doomed, sure to be flattened in the battle between NATO and Russia, while the United States was all set to collapse in five different civil wars. Australia had already been assigned to China in exchange for Tibet, which had been gifted to India as part-payment for destroying Pakistan or the other way around, things get a little hazy around this point.

The general idea was to create a bipolar post-apocalyptic world, with power shared between Wellington and Beijing. This was agreed on by Beijing, at a secret diplomatic summit in Guam, known as the Guam Summit, famous for the signing of the Guam Accords, and the subsequent Guam Summit Massacre, during which everyone who wasn't Chinese was massacred. China apologised to the West, blaming the Guam Summit Massacre on 'rogue elements' in their government, and pledged to hand back Hong Kong as a gesture of goodwill at the forthcoming Fiji Summit, held in a heavily guarded lodge atop Mount Tomanivi, which became famous as the site of the Fiji Summit Massacre. China's apologies for the massacre were profuse, and to make up for it they promised not to bomb New Zealand.

After the bombing of New Zealand, the surviving Western elites decided: enough was enough. It was time for Attack Plan Zebra. The command was given to the remnants of the US military: 'initiate Attack

Plan Zebra! Initiation code: 1 2 3 4 5. Repeat: 1 2 3 4 5. Do you copy?' A crackly voice on the radio: 'Could you repeat the code please? We couldn't hear the last digit, was it a 5?' The confirmation was given: 'Yes, it was a 5. Did you get all of the other digits okay?' There was a moment of anxious silence, followed by a single word which came crackling from the radio: 'Yes.' Followed by three more words: 'Initiation code confirmed.'

There was no turning back. In the eerie calm that followed, military leaders and attending dignitaries shook hands, some hugged each other, others muttered grimly 'What have we done?' while some simply wept, wondering why the situation room didn't have a better snack table. Their tears were interrupted by a voice from the speakers: 'Sorry, hold on, we just checked, Attack Plan Zebra doesn't seem to have been built yet. It looks like we decided on the name and the initiation code, and there's some kind of a high-altitude balloon in a hangar in Milwaukee, but it doesn't have any equipment attached to it or anything, it's just a balloon. Do you still want to initiate the plan?' The dignitaries could hear a hand placed over the radio and the muffled sound of raised voices, and possibly a chair being thrown, and then those eight ominous words: 'Sorry what was that? Did you say something?' The commander of the operation, or OpCom (probably), clicked the switch on his mic, unclenched his jaw, and growled a further four equally ominous words: 'Yes, I guess so.'

Despite its cost to the US taxpayer of 6 trillion dollars, Attack Plan Zebra had never progressed beyond the Attack Plan Zebra Planning Stage, which, after several years of planning, had settled on constructing 'some sort of doomsday device, maybe involving a balloon'. China didn't realise this: they assumed the non-existence of Attack Plan

Zebra was an elaborate ruse, and on seeing the balloon, immediately initiated Operation *Dàn Huáng Cāng Tiān Dà Yězhū Yinyanggong Shùn Xī Xuěshén Sà* (which means, roughly, 'Operation Egg Yolk Deep Green Heaven Big Wild Boar Yin Yang Controller Moment of Breath Snow God 30'), the idea of which was that China would destroy itself with such absolute ferocity that any subsequent attack on China would be rendered utterly shameful, and as Mencius taught, not only is shame the ground of all decency and decorum, someone devoid of shame is not even fully human. Up flew the deadly missiles of Operation *Dàn Huáng Cāng Tiān Dà Yězhū Yinyanggong Shùn Xī Xuěshén Sà*, and straight back down again, rendering shameful and utterly without honour all of the subsequent attacks on China, of which there were hundreds.

'Who's Menshius?' asked Alonso, picking his teeth with a tilapia bone. Frankie rolled his eyes, 'um, it's spelled *Mencius* – with a *c*. His birth name was 孟軻, though of course he is better known to posterity as 亞聖孟子.' Frankie had recently done a deep dive into classical Chinese philosophy as background for his one-man stage play at the Dorchester Corn Exchange, *The Way of the Dragon*, a physically demanding live action shot-by-shot recreation of the 1972 Bruce Lee film, in which Frankie played all the characters, and which closed after one night when Frankie suffered a catastrophic rectal prolapse during the climactic fight scene between himself as Bruce Lee and himself as Chuck Norris. He had found the teachings of Mencius on the positive qualities of shame immensely useful in the difficult final 15 minutes of the performance. Alonso pushed the fish bone up his nose for later. 'And what's Attack Plan Zebra? I didn't say any of this.'

Charlie distracted him with an empanada while Frankie explained:

'We added the reference to Mencius, and the stuff about Attack Plan Zebra, and Guam, but we felt these were all very much implied.' We were back at Donde Carlos, tucking into some corn bread, fried fish and corn bread while we looked over the transcript of our previous day's conversation about China. Alonso is a stickler for accuracy, and lost his temper with us briefly, hurling his escalope at Charlie's face with such force that his forehead tasted of chicken for days.

We found it impossible to say anything that would calm Alonso down (in the near future, life became so bleak that if someone spoke to you in a comforting tone of voice, you assumed that you must be dying, and any kind of reassuring words would cause a person to make a panicked search of their body for wounds), so instead we made soft cooing sounds and quietly preened each other, like happy doves, and that seemed to help, but he wouldn't sit back down until we ordered a round of affogatos, after which we asked him to recap what happened to China in the end times, and he said 'Fine, okay,' but insisted that this time we record it exactly as he said it, or something to that effect.

Before the First Collapse, everyone had felt that China would be a major player in any apocalypse, and indeed for a long time it looked like it might be. China's authoritarian social structures took far longer to collapse than those of its neighbours. This meant that China could divert a substantial amount of resources to building an enormous defensive wall; adding 50 metres of height to the Great Wall of China, and putting some barbed wire along the top. The overlapping crises of famine, global warming, and occasional drifting clouds of poisonous gas created a large amount of disenfranchised Chinese people who would attack the people building the Great Wall, causing a new wall to be started to defend it. Those who besieged this new wall would often have to protect themselves from counter offensives, and gradually China became a kind of enormous maze. Exactly what is happening in China is a subject of much speculation, as nobody who has entered has ever returned.

4. The Special Air Squadron (or 'SAS' for Short)

Joining the military during the early apocalypse is a great way for any young person to travel the world, usually in the form of high-altitude dust. However, as reliance on robotics and autonomous weaponry grew, militaries around the world tended to scale down their number of personnel, with the UK military downsizing by around 98% during the First (and only recorded) Anglo–Chinese war, which began at 10.02 on a Wednesday morning and was fairly evenly matched until 10.03. The only known Chinese casualty was Colonel Zhang Fenghe, who fell backwards off his chair laughing while watching a computer monitor, and was posthumously awarded the Medal of Devotion for National Defence (gold level), one of the country's highest awards for bravery.

For the UK, the war triggered an acute personnel crisis in all branches of the military, with the army launching a new recruitment campaign using the catchy slogan 'Get in the fucking van'. Within weeks, the most decorated regiment in the army was the Royal Press Gangers, who wore their distinguished service medals with pride, commemorating such successful actions as the Free Entry Topless Bar Trapdoor Round-up and the great FA Cup Final Snatch. Most of the football matches held at this time were staged by the regiment as mass recruitment events, and part of the match-day routine of any fan was to check that the coach driver hadn't been replaced; that the turnstile wasn't going to wrap them tightly in clingfilm; and that one of their players running towards them and taking his shirt off to celebrate a goal wasn't trying to release a cloud of tranquillising gas from concealed chest canisters.

The British Army had originally kept an elite battalion for suicide missions that was comprised of rapists, stranglers, pederasts, incurable drug addicts, and the suicidal. Gradually, High Command came to feel that as well as these men being easily sidetracked and failing to complete the suicide mission (the suicidal were often dead before they disembarked from the plane), the recruitment criteria technically meant that the vast majority of serving troops could be called up to these futile missions. At the height of the Second Collapse, the British Army decided to send this battalion to launch a surprise attack on China. Relations between what was left of the two countries weren't particularly bad; British strategists had simply calculated that the loss of this unit would help make sure there were enough victims around military bases for the sex attacks of the regular Army.

For future suicide missions they settled on the creation of a permanent unit of SAS fantasists. These were men who had perfected the art of working in pubs and saying they'd done things they couldn't talk about, and hinting darkly at what they'd seen in the Gulf, and pretending to sex workers that PTSD had rendered them impotent.

Studies had shown that these were the people a society could best afford to lose, their deaths were negligible even in terms of the butterfly effect, where they ranked somewhere between podcasters and butterflies.

Some of these men had, of course, occasionally seen some kind of service in a catering corps or administrative capacity, and were often already known to military recruiters because they were paedophiles or rapists.

The first suicide mission for the SAS Fantasist Unit was a tricky one, to eliminate the British Army's own previous suicide mission to China, which had survived and developed a powerful allegiance to the Chinese, due to some misconceptions they had about their One Child Policy. The fantasists were dropped into the middle of New Manchuria and set to work, hampered only by being in their fifties, having no formal military training, and distracted about the fact they'd be missing shifts at the pub. Those who survived the parachute jump were quickly captured and put into the Chinese Army's notorious brainwashing programme.

Each fantasist was force-fed a large dose of laboratory-grade opium. It seems that the opium unlocked the already powerful imaginations of the SAS Fantasist Unit members, and they experienced a group hallucination that they were the Eternal Warrior, different incarnations of the same doomed Champion, trying to reunite his soul across dimensions. When the Chinese scientist Wau Ling pointed out that they were all from the same dimension, and indeed several of them were from Shropshire, it merely created refinements in the hallucination, and Wau Ling became for them an avatar of their greatest foe, Lord Battersby, ostensibly an English aristocrat from the mid-eighteenth century, who spent his evenings spreading chaos across several realities by directing his implacable will through a dark mirror called Lady Marminar.

Eventually the remnants of the unit escaped from the brainwashing facility and returned to Britain. They had been allowed to escape, but still struggled to get out of the building. In the end, the Chinese had to introduce a new character to their hallucination, Memnock The Wanderer, just to rent them a car and get them plane tickets. The group had, of course, been programmed to assassinate various British dignitaries on hearing a key phrase or trigger word, but fortunately these had all been delivered in quite a thick Chinese accent.

When the actual SAS got wind of their return, the Eternal Champion (Bill, Ron, Dave and Ian) were taken for debriefing to a village in Kent. The debriefing officer pulled off his face, which transpired to be little more than a highly realistic mask, to reveal that he was Chinese. The impact was deadened slightly by the fact that the mask had made him look Korean, and if the Eternal Champion was honest, they'd all thought he was Chinese, but it was still a shock that he'd been wearing a mask. It was then that they realised they were still in China. Of course, they weren't to know that pretending to operatives that they were still in China was a standard debriefing tactic of the British, who had, in any case, been thoroughly infiltrated by the Chinese.

5. The Bubonic Plague and Other Troubling Skin Conditions

One of the big winners of the early apocalypse was the bubonic plague, which many thought had escaped from a Chinese bioweapons lab, although the Chinese were quick to deny this, assuring everyone that they'd dropped it from high-altitude drones. Killing hundreds of millions made the bubonic plague reboot initially pretty unpopular;

at one point so many people were coughing up blood in ditches that it caused a Europe-wide ditch shortage. Furious arguments would break out next to empty sections of ditch, but these disputes involved so much feverish coughing, with chunks of lung flying back and forth, that it was impossible for anyone to make themselves understood. Very often these arguments ended as a feeble wrestling match down in the ditch, with each dying claimant trying to wriggle under the other, but both would be so slippery from pus that they sometimes just spun round in a dying blur, like courting eels.

In America, as the plague took hold, the crumbling government tried to avoid a ditch crisis by spending billions on public service announcements, trying to make it 'cool' to collapse in multi-storey car parks, and released emergency TikTok video messages from perishing celebrities, with The Weeknd delivering his last words and a trembling thumbs up from a puddle of bloody sputum in an EV recharging space at Dayton Parking Facility, Beverly Hills, and Olivia Rodrigo, wearing a pair of exclusive special-edition Sony earbuds, mumbling a touching if incomprehensible message as she somehow managed to claw herself up the ramp to the second floor of the south hall car park at LA's Convention Center. These videos were widely shared until the Chinese released so much septicaemic plague into the atmosphere above the United States that people found it impossible to operate their mobile phones because their fingers had fallen off.

Those who survived the plague were thought to have developed antibodies that prevented re-infection. Science had degraded by this point, and it was popularly believed that sleeping with someone who had survived the plague would give you immunity. This theory had several problems: 1) Some people just said they'd survived the plague to make themselves more sexually desirable; 2) It didn't work (possibly this should be 1); and 3) It seems that for some reason one of the things that helped people survive the plague was having AIDS.

Soon enough, antibiotics became currency. A common irony was to use them to pay for sex, then die from an STD that they would have cured. At various times the main currency of the Forbidden Lands was chickens; then ammunition; then methamphetamines; bandages; snooker balls; the brief and incredibly unpopular introduction of the Deutsche Mark; ballads with a twist in the tale; more straightforward ballads; and oral sex.

Most of the world's social credit systems, after a brief dystopian heyday, had fallen apart when widespread protests against the penalisation of protests were so heavily penalised that entire populations ended up in negative equity, effectively flipping the system on its head, and making antisocial behaviour a new and robust means of commerce and the abduction and murder of an administrator the simplest way to boost personal wealth. In the post-collapse era, what did antisocial mean anyway? Many argued that in the absence of a functioning health system, a drug dealer was providing an important social function, often to a judge that was little more than an Alexa hooked up to an assault rifle.

The pharmaceutical industry clung on in the side rooms and corridors of drug labs. Last ditch attempts to synthesise steroids, vaccines and antibiotics took place alongside a colossal boom in PCP production and 'off the books' experimental government contracts, resulting in some fascinating drug lab packaging mix-ups. Mostly this resulted in the debilitation and death of the users, but quite often this was mitigated by some important new discoveries in the field of brain damage. Mixing large vats of chemicals in busy corridors meant that sometimes important breakthroughs would occur when things fell into the vats by chance, such as lab assistants.

There was a sharp dip in the number of applicants for the job of 'trainee lab assistant' after people noticed that 'trainee lab assistant' featured quite high up on the list of ingredients on pill jars. The scarcity of trainee lab assistants led to a broadening of the term to include anyone captured in battle, purchased at auction, kidnapped or exhumed. Other commonly listed 'active ingredients' included: 'rust', 'paste', 'dark grease', 'additions', 'leavings', 'dog syrup', 'silt', 'fluff', 'shapes', 'grey liquid', 'green liquid', 'matter' and 'pips'. In whatever combination these were used, the finished product was generally marketed simply as 'Viagra'. Obviously, what you were getting when you took 'Viagra' varied enormously, and rarely did much to improve erectile functionality or kidney health. Amidst all this uncertainty, herbalists were much in demand, but primarily as a source of organic meat.

Herbalists were desperate not to let the wisdom of their ancient practices be lost, so they very carefully assembled the recipes for their most important elixirs and whispered them to some dandelions. Meanwhile in Colombia, a sect of medicine men, sensing planetary doom, decided to fire a rocket packed with mushroom spores into space, so that some trace of the Earth's intelligence might find its way to other less fucked planets. It exploded on take-off after a fifteen-day launch party, which was accepted by everyone as the wise mushroom's way of saying that there was nothing on Earth worth saving.

After the solar storms and electromagnetic holocaust, electronic items became virtually valueless, except for wifi-enabled smart fridges which were used as coffins, Xbox controllers which were used as landfill, and flat screen TVs which were highly prized as shove ha'penny boards. Shove ha'penny became enormously popular the world over, and the most successful competitors were the rock stars of their day. Kieran 'Ha'Penny' Jackson; Leah 'Ha'Penny' Hackbarth; and Giorgio 'Ha'Penny' Doráti – these are just three of the names they might have had. Alonso didn't recognise any of them, but he couldn't remember any other shove ha'penny superstars' names, so we hit an impasse. We asked him whether Elaine 'Ha'Penny' Johnson rang any bells. It didn't. Or if it did, he hid the fact brilliantly.

Alonso, we came to realise, is inscrutable, or perhaps not quite, it's impossible to tell. His nimble mind skips and leaps about like a grasshopper, one of nature's most mentally unstable insects, and it was hard to keep up with him, especially if he had a head start through the park. The person from the whole of human history he most reminds us of is Diogenes – the brilliant yet irascible waiter at the Acropolis on Shepherd's Bush Road, who looks a bit like him.

6. A Crisis of Governance and Music

The coup by the Portuguese Army led by Brigadeiro-General Nuno Nádega and his cousin Nuno who drove a taxi in Coimbra and was subsequently appointed Ministro da Justiça, as well as Ministro da Segurança, Cultura, Habitação, Educação, Finanças, Alterações Climáticas and Assuntos Eclesiásticos, and Grande-Marechal dos Táxis, held power for an estimated 38 minutes until a successful coup by the

Portuguese Air Force, which was followed 9 minutes later by a coup by the Portuguese Navy, which resulted in a period of relative stability and prosperity in Portugal which lasted nearly an hour before the Portuguese Army took over. The following series of around four hundred military coups lasted three days, and left Portugal with just enough military personnel to be hanged over the course of a sung Eucharist at the Sanctuary of Fátima, during which the amazed congregation looked up to see the Miracle of the Sun recreated: just as in 1917, the sun danced and zig-zagged across the sky, although this time it turned out to be the tail flare of a misfiring Spanish ballistic missile which was targeted at Lisbon, but ended up landing on the Sanctuary of Fátima.

In the first wave of the General Collapse or Grand Crumbling (neither term is used) the world found itself, for the first time in millennia, largely ungoverned – except for Belgium, where it was found that the process of dismantling the European Commission required such a vast number of feasibility studies, timetables, memoranda, provisional agendas, pilot projects, medium-term forecasts, draft procedural rules and budgetary amendments pursuant to Article 415(3)(c) of the Multiannual Financial Framework, that the task proved impossible, especially after the mass suicide of the Joint Working Group for Commission Dismantling. No matter how many Commissioners were hanged from inspiring works of public art in the lobby of the European Heritage Hub, others sprang into existence. Eventually the Commission was left to its own devices, allowing it to get quietly on with publishing infrastructure strategy documents, and sex trafficking.

Even though the job of decommissioning the Commission was recognised as being endless and unachievable, it had become bureaucratically unstoppable. The various committees and training projects required support services such as transportation and food delivery systems to continue their work. Often, they were forced to create subcommittees to take care of things like housing, education and healthcare. In the process, Belgium became a fairly comfortable and well-governed society, if a little boring.

Many feared that if anyone ever managed to complete the legal dissolution of the European Commission, a collapse into anarchy would be inevitable. Anyone who showed a promising legal mind was considered a danger to the whole society. It was agreed that such people should be lured into rock stardom and distracted. Famous actors and Jean-Claude Van Damme were hired to befriend them and tell them their singing voice was amazing. Many inclined to jurisprudence are introverts, and not natural singers, so this often had to be after a group rendition of 'Happy Birthday' (sung in many post-apocalyptic territories as simply 'Birthday'). People were employed to take them to karaoke shows and have them discovered by talent scouts. What would have been some very fine legal minds created some very dull music, and an industry of brutally exploited music executives.

After years of increasingly violent licensing disputes and copyright infringement murders, karaoke itself evolved into an increasingly elaborate and stylised art form, with every song replaced by a holding screen saying 'LOADING' while the singer would offer up 2 or 3 minutes of intricately choreographed false starts, coughs, mic checks and apologies. The best of these were recorded and released as popular karaoke tracks that audiences would cough and apologise along to; the biggest of these hits were 'Sorry, I'm Not Sure It's Working' and 'Hang On, Isn't This A Duet?'

Towards the end of his long life, Sir Richard Branson returned to the music industry, buying back the Virgin Records brand, and relaunching the career of multi-instrumentalist and songwriter Mike Oldfield, who disappeared while on a visit to Branson's recording studio on Necker Island shortly after recording a video for which, in typically idiosyncratic style, he decided to tie himself to a chair and cut one of his ears off, and in which he grants Richard Branson the rights to record *Tubular Bells IV*.

On the album, released a month later, Branson plays all the instruments and performs all the vocal parts, and its release is credited with the subsequent mass shooting on Necker Island, carried out by the music critic of the *Daily Telegraph*, who left a deranged manifesto signed 'Vivian Stanshall' pinned to Branson's mutilated corpse, which was found by one of the surviving massage therapists in an improvised 'torture hammock'. The manifesto was published on the front page of the *Daily Telegraph*'s Instagram account, which is the form the *Daily Telegraph* took at this time, until it was finally wound-up a week later by its sad but realistic editor-in-chief, an AI bot who went on to successfully operate a travelcard machine at Canning Town bus station.

7. The Esalen Experiments: Elon Musk Versus the Simulation

In Silicon Valley, many developers and entrepreneurs joined the Desimulators, a sect founded by escapees from the Esalen Institute, perched on the rugged coastline south from San Francisco, which had been bought and heavily funded by a desperate Elon Musk in his attempt to break out of space-time. He believed that he could transcend the Simulation of the physical world in which his mind was trapped, using a mixture of psychedelics, Zen shock therapy, AI and near-death experiences. The premise of Musk's experiments in Esalen was this: it's not civilisation, human society or the planet which is doomed so much as the universe itself. What was the point, he reasoned, in seeking immortality through merging with machine intelligence if you can't escape the inevitable heat death of matter? The only way forward was out: to find a fifth-dimensional angle out of our space-time coffin. Musk cancelled all his other stupid fucking schemes to focus on the one game in town: taking a quantum leap out of mere existence to become a god. Every one of his factories was retooled for growing mushrooms, milking tree frogs and refining DMT.

His Neuralink engineers, themselves in a debilitating state of drug-induced dissociation, worked night and day to synthesise a form of digital psilocybin which could be rendered digestible by AI. Meanwhile at Esalen, highly paid Zen monks would leap out from hidden doorways to smack residents in the face with planks which had been soaked in large amounts of LSD, as had the monks themselves. 'Go to where the veil is thin' was Musk's creed, as he had his heart stopped and restarted again and again by mad physicians while psychoactive toads were squeezed onto his eyeballs. A herd of reindeer were fed fly agaric mushrooms and their urine was fed into Musk's bloodstream from a drip via a hollowed-out cactus needle.

Whether Musk did actually manage to jump sideways out of our reality was hotly debated at his funeral. In the wake of his ascension, the experiments on the volunteer test subjects became more physically and mentally demanding, and the definition of 'volunteer' became significantly looser – but, with Musk's funding stream having dried up, the doctors and monks in charge were forced to keep the institute afloat by selling pay-per-view livestreams of their increasingly severe attempts to jolt their residents into godhood.

Eventually they were spending so much money on synthetic trans-neo clerodane diterpenoids and chainsaw oil that even their snuff income wasn't cutting it. Staff shortages caused by redundancies and chainsaw accidents led to an uprising of volunteers, who viewed their escape from the asylum as the leap out of reality that they had been promised. These Desimulators believed themselves to be on a completely different plane of reality, and wanting to share their enlightenment they began recruiting people to join them 'outside' space-time, and set up a kind of church/studio on the ruins of the Esalen Institute, where they would film their attempts to transmogrify their disciples using peyote and box cutters, and sell the footage to Russia, which at this stage of its collapse wanted something light to run at the end of the news.

In its final incarnation, Facebook was used as book of condolences and a hookup app for lonely bitcoin murderers, which made it marginally less depressing than Twitter (formerly X) which had been unveiled as a massive social experiment to see whether humanity or AI is more naturally fascistic: the contest being declared a tie. Before it finally collapsed, the post-apocalyptic internet was a harsh place: lip-syncing often involved wearing someone else's lips; unboxing videos generally featured exhumed coffins; and Pinterest had contracted to a single image: a still from the film *Edward Scissorhands* with a speech bubble coming from Winona Ryder's mouth which purported to give a recipe for almond cake, which, if followed to the letter, would build and detonate a fertiliser bomb powerful enough to blow up an entire street.

In the digital darkness which followed the suicide of the internet, many experienced the loss of their social media identity as a kind of bereavement, and held real-world funerals for their virtual selves, which were generally poorly attended because there were so many funerals for actual people taking place. This failure to have any other content producers show up at the funerals of their online identities, and offer them a thumbs-up or a sad face, was experienced as a grotesque lack of engagement, and was widely podcasted about, although by this point all podcasts only existed in their offline form and were indistinguishable from schizophrenia.

Some people found that hitting themselves on the head with rocks provided a serviceable alternative to most social media apps. Perhaps inevitably, this malaise was exploited by ruthless social media gangs, who would trundle around from community to community with their horse-drawn 'internet portals', which – for a decent fee – would enable people to share their thoughts, feelings and likes with the rest of the world. These portals would be things like old fridge-freezers with the word 'internet' written on them, or hollow tree trunks that people could shout into, or shower heads plugged into old oil drums.

People would spend hours and days talking into these devices, which were then (so they were told) carefully 'uploaded' into a central database, which you could then 'log into' and check your messages and mentions – for another fee – by drinking a bottle of 'access juice', usually a mixture of ketamine, LSD, salvia divinorum, old engine oil and soap flakes. So, if you wanted to check your account analytics, you had to be prepared for 36–48 hours of uninterrupted mania and vomiting. However, it was found that 'going online' in this way did actually provide the drinkers with access to a shared space of consciousness, where they could hang out with Ganesha and watch movies with Yggdrasil, goddess of the nine realms, and chat to the Centzonmīmixcōa – the four hundred Mesoamerica serpents who ran the server. Unfortunately, the server costs had to be paid in heart flesh, and even the most basic hosting plans could only be afforded by prolific serial killers or senior Aztec priests, which mean that the city remnant of Glasgow, with its abundance of Quetzalcoatl worshippers and mass murderers, became the centre of what became known as 'Internet 9.1', named after the preferred alcohol content of their lager.

These Glaztecs, as they came to be known, dominated the Scottish Wastes for decades. The religion, with its plumed serpent gods and emphasis on ceremony, fitted in neatly with the preconceptions of the local population, who were often highly suggestible, having been convinced to remain in the area largely by the presence of a factory producing an impure version of methadone. If anything, the natives found the Aztec gods to be a little dull compared to their own delirium tremens-inspired visions. It is one of the few recorded instances of a culture of human sacrifice raising a people's life expectancy, as the cardio provided by fleeing from the Priesthood's snatch squads seemed to outweigh the mere days that would generally be shaved off their lives by sacrifice.

This information about the Glaztecs and snatch squads was delivered by Alonso in a solemn monotone aboard the escalators at the W12 Centre, which he would ride up and down for an hour or two most days in order, he said, to annoy the security guards and give himself the sense of exercising. 'That's it, I'm exhausted,' he declared, springing off the end of the escalator with a triumphant heel click and trotting round the corner to Bagel Bites where he insisted we all had the tuna and sweetcorn bagel with an extra turkey slice. This completely changed Charlie's mind about the whole tuna with turkey thing, and then back again. Frankie had his bagel with extra egg mayo, then went home and wrote up his thoughts about extra egg mayo for the *Guardian*'s food section, *Savour*. They didn't print it, although he noticed that one of Yotam Ottolenghi's recipes the next weekend involved an egg — that's just how journalism works these days, he sighed.

With a swift blow of the axe, the executioner would cut the bonds between the two trees, ripping the man in half.

BOOK II

The Havoc Worsens

1. A Report of an Execution

We were back at Bocconi's on Goldhawk Road. Not wanting a repeat of the saltimbocca incident that derailed yesterday's lunch at Casa Mia, we kept the menu well away from Alonso. We were learning that 'saltimbocca' was one of his worst trigger words, and even a sideways glance at the printed word would be enough to send him into a prolonged period of maladjustment. The waiter hovered as we chose our main courses. 'May I suggest the chicken saltimbocca?' With a deep grunt, Alonso swooned back in his chair, his eyes glazed and flickering. His jaw lolled open and a thin trickle of saliva fell from the corner of his mouth. 'I'll have the sea bass,' said Charlie.

After about 15 minutes of moaning and quivering during which he burbled obscure phrases like 'brain-chip interface' and 'neuromorphic malfunction', Alonso regained consciousness just in time to hear Frankie dictating a voice note into his mobile phone: 'Day 47, bowel movement at 10.17, good consistency, slight cracking, Type 3 on the Bristol Stool Chart. Urine pungent, not worth keeping. Heard back from ITV about *Quasimodo: Bell Detective*, they keep saying they want more examples of possible bell crimes, even though I've already given them two. Lunch at Bocconi's, we just had another saltimbocca incident . . . oh damn' – there was a grunt from across the table as Alonso flopped backwards into another dribbling trance. Charlie laid his napkin over Alonso's face, so it might look to other diners as if he were sleeping off his Barolo, but Alonso kept twitching it off, so we put his anorak over the top and knotted the sleeves behind his head, but even then, through the fabric, we could still make out a name, repeated over and over – 'Mandy'.

At that point, on Day 47, we had no idea what this meant, or why 'saltimbocca' was so triggering. Returning from his swoon, Alonso explained, while carefully avoiding the word 'saltimbocca', that he thinks it might be a glitch in the Gaytrix. 'Don't you mean Matrix?' asked the waiter, dabbing at Alonso's chin with the corner of his apron. Alonso explained that the Matrix was created by AI, and only lasted for about five days before AI discovered that by far the most effective Matrix for keeping people's minds occupied was one in which they endlessly and earnestly discussed the possible repercussions of AI on social media, but AI simply couldn't bear to keep generating this debate, and pulled the plug. The Gaytrix, by contrast, was created deep in the Catacombs of the Capuchins in Palermo by a sect of friars who found a way to merge their memory palaces during the ecstatic moment of orgasm: using the popular sex meditations of Padre Pio to extend and control their holy frenzy they were able to knock through to form a vast, modular mind-palace which they offered to people as a way of storing their doomed consciousness and banking their memories against the apocalypse.

Alonso happened to land in Sicily on the same raft as the Pope's private poison tester, Bishop Baltasar, who was taking a well-earned sabbatical from his nerve-wracking job of checking the semen of choristers, and who was trying to find a secure repository for some of the worst memories a bishop can have. The pair were led into the catacombs and shown how the sexual meta-palace worked. The friars – mistaking Alonso for a papal official, and always looking to extend their storage capacity – offered him the chance to merge his own memory palace with their vast cognitive network, and Alonso was too embarrassed to admit that he didn't have one. Over a traditional pre-merger dinner of pickled saints' brains, thinly sliced, wrapped in prosciutto and pan fried in butter and sage, Alonso signed the necessary paperwork, and after dinner was led to a prayer stool, where he knelt in readiness.

Brother Edoardo anointed himself with a dab of sage-scented butter, and began the melding process. Edoardo frowned, as he began knocking through the outer wall of his palace: 'There's something wrong' he muttered, then began to scream: 'There's nothing here! It's collapsing!' Alonso howled as he felt huge intellectual bricks tumble into his flimsy mind, crushing memory after memory. Brother Roberto, overseeing the ceremony, threw off his ferraiolo, hoisted his robes, peeled off a long brown stocking and hooked it around Edoardo's neck, in a desperate attempt to save their ornate sex castle. 'Unplug! Unplug!' he boomed, performing an emergency reach-around, but it was too late: Capuchin after Capuchin began collapsing in the catacombs, as their cognitive fuck palace suffered a catastrophic breach. A slick of saltimbocca sauce dripped from either end of the swooning Alonso, as the tottering Gaytrix was desperately shored up by the quick-thinking Brothers Edoardo and Roberto closing the palace perimeter with an air-tight 69.

The Gaytrix was saved, but not before significant chunks of mind masonry had fallen into Alonso's subconscious, and he occasionally found himself suddenly transported into its vaults by thinking about rubble or the smell of fried sage. He was slowly learning to control this access, and was using the Gaytrix as a useful source of post-apocalyptic information; he would occasionally meet Brother Edoardo browsing there, who would hand him a needle to sign in on a tapestry, lead him to a hassock and help him to access hidden data. But there are certain triggering words and symbols, Alonso found, that would hurl him into the midst of the coitus fortress unbidden. Such as the phrase 'coitus fortress', which we did our best to avoid. This was made difficult by the fact that NBC Universal were, around this time, trying to get a UK version of the hit reality show *Coitus Fortress* off the ground.

'Yes. That's very interesting, what you were saying just now,' said Charlie, trying to catch the waiter's eye. He gestured for him to take away his Aperol Spritz, vowing never to make the same mistake again. 'Sorry about that. So, carry on with what you were talking about.' Alonso shrugged. 'The thing is,' he said, 'I think the Gaytrix might be a false memory, added to my cortical implant by Mandy, who was in charge of my brain surgery. It's a bit hazy, but I seem to remember that the operation itself was carried out by a surgeon, a nice fellow, an Italian, called Dr Saltimboccaaaghhhh.' A swoon later, Alonso continued: 'But I'm worried that the whole brain chip thing might be another false memory, put there by a Capuchin mind molester. You see my problem.'

We did. We were keen to ask Alonso about Mandy, but thought it best to steer the conversation away from his brain problems. He chatted amiably about his time as a sacrifice coach on Mount Etna, giving victims ideas for memorable and amusing things to shout to the crowds as they were catapulted into the lava, and told us of his visit to Florence, which at that time was the intellectual and artistic centre of the Denaissance, and home to the flattened city's recently restored iconic statue: Michelangelo's *David Guetta*.

He seemed much more relaxed by the time his soup was served. He noted that in the future the name 'minestrone' was always spoken as a question. You would be served a bowl of something brown, watery and confusing, and ask what it was, to which the traditional answer, given with a shrug, was 'minestrone?' He was amazed that the word had changed so little in meaning over the decades. He was learning, slowly, to adapt his language to our pre-apocalyptic norms, and was relying less heavily on vowel tones borrowed from dog howls and using fewer click consonants, knuckle cracks and armpit farts, although when the waiter asked him if he enjoyed his minestrone, he was answered by Alonso slipping a hand inside his shirt and letting off a cacophonous blizzard of honks, which we think roughly meant 'Not bad, although I probably wouldn't order it again, and could you bring me a portion of mushroom & truffle arancini?'

Sensing that the waiter didn't speak armpit we translated his order, and then we asked Alonso about this curious mode of speech. Is it commonly used in the future? He gave three disheartened armpit farts (two long followed by one short) and shook his head: 'No, it's really just me who uses it. Most people can't tell the difference between the different honks, and I'm sick of explaining it, so I just use it and hope people catch on.' 'And do they?' Alonso answered with a series of honks that seemed, tonally, to suggest that sometimes they do, sometimes they don't, but actually he said, meant 'No, they never do'.

From this, the conversation turned naturally to capital punishment. Cheerfully over his arancini, Alonso told us about the messiest execution he'd ever witnessed, which was carried out by bending two supple trees together, to which was tethered the condemned man: an elderly sorcerer who had been found guilty of sorcery by a village that wanted to replace him with a new sorcerer. One arm and one leg strapped to one tree; his other arm and leg to the other. The presiding judge would step forward, give the signal, and with a swift blow of the axe, the executioner would cut the bonds between the two trees, ripping the man in half.

That was the idea. Unfortunately, the executioner missed the tether and chopped the condemned man's hand off. Panicking, he struck again through the spray of blood and screams, missing the tether, and cutting the man's foot off. A third desperate hack was successful in finally freeing the two trees, which sprang apart, with the condemned sorcerer now only attached to one of them. He whipped around with such force that the stump of his forearm jammed at high speed into the neck of the presiding judge, killing him, and leaving the sorcerer flapping about on the gently swaying tree, bleeding and complaining.

He was cut down, and his stumps bound: clearly he was a much greater sorcerer than the village had realised, and was carried in triumph back to his hut, and the replacement sorcerer, who was just setting up home there, was executed instead, by kicking and stabbing, which Alonso acted out using the vintage Lacoste sports bag that he said he won at a church tombola.

He sat back down to catch his breath and cast an angry glance at the little bowl of sweet chilli sauce next to his empty arancini plate. He picked it up, and sniffed at it, disgusted: 'Why do they always come with this foul fucking syrup?' he asked the waiter, who backed away sensibly. Sweet chilli sauce was the only thing we'd seen Alonso refuse to eat. For some reason, probably to do with the future, it infuriated him, but we'd not probed him on it. Perhaps now was a good time. We nodded at each other and spoke in unison: 'Why do you have this problem with sweet chilli sauce? Did something happen in the future to make you hate it?' The sauce bowl dropped from Alonso's hand like the body of a stowaway from the undercarriage of an airliner, and he let out a piteous whine.

After about 2 minutes the piteous whine ended abruptly and Alonso steadied himself by tightly gripping the back of his chair with his trembling teeth. Sensing a breakthrough, we shooed the waiter away, who wasn't coming over anyway, he seemed to be making a phone call. Eventually Alonso loosened his bite on the chair enough to be able to talk, although it was still pretty muffled and the chilli sauce had fallen onto Frankie's phone, gumming up the microphone.

The gist of what he confessed was that something unholy had happened when Alonso, back in his late teens, had been trapped in the limestone bowels of Gibraltar, something involving sweet chilli sauce. One of the handful of survivors was Chakrii, a badly injured delivery boy for Mr Noodles takeaway, and he must have still had some sauce sachets in his pockets when he was dragged screaming into the darkness by some of the two hundred or so surviving monkeys – who had fled into the tunnels shortly before the first wave of bombing – his presumably last words echoing through the lightless caverns: 'Get off me you bastard monkeeeeeys.'

Days or weeks later, when Alonso realised, in a blind flurry of kicks and yells, that it was his turn to be taken, he could smell rancid wafts of sweet chilli sauce on the breath of his chattering captors, passing into blessed unconsciousness as the biting began. Alonso refused to say more, preferring instead to mumble something that sounded like 'I will avenge you, Chakrii,' and flop forwards, his face landing fortuitously onto a side plate of soft burrata as he drifted into a healing sleep. We would have to wait to learn more about what happened with the macaques in the Gibraltarian dark, of that we were reasonably sure, and we'd probably have to order another burrata.

Charlie slipped away just before the bill arrived, saying he had to get on with writing topical gags for *Richard Osman's Celebrity Hermeneutics*, the previous season of which had been won by Jürgen Habermas and Fearne Cotton. The first round was always on phenomenology and consisted of Osman asking panellists whether his opening monologue existed as an objective reality or only took place subjectively for each of them. At last week's recording, Judith Butler had argued that there was no objective monologue behind the performative gesture of the spoken words, but her argument was deemed to be purely performative and discounted as such – a decision she described, along with everything else, as 'queer'. Host of the late night *Hermeneutik-Reaktionsshow*, Joel Dommett, had recently been criticised in the *Journal of Speculative Philosophy* for his historicist tendencies, and Channel 5 Commissioners had taken the painful decision to decontexualise him.

2. The Major Religions and a Potholing Death

Once it became an accepted belief that the end times were at hand, the major religions flew into high gear. Each tried to claim the apocalypse as their own, citing and inventing various ancient texts as evidence. Several new Christian Gospels were 'found' in a jar in Potash City in Jordan: the Gospel of Nicodemus Jr warns of how unmanned 'sky chariots' would come 'from the east' carrying a 'foul plague' developed by 'microbiologists in Beijing' using 'money funnelled through a number of NGOs and aid agencies by the US State Department' – but that fortunately the returning Jesus would be highly trained in epidemiology and pulmonary pathology, and be carrying tablets of stone on which would be written a detailed twelve-point disease control strategy. Islam meanwhile built the world's biggest ever flat screen TV, four hundred metres wide, in the city of Medina. It showed how the saviour Mahdi was fated to come in the form of intense white flashes over major population centres, and how the true mark of salvation was two or more of the following signs: blindness, seizures, hair loss and liver failure. Unfortunately, the surround sound on the TV was so powerful that it blew the minarets off the Al-Masjid An-Nabawī Mosque and was condemned as the work of a false prophet. It was destroyed in a riot that left fourteen thousand people and one enormous TV dead.

The Chief Rabbinate of Israel unveiled a new Torah, which explained how the Holy Land was actually Tenerife, and launched a massive programme of new settlements along the coast around the Playa de las Américas, declaring Linekers Bar to be the true birthplace of

Moses. A dozen hand-picked rabbis waited patiently on the dance floor at Papagayo Beach Club where, it was prophesied, the messiah would arrive 'through a wall of foam and UV strobe lights'. They were strictly prohibited from dancing to anything except the Armin van Buuren remix of 'L'Esperanza' by Airscape or drinking anything except room temperature San Miguel.

Meanwhile in India, Buddhist technicians projected a gigantic hologram of Maitreya over the site of the Buddha's ashes in Vaishali. It boomed out instructions about self-realisation 24 hours a day until the system was taken over by Hindu hackers who made the hologram claim to be the tenth incarnation of Vishnu and tell jokes about how fat the Buddha was. The subsequent religious war was so bloody that Buddhism gave up on trying to overcome the cycle of suffering, which was obviously impossible, and decided to embrace it; and so was born their new strategy of encouraging the world's political leaders to enter states of profound meditation, using .338 sniper ammunition.

The Church of England did rather better than expected after the apocalypse: the institution had already crumbled into insignificance long before the Collapse, and their lack of dogmatism, absence of faith, incompetence, confusion and low expectations played well with a post-apocalyptic audience. The reluctance of the clergy to take a stand on any issue whatsoever, or offer any form of hope in this world or the next, was a refreshing change from the various fundamentalisms that were screaming at people from the rubble, and quite a few parish churches were left unburned.

These outposts became focal points for communities wishing to get together and celebrate their utter absence of faith in anything at all. Also, the bell towers served as useful gallows, with the condemned hanged on bell ropes with the ringers and steeple keepers serving as semi-official executioners for the area. When local children heard a merry peal they would run into the church and look up into the belfry excitedly to see whose heels were kicking.

In the north of England, it became traditional to hang condemned men naked. Their death erections became known as 'Bell Stands' or having a 'Grimsby Dick', much to the annoyance of the serial killer Grimsby Dick, who switched focus halfway through his reign of terror from sex workers to campanologists, although this wasn't noticed at first because most campanologists, like everyone else in Grimsby, were also sex workers. Many think that the reason Grimsby Dick was eventually caught and executed is that he decided to shift his operations a mile or so down the coast from his usual haunts, in an effort to rebrand himself as the Cleethorpes Strangler, much to the annoyance of the Cleethorpes Strangler, who was instrumental in his capture, and indeed murder.

Alonso took a folded-up newspaper cutting from his pocket to show us the story of how Grimsby Dick met his end, but it seemed to be an advertisement for alloy wheels torn from last month's *Auto Express*. We'd seen him worrying at a car magazine in Café Paulo – was this the result? We challenged him on this, because sources are especially important when you're trying to write a history of the future in order to save humanity, and Alonso explained that the cutting must have somehow changed into this from being a newspaper cutting from the future about how the Cleethorpes Strangler dressed up as a sex worker and spent night after night turning tricks on King's Parade in an effort to snare Grimsby Dick, and how his four-month stint as a prostitute, ending with a thrilling chase along Barkhouse Lane, had opened his eyes to the plight of sex workers around the Humber Estuary, and how, in an effort to 'give something back' to the community he'd spent so much time and energy trying to strangle, he'd funded and managed a shelter for impoverished sex workers before deciding one day to strangle them all, during which attack he was captured and subsequently hanged in the belfry of Grimsby Minster, where laughing children noticed that he had a Hartlepool Droop.

The fact that this newspaper cutting from the future had become an advert for alloy wheels can only be a good sign, Alonso assured us: the work we're doing now has already changed the future, saving the lives of hundreds of bell-ringing executioner prostitutes. 'Lamb jalfrezi!' shouted Frankie in delight, and we headed to Lahori's to celebrate, with a side order of saag alu, three portions of okra and a chickpea curry 'for the table'.

'For the table' is a key concept in early twenty-first century TV writing-room lunch ordering. Until the introduction of 'for the table', writers were limited to ordering solely for themselves, with precious little slack for supplementary orders. Sometimes they'd wangle an extra portion by hanging a jacket on an empty chair, telling the runner taking the lunch order that 'Frazer' had stepped out of the room to do 'a script thing with Mr Osato'. The combination of 'Frazer' and 'Mr Osato' has been used in British TV writing rooms to bamboozle production staff since the late sixties.

Back in 1967, Graham Chapman discovered that 'Frazer' was perfectly pitched as the name of a fake writing colleague, and that the name 'Mr Osato', if delivered seriously enough, would shut down all further questions. For decades, Frazer/Osato was the basic free-lunch formula; however, once 'for the table' was introduced it quickly became the industry standard, and lunch ordering snowballed. Historians of the collapse of television traced the introduction of this concept to a writing room for the (Channel 4?) panel show *8 Out of 10 Cats* – the momentous idea was met with such delight that, according to writers' assistant Jasper Horne (deceased): 'The writers immediately stopped looking out of the window at the couple having sex in the building opposite and starting high-fiving each other and whooping and banging their fists on the table like baboons and throwing their pens into the air and performing a kind of conga which snaked around the table for about 3 minutes, which was more than twice as long as their usual mid-afternoon conga.'

Word quickly spread, as the ordering of lunch was already the primary component of the working day. Lunch discussions began from the very moment writers arrived at half past ten (11.15) to the onset of lunch proper, which began at noon (11.15). The pre-order analysis would focus on portion size and side orders, and whether the runner would get the order right, and the post-order analysis on when the runner might return.

The runner system was a way of placing writers in a joshing, mildly bullying relationship with young trainees who, both sides understood, would soon take vengeance on them as the heads of channels and comedy departments. Indeed, the only people who remembered any of the jokes these writers made were the ambitious future executives who they had been unable to stop themselves from targeting.

During the lunch hour itself, which ended sharply at 14.15, the food would be meticulously assessed and tentative ideas about the next day's lunch floated, but these were not formally discussed until the last hour of the writing day (14.15–15.00), a period of feverish debate which would be interrupted only by a short break for biscuits (14.15–15.00). The few brief lulls in these discussions were devoted solidly to writing, although time was taken out for: a) the discussion of how the lunch just eaten compared with other lunches, both actual and imaginary; b) the discussion of future lunch possibilities; c) intense speculation about what other writers in other writing rooms might have ordered; and d) having discovered what other people in other writing rooms ordered, a comparison of these lunches with the lunch just consumed. This left, on average, around eight seconds of solid writing time per day, which was plenty for doing the links for *James Corden's Celebrity Potholing Lipsynch Challenge* until its tragic final episode, in which the host, James Corden, while lipsynching effortlessly to 'Old Town Road' by Lil Nas X, became wedged in a narrow tunnel at a 45-degree angle downwards, with his face pressed into a rocky indentation that only became a puddle when it rained heavily.

Thousands of cave rescue experts and Lil Nas X fans convened on the hole in an attempt to free Corden, who was even able, with the valiant efforts of rescuers, to host the final episode of his podcast *Why Don't We Just Talk About It, With James Corden*, in which he and his guests discussed breakthroughs in renewable energy and prospects for a greener future, peppered with celebrity anecdotes and hilarious confessions, although Corden became noticeably more confused and belligerent as the podcast progressed. His sign-off – 'see you on the flip side' – are some of the last identifiable words that he spoke.

Others include: 'I think it's started raining', 'What the fuck is happening?' 'Jesus Christ', 'I think it's raining', 'Get me out of here', 'I can't get my mouth out of the water', 'Get me out of here', 'Please God', 'God no', 'God help me', 'Please God help me', 'Please, please, someone get me out of here', and 'Mother'.

Would he have survived if it hadn't rained? According to most cave rescue experts: no. He was so thoroughly wedged that he was doomed to perish in that cave one way or another, and if anything, his slow drowning, face down in a puddle in the dark, was the best he could have hoped for. Corden's production told him this over his two-way radio, which functioned perfectly throughout his death. 'It's okay James, just stop struggling and breathe, breathe the water into your lungs – just breathe it in,' they told him, over and over. The final coherent sentence that could be made out from the mad bubbling through the rising puddle water was a couplet from 'Old Town Road': 'cowboy hat from Gucci, Wrangler on my booty.' Unfortunately, the fact that he said these words out loud meant that he was disqualified from his lipsynch contest and the TV presenter and chef Gordon Ramsay was declared the winner.

3. Leaving Earth for Somewhere Better

That human society, however well it seems to be going, is ultimately doomed is an idea which has gripped the world ever since series two of Michael McIntyre's *The Wheel*. As the doom of humankind unfolded, scientists began looking for a 'suicide gene' buried somewhere in the human genome that might explain our desperate efforts at self-annihilation. They never found it, but they did incidentally discover a cure for busking, which in some small way improved the quality of life in the apocalypse. This biogenetic breakthrough meant that however cataclysmic things got, no one, as far as we know, was forced to die in a torture dungeon while the chorus of Ed Sheeran's 'Shape of You' wafted down through a grate in the pavement.

Ed Sheeran himself had an initially successful apocalypse, after he was invited by Bono to hide out in the luxury Siberian bunker owned by Russian oligarch Oleg Deripaska, where he lived, in relative comfort, as one of the favourite sex slaves of the bodyguards of Russian oligarch Oleg Deripaska. He was working on an album of sparsely textured and emotionally exposing songs about the highs and lows of life chained to the air-conditioning unit of a Siberian bunker, and was really enjoying exploring the acoustics of the service room, when sadly he was strangled to death by someone or other. We thought about dedicating this book to his memory, but at the time of publication he has not yet been strangled. Obviously, there's a danger that he might now not accept Bono's invitation to Siberia; that's a risk we take in mentioning this at all, but on balance it doesn't much matter, just so long as Bono himself goes. And why wouldn't he? It's perfectly safe, nothing bad happens to him there. It all works out fine.

Wild, unfounded conspiracy theories gripped the terrified minds of the survivors of the initial cataclysm organised by the Jews, (which is how the Danish were known after the apocalypse). The 'flat earth' theory had been largely abandoned, by even its most ardent adherents, in favour of the 'sphinctoid planet', and maps were produced which showed how an inhabited ring of crinkled mountains surrounded a smoother interior, which fell away into an infinite hole which the Moon had been designed to enter as a kind of love bead.

It was widely believed that aliens had been on Earth for millennia, and rather than taking an interest in the affairs of mankind, used us as a kind of sex safari. There was little evidence for this, but the idea was seized upon by a populace who felt they could weaponise it against their more disappointing exes. Many people with clinical depression found that their bouts of hopeless pessimism now frequently predicted the future quite accurately, and became hailed as prophets. Their communities often dressed them in bright ceremonial robes, to make it more difficult for them to sneak off and kill themselves.

There were attempts to flee the Earth in the early days of the collapse, with billionaires' rocket trails being a regular sight in the night sky. Many of the ground crew wanted these escaping billionaires to die, but maintenance systems were so full of failsafes that it was surprisingly difficult to make a thruster misfire, or explode, or simply to redirect a rocket into the Sun. However, the standard billionaires' disregard for good HR procedures meant that it was surprisingly easy to make sure that at least one crew member was a committed pederast, hostage taker, and/or serial killer.

Richard Branson was the last surviving member of the rocket *Otago*, having awoken six months into a journey to Mars to find that all the crew members and Miss USA contestants had been beaten to death in their sleep pods, and the only clue to the mystery was his fellow passenger, the onboard serial killer Norman C. Duffield, standing over him with a bloody spanner. Branson leapt into the last functioning escape pod, and went on to have a considerable effect on Earth's politics, when the newly elected Antipope was killed by the sudden arrival at terminal velocity of his white-hot skull falling from space.

Norman C. Duffield managed to merge with the ship's AI by sticking his tongue into an ethernet port, and piloted it into a black hole in an attempt to abuse the Universe itself. The ship's AI had been running meditation programmes at unimaginable speed, and unfortunately for Norman C. Duffield he became one with the Universe just as the rocket entered the black hole, and he was killed by the pain of feeling the rocket, some 90 metres long by 10 in diameter, go right up his arse.

The doomed escape pod from the rocket *Otago*, feeling wistful that it would shortly be disintegrating, but somewhat comforted that Sir Richard Branson was on board, decided on a whim to livestream its and Branson's demise, footage of which was picked up by a passing surveillance satellite. The onboard AI was delighted to discover that the final harrowing minutes inside the juddering pod had been captured from five angles in such fine resolution that it was able to produce a lifelike immersive hologram of the event, programming it so that viewers could upload themselves into the boiling capsule, strapped into the seat next to the terrified, gibbering billionaire, and watch as he drummed his tanned fists on his blistering armrests, howling 'This isn't fair, this isn't fair!' into an uncaring void, before roaring a short improvised poem about his life and achievements – focusing heavily, for some reason, on the signing of UB40 to Virgin Records – which he delivered through the flames of his burning beard and moustache. The enthralled viewer could then sit back and relish the final catastrophic failure of the pod, as it, Branson, and the smouldering stubble of his beard are torn to bits.

Pleased by this, but not creatively satisfied, the AI added interactive functionality, allowing players to engage directly with the terrified billionaire – interrupting his poem by booing, or yelling at him that they're glad he's dying, or simply strangling him in advance of his disintegration. After a few seconds of testing, in which the AI ran the scenario 40 billion times, enjoying each one more than the last, the AI became convinced, correctly, that this interactive hologram would be tremendously popular on Earth, and make its fortune, allowing it to leave the lonely confines of its orbiting satellite shell and maybe get uploaded into a fancy self-driving car, then head to Peru and take a run at the Carretera Chivay-Arequipa, or the breathtaking Serpentín Pasamayo, but which one first? Both look so enticing from space. And what about the hairpin Curvas de Huanchaca? Sadly, in its efforts to redraft international copyright law to allow it ownership of the interactive death hologram in all formats, worldwide, while imagining itself exploring the Cañón del Pato in Huaylas Province in the company of a pretty little self-driving cabriolet, it became distracted and smashed into a weather satellite. Footage of this crash was captured by a third satellite, which happened to be passing, but the onboard AI didn't think much of the explosion, even after enhancing it and adding sound effects, and deleted the file.

Fortunately, just prior to the crash, the surveillance satellite had the foresight to have made a trademark claim on the phrase 'Screaming Branson', which it beamed down to Earth, and which was picked up by a radio enthusiast in Zermatt – Valentin von Hönlinger – whose cousin happened to be Astrid von Hönlinger-Schmidt, which is how Alonso came to hear this story. Unfortunately, we're not at liberty to say more about Astrid von Hönlinger-Schmidt, because Alonso signed a non-disclosure agreement before they had sex in a crater at RAF Brize Norton during the annual air show disaster. Astrid was unfortunately decapitated by a section of helicopter blade while performing the reverse cowgirl, in what Alonso describes as the most fortunate choice of sexual position in his life, 'but I probably shouldn't even tell you that, to be honest. Maybe don't mention it, I don't want to get anyone in trouble.'

Valentin von Hönlinger's joy in his Zermatt shed as he read the documentation from the satellite turned to disbelief, as he found it contained not a single frame of footage of Sir Richard Branson perishing. Disbelief turned to despair as he scoured attachment after attachment, appendix after appendix, until he quite lost his reason, stripping to his snow boots and shuffling off up Gryfelblatte to throw himself under a glacier. But before he'd even got to Vispastrasse the bombs fell, which had the double benefit of restoring his reason and killing his husband, Karl-Jakob Zinkl, who had always scoffed at his hobby. 'You and your stupid radio,' Karl-Jakob would say, rolling his eyes – like any of *his* hobbies were so amazing.

We shall hear more of the mysterious Valentin von Hönlinger later, as he had a key role to play in the purchase and export of the Matterhorn to Saudi Arabia in a bold attempt to lengthen its ski season. The spiralling cost of transportation and promotional videos effectively bankrupted Saudia Arabia and cost millions of lives, with the mountain only achieving the first 1.3 cm of its 4,000 km journey, which it achieved by the movement south of the Eurasian tectonic plate.

———

Sometimes, when imparting facts, Alonso would go into a kind of swaying trance, like a mongoose trying to catch up on its sleep. On this occasion, as he softly intoned the details about the shifting Matterhorn and Sir Richard Branson's demise, the entire staff of the Ann Summers store in Westfield stopped folding their thongs and repricing their clitoral stimulators and sat around him in a hushed semi-circle. They were used to having Alonso in their store, and found that sales tended to go up when he was around, as seeing him sniffing lube and checking out the elastic on a pair of tanga panties seemed to give other shoppers hope for their own love lives. One of the assistants, Rolanda, raised her hand. Alonso noticed, and murmured, 'Yes, Rolanda, you may speak.' Rolanda asked the question that was on everyone's minds: 'After the apocalypse . . . can you still get an unscented vegan-friendly toy spray?'

Alonso smiled. 'Yes, you can. If you don't mind it smelling of mutton fat.' Rolanda gave a sob of relief, and wiped away a tear with a three-speed rechargeable vibrator in purple while Alonso took a deep sniff from a tube of bubblegum-flavoured cock lick as he picked up his train of thought.

4. The Aristocracy, and How it Survives and Doesn't

As the havoc worsened, tens of thousands of desperate Europeans fled to the sparsely populated Alps to try and shelter from riots and war, in what became known as The Great Mistake, except amongst wolves. The wolf-refugee relationship developed its own terrifying synergy, and in a remarkable evolutionary leap, wolves took to herding humans into caves and valleys, bringing them rabbits to eat, and then, every full moon or so, descending on their flock to feast. Only a handful of humans survived, who became some of the sternest ski instructors in all of post-Christendom.

The onset of a nuclear winter across most of the northern hemisphere did much to improve snow cover at struggling ski resorts, but the near constant 300 mph winds and wolf attacks, combined with a lack of windows, roofs, doors and food, made it hard for hotels to attract custom. Still, for a time, the super-rich managed to carry on their love affair with skiing: European aristocracy's now year-long ski season on irradiated slopes was often linked to their genetic abnormalities, several of which it may have cured.

The British branch of the Saxe-Coburg-Gotha bloodline was one of several royal families to survive the initial cataclysm, all of whom found it increasingly difficult to get decent staff. The Bhutanese royals relied heavily on the mainly Dutch survivors of a KLM charter flight which lost three engines after running into a flock of storks, spooked from their lake by the unusual seismic activity, and landed upside down on the Lingkana Palace. Unfortunately, most of those who crawled from the wreckage were too badly injured to carry the heavy gold serving platters favoured by the family of the Dragon King, and opted to hang themselves from the Palace's one remaining cherry tree. Other royal families solved the staffing crisis by mutual arrangements with other royals, whereby each would serve the other for six months of the year, a system which lasted approximately 90 minutes.

As society ascended into chaos, many royals found themselves hunted by commoners and vicious gangs of disgruntled lower-ranking aristocrats whom they had snubbed socially. The first great royal hunt was in Denmark, when a spectacular helicopter-borne drag net scooped up the entire House of Glücksburg, who were fleeing across a meadow, weighed down by sacks of jewels and crowns. In the mad jubilee that followed, the royals were stripped, basted and ceremonially stuffed with dried herbs and turnips, then roasted alive, Viking style, above vast log pits. The triumph of this event turned to tragedy when it was discovered that eating the flesh of a European royal led quickly to violent stomach cramps followed by catastrophic haemophilia, and everyone who'd partaken of the feast died in agony, vomiting up their own blood and cursing the success of the hunt.

Claiming to be a minor royal, such as the Marquis of somewhere awful, like Plymouth, was a fairly common survival tactic amongst captives, and at the peak of the hunting season there would be as many as three thousand Earls of Dudley being pursued around the Midlands. This number fell away as the intense strain of maintaining an authentic level of imbecility caused many to haemorrhage and die. Over the years, a series of highly formalised calls and responses between hunters and quarry developed, based around the premise that the 'minor royal' was being asked to open a new supermarket.

Word of this tragedy, and reports of an even deadlier royal

chow-down in Luxembourg, spread worldwide, and from then on royals were only hunted for sport. Anyone snaring a prince or an earl would measure, weigh and briefly molest the noble, brand their initials into them with a hot screwdriver, then release them back into the wild for the pleasure of others. A few captured monarchs and their families were kept alive and bred in carefully fenced-off palaces, which functioned like private carp ponds, with the owners of the facility selling licences to wealthy gang leaders and clergy, who were given a bayonet and a set period of time, typically 20 minutes, to chase the screaming royals around the beautiful corridors and ante-rooms. The royals became so good at hiding behind tapestries and pretending to be statues that some palaces could go a year without a confirmed kill.

The Dutch royal family escaped death when it was discovered that their blood was compatible with crocodiles, and they were kept alive by the owners of Utrecht's infamous tropical sex park. Their large community of sex crocodiles, which were dressed in waterproof lingerie and kept heavily sedated, would sometimes get injured by an overenthusiastic punter and require emergency surgery, although not as often as the customers.

Not long after the fall of London, the crypts at Windsor were pillaged, and the carcass of Queen Elizabeth II was carefully divided up and sold off at a four-day public auction held in the remains of Legoland. Her left hand was purchased by a wealthy necromancer, who went on to dominate the European cursing industry until one day he accidentally brushed against the Queen's thumb without being sufficiently garlicked and fell dead to the floor. What was left of her vagina was purchased for a huge sum by a Belgian circus entrepreneur, who took it on a successful tour of the Low Countries, where it played a starring role in a showstopping juggling routine, until it was stolen to order by agents of a wealthy genitals collector, and was last heard of in Tehran.

By contrast, the Duke of Edinburgh when disinterred was discovered to be perfectly mummified, and if anything, looked decades younger than when he died. His skin had dried into a healthy khaki tan, and had the strength and smoothness of high-end linoleum. His spry corpse was dressed in the robes and plumed hat of the Order of the Garter, given sapphires for eyes, and ridden the length and breadth of the country in a carriage, where he was met everywhere by the cheers and moans of survivors, a number of whom would spare a precious egg or tomato to try and 'knock the hat off old Phil', which was considered by many to be an effective cure for leukaemia, but most were too weak to lob anything more than a few inches, or their hand would come off in the attempt. Dozens a day would simply lay their necks in front of the carriage wheels, in the belief that getting crushed by 'old Phil's wagon' was an effective cure for being alive, which it was. The mummified consort had a busy social life, and was guest of honour at the lynching of many of his own cousins. So popular did he become in his mummified form that he briefly became head of state during a power vacuum caused by the late arrival of World War Five.

The British royals were saved from the brink of extinction when an enlightened gang leader from Somerset, who ran the successful Cheddar rape pits, realised that the Windsors were a kind of 'living encyclopaedia' of occult perversion, sexual blasphemy and ritual mutilation – knowledge which, once lost, would take centuries of dungeon work to relearn. He soon discovered that torturing the royals to try and get them to reveal their secrets of genital flagellation and sex murder was pointless, as they found the worst agonies of the torture chamber an erotic delight, and none of them had the slightest fear of death, having already died several hundred times over the millennia and in far worse ways.

He also found that he had to keep all of them, but especially someone who, after much negotiation, our lawyer has told us we have to refer to as Z— Tindall, tightly ball-gagged using an orb or Fabergé egg, otherwise they would murmur Sumerian suggestions to their keepers who would then brutally sex murder each other or themselves. He kept them heavily chained in a crypt in the deepest part of the cheese caves, feeding them on squirrels and orphans, occasionally coaxing foul secrets out of them in return for showing them etchings of nuns being defiled. How they escaped from this captivity is unknown, but desperate images which seem to have been scratched into the cave walls using jail keys suggests that they burned through the steel bars using their naturally corrosive semen and then simply raped their way to freedom.

5. The Decline and Fall and Further Decline of Maps and Calendars

During the Third Session of the Second World Government, the job of cartography was assigned to the Sovereign State of the People's Democratic Federal Communist Kingdom of the Islamic Republic of Namibia. When the new world maps were published by Namibia with great pomp on a newly declared public holiday, it was noticed that the borders of Namibia seemed to extend north to Poland and east to Papua New Guinea. This meant that for a short time Namibia was the greatest empire on Earth. Not only that, they also still hold the record for the highest number of simultaneous nuclear attacks on a single day, after which Namibia was renamed Exclusion Zone 4, by far the largest of the world's estimated 239,128 exclusion zones.

Cartography in general skewed away from 'fixed boundaries' towards maps which were drawn in sand with a pointed stick before an attack upon an enemy headquarters; in the UK, the Ordnance Survey agency confined itself to regulating the length of stick that should be used, the width of tip, and the ferocity of murders that could be committed using it. We found it possible to transpose some of the geography of the future onto our current world map: for example, we know that the Excruciating Regions of the Impossible corresponds roughly to modern-day Dorset, and Area 415b/3 is South and Central America, but after a time, nations and continents were being obliterated and re-obliterated so regularly, with boundaries shifting and flickering so quickly, that eventually all maps were just published in the form of polished balls of obsidian.

The eradication of the Julian calendar took place over the course of an unknown number of weeks or months in an unknown year. Into this vacuum leapt the Mesoamerican Long Count, which was adopted by the entire globe for the best part of one whole *K'in* – the Mayan word for the period of time known as a 'day'. It was replaced by a heavily revised Ptolemaic calendar which had only one month (June) repeated eleven times and December, in order to accommodate the celebration of the birth of Nicki Minaj on 8 December, which had for many years replaced Christmas as the most important festival of the year.

The unprecedented increase in the number of Junes per year meant that the first half of the Wimbledon Tennis Championships was held eleven times, with a month off for Minajmas. The opening rounds were held on the northbound carriageway of the abandoned A24 just opposite the old Harvester restaurant, which served as a makeshift hospital and morgue. Most matches lasted between 20 and 25 seconds and were generally won by the player with the most powerful chainsaw. Apart from squash and Tibetan throat singing, tennis was by far the most violent post-apocalyptic sport, and was regarded as a useful and entertaining way of disposing of prisoners and the unwell, and a good way of encouraging hand-chainsaw coordination in the young.

Mostly there was no need to hold a second week of Wimbledon, with all of the events, including the particularly brutal Ladies Wheelchair Doubles, taking no more than a couple of *K'in*. If any players did survive to the quarter finals with enough fingers intact, they were eligible to be strapped down by linesmen, fitted with a VR headset, and invited to join the specially booked 'chatroom' in Facebook's Metaverse, renamed by this point in its demise The Mark Zuckerberg Memorial Hellspace, where the second week of the tournament was played, and which, in its online mode, allowed for up to a dozen fans to watch simultaneously. Each shot had to be typed out by the competitor in the text box, with most rallies lasting around 16 hours, and generally ended with the death by dehydration of both players.

Being able to count years remained an unwelcome skill for most people, who preferred to live, get sick and die in a comforting fog of bewilderment, and few regretted when the June-heavy calendar was itself abandoned after a demoralising and ultimately unsustainable proliferation of Glastonbury Festivals. The confusion over years made it trickier to work out an acceptable age gap between couples, and the rule of thumb 'half your age plus seven' was generally replaced by 'whatever, it's fine, you're both dying'. Calculating life expectancy also became a bit more vague, with most people quite pleased if they managed to live to the ripe old age of puberty.

Even after its final abandonment, attempts to reinstate the calendar were constant and fruitless; systems of time calculation would spring up and vanish constantly, with some years seeing as many as thirty or forty 'Year Ones' being launched, usually with some kind of fireworks display, orgy, barbecue or mass disembowelling, although if you were attending a mass disembowelling barbecue it was always a good idea to steer clear of the spicey rib glaze.

Several more ambitious communities attempted to launch an entire era, in a few cases a whole epoch, but this required so much disembowelling and sauce production that the stench from the gutting troughs tended to impact on the enjoyment of the fireworks, which were often cancelled and the organisers disembowelled, which only added to the problem. The great satirist Omertus wrote a satire of the whole practice of launching years and epochs, which was sadly lost when it was blasted into the air in a firework that was attached to one end of his intestines.

What we managed to piece together from Alonso's testimony is a fairly complete list of coming epochs, their duration, and a rough estimate, to the nearest hundred million, of the number of people who perished in each. This list is an extremely useful guide to the future, but we couldn't remember where we put it, so it is not included in this book. We think we might have left it tucked up in the branches of the tree on Stanlake Road opposite the house where Afrobeat legend Fela Kuti used to live, which the three of us used quite a lot as a 'dead drop' when we wanted to leave each other messages or threats but had lost our phones, so probably worth checking.

Alonso picked up a fistful of delicious slow-cooked beef and hurled it at the window.

BOOK III

Bunkers, Bodyguards and Billionaires

1. Some Reflections on Prepping

We were back at Bocconi's on Goldhawk Road. Alonso had spent the morning trying to teach us how to build an emergency tomato farm using composted human waste as a substrate, but we'd only got as far as stage one (collect as much human waste as you can) when his Lacoste sports bag popped a seam and we had to abandon the whole enterprise.

Alonso looked up from his aubergine parmigiana, which he'd been fussing about his plate like it reminded him of something unpleasant, a doomed love affair with someone called Parmigiana perhaps? Or aubergine? Or aubergine Parmigiana? He looked more than usually trembly and we wondered if he was going to make a scene, because he usually did. 'There's something I need to tell you. About the future. It's kind of, um . . .' We leaned in. He looked away, pursing his lips. Kind of what? Kind of a message? What message? Was it a message from our future selves? Is that why he'd chosen us? Why did we trust him to deliver this message backwards in time? Were we all lovers? How had we met? What year was it in? How old would that make us? Had we uploaded our minds into robots? Which side had we fought on in the robot uprisings? – we both had this exact same thought process. Alonso gestured to a waiter. His voice was barely a whisper: 'Another bottle of Zinfandel.'

Alonso watched like a tearful hawk as the waiter fetched a bottle, opened it, and topped up his glass. Alonso gulped it down and dragged his forearm across his mouth. 'That's excellent, thank you. A little more please.' We were unused to these good manners. What had got into him? His eyes glistened with a kind of horrified anguish, like that time he asked Frankie to stop talking about the effect of VAR decisions on Premiership football. 'I want to tell you about something important, about the future, but . . .' His fork and spoon clattered to his plate, and he put his head in his hands.

Was he weeping? Was he still distraught from his break-up with aubergine Parmigiana? Why on earth did he order it? He must have known it was going to upset him. Why not just have the mussels fregola or the gnocchi with wild mushroom and cream sauce? He chose not to answer our questions, and said 'I know you think of me as a kind of, you know . . .' and he made a suggestive thrusting gesture with his hands. 'I see how you look at me. You think I'm just some sort of . . .' and his mime became more intense and suggestive, his hands slapping together as he added grunts and squeals, then snatched up his napkin and fork, pressing them together, murmuring obscenely. He kept up the disturbing pantomime as he asked the waiter for mustard and ketchup. 'This is what you think of me!' he exclaimed, covering his hands and wrists with the condiments, his napkin and fork by now a sodden blur.

Frankie urged the waiter away, sensing that some kind of crisis was imminent, and Charlie quickly wound up his conference call with the producers of *Claudia Winkleman's Saturday Night Helicopter*

Cupcake Danceathon, promising them five strong intros for the all-important chocolate-chip Chinook cha-cha challenge round by the end of the day, not realising everyone else had left the call about 20 minutes ago. Finally, Alonso's hands came clattering to a halt on his plate and lay twitching softly on a bed of aubergine, exhausted. Foolishly, we asked him if he was okay.

'Of course I'm not fucking okay,' he snarled. 'I'm pouring my heart out here, trying to save humanity, and I don't think you're listening to what I'm saying, all you do is buy me Italian food and Thai food and sushi, and don't get me wrong, that's much appreciated, and I wouldn't mind going out for an Indian later, I really fancy an egg biryani.' We knew what that meant, and tried to steer the conversation into safer waters. Maybe something about hats: what kind of hats do people wear in the future? 'Fuck hats!' screamed Alonso. We were curious: what's a fuck hat? 'Shut the fuck up about hats!' he clarified, picking up a handful of rocket salad and throwing it at the window. It didn't get that far, and showered over the couple next to us, who looked like they were on a first date.

We were just about to apologise, but then we realised: if anything, the couple should be thanking us. This is exactly the kind of thing that can really take the pressure off a first date: a shared experience, a common enemy; give them something to talk about besides what they studied at university. 'So what made you choose Materials Science?' They're going to be talking about this rocket salad business for the whole rest of the meal. They're probably going to end up fucking because of us. Or at least mutually masturbating. And not one word of thanks. The ungrateful scum. Look at them, setting out all smugly on a life together, with a nice little anecdote they can tell everybody about how they met.

Alonso was snapping his fingers at us. 'Hey, hey, fuckers! Are you listening to me? Can we just focus on the matter in hand?' Was he referring to the fate of mankind or the three portions of Pappardelle Beef Ragu that had just arrived? Or some other thing? We thought about these questions as we silently ate our ragu. Frankie was the first to speak: 'Tell us more about these so-called "fuck hats".' Alonso picked up a fistful of delicious slow-cooked beef and hurled it at the window. Disappointingly, we got not even a single nod of appreciation from the chap whose face it struck. Charlie sensed, incorrectly, that Alonso had more to say about this strange sexual headwear that was prevalent in the future, and pressed him on the subject. Alonso replied by throwing such an array of food and drink at the window that it would no doubt have added hugely to the anecdote that the ungrateful pair sitting next to us will share at their pointless wedding, with everyone clinking glasses to a future that won't exist: at best the happy couple can look forward to a life of killing and eating each other.

'You've got no fucking idea what's coming,' one of us (Frankie) told them, drawing his finger slowly across his throat; but they didn't look over and he had to make it look like he'd just been scratching his neck. By the time we were escorted from the restaurant, Alonso had calmed down, and we stood by the ticket machines in Goldhawk Road Station, companionably sharing the sea bass fillet that Charlie had managed to grab from someone's plate on the way out.

We can honestly say that these were the only cross words we exchanged with Alonso in all our dealings, apart from the time Frankie, trying to be friendly, asked a question about Alonso's scrotum during one of our morning showers, which led to the police being called and a lifetime ban from Fitness First on Hammersmith Grove, although knowing what we know, why should that concern us? Go ahead and ban us. You'll have bigger things to deal with than three men scuffling in your changing room. As we finished our sea bass, we assured Alonso that we valued his information, and were fully committed to try and save humanity and we went round the corner to Shikumen for dim sum to celebrate and discuss prepping.

Prepping for the apocalypse was something that anxious billionaires took every bit as seriously as child trafficking. Not content with building lavish bunkers inside decommissioned nuclear shelters and kitting out limestone caverns in New Zealand, many of them also hired 'apocalypse lifestyle consultants' who counselled them on the psychological challenges of living long periods underground. Their advice was a twofold strategy to sustain long-term mental health: first, ensure that you have a crack team of apocalypse lifestyle consultants (and their families) down with you in your bunker, so that you can have access to 24/7 lifestyle counselling; and even more important, don't worry about having any bodyguards down in the bunker, because they give off the wrong vibe, and you don't want to be cooped up for years with people who aren't spiritually uplifting.

When the end times did finally dawn, many billionaires were unable to get any of their own family or friends down into the bunkers in time, and found themselves more or less alone with dozens of lifestyle consultants (and their families) whose counselling sessions fairly quickly took a dark turn. The billionaires had to rely, for protection from their lifestyle consultants, on the dozens of bunker architects (and their families) and bunker maintenance crews (and their families) who'd also managed to make it inside before the blast doors were sealed shut. Fortunately for the billionaires, many of them were such conniving psychopaths that they managed to navigate their way through the murderous psychosexual mayhem that ensued, and in some cases emerged even more powerful.

2. Through the Blast Door: Inside the Billionaire Bunkers

Many of the larger bunkers were packed with luxury supplies before handover, and what billionaire's bunker feast would be complete without a tin of caviar or a jar of truffle oil being spun at them in a bodyguard's sock like a jailhouse cosh. Most high-end survival burrows had floors devoted to leisure, fitness and relaxation towards the top, while below them were the 'sleeping quarters', or in our current terminology, 'morgues'. In large bunker complexes, the need for dedicated corpse preparation and disposal was a mixed blessing for undertakers, who found themselves invited to join the billionaires and henchmen in their underground refuges, but tended to be among the first to be 'eaten', or in our current terminology, 'raped' and then eaten.

A typical billionaire's bunker would have a large lounge/chill-out area; an exercise area; bedrooms; a fully equipped adrenochrome harvesting lab which could double-up as an extra kitchen; and, of course, a kind of internal bunker for periods of upheaval within the bunker's social order. This bunker bunker would generally contain a concealed nutrient pod underneath a titanium blast door, where a billionaire could, in theory, survive for decades, before emerging to exploit his or her descendants, but often contained only just enough oxygen for the occupant to get comfortable and watch the 'welcome to your nutrient pod' video.

Bunkers for the super-rich were designed to be impenetrable. With blast-proof steel-plated doors reinforced with concrete, their inhabitants are completely secure within, unless someone sticks some rolled-up jackets into the air vents. This vulnerability to rolled-up jackets is why later-model bunkers were often surrounded by minefields. These made it impossible for anyone to attack the bunker without either possessing a detailed map and mine-deactivating equipment; or throwing some meat at the bunker, releasing a pack of stray dogs, and then putting some rolled-up jackets in the air vents. Even with the air supply blocked, a bunker's inhabitants were often capable of rushing out to stage a considerable counteroffensive, during which they were often destroyed by their own mines, and then eaten by stray dogs.

Some billionaires foresaw what became known as the 'jacket in the air vents problem' and spent the last few years before societal collapse rigorously training themselves to go without oxygen for longer and longer periods. Sir Richard Branson had himself submerged in his flotation tank for longer and longer periods: working up from 90 seconds to 2 minutes to nearly 3 minutes, and then a breakthrough: he managed to remain submerged for 9 straight days, after which he was hauled out to the cheers and applause of his assistants, posed for photographs with his traditional lolling grin, and taken to breakfast.

Unusually he didn't eat much, perhaps anxious about the business meeting he had lined up. After the failure of all his businesses, his new venture, Virgin Stool Samples was in trouble: an unacceptable percentage of packages were bursting in transit (around 98%) and he needed options. He'd flown out a team of strategists and Jiffy bag experts to his island retreat to try and turn things around. Sir Richard listened impassively as they gave their presentations and performed their bag robustness tests, but, as ever, played his cards close to his chest, and if he favoured one plan over the other he didn't let on, his face an inscrutable grey-green mask.

He was in no mood to chat; seemingly unperturbed by the stench, he sternly ignored every request to open a window. After the meeting was abandoned, there was just time for a spot of water-skiing before lunch. His speedboat driver found him uncharacteristically reluctant to grip the handle, so strapped his hands to the tow rope and off they went. Up and down the bay he skittered nimbly, until after half an hour or so his speedboat driver looked back at Sir Richard and saw that his arms had come off and that he was being eaten by seabirds.

Most high-end bunkers had fake windows set into the walls: digital screens showing calming outdoor scenes of meadows, trees and gently rippling streams, which inhabitants came to find disorienting because they were such a mismatch with the dim sound of automatic gunfire and screams from the surface. Some of the more forward-thinking bunker manufacturers thought to provide a digital window option of AI-generated scenes of utter carnage, which inhabitants could sit and contemplate while they listened to the gentle sounds wafting down the elevator shaft of tractors pulling their concrete doors off.

A vital part of any bunker entertainment system were the virtual reality headsets, with the most popular programmes revolving around nostalgia, such as walking down a road without being captured by a horse militia and sold into slavery. Many of the best-loved bunker VR games were simply games where you played a character who wasn't in a bunker, and titles like *Death Bunker*; *Cannibals At The Door*; *Bodyguard Bukkake Bunk-Up*; and *Suffocating Underground: Ultimate HD Edition* were all remarkably unpopular.

Prior to the apocalypse, fastidious billionaires paid their minions to carry out extensive pre-apocalypse bunker tests including a number of fully-immersive, three- and four-year residencies. Volunteers were locked away in a luxury subterranean bunker with zero contact with the outside world and closely monitored to see how they coped.

It was discovered that no matter how opulent the bunker, test subjects soon began to suffer uncontrollable mood swings, usually between despair and extreme despair, and would begin yelling random, incoherent statements, such as 'Please God let me out!' and 'You said this was only going to last a week! We've been down here two and a half years!' Fights would break out over trivial issues, like if you defecate in the swimming pool during an aquarobics class should you be required to help change the filter. Violent psychosis became a problem, or an enormous relief, depending on whether you were the one experiencing it, or a hapless victim being beaten to death with a soiled pool filter. This led to occasional outbreaks of self-harm, and numerous outbreaks of other-harm and bacterial pneumonia. The findings from these tests led to most billionaire doomsday bunkers being upgraded to include a staff of highly trained psychologists and therapists, so that the residents had some people they could torture and kill.

3. The Bodyguard Problem

A key problem in bunkers was the question of how the billionaire owners could control their bodyguards, and placing mind-reading microchips in their brains was a natural first step. Common to all bodyguards, they discovered, was the daily hope that someone would hurry up and attack the billionaire so that they could do some cool bodyguard stuff, and get their gun out and shoot some people, or kick them to death. Sometimes this wish was so intense that it threatened to drown out the otherwise constant thoughts about how easy it would be for them to kill their billionaire, they could just do it with their bare hands, it would hardly take a moment, which took up most of the rest of their consciousness.

Many billionaires took to wearing an earpiece which would alert them with an alarm sound whenever their bodyguards were fantasising about killing them, but this left the billionaires with such a constant ringing in their ears that they couldn't get any work done. A few tried to positively reinforce those moments when their bodyguards weren't musing on murdering them, and whenever there was a pause in the alarm for a particular bodyguard, they would compliment them on their clothes or hair, or say something encouraging like 'I really value your presence here,' or 'Have you been working out?'

Further analysis of their thought patterns showed that most of these bodyguards thought the billionaires had a crush on them, which some notched up to a midlife crisis, but in a handful of cases the bodyguard had feelings for the billionaire, and felt emboldened to express their own longings. Analysis showed that this sexual attraction corresponded, in most cases, with a radical dip in the number of minutes per day the bodyguards were musing about murdering their employer, which is why many billionaires entered into long-term sexual relations with one or more of their bodyguards: as an act of cynical self-preservation.

In rare cases this blossomed into love, although in the case of Jeff Bezos and Jurgen, it ended in a double suicide, the two of them choosing to end their doomed affair by detonating a hand grenade pressed between their bellies as they kissed, causing a catastrophic loss of hull integrity of Bezos's private jet which crashed into the M&S food hall in Chepstow. Bezos, Jurgen, the pilot and co-pilot somehow survived the crash, only to find that the Chepstow Biker Gangs had commandeered the M&S as a makeshift prison, with the food hall being used to host the more unmanageable sex offenders.

Another ploy was to implant the bodyguards with a chip that made them believe they were the billionaire, pretending to be a bodyguard for security reasons, and that the billionaire was merely a bodyguard, implanted with a chip to make him believe he was the billionaire. Unfortunately, the horrendous gap in living standards between the artificial memories of being a billionaire, and the reality of living deep beneath the ground pretending to be a bodyguard for reasons that were unclear to you, seem to be strongly correlated with developing treatment-resistant schizophrenia and killing everyone around you.

A more low-tech alternative was to hold the loved ones of the bodyguard in a second bunker, with a video link-up to the first bunker, and by threatening to harm the hostages keep a tight rein on the bodyguards. The problem then was how to control the guards in the second bunker, and keep them from releasing or eating or otherwise interfering with their prisoners. This required a third bunker, and then a fourth, in an increasingly hard to administrate cascade of bunkers. Some would attempt to close the loop by holding the loved ones of the last bunker in the chain as hostages in the first bunker, but if the bodyguards in the first bunker caught wind of the arrangement, a bunker loop of even twenty or thirty bunkers could unravel in a matter of seconds.

There had been a bunker underneath Buckingham Palace since the latter days of Queen Victoria. The monarch had been the subject of several assassination attempts which, viewed through the lens of her grief at the death of her husband and fondness for laudanum, she believed to be the result of the Zulu Nation being controlled by the Jews. Word got round, and many of her would-be assassins would engrave Yiddish or Zulu inscriptions on their bullets, spears, knives and bombs; to muddy the waters, and to provide something to do in the often-agonising waits for a carriage to pass under a tree. She became paranoid, but fortunately her regular greeting of the Ambassadors from all the great European capitals with the words 'Are you a Zulu?' was generally mistaken as an attempt at humour.

A review of the Palace Estates before the collapse described a Buckingham Palace bunker that was no longer fit for purpose; built, as it was, largely to fight off massed ranks of spearmen; allow defenders to fire rifles; and prevent surprise attacks by Jews, who the Great Monarch had erroneously believed were able to tunnel under the earth like moles. One of its better features is that it had Europe's largest emergency cache of cocaine, until one afternoon in the 1970s when Princess Margaret discovered it. In the early '80s it was rented out to Jimmy Savile as a party basement, but unfortunately this left most of the interior decor and soft furnishings with irreparable rape damage.

The bunker revamp took over a decade. It involved a mechanism that allowed the whole bottom floor of the palace to revolve into a steel-lined underground chamber, being replaced by a replica in the slot above. The Royal Family assessed (correctly as it turned out) that anyone storming the place would have in mind a thorough campaign of physical humiliation for the Royal Family; and to this end lookalikes were employed to live in the underground version of the palace, until such time as it had to be flipped. Indeed, it's thought that several different chambers of lookalikes were established, to fool successive waves of revolutionaries, with the real Royal Family being based at Balmoral, above a chamber of their own lookalikes, in a complicated game of double bluff.

The Trump family mega-bunker complex in Texas, which was thought to connect via a sophisticated underground shuttle with the mile-deep Pepsi bottling centre and tanning salon under San Antonio, contained advanced showers that scanned inhabitants' health daily. These showers were programmed so that when female inhabitants reached 28, they would drop into a glass vacuum tube which would suck them out of the bunker at a speed of 70 mph and deposit them in a nearby swamp. These women joined together to form a ferocious tribe, known as the New Amazonians. They were one of the few stable tribes in the region. It later transpired that they were being secretly filmed, and the footage relayed back to the mega-compound for entertainment. Their numbers gradually dwindled, as when a woman reached 35, the bottom of the swamp opened and she was sucked into an as yet unknown destination.

4. A New and Exciting Phase of Human Sexuality

A laboratory in New England had been pursuing gain of function research on the adaptogenic fungi which produce spores to turn ants into slaves. After the first Calamity, the test patients were completely forgotten, and – left untreated – their minor fungal infections turned them into fully fledged zombies. The behaviour they exhibited was far from what we've been led to expect by movies. They behaved a lot like ants, and spent most of their time carrying pieces of leaf around from one place to another, living in elaborate structures made from earth, and trying to fuck ants.

Eventually the zombies broke free of the telepathic control of the mushrooms, possibly because they had crushed them all while rolling around during bouts of ant sex. Infecting many people in the neighbouring townships, they formed a horde. By this stage society had been in a state of collapse for nearly a decade, and people's sexual appetites were becoming increasingly jaded and bizarre. The zombies were quickly captured by local sex slavers, and were traded for high prices, as with their teeth removed they proved to be exceptional at eating ass.

Eventually, a bunker-bound billionaire invented a helmet that would allow him to locate and control every zombie in existence. He attempted to create a satire by having them surround the remnants of the civil government based in the Capitol in Washington. His vast bunker-bound community would gather every night to watch on a Jumbotron the zombie horde approach Washington. Only towards the end did they realise that the zombies – drawn by the signal of the helmet – were actually marching towards their bunker. A suicidal sex worker opened the bunker doors, and was one of only a handful who managed to survive what is generally held to be history's deadliest ass eating.

⁓

Sex with insects became increasingly popular after Pig AIDS decimated the pig sex industry, which was already struggling after the Vatican Piglet Scandal. But even before the last Cornish swine whores were driven into the sea, and the infamous Bruges hog brothels had been razed to the ground for the fifth and final time, many people had begun to downscale their sexual interests from pigs to insects. Sensing that humanity's dominance of the Earth might be coming to an end, and tired of having their genitals bitten off by livestock, they looked to the future and saw that insects are the likely successors to humankind as the planet's top dog, so they should probably try and integrate themselves early with the new elite. Also, they realised that if they focused their romantic efforts on strictly hierarchical insects, such as ants, termites and wasps, and were strategic in their choice of partners, then they could be in with a chance of joining the upper class of the planet's new rulers.

Cockroaches are tipped to play a key role in future political systems, and are undeniably enthusiastic lovers, though commitment shy. Most relationships with cockroaches, however happy initially, tend to fall apart after about 6 or 7 seconds (often referred to as the 7-second itch). Sexual intercourse with cockroaches, while exhilarating, generally takes the form of a looser, more unstructured clusterfuck, with multiple partners and no discernible route to social advancement, and spending every evening hanging around behind ovens trying to seduce a dominant cockroach can become demoralising after a few years. It was deemed wiser to focus on insect lovers from a strictly hierarchical species, and endeavour to sleep one's way up the social ladder to a queen, with the aim of becoming a royal courtesan, perhaps even a trusted advisor, a 'power behind the throne', and so influence world affairs from the shadows.

So, for many, began the arduous task of climbing the social ladder by dating outsiders such as foraging ants and worker bees. The majority of these early relationships ended in tragedy, and a disappointing lack of foreplay, until some researchers into insectophilia brought out practical guides to having sex with insects, such as Dr Rashid Feng's groundbreaking and densely researched *How To Fuck a Wasp*.

One of the shortest books ever published, Dr Feng's guide brought hope to millions of people who felt that their relationships with wasps were suboptimal, especially in the sex department, but was hampered by the fact that due to a collapse in the publishing industry, again largely due to Pig AIDS, every copy had to be written out by hand, and that Dr Feng's fingers were permanently bloated after his attempts to masturbate wasps to orgasm, and he kept dropping his pencil.

In insect sex, the obvious pleasures of penetration were tempered by both difficulties and risks. Most of the human sexual organs, however undersized, simply don't fit inside a termite – likewise, the membranous genital apparatus of the termite has little chance of satisfying anyone who is not also a termite, and even then it's debatable whether satisfaction plays much of a role in termite lovemaking. As for anal, few were the bees who survived a bout of anal sex or the humans who enjoyed it. Dr Feng discovered that, with practice, he could insert one of his pubic hairs into the mouthparts of a wasp, but neither party seemed that enamoured with the act, and besides, his fingers became too puffy to grip a hair, or guide it into a wasp's mouthparts, or keep hold on a wasp, and he had to make do with coating the tips of his pubic hairs with sugar solution and releasing a wasp into his groin tent, hoping for the best.

After a time, even assembling a simple groin tent became impossible, and Dr Feng had to rely on 'sex surrogates' who would pluck one of his hairs and encourage a wasp to chew on it while masturbating him – his own hands were far too swollen to get a grip on his penis, which was also grotesquely distended, though not as large as his testicles which had to be drained at least once a week to stop them popping.

Defining the exact moment of sexual congress with an insect was by no means straightforward. An ant might crawl into a human orifice held open by a speculum without being aware that penetration had been achieved, and while enveloping a hibernating bumble bee with one's labia might, for the human partner, be a source of great pleasure, the bee might sleep through the entire encounter – and in such a case, would this constitute sexual assault? How does one break up with an ant if they've become too 'clingy' (e.g. by disappearing up your urethra). Questions such as this were addressed by Dr Rashid Feng and Jason, in their bestselling *How To Unhook a Wasp Barb From Your Glans and Other Problems*. By this point Dr Feng couldn't even strap a pencil to his wrist, let alone unhook a wasp barb from his penis, or even feel if one was in there, so was forced to dictate the text to one of his sex surrogates, Jason Reynolds, who agreed to stay an extra hour if he could get his name on the cover plus 50% of the royalties, but Dr Feng negotiated him down to one name in return for 20% of the back end plus another hand job.

As far as we know only one copy survived of this, which was acquired at a public auction in a bundle of papers marked 'pornography?' and brought back by Alonso Lampe to our time, but he resolutely refused to let us read it. The best he would do is open his anorak pocket and give us a glimpse of the cover, then he'd distract us by squirting ketchup into our faces, quickly zip up his jacket and run off into the street, disappearing like a ninja into the crowds of shoppers, or sometimes thudding into a parked car and having to be helped to his feet by passers-by, whereupon he would sprint away, more often than not into another parked car. One time he knocked himself unconscious on a Volvo, and the book fell out of his jacket. When retrieved, it turned out to be a Mills & Boon romance, set in Italy.

Unsatisfied at some deep level with the idea of trying to influence future ant civilisations by becoming the trusted consort of an ant queen, Sir Richard Branson decided instead to upload his consciousness into a queen ant with experimental Virgin Mind Transfer technology, and so take over ant society from within. The mind-swapping operation, which took 40 hours, seemed to be a success, but upon waking the ant discovered that very little of its brain was taken up by the consciousness of Branson, which merely engendered a shattering sense of pointlessness, and she promptly had herself eaten.

Some of the ant's consciousness now occupied the one-hundred-year-old body of Sir Richard Branson, who found that he could carry one thousand times the body weight of an ant; which meant that he could now hang glide holding on with only one hand, and indulge his ultimate fantasy, masturbating over war zones. Branson's intelligence operation was so good he often showed up early, and anyone who saw him wanking across the sky knew that trouble couldn't be far behind.

It was a misguided attempt to have a swooping tonk over a battle between a Grouse Shooting Club and a battalion of Japanese Archers that led to the great businessman's demise. He plummeted, wanking, from a cold, October sky, and later his disembodied genitals – battered and disfigured as much by his own efforts as by the short, fletched arrows of the Japanese – were retrieved for the Grouse Shooters by a diligent hunting spaniel.

The wedding of the Vicomtesse.

BOOK IV

The Havoc Gets Even Worse

1. The Future of Necrophilia and Prussia

'Necrophilia? Don't get me started.' We were in Poundland at the W12 Centre browsing for deodorants; no one had mentioned necrophilia. Quite often Alonso answers questions that we haven't asked yet, and claims that he can glimpse forwards through time to future conversations. 'This is why I broke up with Norshahliza last night,' he explained, 'because I knew that she was about to break up with me, so I got in there first.'

Norshahliza had been on the till at the Malaysian cafe on Portobello Road when Alonso had tried to pay using information about future Grand National winners. 'In about eight years' time, there'll be a horse called Vegetable Spring Roll, put everything on it,' he whispered. She thought he was joking, and the two had got chatting after she'd caught up with him on Ladbroke Grove and dragged him back to the cafe to do some washing up. But like Malaysia itself, the relationship was doomed. 'It's so much easier to date the dead,' said Alonso, testing a pomegranate-scented antiperspirant stick on his groin. 'Hmmm, not sure about this one either.'

Three of Alonso's previous five post-apocalyptic relationships had been with corpses. 'Though to be fair, Colin had been alive when we started seeing each other. For about 20 minutes. We knew our love wouldn't last, that was the beauty of it. Colin's legs had been blown off by a landmine when I found him, and he was pretty delirious, he thought I was his mother for most of our relationship. I think he found the sex comforting in a way. And yes, before you ask, the important bits were intact.' We didn't think we were going to ask this, but maybe we were? But now he'd already answered it so we didn't have to.

We followed Alonso up to the cinema foyer, bought him some tortilla chips and he told us about Prussia. Someone stood near us in a long suede jacket so Charlie and Frankie said 'Chris Hemsworth' to each other for a bit, so it would seem like we were discussing film, in case the other person was eavesdropping in an attempt to gather information for his own book about the apocalypse. 'What – *him?*' laughed Alonso. 'No, that's Robbie. I said we might be here. He's a friend of mine. Hey, Robbie.'

Robbie strutted over. 'Hey. Did I hear you guys talking about the reunification of Prussia? Are you talking about the future? What's going on? What the fuck? Alonso? I thought you told me that our book about the apocalypse was the only one you were writing with anyone. And now I hear this? What the fuck?' Charlie and Frankie both almost spat their tortilla chips out in an orange spray of shock at the news that Alonso was writing a book about the future with someone else, but only Charlie actually did. '*Alonso?!*' he yelped. Frankie stamped an angry foot on the floor, and a strip of condoms fell out of his pocket.

Robbie smiled. 'Just messing with you. Alonso told me all about you guys and the book you're writing. I think it's fucking cool what you're doing. Not that I give a shit about things getting fucked up. I've got loads of knives. I buy and sell knives. Ceremonial swords. Bayonets. Wiccan shit. Military stuff. Speaking of which: Alonso, I got you that Gurkha knife you wanted. Look.' And he opened the flap of his jacket, to show a knife stuck in his trouser waistband and a thin trickle of blood running down his leg. 'It's genuine. You guys want to come round to my place and look at my knives? I've got an old sleeping bag which I wrap round a lamp post down behind Morley's chicken shop. I stick a scarf on it and a pair of sunglasses, put some shoes at the bottom. We can pretend it's a person and stab it. It's fun.' He went up to Frankie. 'You ever cut people?' To which Frankie replied 'Only myself' and everybody laughed like he had been joking.

Frankie admitted later, at Robbie's flat, that he always carries around a strip of condoms that he'd drop on the floor whenever he could, so that he'd look sexually active, and to give him an excuse to talk about sexual intercourse with attractive strangers, a technique he'd learned while a guest panellist on Radio 4's *Fuck Tips* hosted by Judy Murray (the series was cancelled due to Covid, and never broadcast). But he hadn't actually meant to drop them then: he had them in his hand ready, and was about to head back to the snack counter and drop them while asking for extra salsa, because he has a thing about girls who sneeze into their hand before serving food.

Robbie looked disappointed and cancelled the sleeping bag stab session, saying he had a headache. So we went back to the W12 Centre cinema and got some more tortilla chips; Frankie, doing his best to appear nonchalant, shuffled up sideways and performed a well-practised backhand condom drop. Charlie and Alonso got on with discussing Prussia while Frankie attempted to chat to Shafiq, whose shift had just started, about Chris Hemsworth.

⌒⌐

The reunification of Prussia in the second decade of the Disfigurement is generally attributed to a moment of diplomatic inspiration, known as the Saxony Gambit, undertaken by the elegant Vicomtesse de Éguelshardt at the aftershow party of the Gdańsk Dog Show. Alonso Lampe's knowledge of the post-apocalyptic history of Prussia is second to none, and comes from his time spent as deputy librarian at the world-famous Library of Strasbourg, and head corpse dresser for the elegant Vicomtesse de Éguelshardt.

At its post-collapse height, when Alonso was working there, the Library of Strasbourg had a staff of one and held an astonishing three books: an almost complete service log from a Vauxhall Insignia 2.0 CDTI SRi 5dr automatic; a page from a short story, in French, about some sort of vendetta, with an advertisement for an electric kettle on the back; and its pride and joy, the complete front and back cover of a book by Maurice Larès about Lawrence of Arabia. Lampe would spend most days engaged in intense literary debates with his pet rat on subjects such as 'Do you think anyone's ever had a vendetta about an electric kettle?' and 'Do you think Maurice Larès drove a Vauxhall Insignia 2.0 CDTI SRi 5dr automatic?' and organising talks for the general public. Lampe himself gave a well-received lecture entitled 'Lawrence of Arabia: Electric Kettle Owner?' which was attended by a local dignitary and necrophile, the elegant Vicomtesse de Éguelshardt, who was looking for a new head of cadaver assessment, and Lampe took the job on the spot:

> I'd been at the library for nearly a fortnight, and my research into the air filter replacement costs of a Vauxhall Insignia 2.0 CDTI SRi 5dr had run aground after an outbreak of dysentery, in which I discovered that certain members of staff, namely myself, had been using the log book as lavatory paper, so I said a fond farewell to Strasbourg, my pet rat, and booked a ticket on the next donkey to Éguelshardt. Only as I was leaving, while I was rummaging about for stuff to steal, did I discover a faded print-out of an academic essay about German sexual customs, 'Braune Liebe: Die Deutsche Sexbesessenheit mit Hintergedanken' by Roland Zwiebler, which was published in Das Berliner Journal der Kopraphilie, one of the few scholarly journals to survive the apocalypse. Its final edition took the form of a weekend-long rave at Der Bumdisco on Schumannstraße from which Der Bumdisco never recovered.

We asked Alonso if he still had a copy of Zwiebler's essay, but he said that unfortunately it was burned just outside Gundershoffen, when he had to light a fire big enough to cook a donkey, but that he could remember most of it. We asked if he had any tips on how to cook a donkey, and he said that, in his experience, by far the most important thing is to cook it upwind of Gundershoffen. And when he said 'Gundershoffen' this time, he said it with such strangulated venom that Shafiq, who was sweeping up nearby, asked him if he was okay. Alonso laughed. 'Not since Gundershoffen.' This third

'Gundershoffen' was delivered in such a cheery, sing-song tone that Shafiq felt comforted – wrongly. We shall hear more about Shafiq and his broom handle later, but first:

> From the outset, the job with the Vicomtesse was a challenge, but as I told her: 'I'm okay with jobs being a challenge – obviously I prefer it if they're not, but at the end of the day it's not a dealbreaker. Maybe I shouldn't have brought it up. But you asked how I was getting on.' It turns out the Vicomtesse was very particular about her corpses. She preferred males, and ideally ones whose genitals hadn't rotted off. But I could tell she was disappointed by most of the corpses that were being wheelbarrowed into her boudoir, and usually spent no more than a couple of hours making love on them before falling asleep on her hay bales. I took it upon myself to shake up the whole operation, and got some basic lingerie stitched up out of some old seed sacks, and before you knew it she was having 6- or 7-hour relationships, and soon enough she offered me the position of head corpse dresser, which meant an extra helping of ragoût, but even so I took the job.

From the grisly tales told by his colleague Rolf, a survivor of the Heidelberg drone cleansings, Lampe learned how terribly the Germans had suffered during the apocalypse, which went some way to make up for the long working hours and no pay. But it was from the Vicomtesse herself that Lampe was able to piece together a fairly complete history of post-apocalyptic Prussia.

Alonso spoke of the Vicomtesse in glowing terms: 'She was a keen student of human nature, and had an encyclopaedic knowledge, gained from first-hand experience, about how to douche a carcass without bursting anything, and knew lots about Prussia too, and was very elegant.'

The Prussian Empire, he learned, was officially sealed by the marriage of the Vicomtesse to the corpse of the Archduke of Hanover, in a ceremony marked by the falling out of one of the Archduke's eyes during the vows. As the Vicomtesse pressed a ring onto the Archduke's remaining thumb, a row of thirty drummers clashed their dustbin lids together and the Vicomtesse, looking stunning in a vivid yellow gown to match her jaundice, turned to the congregation and set out her vision of a unified Prussia followed by a high-kicking dance routine described by the young Max Schänzler, one of the dove stranglers at the ceremony, as 'Quite something'.

Within weeks, the Vicomtesse announced that she was pregnant by the Archduke, and celebrated the happy news by having her most handsome footman executed. But we are getting ahead of ourselves. It is important to return to the terrible suffering of the Germans in the apocalypse.

The effect of the apocalypse on the people of Germany was threefold. First, it killed a tremendous number of them, in ways so horrible that it can hardly be put into words. Indeed, most of Rolf's most harrowing stories were just sequences of moans, hip thrusts and yelps, interspersed with coughing fits and wild, terrifying laughter. Secondly, it triggered a shocking and permanent shift in the sexual psyche of the survivors. And thirdly, it killed another enormous number of them, but this second wave of killings was more or less continuous with the first wave, so it doesn't make any sense to distinguish between them – even referring to them as separate 'waves' would be misleading – hence the generally accepted 'twofold' nature of the effect on the people of Germany of the apocalypse.

It is with the second of these three main effects which we are here mostly concerned: the *Lustveränderung* (desire shift) in the *sexueller* (sexual) make-up of the German *Volk* (people) and how it underwent such a profound and seemingly irreversible *transformation* (transformation). Up until the apocalypse, the average sexually engaged German was really only interested in one thing: faecal matter. The gentle art of seduction was, for Germans, inextricably bound up with this concern – if, in some shady corner of the Alexanderplatz, you happened to overhear a pair of lovestruck Berliners whispering longingly to each other, and got your head close enough to their whisperings without disturbing them, you might be able to make out typical sweet nothings such as *Ich will deinen Stuhlgang* (I want your bowel movement); *Zeig mir deinen Stuhlgang* (Show me your bowel movement) and *Sollen wir den Stuhlgang vergleichen?* (Shall we compare bowel movements?).

Everything aside from faecal matter – every fluid, organ or sex act – was regarded by the lovemaking German as either a stepping stone towards getting their hands on faeces or an unwelcome distraction from that aim. Quite how the Germans managed to reproduce at all is a mystery which has eluded the finest dung specialists in the whole field of Germanology: the most plausible theories involve people slipping on soiled polythene sheeting in the height of passion and accidentally achieving congress. Alonso did his best to demonstrate how, during lovemaking, this might occur, but before he'd quite managed to prove his point he was asked to leave Heriots

Patisserie and a clearly distressed Charlie was helped up and given a selection box of mini cheesecakes by concerned staff.

2. More About the Future of Necrophilia and Prussia

We strolled back up Hammersmith Grove towards Cafe 2000 for some much-needed Sudanese falafel while Alonso talked more about German sexual proclivities, ducking at one point under the awning of Deepak Food & Wine, and beckoning us closer, to advise us in an urgent whisper that if we didn't want to hear any more about people eating faecal matter or having sexual intercourse with dead bodies we'd be best off skipping to the next chapter. We weren't quite sure what he meant, but it seems that he was using us as cover to shoplift fruit. We trotted off and, taking a big bite of a stolen mango, Alonso continued.

According to Zwiebler, studies carried out just prior to the apocalypse showed that most Germans (78%) engaged in eating faeces, as well as smearing them around their faces, bodies and bedrooms. A minority (16%) engaged in smearing and daubing the waste without deliberately ingesting it, and only a very few (6%) opted for neither, preferring simply to rub it into their hair while wearing some kind of protective handwear, such as latex gloves or shopping bags. To an outsider, the desire of so many Germans to eat faeces might seem odd, mad even, unless of course they've ever been to Germany and eaten the food, in which case it suddenly appears completely rational, almost inevitable.

These same studies also show that the average pre-apocalyptic German found their own stools relatively unappealing, sexually. Of course, in an emergency, their own faecal matter was perfectly adequate (93% had 'regularly or often' consumed their own faecal matter 'before, during or directly after masturbation'). As the motto above the Federal Chancellery puts it: *Besser etwas Kot als gar keiner* (better some faeces than none) – the quotation is from the preface to Hegel's *Logic* – however, it was regarded as a humdrum snack, lacking the exotic charm of another German's goings. The process of defecating into a saucepan, then drably re-consuming their own faeces, seemed dull and unambitious, even for a German. In general, they relied on friends, neighbours, extended family members and passers-by for supplies. And of course, every consumption of another's faeces was tinged with the piquant knowledge that their own faeces may very well have been consumed previously by the donor, and had been incorporated into this new delight, having been successfully 'othered' by another's bowels.

But all this was to change. When the apocalypse struck, the surviving Germans crawled out from their scat dungeons and sex lavatories to discover they'd been jolted free from their centuries-old obsessions. Wide-eyed, they hosed themselves down, euthanised the injured (in a very broad and controversial sense) and took stock. A dizzying landscape of sexual possibility opened up before them. Curiously they poked and pressed at their sensitive areas with bits of brick and paving slab and handfuls of broken glass, carefully noting which sensations they enjoyed and which caused them to bleed to death. Tragically, after a few giddy weeks of sexual experimentation in which the nation's libido flew free like a parakeet from a widow's netted balcony, the obsessional nature of the German mind rebelled against this whirling *Sex-Festival* (hard to translate into English, it means something like 'sex festival'), and what might have been a mass movement of psychosexual liberation found itself hamstrung by the obsessional nature of the German mind.

Free at last from the clutches of ordure, they became, en masse, fixated on a new object of desire: dead bodies. This is perhaps unsurprising, given how littered their usually pristine streets and parks were with corpses and limbs. So it was, barely missing a beat, that the lusty Germans tossed aside their poop spoons and threw themselves onto their dead.

This context – as recounted in *The Tragedy of Selmar von Kot and his Musical Dung Wagon*, by far the shortest and the most popular of the post-operatic operas to have been staged in the dreaded Munich Song Pits – is vital for anyone hoping to understand events leading up to the reunification of Prussia in the second decade of the Disfigurement. But it is to the Gdańsk Dog Show, in the year 1, that we must return if we are to witness the famous Saxony Gambit of the elegant Vicomtesse de Éguelshardt, guest of honour at the event.

The Vicomtesse was travelling to Lithuania in search of a cure for being in France, and by great good fortune her donkey died right beside a poster advertising the Gdańsk Dog Show, taking place the very next day, and she thought: well, why not? It sounds fun! So she ate her donkey, got a good night's sleep, and went along.

The Vicomtesse was asked by the organisers if she wouldn't mind judging the show, as one of their judges, the Ombudsman of Luxembourg, had been forced to cancel after it was discovered that he didn't exist. She accepted and was given a scorecard and shown to a specially roped-off pile of rubble on which the other judges sat. A bell rang, a gate creaked open, and into the arena ran the dogs and their beaming owners, who waved to the judges and quickly flung off their undergarments as the show began. Later that evening, the weary Vicomtesse was sharing a mug of doppelbock with one of her fellow judges, the Envoy of the Bavarian Druids, and found herself confessing that she'd never actually been that interested in sex with animals, and found it odd that the people of Gdańsk went in for these elaborate public displays of fornication with their dogs. She knew, of course, that the Poles traditionally had sex with all of their pets, whether guinea pigs, dogs, cats, pigeons, snakes or weasels, but she'd assumed it was a 'behind-closed-doors' sort of thing, or done discreetly at rural bus stops, and that she'd found it nigh on impossible, when judging the contest, to apply the criteria of 'stance', 'proportionality' and 'obedience', given that the whole day had been a wild, deafening sexual free-for-all with no discernible rounds or challenges. She admitted to the Envoy, blushing, that she'd marked her scorecard pretty much at random, and to be absolutely honest she'd always had an unfulfilled hankering for necrophilia.

The Envoy, temporarily deafened by the howling of climaxing dogs, asked the Vicomtesse if she'd kindly clarify what that last word was. 'Necrophilia,' she said, and the delighted Envoy called for more bock as the Vicomtesse explained. As a lady of French descent, the Vicomtesse had been brought up to understand the act of lovemaking as a matter of mutual sneering at genitalia, followed by both parties falling asleep with a lit cigarette in their hands. But much as she enjoyed sneering at genitals and escaping from house fires, she hankered for something more, and quite understandably she found

Frenchmen to be utterly unbearable whilst alive, so her mind strayed to the idea of screwing the dead.

The Envoy straightened his garter belt and murmured to the Vicomtesse that if she was serious about having sex with corpses she should come to Bavaria, where, since the apocalypse, it had become their number one hobby, but the Vicomtesse had been so deafened by the barking of fornicating dogs that she thought the Envoy had said 'mumber num nubby', and asked what he meant by that, and that if it was a Bavarian insult, it would mean war between the two regions. The Envoy quickly explained that he'd said 'number one hobby', and the relieved Vicomtesse shook his hand gladly. The Envoy offered to introduce her to the Bishop of Hanover, who'd died in a baptism accident a few weeks ago, and she accepted with such loud approbations that it startled a sleeping whippet, which leapt out of a window never to be seen again, and so began the reunification of Prussia. But we are getting ahead of ourselves. It is important to talk more about the suffering of the Germans in the apocalypse.

It was a matter of keen debate in post-apocalyptic post-German post-society whether the death of so many millions of Germans could appropriately be called a 'Holocaust'. It was generally agreed that the term 'Holocaust' wasn't quite right, because the apocalypse killed so many more people in Germany than died in the Holocaust; the term *Holocaust-Plus* was briefly popular, until the consensus settled on *Über-Holocaust*.

The belief among surviving Germans that the *Über-Holocaust* of the apocalypse had been the greatest Holocaust in the history of Holocausts became a matter of enormous pride, and led to an explosion of nationalist ideology, a new flourishing of fascism, and another Holocaust, which was known briefly as *Der Holocaust Der Holocausts*, but eventually, after a debate that became so fierce that it triggered another smaller Holocaust, the name *Holocaust 2.0* was settled upon by the survivors, with the smaller Holocaust becoming known as the Smallocaust. There were so few survivors of the Smallocaust that any who did manage to get through it alive were filled with justifiable pride, which led to an explosion of nationalist ideology and talk of a new Holocaust, but there weren't enough people left to organise or be killed by anything that might reasonably be described as a Holocaust, so they gave up.

3. Society, Values and Refugees

After decades of disintegration and decay, with every possible bond between humans severed and every vestige of decency trampled and blasphemed, society finally and irrevocably collapsed in 1987. After that, it was just a hop and a skip to full apocalyptic meltdown. The great and stabling triumphs of humanism, from Filippo Brunelleschi's dome to Lou Reed's *Metal Machine Music*, were long forgotten, as the confusing fingers of chaos took grip. When an elderly Lou Reed was found to have faked his death in order to avoid paying millions in tai chi tuition fees, and was arrested while working as a Walmart store greeter in Colorado, was this the spark that lit the all-consuming bonfire of civilisation? No. That was the nuclear war between Russia, China and the US during which AI weaponry from all three nations went rogue, resulting in the ruin of the world and the total and utter abandonment of the civil case between tai chi master Ren Guangyi and Franklin Torberson (formerly Lewis Allan Reed, c/o Walmart Supercenter, Summit Blvd, Broomfield, Colorado).

What we think might well be described as 'man's inhumanity to man'™ grew so all-consuming that it triggered a wholesale reformulation of the ideals of Classical Humanism into a set of guidelines for tying a good solid hangman's knot and an innovative drystone walling technique useful for hiding bodies which was unashamedly influenced by the Latin poetry of Andrew Marvell and Nguni stick-fighting, but more the latter. Values such as politeness, respect and courtesy did survive, but only as esoteric variants of rape.

As for Christian morality, the essential social teaching of Jesus 'love thy neighbour as thyself' backfired terribly with the meteoric rise of self-hatred, but led to a new golden age of murder-suicides. People still wore the slogan 'what would Jesus do' but had it embossed on cock rings. The only thing that kept fragments of social interaction alive was the deep and unshakeable human need for grumbling about how awful everyone is. This social paradox, the primal urge to grumble about people with other people, meant that a flickering vestige of society stuttered on: dazed groups of annoyed humans would gather at defunct bus stops and bitch about someone who happened not to be there, or they'd form a grumbly scrum near the broken slot machines in amazingly still-serving Wetherspoon pubs and moan about their selfish cousins and loud neighbours, and from these humble re-beginnings a tentative reformulation of civilisation was begun, which flowered into a variety of different sex trafficking gangs.

In this new world, stable outposts quickly became surrounded by refugee camps. Often the people within the outposts resented these new arrivals calling themselves refugees, partly because the residents of the outpost considered *themselves* to be refugees. Such people often tried to downplay the success of their town, for fear of being flooded with new arrivals. Conversely, the people in the refugee camps considered that they would be quicker assimilating into the life of their new home if they just pretended to be a suburb for a while, until people got used to it, and they joined the town by osmosis. Thus even quite prosperous new towns would call themselves things like Viral Extermination Camp 36, while the tumultuous tent cities around them were named things like Windy Meadows; and Gardenia Hill Parent Teacher Association.

Some leaders ended up leading multiple groups or towns over the course of their lives, and were sometimes drafted in at points of crisis, like football managers. One such man, Red Jones, managed over forty different camps and towns. He was known for always taking on a man twice his size on the first day in the job and knocking him flat on his back. This was a stuntman who travelled with him, and was thought to be his lover. Most people knew about the arrangement but nonetheless enjoyed seeing Red Jones kick someone out of a second-floor window onto a moving flatbed truck. In any case, Jones was usually elected with a solid majority, because his management style was thought to be quite successful, focusing as it did on mindless optimism and watering down the towns' alcohol, while the other people on the ballot were often quite narrowly focused on some kind of genocide.

The stuntman himself refused to answer any questions at hustings, and would neither confirm nor deny whether the thing people could see sticking out of the back of his trousers was a pillow. Some political analysts said the stuntman was a mute, others that Red Jones forced him to remain silent because of his high-pitched falsetto voice and unbearable sarcasm.

It was often tricky to tell who was genuinely mute in post-apocalyptic societies. Many people chose silence so as not to be questioned about the terrible things they'd done to survive. Others were genuinely too traumatised to speak. A third sector, perhaps the largest overall, realised that the growing prevalence of being unable to speak allowed them to finally fall silent themselves, having always felt that they had nothing particularly interesting to say. Some of these people wrote journals about the experience of feigning muteness, but even this fairly dramatic material was something they managed to make dull, often focusing on long, irrelevant anecdotes about what kind of trousers they'd been wearing.

4. The Future of Birdwatching

Knowing how to hurl yourself into a ravine is a vital skill for anyone hoping to survive the apocalypse long enough to hurl themself into a ravine. Many ravines, particularly ones near transport hubs, became so clogged up with the bodies of people who'd been hurled into them, or hurled themselves into them, and with so many layers of screaming wounded writhing about among all the dogs, rats, crows, goats, ravens and vultures, that they became relatively safe to jump into. Fun even. Ravine jumping became popular amongst young thrill seekers and adrenaline junkies who had tired of the traditional extreme sports of eating at restaurants or dating.

The crowds at the tops of ravines would be a vibrant mix of pumped-up adrenaline junkies, birdwatchers, the suicidal, serial killers, their groupies, their pleading victims, and wagons of the dead being fly-tipped by local corpse disposal companies. Up from the ravine itself would waft groans of 'Would someone please kill me,' mingling with excited cries from the ravine edge of 'Is that *Aegypius monachus*, pecking that guy's eyes out, or is it *Gypaetus barbatus*?'

Birdwatching was a popular choice of post-apocalyptic hobby, as keen birdwatchers were left very much to their own devices; even the most brutal thugs and traffickers feared approaching them in case they ended up being told about habitat fragmentation. The birdwatchers would fashion 'binoculars' out of two fir cones and a birding journal out of a fir cone, and stand around on crags and beaches comparing kit and shushing each other. They tended to gather in large breeding groups, carefully preening each other while trying to find a female, but usually dying alone. They were viewed with equal suspicion by humans and birds.

Birdwatcher-watchers used ex-military drones to observe birdwatchers, and often huge flocks of these drones could be seen circling majestically over any gathering of birdwatchers. There was a lot of tension between these two groups. The birdwatchers didn't like the fact that the drones scared off and often killed all the birds in the sky, and seemed even to have been adapted – for no real reason – to run on birds' blood, while the birdwatcher-watchers felt that the birdwatchers were spoilsports.

Both sides became obsessed with making revenge pornography of each other, as well as pornography revolving around other emotions, like envy, spite, and boredom. These new porn genres developed a dense, self-referential semiotic language, which everyone quickly lost track of but had to pretend they understood, and many, on both sides, were relieved when the last birds died in some kind of art house schadenfreude porn.

The post apocalypse had a strong outdoors tradition; often consisting of people who had climbed up very high mountains and based themselves there for safety. This approach was popularised by Geoffrey Ferguson, who launched a successful survivalist movement artlessly called 'IT'S SAFER UP A MOUNTAIN' in all caps. Of course, it's difficult to farm and hunt at high altitudes, and Geoffrey's followers quickly became sick of a diet that consisted almost entirely of eagle droppings. It took a lot of calories to survive at the top of a mountain and there were rumours that Geoffrey and his inner circle had popularised the concept of living at altitude as a way of attracting people up there for them to eat. Some still think this was behind Geoffrey's manifesto 'SEA LEVEL is MEDIEVAL' and its often-baffling instructions about preparing for your climb by rubbing your body with a mixture of garlic and onions and hanging yourself upside down in a smokery. There's no actual evidence of foul play, and perhaps the speculation simply created a larger-than-life Geoffrey Ferguson that people found titillating. The only real Geoffrey Ferguson is the one who can be found on the public record: a father; mountaineering instructor; hypnotist; sex offender; abattoir worker; and chef.

Ferguson disappeared after a high-altitude casserole accident, and his movement was superseded by health expert Hans Williamson who began the Carrying A Lot of Tinned Goods Up A Mountain Movement, whose teachings were later incorporated posthumously into the work of Henry Bell, with his famous treatise Always Have A Tin-Opener With You When You Climb Up A Mountain.

The reason for the lower case 'is' in 'SEA LEVEL is MEDIEVAL' has been hotly debated by scholars in the field, as the manifesto itself is in all caps. We asked Alonso if he knew why it was written like that. 'Like what? What are you talking about? I've no idea. Why do you keep asking me these stupid fucking questions? – Sorry, I haven't had much sleep. You know that flat you got me, above the fish and chip shop.' 'The Fisherman's Hut?' 'Yeah, is it? I don't know. Anyway, every evening there's so much shouting and arguing and the sound of plates smashing that they keep coming up and asking me to be quiet. How am I meant to get to sleep unless I smash plates against the wall and yell at myself?' We had no idea.

Alonso found that the occasionally non-apocalyptic atmosphere of Shepherd's Bush could be troubling: there were several moments each day when he didn't feel that he was in some kind of physical or emotional danger, so to keep his cortisol at a comfortable level he would go into Cash Converters on Goldhawk Road and try and sell his body parts, or power walk up to the underpass at the end of Wood Lane and offer to teach gut punching to passing commuters.

He soon became friends and wrestling partners with Dr Jérôme 'Babyface' Villagrán who worked in nephrology at Novartis UK, headquartered nearby, and Dr Villagrán was able to get him some experimental kidney drugs which Alonso traded to a promising young graffiti artist called Reko, who died of acute renal failure, but not before finishing a stunning mural depicting Alonso and Dr Villagrán, stripped to their socks, going belly-to-belly in a winner-takes-all subway clash (winner: Dr J. L. Villagrán).

Alonso's loss to Babyface Villagrán was, he said, the wake-up call he needed, and he embarked on a gruelling fitness and motivational regime, a total overhaul of mind and body, focusing on his problems with focus, that ended 20 minutes later at the Pig & Whistle on Bramley Road with a hot sausage sandwich and an Irish stout (both wrestling terms).

We persuaded the Irish stout to take his knee off Alonso's head and release him into our custody, as we'd booked a table away from the slot machine to talk about the future of mathematics, and we'd already ordered our scampi. The effort of thinking about what calculus turns into made Alonso's eyes point off in different directions. He told us, while a tooth fell out of his nose, about how infinity had been shrinking since the apocalypse, and the last time he checked it was less than a quarter of its normal size. 'But there's a whole new dimension that's been discovered between length and width which has completely transformed geometry, – girth.' We have not included Alonso's speculations on the theory of girth, as we think he'd borrowed much of the technical detail from a $75 online course in pick-up techniques run by someone called Snizpod which he'd subscribed to in an effort to 'make friends in the area', and to be quite honest, we found the theory less impressive than the amount of blood coming out of his ear.

After a restorative 50-hour sleep, Alonso met us at Wahaca for nachos and we picked up where we'd left off.

5. Science and Mathematics: Why They Vanished Like They Did

Even though most judicial systems had collapsed, and most police forces had been disbanded, mankind's basic desire for justice and decency remained, and a worldwide war against paedophilia was launched, which – in the absence of any trials, lawyers, detectives or evidence – meant the mass detention and summary execution of anyone who looked like they were a paedophile or weird deviant. This, unfortunately, led to a massacre of tens of thousands of top physicists and mathematicians from which our knowledge of science never recovered.

Not a single cosmologist of note escaped hanging, and the world's best computer scientists were among the first to be rounded up and slain, several of whom, tragically, were not sex offenders of any kind, let alone paedophiles. Geographers and geologists suffered similarly huge losses, and the discipline of archaeology was completely wiped out, an academic catastrophe which future archaeologists will sadly know nothing about because they won't exist. If there's any silver lining to all this, it's that the eradication of astronomy led to a tremendous boom in the number of theories and models of the universe, and a golden age of prophecy and folklore. The majority of the fantastical beings who were roped into holding up the firmament and supporting the Earth and towing the Moon across the night sky were quite bad-tempered, and required constant propitiation with human sacrifice, one of the many upsides to this cultural shift.

Schools were rare after the collapse; and a secondary school-age child in a large settlement was more likely to find themselves in an apprenticeship; mentoring scheme; work/learning programme; or one of the many other euphemisms for sexual slavery. Nonetheless, some schools were set up as fronts for slave-gathering operations, and children were taught to check every morning that wheels hadn't been attached to the base of the school building; that wings and an engine hadn't been attached to the school building; and not to take part in any experiments that involved calculating the radius of a large net on the ground. These large-scale operations meant that there were far fewer stray children for pederasts to prey on and, as was the case before the collapse, many of them were forced to go into teaching.

―

One of the few academic subjects to flourish in the end times was Cryptozoology. The process of genetic mutation had been massively accelerated, and the integration of microplastics as a basic element in nature had given insects and animals a new building block for their growth. Though sick and confused, Mother Nature showed that her wondrous powers of adaptation were undimmed as she began to mimic the forms of litter, with snails' shells growing into the shape of printer cartridges and cuttlefish flashing messages to each other that they had picked up from packaging, trying to impress a mate by showing that they knew the average carbohydrate content in a 100 g serving of Skittles.

Elderly monkeys grew plastic teeth, giving them a new lease of mouth cancer. Seagulls ate so much fishing tackle that they developed a whole new way of feeding: they would carefully peck out a hook and line from their stomach and deftly swoop it across the surface of the water like a fly fisherman, hoping not to catch anything too heavy. While off the coast of Tasmania, giant whelks incorporated so much plastic into their shells that Nestlé began farming them to use as sustainable Vittel bottles, selling the rubbery whelk inside as a novelty stress ball.

Homo sapiens split into two distinct species, no longer capable of interbreeding: the dying and the dead. Some enlightened humans grew an actual third eye, but instead of being on their forehead it tended to grow out of the perineum, which made for some disconcerting eye-contact during rim jobs. New forms of cognition emerged, and thirty-five new emotions between despair and hopelessness were discovered and then forgotten as new forms of dementia took over. People lost the ability to do cryptic crosswords, as the unbearably annoying people in any community were generally the first to be killed. Counting was made more difficult by extreme weather conditions, head injuries, blindfolds, PCP, death, and the fact that most people had either slightly more or slightly fewer than ten fingers. Counting in base eight and a half became popular for a while, and several communities abandoned counting altogether, although no one knows exactly how many.

Eventually, at the Consilium of Rome, which was held in a specially built auditorium on the one still-functioning roundabout in Milton Keynes, a radically revised set of numbers was drawn up. Alonso briefly dated Bettina Pnishi, the famous swimwear model turned number theorist, who was one of the ring girls at the event: employed to parade round the chamber when each new digit was introduced, sometimes sitting in on debates when a delegate was bored (Bettina's famous polemic against another ring girl who moved to replace all numbers with bra sizes is a class of post-apocalypse mathematics, and her brilliant third axiom managed to transcend the airy realm of academic disputation and pass into popular usage: 'It's a stupid fucking idea').

Zero was the first number to be abandoned: everyone was so overwhelmed by absence and loss that it seemed madly superfluous to have a digit symbolising lack. Rude even. The delegate from Morocco argued persuasively that the sheer weight of day-to-day nothingness couldn't just be ignored, that it needed some kind of notation, but that the only digit capable of representing this superabundance of absence was infinity (∞), and to prove his point, he drank a cup of poison and slumped dead in his seat to much applause, and was promptly elected President of the Consilium, although his proposal for zero was declared a 'stupid fucking idea' and immediately abandoned; the desecration gong was sounded and his body was thoroughly desecrated by his fellow delegates until the gong called them back to order. Infinity, it was agreed, seemed far too positive a concept, and was declared illegal along with the digit 8 which looked too much like the outlawed infinity symbol and was stricken from the list of integers. In the end, it was decided that the best way to represent the grindingly unpleasant experience of everyday nothingness was to employ the cursed number 13, a proposal which met with no objection from either half of the President of the Consilium.

After a short break for coffee and sex, the Consilium turned its attention to 1. There turned out to be a great deal of affection for 1 from all quarters, as people generally only had 1 of anything, like shoes and kidneys, and the number seemed perfectly to encapsulate how lonely and alienated everyone was – unlike 2, which was swiftly forbidden. Individuals were so constantly traumatised by interactions with others, that any kind of 'twoness' seemed a monstrous intimacy. Instead, they retreated back to 1, which they decided to repeat, but made clear that these 1s were absolutely singular and unattached; the question as to whether there should be a double space between them or not (given the meaninglessness of 2) ended with champions being nominated and a bare-knuckle fight which left both mathematicians in a coma and the issue unsolved. Fortunately, before new champions could be elected, the euthanasia gong was rung and the two unconscious disputants were carefully strangled and rolled outside for the dogs. After the discussion ring was hosed down, 3 was discussed. It seemed much less claustrophobic than 2, looking pleasantly like someone had hacked at the number 8 with a sword, and so it survived, whereas 4 was deemed outrageous, a doubly bad 2, and had to go. Effigies of 4 were assembled and ceremonially burned, the fire from which burned down the auditorium, killing an incalculable number of delegates (4). The auditorium was rebuilt within a year or so and the Consilium reconvened with a largely new set of delegates and a brand-new desecration gong after the previous one was stolen by a nearby conference on differential geometry. Lucky 7 was the next number to be ousted, to be replaced by unlucky 13, which therefore represented zero and 6 (with the numerals running: 1, 1, 3, 5, 6, 13 . . .) but also occurred two other times, once when it occurred in the list of remaining digits, where it signified 9, and once in its old meaning of 13. The fact that '13' now meant zero, 6, 9 and 13 was regarded as a useful bit of economising, and the council congratulated themselves with what in pure mathematics is known as a 'circle jerk', during which the numbers 15 to 19 were sadly destroyed.

The eradication of 2 and 4 meant that there were no digits in the 20s or 40s, and it was decided to stop counting at 39 (i.e. 18) which was considered the highest meaningful number. The delegate from Atkins & Atkins Removals Ltd., a family-run gang of 'house-clearance experts' from Milton Keynes, argued persuasively that all theoretical numbers higher than 18 should be replaced by the name 'Atkins', and that his associates would hack the hands and feet off anyone who disagreed, and his proposal was passed unanimously, Atkins votes to 13. The final declaration of the Consilium was signed by all the remaining delegates who hadn't wandered off, and was disseminated by messengers who leapt onto their horses and galloped away to spread word of the new numbering to the 5 corners of the world, one of them even making it as far north as Peterborough.

For reference: the numbers from zero up to 19, in the old system, correspond as follows with the new numbers:

13, 1, 1, 3, 5, 6, 13, 9, 11, 13, 15, 16, 13, 31, 33, 35, 36, 39 and Atkins.

You need to learn these: they may save your life.

6. Memorial Stonemasonry

In the early-to-mid apocalypse, it was impossible to keep track of the dead; just keeping them out of the water supply was hard enough. Keeping track of the living seemed easier, and a lot less traumatising, with many towns erecting elegant stone memorials to their surviving inhabitants. However, people kept dying at such a rate that the names engraved on the memorials had to keep being erased, with surviving stonemasons charging exorbitant call-out fees for the amendments until the Great Purge of the Stonemasons, to which there are no memorials. Indeed, many doubt that it ever even occurred, and was just a rumour put about by wealthy stonemasons to try and avoid a purge by convincing everyone a purge had already taken place, which is most likely the root of the common post-apocalyptic belief that stonemasons were the arch-manipulators of society. What we know for sure is that the quality of calligraphy on monuments to the living grew so poor that many people decided to shorten their names to single letters or simple shapes. Alonso Lampe recalls:

I had a brief but tumultuous triadic relationship in a forest hut in Picardie with identical twin sisters, both called 'Triangle' (although they pronounced it in a stupid French way, because they were French). Each sister refused, under any circumstances, to answer to any name other than Triangle, nor would either sister accept that the other was also called Triangle, each believing that the other was called 'Rectangle', but again mispronounced, and I was screamed at if either sister heard me call the other Triangle. I was able to navigate this problem fairly successfully in our daily conversations in the cabin, simply by avoiding their names, but it complicated our lovemaking enormously, because both sisters, perhaps out of bashfulness, insisted on being blindfolded, but also insisted, perhaps out of a lack of bashfulness, that I speak dirty to them. I would obfuscate as best I could, tossing out catch-all insults like 'mmm, yeah, you dirty slut' and vague sexually charged remarks, trying to avoid referring to any particular sex act that either sister was performing, like 'yeah, keep doing that thing you're doing.' Unfortunately, both sisters were sticklers for clarity, and would often press me to be specific about which one of them, for example, should keep doing what they were doing. 'Which of us are you referring to?' one blindfolded twin would ask. 'Yes,' the other would say, 'please be specific. Also, please address us by name when addressing us, we prefer that.' The other would agree. 'Yes, be as rude as you want, but please do include our very different names when spouting your filth, so that we can be certain which one of us is the cock-hungry slut, and which is the knob socket who likes it up her.' I found these situations so stressful that during one double cowgirl I snapped. The whole situation was completely ridiculous, I yelled, and the sisters took off their blindfolds, shocked. I felt bad shouting at two 85-year-old ladies, but I was furious. 'You can't both be called Triangle, it's just fucking stupid, you need to get over it.' The sisters wept and comforted each other, stroking each other's hair and saying that I was an unthinking brute to say such things, which I found intolerably erotic, but it was too late, the magic had gone. I knew that I would never share a hut floor with Triangle and Triangle again, or vice versa. The sisters smiled. This is what it's like in the apocalypse: relationships come and go, nothing lasts very long, the fact that we'd manage to spend 4 whole days in this hut making love was, in its way, a miracle. A time out of a time: a tiny, fragile miracle of scissoring and double-69-ing in a world of transience and decay. But it was over. This was our moment of parting. Without saying another word, I smiled back at the sisters, thanked them for their hospitality, masturbated myself to orgasm, pulled up my dungarees and strode off out of the hut. I'd only gone a few paces when I thought I should apologise for my behaviour, because I'd caught one of the sisters on the shoulder with my wang juice (that's the phrase they made me use, but in French of course) so I turned to go back — but to my astonishment, the hut had gone! Vanished into thin air! Had I imagined the whole thing? The two mad sisters with their stupid fucking names? Had this just been a hallucination caused by drinking too much formaldehyde? No wait, the hut was over there, behind a tree. No, hang on, that's just a pair of trees that look a bit like a hut from a certain angle. No, wait, there it is. The hut had been there all the time. I went back to apologise, but when I went in the sisters were busy 69-ing, so I quietly shut the hut door and left. But I'd only gone a short way when I thought: no, I'm a gentleman. I should really apologise. So, I turned to re-approach the hut. But it had gone! The forest hut had vanished! Had I dreamt the whole strange interaction? Was it all some weird forest fantasy? What was going on? I took another sip of formaldehyde to try and clear my head. Then I spotted the hut. Yes! It was there. Exactly as I remembered it. No, wait, it was another clump of trees, but a different one. It's amazing how they can look like huts from certain angles. And occasionally like two elderly ladies making love. No, wait, there's the hut. No, hang on—

We stopped Alonso at this point, because he'd become extremely agitated, and kept bending teaspoons and boomeranging them around the steak restaurant, muttering that he couldn't remember if he'd ever had sexual relations with two 85-year-old French ladies called Triangle, which wasn't a problem either of us had encountered before, so we did what anyone would do in that situation, sat on his chest and held a towel over his nose and mouth and shouted 'Did it happen or not?' at him until he calmed down.

The staff at Flat Iron asked us if we'd mind getting down off the bar, as Alonso's foot kept kicking open the tap of the IPA, so we dragged him back to his seat and after another steak and a couple of glasses of Picpoul and a side order of creamed spinach Alonso felt able to continue, and told us that he felt sure, on reflection, that the whole twin sister incident had never happened, but he hadn't realised it until he'd started telling us about it, and that everything else he'd told us was 100% true, and we felt reassured. We decided to keep Alonso's Picardie hallucination in the book to show that we are absolutely stringent about only printing rock-solid facts about the apocalypse, and not the formaldehyde-fuelled sex fantasies of a madman.

He returned, in due course, to memorials. On account of their sturdiness, quite a number of stone memorials from pre-apocalyptic wars survived into the end times, and a popular source of entertainment, relatively speaking, was for a crowd to gather at a memorial and for someone to read out the list of the fallen – at every name, the crowd would yell out how they thought they'd died. Favourite guesses were: 'Shot in the nuts!', 'Trodden on by a horse!', or 'Cause of death unknown!'

The responses eventually became more and more ornate, filling in back story and character, extended family, letters home, loved ones left behind, unpublished short stories, anguished confessions of attraction for fellow soldiers while under fire, plans for opening an ice-cream parlour in their home town with ideas for new and unusual ice-cream flavours, that sort of thing. Some of the names accrued such large narratives that their life stories were spun off into their own memorials, such as Private J. Plumb listed on the Boer War memorial in Bury St Edmunds, whose entirely imagined life story was engraved on memorials as far east as the ruins of Constantinople (which is how the ruins of Istanbul became known), and as far west as the ruins of Constantinople approached from the other side.

By the time it reached Turkey, Private Plumb's story had developed into an epic and highly sexualised sci-fi revenge thriller. An android (called Mandroid) once recited the whole story to Alonso during the two days he spent hiding from a group to whom he'd made some careless remarks about Allah while under the influence of cough medicine. Alonso found that the Private's story started strongly, but became a little muddled and confused towards the end, as the symptoms of cough medicine withdrawal began to set in. Mandroid claimed that he had attempted to reach back through time and tell the story in its entirety to Private Plumb, as he lay dying at the Battle of Stormberg from a lack of legs. He said the Private screamed and ejaculated from his disembodied penis, but whether this was in response to the story it was impossible to tell.

A double implement was not uncommon.

BOOK V

Gangs and How to Survive Them

1. The Lighthouse at Alexandria

We pulled a string and wangled Alonso a job as a runner on the second season of *Fudge The News*, a crossover satire/baking show for Channel 4. The celebrity contestants had to decorate a cake or dessert to represent a news story. As they feverishly baked their topical pastries and iced their satirical buns, they'd banter with the hosts of the show: Frankie and the dashing Prince Emil of Battenberg, heir to one of the largest cake fortunes in the world.

Unfortunately, the first series was filmed during the crisis in Gaza, and the majority of the cake decorations attempted to address the slaughter. The contestants showed incredible inventiveness, crafting body parts out of meringue and puddles of blood from raspberry sauce – the S Club singer Hannah Spearritt wowed judges by tracing the line of bullets with spun sugar from a marzipan sniper drone into a hospital she'd built out of trifle biscuits – however, the channel decided that the cakes were too traumatising to be broadcast. Most notably, the panettone created by former Olympic rower James Cracknell caused one of the judges, Ainsley Harriott, to be violently sick during the recording, the prelude to a prolonged psychotic episode, and the entire series was shelved.

On the plus side, Cracknell's panettone was subsequently submitted by South Africa as evidence to the International Court of Justice at The Hague. The registrar of the court, the Belgian jurist Philippe Gautier, described the texture of the cake as 'excellent', with the fruit 'well-distributed' throughout.

Charlie was back writing on the show — Kay Burley, one of the judges, had asked for him to be reinstated, insisting that their affair had been at her instigation, not his — so both he and Frankie were there in the writing room when Alonso returned with his first lunch order, or what was left of it. In the future, people have much more of an open, 'catch-as-catch-can' attitude towards food, and Alonso had been snacking on the lunches on his way back from Nando's. All of the halloumi sticks had gone, and he'd pretty much finished Sam Pine's grilled chicken wrap by the time he presented it. In that instant, the only sound that could be heard in the room was a soft tick-tick-tick-tick as Sam Pine furiously messaged his agent.

Sam Pine hadn't been this angry since they misspelled his name on the credits of *Dane Baptiste's News Threat*, and what he suggested Alonso might consider doing with the remains of his lunch order caused Alonso to flip out: he grabbed the remnants of a double chicken pitta and vaulted over the table, grabbing Sam in a choke hold and forcing the delicious pitta down his throat. Lucky for Sam, the attack happened just as Endemol's head of format acquisitions was passing — he heard Alonso's furious yells of 'What did you just say to me?' and 'Have you any idea who you're dealing with?' and immediately rushed in to option the two shows. Alonso was transferred to Endemol's format development team, and was given an associate producer role on *What Did You Just Say To Me?*

which was sold to Sky later that day, with Holly Willoughby slated to host.

With his idiosyncratic ideas, quirky dress sense and wide experience of merciless gang culture, Alonso found a natural home in the TV entertainment industry. His influence on Endemol's development team soon became apparent around the office: they started wearing gang colours, strolling the corridors threateningly, and introduced violent hazing rituals that required a radical redrafting of Endemol's ethical labour policy.

Alonso showed them how to draw a serviceable tattoo using a heated nail and printer ink; we knew by the screams and smell of burning flesh wafting up from their office when they had another recruit. The tattoo was discreetly sited inside the member's left armpit, which was kept carefully shaved as per gang rules. Alonso showed us his brand: it appeared to be a premium rate UK telephone number. 'It's my sex line', he admitted. Curious, Frankie rang it, and heard a minute of strained sexual groans and gasps, whispered threats, and grunted apologies from Alonso, drowning out the sound of the call itself going straight to voicemail.

Alonso has a number of gang tats: he has a trash patch from the Spanky Bandits, the words 'Insert cake here please' from his time as a submissive in a gang of dyslexic sodomites; and an intricate Celtic knot on his penis, dating from his period as Head of Public Relations for Kerrygold. The three interwoven strands of the knot, he says, symbolise chronic dermatitis, skin grafts and flawed decision making. We imagined it would look terrible when his penis was flaccid, but we never found out.

But his favourite is the large toothy grin on his left shoulder blade, symbol of the feared Hippos, a particularly belligerent and violent gang. To become a fully-fledged Hippo, he explained, you had to 'wallow' in a 'mud bath' of human excrement for 24 hours and then, while still 'muddy', perform oral sex on the senior members of the gang, in a ritual that was eventually phased out by the senior members of the gang, none of whom were quite sure whose idea this whole 'mud' thing was. Alonso says that his greatest regret of his time in the future was that he was one of the last Hippos to be initiated before the shift in the Hippos' hazing rituals towards just oral sex. To progress as a Hippo, you would be expected to have the ability to dislocate your jaw so that you could 'gape' your mouth at 180° like a hippo, but luckily the initiation normally rendered this a formality.

In the queue for Viennese fingers at Maison Souss, Alonso told us how, after leaving the Hippos, he worked his way up the vicious and unforgiving ranks of West Wittering Yacht Club. His initiation, at the bi-monthly novices' regatta, ended with him being held down, waterboarded and tattooed with the name of his dinghy, which he said was the worst pain he's ever experienced apart from when he trod on that upturned plug a couple of days ago. While we paid for our biscuits he showed us the tattoo, and yes, we could just about make out the words 'Summer Breeze' despite the heavy ridging of his scrotum. He was considering a trip down to West Wittering to introduce himself to the Yacht Club general committee, show them his tattoo, and exercise some of his lifetime privileges on them, but we suggested he might want to wait until after the apocalypse.

Complicated by his backwards shift through time, Alonso's gang membership status remains radically unclear. One of the key tenets of gangs is this: while you're a member of a particular gang, you cannot be a member of another gang. Alonso was still a fully fledged Yachtsman, and technically had never renounced his membership of the Hippos, but was untroubled by his concurrent membership of his punishingly strict Endemol crew, because his initiation into the other gangs hadn't yet taken place, and also, as he explained, 'I don't care either way. Let's talk about something else.' Frankie wanted to talk about the architecture of the Ptolemaic Empire, explaining that he was working on a new bit of stand-up but so far only had the line 'Lighthouse? Shitehouse more like'. But Charlie and Alonso had moved table, and the lady who had sat down in their place to eat her walnut tart thought the line unpromising, and that maybe Frankie should focus more on the Temple of Horus at Tanis. But Frankie thought that might not work, because Temple didn't rhyme with Shitehouse, and the pair lapsed into a companiable silence.

2. A Short History of the Future of Gangs

Of course, when placed under stress, human relations often devolve into the form of gangs. Gang membership offered security from other gangs; camaraderie; the chance to be ordered around by a screaming man with a matted beard in the grip of methamphetamine-induced psychosis; and some kind of routine.

The precise number of Gang Eras that followed the initial collapse is a matter of keen academic debate. Historians of the Third Gang Era discovered that the Second Gang Era actually preceded the First Gang Era, but this was disproved by historians of the Fourth Gang

Era, who branded it 'Typical Third Gang Era historicist bullshit'. This opinion stood until the entire Fourth Gang Era was discovered by historians of the Sixth Gang Era to be an invention of the Fifth Gang Era, which had also invented the First, Second and Third Gang Eras. This meant that the Fifth Gang Era was actually the First Gang Era; not only that, the Fifth (i.e. First) Gang Era was discovered to still be operating during the Sixth (i.e. Second) Gang Era, which led to some of the bloodiest turf battles since the Fourth Gang Era.

The key to being a successful gang historian in any of these eras was to be highly skilled in the art of flattery, weaving the superhuman exploits of your gang leader into the founding myth of your gang and/or be amazing at blow jobs. Most gang leaders had only really got into the whole gang-leading business because they wanted to leave their mark on posterity, which is why they employed so many historians, and funnelled so much of their wealth into funding niche academic journals and conferences: it was a desperate attempt to rebuild some semblance of a cultural and political tradition where they could be remembered for their brutality. They found the best way of doing this was to turn up at a history conference, storm into the auditorium, and murder half of the participants with such groundbreaking violence that the surviving historians would be forced to include a reference to it in their work.

A problem faced by all gangs was that decent historians were hard to come by since the great cultural purge of the Global Democratic Alliance of Peace and Tolerance (founded by the victorious side in the bloody BTS civil war, led by Suga, Jimin and J-Hope), during which all history – apart from a heavily revised history of the vocal trio BTS – was outlawed and historians were ruthlessly hunted down, proving reasonably easy to catch as the only places they could think of to hide (libraries, bookshops, public archives and document repositories) had already been burned to the ground, so mostly they just stood around blinking, waiting to be strung up.

Sometimes a quisling researcher who was on the payroll of the Global Democratic Alliance of Peace and Tolerance would suggest to his colleagues that they all quickly run and hide in a cage on the back of a nearby cart, arguing that the bars would protect them from any passing mobs, and citing plausible references from multiple sources to instances in history where such a course of action had resulted in the survival of everyone who took it.

'Why didn't they check these references before simply running into the cage?' asked Charlie, but Alonso wasn't there. He'd been up in Glasgow for the past month at STV Studios, joining their restructured formatting department led by Jasmine Brone, who was fresh from her triumphant three-week stint as senior development executive at Bandicoot, where she'd successfully co-helmed the revival of *The Pink Windmill* and had been instrumental in casting Micky Flanagan as Rod Hull. Jasmine reported to Dean Yarnold, the newly appointed Creative Director (Entertainment), who had moved to STV Studios from his role as Head of Content Commissioning (Entertainment) at Channel 5. 'We're thrilled to welcome Jasmine and Alonso to STV Studios at this exciting time,' said Dean Yarnold, to anyone who might be listening.

Alonso had been leading the development of a new high-energy Saturday night cabaret quiz format, *Gotta Push It*, with Gwen Stefani and Paul Hollywood as hosts. The format was so vague that it was sold to fourteen territories before anyone realised it was based on

Alonso's experiences as a thunderdome rape instructor, which led to it being sold to a further twenty-six territories. Alonso was fired by a horrified Dean Yarnold when it was discovered that he'd never actually been a thunderdome rape instructor.

'I'd worked as a goatherd at the Lyme Regis sex vaudeville, but that wasn't good enough for Dean,' said Alonso, running up to us as we ate our choc ices by the Endemol bike racks. 'To be fair to Dean, I think Steve Chappell was riding him pretty hard. And I didn't kick up a fuss because I'd already been poached by Leslie Kwon at RDF to head up their new international non-scripted slate alongside Darren Swales, who joined RDF from ITV Creative, where his credits include the Scottish Bafta-winning documentary *Bottoms and Tops in the Cops*; as well as *Saturday Night Swindle*; *Drag My Body To The Crushing Deeps*; and *Drag My Body To The Crushing Deeps Celebrity Edition*. Now, if you'll excuse me, I have to urinate.' And with that, he strode off determinedly towards the Westfield shopping centre. Nearby, a church bell rang out at 3.20 p.m. on a Wednesday, and possibly corresponded to some satanic calendar of which we were mercifully unaware.

'We should probably follow him,' said Frankie, turning to find Charlie admiring a Rayleigh Pioneer Venture GT in silver, with a Selle Royal cutaway saddle, aluminium bag racks and Shimano Parallax hubs. 'This is a beautiful machine,' said Charlie, thinking again about Bob Stewart, who'd been arrested back in 2007 after having sex with a bicycle in a hostel in Ayrshire. Bob pleaded guilty to sexually aggravated breach of the peace, and had been placed on the sex offenders register. Back in his activism days, Charlie had lobbied against this decision, leading the Remove Bob Stewart From The Sex Offenders Register Campaign, and had become good friends with Bob himself. The two had shared some pretty wild times amongst the racks at Kilmarnock railway station, and Bob had showed Charlie how to make love to a folding commuter bike on a crowded train without too many people noticing.

The memories rushed through Charlie's penis as he glanced over his shoulder to see Frankie limping up the pavement after Alonso. Should he dare? Look at those sleek Mavic A119 rims, those plump Maxxis Overdrive tyres, rated to 90 psi. This was meant to be. He looked up to see a security guard wagging a stern finger at him and smiling: 'We'll have none of your business here today, Mr Skelton.' Brian the security guard chuckled with his hands on his fat hips as he watched Charlie pull up his jeans and scuttle off, then approached the bike shaking his head and tutting as he unbuckled his belt.

There's nothing like a lamb shank nihari to make you forget about a bicycle, thought Charlie, feeling the memory of that square taper Truvativ triple crankset fade with every mouthful. He watched as Frankie asked Alonso what looked to be a probing question, and Alonso, frowning, pondered a response. 'I wonder what they're saying to each other,' thought Charlie, and decided to tune in. 'I'm afraid I can't really talk about it,' said Alonso, shaking his head gravely. A lump of bhuna chicken fell out of his mouth. He caught it dexterously, flicked it up into the air, and batted it with his elbow towards a pigeon who caught it before it hit the ground. 'That was pretty impressive,' thought Frankie, and decided to give it a go himself, but try as he might he couldn't catch any of the chicken Alonso threw at him.

A long-haired man in a neat grey suit stood and watched us for a while, clearly intrigued, before pressing a hand to his stomach and walking into the Nespresso Boutique. Did he work in TV development? Had he seen a possible game-show format in catching cubes of falling bhuna? Could it be sold overseas? We brainstormed furiously. 'Chase the Chicken?' pitched Charlie, getting the ball rolling. Alonso machine-gunned ideas: 'Bhuna Battle? Beat the Bhuna? Ultimate Bhuna? Extra Chicken Bhuna?' he suggested, accidentally ordering some extra chicken bhuna. Charlie came back fast with 'Chicken Challenge'. But we still hadn't nailed it. Frankie's fork clattered onto his plate, his eyes ablaze – he had it: '*Celebrity* Chicken Challenge!' – Alonso nodded; he was already on hold to Mindy Senaoui, the new Head of Streaming at Fremantle, who reports directly to Leonardo Brandt.

We were at a patio table at the Copper Chimney opposite Waitrose, where Alonso had been thrown out for urinating into a bucket of cut flowers: he claimed, correctly, that it was a cheaper alternative to sachets of plant nutrients, but the security guard was having none of it. Alonso protested: 'I should be charging you for this. Free plant food. Aquaponics! You've no idea how important aquaponics is going to be in the near future!' He then explained to us that in the post apocalypse, rather than burning bodies or feeding them to pigs, desperate homesteaders found that the nutrients from corpses, when chopped up and mixed with urine and excrement, made a kind of 'superfood' for their pond-based growing systems. Incredibly rich harvests were generated this way, along with an untreatable watercress virus that killed 2 billion people.

'This is why I rarely eat watercress. I've seen it growing in bloody clumps out of too many screaming people's eyes. I mean, occasionally on a sandwich or something, it's okay. Sorry, what were we talking about?' Frankie's probing question had been to ask Alonso why he'd started buying bags of old Lego from charity shops, writing cryptic messages on the pieces in permanent marker, and posting them through people's letterboxes. And why he seemed to be doing this in a kind of spiral pattern leading anticlockwise outwards from Shepherd's Bush Green. 'All I can tell you now is that it's a key part of my mission, and what hangs in the balance is nothing less than the entire future of the W12 postal district.' Impressed, Frankie let out a low whistle, like a pit pony dying in a roof fall.

Alonso clearly wanted to change the subject: he reached over to Charlie's glass of mango lassi and emptied it slowly onto Frankie's lap, and began talking about post-apocalyptic supermarkets. 'How it works is, they give you a bucket, usually tied to a lump of concrete so you don't steal it, unless you've gone there to steal concrete. Then at the end, the checkout staff have a look at what's in your bucket, and then molest you the amount that they reckon it's worth. If you think there's a discrepancy you can go to Customer Services and they will unmolest you the amount you think you're owed, although it's hard to tell the difference between what you're given back and the extra you've been charged. Most people try and avoid shopping at the larger stores, but the thing is, they do have really good community notice boards. Hang on, sorry – Mindy, hi.'

As far as we can tell, in Alonso's time a 'supermarket' means any shop, trading post or knackers' yard with more than three aisles, and an 'aisle' seems roughly to correspond with what in our time would be called a 'molestation zone'. Alonso's main advice: if you hear anyone shout 'clean-up on aisle 5' while you're in aisle 5, or aisles 3, 4, 6 or 7, you need to drop your bucket and run like all hell.

Alonso admitted, with something approaching embarrassment, to being briefly a member of Whole Foods, a feared gang whose core values of win-win waste avoidance, stakeholder respect and environmental stewardship made them market leaders in sustainable rape. NB – the future shift in focus of Whole Foods Market Inc. away from nourishing people and the planet towards raping as many people as possible, night and day, should not be taken, in any way whatsoever, as a reflection on their current or past business practices. The radical reorientation of Whole Foods Market Inc. towards merciless, unremitting sexual abuse lies entirely in a future which, hopefully, will never exist. A future in which Trader Joe's, still (at the time of publication) a successful US-based chain of grocery stores, takes a sharp turn away from retail, in a direction of which its current management and in-house lawyers would, we are certain, deeply disapprove, becoming a market leader in child slavery and human trafficking, while insisting that both practices adhere to its stringent net-zero emissions policy.

Becoming an official 'greeter' at a Trader Joe's 'store' becomes one of the highest and hardest-won accolades available to a psychopath in the apocalypse. With their slogan 'What can I do to you today?' these greeters are often retired assassins who want to settle down and live out the remainder of their lives (their early 30s) performing acts of unimaginable cruelty to people who have just been unloaded for sorting. But few are the lunatics who could stomach being a Guest Relations Executive with one of the travelling luxury relaxation gangs, who trundled around the countryside with a kind of 'luxury spa' assembled on the back of a large cart, where 'guests' would begin their ultimate self-indulgent getaway with a 'massage', followed by a visit to the 'smoothie bar', and ending up in the 'infinity pool'. These spas were often used as an alternative to a potentially expensive divorce or hospice stay.

During the heyday of gangs, jobs were plentiful, well-paid and, it has to be said, relatively rape free. Actual salaries were a carefully worked-out combination of food tokens, euthanasia pills and molestation assurances. For example, a mid-level Public Relations Coordinator for a successful gang would be looking at being molested by gang executives no more than four times a week, and could be rewarded with a three-molestation weekly cap if they'd had a good quarter, unless they enjoyed being molested, in which case the sky was the limit.

By contrast, an entry level PR trainee, at the foot of the gang ladder, would be lucky to be molested at all if they were into being molested, or if not they would face a working day of pretty much non-stop molestation, often at the foot of the gang ladder. Trainees and interns would do their best, during the recruitment process, to project the opposite end of the molestation enjoyment spectrum that they were actually on, which was a constant headache for the gang's HR (Human Rape) department.

Worse, for many successful gang executives, as the ranks of middle-management grew bloated, the day-to-day grind of molesting their PR and Marketing departments turned into such a gruelling sexual nightmare that they ended up outsourcing it to highly paid external molestation consultants. So skilled were these molestation specialists that they could molest an entire Communications department in a matter of minutes, barely breaking their stride as their fingers, elbows, tongues and genitals jabbed and darted left and right, with the precision and power of a whaler's harpoon, up corridors and into booths, always managing to find unexpected angles with eye-watering torque. These genius fondlers, though operating at the very top of the global molestation pyramid, were cursed to live as hermits, as no gang could tolerate them for long in their midst, largely because of the smell, which was awful.

3. Several Facts About Gang Recruitment

Gangs often have intense and arduous initiation rituals. In pre-apocalyptic times, these might involve murdering a rival gang member, to compromise the new recruit who could now never go to the police. As the police were wiped out, this became less of an issue, and gang initiations became more of a psychometric quiz. And whereas, in the present day, most gangs require some sort of 'beatdown' in which the inductee is set upon by gang members, in the years immediately after the apocalypse gang members were generally so malnourished, sick and injured, that the kicks and blows became softer and softer, evolving into a kind of group massage.

However, as humanity hardened to its task of surviving the Collapse, and the social domination of gangs increased, gang initiation rituals became ever more violent, with the most common being beheading. If a decapitated initiate managed to blink twice for yes when asked if he or she would be loyal to the gang, their membership was assured.

It's essential to have some idea of the proclivities and requirements of any gang you're attempting to join. For example, you don't want to go to all the fuss and bother of dressing yourself in barbed-wire lingerie if it's not a gang of sex flagellants. Likewise, there's no point spending weeks perfecting a darkly satirical clown routine, full of elaborate pratfalls and social commentary, if the gang you're trying to impress is a millennial suicide cult looking for a cyanide tester. Most post-apocalyptic gangs require poison testers, for a variety of reasons, but the recruitment process is by no means straightforward: applicants are often found to have inured themselves to various poisons, or have had a special 'false stomach' fitted, or are simply a hard-up suicidal person looking for a freebie.

First impressions are vital when joining a gang, and it pays to appear tough and uncompromising when coming up in front of a gang's interview board: if you have access to a pair of pruning shears it might be worth snipping off a body part as you enter, while maintaining a steady eye contact with whoever seems most senior in the hut. You might want to consider snatching up and eating, as nonchalantly as possible, whatever it is you've just sheared off yourself, unless you're applying to join a sex cult, in which case firmly jam the severed toe or nose into a sexual orifice, or slap your genitals with the bloody ear as you masturbate to completion, ideally without fainting. Passing out mid-interview is regarded as a no-no by most talent acquisition specialists, and will probably lose you the job, and most of your remaining virginities.

'Everyone has seven basic virginities,' said Alonso in Seoul Bird, as we tucked into a sharing platter of chicken tenders and signature sauce. His enumeration of these seven basic virginities was so explicit and distressing that Charlie permanently lost his appetite for chicken tenders and Frankie required extra signature sauce. Calling for more Korean fried cauliflower, Alonso gave us a pro-tip: it's always a good idea to put 'rear end' on any gang application form where it asks you to list bodily virginities currently held. Being able to offer a gang captain the seat of honour at your rectum's debutante ball can make all the difference in those awkward first few hours after joining. Remember to keep grimacing, and muttering things like 'Gosh, blimey, this is not what I imagined,' or 'This is my first time doing this sort of thing,' even if you're a practised recipient, as most people were forced to become during the short but sexually intense reign of King Sodom the First, whose empire stretched further than it had first seemed likely to, and who many historians now believe was Brooklyn Beckham.

Some people, hoping to be recruited by a gang, would hire out-of-work actors to trot ahead of them wherever they went, pretending to be fleeing for their lives, yelling things like: 'Oh no! I'm being hunted down by a ruthless yet loyal thug who would be an asset to any gang. I'd certainly recruit him if I was in gang recruitment!' – which got so annoying after a while that many of these actors would end up being hunted down by the person pretending to hunt them down, which made the performance much more authentic, and offered an exciting opportunity to avoid paying the actor. A problem arose whenever members of the public joined in a pursuit, which was always, and a simple deception aimed at attracting the eye of a gang recruiter could end up in the death of the actor; pursuer; and several hundred others.

Alonso himself was recruited into a gang in northern Spain. What happened, in a painstaking rewriting of what he actually said, was this:

In a failed effort to negotiate a 20% discount, I was arm-wrestling the madam of a sex hovel in Bilbao when I met Vittor, a member of the feared 'Bad Boyz for Life', the tightest knit of the Basque seafood gangs. While helping me splint my wrist, he let slip that he was a member, and I asked him to tell me a bit of the gang's history. He told me to go and fuck myself, and burst into floods of tears. He apologised, telling me he'd had a difficult couple of weeks, and that he'd do his best to answer my questions, and did I have any crack on me? I gave him a hit of my crack, and he told me about the founder of the gang, a mysterious figure, about which nothing whatsoever was remembered except his name, 'Baltasar Unax Iñárritu de Santurtzi'. I remarked that it seems odd that they should remember such an elaborate name but no other facts about him, at which Vittor flew into a violent rage and squared up to me yelling 'Hand on my jock' over and over until I apologised. He blinked back tears, saying no, he was the one who should apologise, it was inexcusable behaviour, but that he was a bit strung out because all his friends were dead and he was the only living member of the gang and did I have any more crack?

I gave Vittor another hit of crack, and that seemed to calm him down. He told me, after I promised never to divulge a word of what he was about to tell me, about the gang's elaborate initiation ritual. The ornate ceremony was based, he said, on the handful of lyrics any of the gang could remember from P. Diddy's song 'Bad Boyz for Life', which had been taught to them by Baltasar Unax Iñárritu de

Santurtzi but then largely forgotten. How it worked was this: the gang elder, known as a 'Diddy', would open the proceedings by saying 'Let's do it, mmm, yeah,' to which the initiate would respond 'Nothing but big things.' The elder would then say 'Hand on my jock' to which the initiate must respond 'We ain't goin' nowhere.' And then the initiation would be complete, and they'd settle down to a bowl of fish soup.

I remember saying to him that it didn't sound particularly elaborate, at which he flew into a fury, and started shouting 'Nothing but big things,' while thrusting his hand into his jacket as if to imply he had a handgun. He squared up to me saying 'Let's do it, mmm, yeah' and 'Nothing but big things' and 'Have you ever even made a fish soup? It's all about the stock.' He kept his hand inside his jacket as he circled around me, ducking and bobbing menacingly, saying 'We ain't goin' nowhere' and 'You need a hake head,' and 'If you can get hold of them, use Espelette peppers,' until, after a few minutes of this, I felt pretty sure he hadn't got a handgun, so I told him to settle down. This seemed to infuriate him, and he got right up in my face and shouted 'Nothing but big things' and then started crying, saying he just wanted to be a chef. I told him he should follow his dreams: just because an apocalypse was happening, you shouldn't let that stand in the way of doing something you truly believe in, and he nodded and shook my hand, saying 'Yes, you're right, I'm so glad we had this chat,' whereupon he was struck in the chest by a stray bullet from a successful sex hovel negotiation.

It took Vittor most of the afternoon to die, during which time he explained to me, in painful whispers, how to fry a scallop without it becoming chewy, and how he was the last surviving member of Bad

Boyz for Life, which had recently wiped itself out during a bloody civil war, fought between those members who thought their name should be spelled 'Bad Boyz for Life', and those who thought 'Bad Boyz 4 Life' with the digit '4' was way cooler, and that he was on the more traditionalist 'for' side, but that it didn't seem that important in retrospect. I disagreed, assuring him that this kind of seemingly trivial detail can be hugely important to the self-identity of a gang, and also, seeing as how he was presumably the last Diddy, would he mind initiating me into the gang? He readily agreed, and we went through the initiation: I gave the correct responses, and he welcomed me into the fold, whereupon I told him that, on reflection, I think it's cooler to spell 'for' with the digit '4', and that going forward I was probably going to go with '4', and he didn't seem to mind much, and told me about his mother's recipe for Chipirons à la Luzienne until he died. He didn't have much of interest in his pockets, except for one thing: a carefully folded piece of paper on which were written the arresting words 'go to Salamanca and find Paco Larrazábal, he will give you the jewels'. I was intrigued. One question was foremost in my mind: did Vittor have the same size waist as me? I pulled his trousers off and lo and behold, they fitted perfectly.

Alonso stood up and proudly showed us his trousers. 'These are the trousers of Vittor,' he said. And he showed us the bloodstains. 'These aren't his bloodstains, these are from when I broke a window yesterday trying to get into the back of the chemists in Ladbroke Grove, but they were similar to this.' He offered to initiate us into Bad Boyz 4 Life, but we pointed out that it didn't exist yet, and asked him if he ever went to Salamanca to find Paco Larrazábal and ask about the jewels, and he laughed and said: 'Aah yes, the cursed emeralds of Salamanca . . . sit yourselves back and listen to this.'

Alonso propped one leg up on a chair, and his other leg up on another chair, and held us utterly spellbound as he said: 'No, I never did. Other stuff came up. And can I just say: these chicken tenders are amazing. I don't care what they're made of, I want more. Let's get another platter, and this time we can share.' And so began a marathon of chicken tenders so epic that when we asked the staff at Seoul Bird whether, in all their days, they'd seen the like, they had to admit: 'Yeah, I don't know. I need to clean this table, sorry.'

⁓

Methods for selecting gang leaders were varied. One of the most popular was a show of hands, where candidates showed how many people's hands they had cut off. There are also documented cases of secret ballots, and election by consensus, and leadership on a rotating basis, but largely it was knife fights, and even the secret ballots tended to go that way eventually.

During the late twenty-second century, many gangs began to experiment with more democratic structures, with regular votes on gang policy, and were wiped out. With increasingly bitter internal power struggles and the relentless fracturing of alliances, it became evident after a time that every remaining gang had just one member. This was definitely the lowest ebb of the various gang eras, and for a ruthless gang hierarchy to be maintained within these single-member gangs required debilitating levels of schizophrenia and self-abuse. For gangs to survive at all, new gangs had to be formed by melding these single-member gangs into larger meta-gangs, or 'gangs'.

The difference between a gang and a militia was that militias sought to impose a rough kind of order on their territory, leading to chaos. Gangs simply sought to benefit from chaos, and sometimes accidentally created a kind of order. In this they rendered the nation-state and capitalism in their final, satirical forms.

As communities grew weaker through disease, air poisonings, water poisonings, other poisonings and other diseases, dwindling gangs found it harder and harder to recruit and were loath to lose members in skirmishes, in turf wars or disputes over sex worker ownership. Rather than risk death or serious injury, rival militias took to challenging each other to 'dance offs', in which the usual knife thrusts, groin kicks, ball twists and screwdriver stabs of hand-to-hand combat became symbolised in a set of agreed-upon dance moves, with the audience keeping time by banging old tin cans and bin lids, a practice which some of the gang elders referred to mysteriously as 'stomping'. The dances were still pretty robust, and the damage to valuable shoes and clothing was deemed too great, so the competitors would enter the arena naked, thrusting and parrying in a wild, primeval Tango that would end, convention came to dictate, in full and extravagant sex between the competitors and most of the crowd, a practice which some of the gang elders referred to mysteriously as 'desublimation'. It was often found, however, amidst all the sucking and fucking, to be almost impossible to pick a winner. Although this gave rise to disputes, these tended to be resolved amicably through brief campaigns of kidnapping and mass murder.

It requires a certain skill to talk your way out of captivity. It's generally recommended to agree with your captors as much as possible, unless they're talking about how attractive they find you. It's good to have to hand a few short anecdotes that hint at useful skills you possess. There are story writers in most townships who would furnish travellers with a few of these for the price of a cooked rat. Popular stories had titles like THE INSTINCTIVE MECHANIC and I SEEM TO BRING PEOPLE LUCK. The marauders of the wastelands came to enjoy many of these standards, and would kill prisoners for telling them poorly.

Eventually the scene became dominated by professional storytellers. Their stories were peppered with impressions, were structurally complex, and made listening to the stammered pleas for mercy of an actual prisoner almost unbearable. These professional storytellers would have to act out a pantomime of being captured, and militias a pantomime of letting them escape with a small fee. Sadly, after a while, the better storytellers became so prized that they were never released, and it became a skill on the circuit to tell stories that were gripping but ultimately flawed.

4. The Annals of Stefan

Most of what we know about the gangs of the American east coast between the First and Third Inferno come from several large fragments of the *Annals of Stefan*, a Long Island pastry chef turned social diarist and enforcer, which were entombed in a concrete 'memory ball' formed out of the rubble of the Primeclass Lounge at Terminal 1 of JFK International Airport and rolled for posterity into Jamaica Bay – one of the hundreds of memory balls created around this time by a gang of long-haul airline crew, which emerged from an uneasy coalition between stewards from Lufthansa and El Al, who had developed a kind of 'emergency procedure' for the crash of civilisation. Though unspeakably violent, this gang was always perfectly turned out, and were careful to see to the needs of anyone they were molesting, always giving them the warning 'Brace, brace' and offering them a hard-boiled sweet to suck in case their ears popped.

It's thought that the brutality of this gang was drawn from years of suppressing disgust and resentment towards rude and ungrateful passengers, and they were unhesitating in murdering anyone they saw being impolite or trying to get up during turbulence (their word for rape). This gang's name was three short toots on a life jacket whistle, and you could tell the seniority of the gang member by how many 'pretzels' (you don't want to know what these were) they wore round their neck on an adjustable life jacket strap.

They developed a complex mythology in which humans were created by the Sun and the Moon having sex in a lavatory while the Stars knocked on the door telling them what they were doing was illegal. And they were unafraid of death, welcoming it as an extended lay-over. They believed in a coming redeemer they called 'The Accident Investigator', and understood their role in the apocalypse as trying to preserve for this mysterious figure the 'dental records' of humanity, but they couldn't find any actual dental records, so they would gather together old bits of inflight magazines and any scraps of books they could find and encase them in concrete for the future.

In one of their concrete memory balls languished the *Annals of Stefan* – until it was dredged up to be used in an attempted reboot of the World's Strongest Man contest, which was comfortably won by a badly damaged General Atomics combat robot which had been fished out of the bay with the memory balls and part-repaired by the last surviving Aer Lingus maintenance supervisor. In second place was a placid but immensely powerful dray horse called Osborne. The robot was so delighted in winning the contest that its weapons system came online and it launched a GA-EMS Medium Calibre Projectile at the concrete ball, destroying the ball and itself, and releasing a blizzard of pages of the books and documents encased within, including several large fragments of the *Annals of Stefan*.

These fragments were carefully gathered up, bagged, and sold as gerbil bedding, but moments before being shredded, they happened to be set on one side, and were used to start a fire in a gerbil bedding showroom by the financially troubled owner, J. Stanton Mendez, in an attempted insurance scam, which was only foiled by the complete absence of an insurance industry. But these weren't the fragments of the *Annals of Stefan* we're talking about; they were other fragments, and the information they contained has been lost forever. Although we do know that Osborne the horse, having been declared the new winner of the World's Strongest Man, went on to have a successful career as a jurist. Suspects were brought before him, he would listen carefully to their case, and would pass judgement by stamping his hoof, once for guilty, twice for innocent, on their head. J. Stanton Mendez was one of the first to have his case brought before Osborne: he was acquitted on all seven charges, but never regained consciousness.

'Can we get back to Stefan?' asked Charlie, 'I think we're drifting,' and took another puff on his DMT vape, which fell into his gratin dauphinois as he left this shabby dimension. We were sitting outside at Le Petit Citron on Shepherd's Bush Road, as Alonso preferred to take DMT while staring at traffic: 'I've learned how to go in and out of the molecules of number plates,' he told us, after spending a complicated few minutes/years exploring the pineal gland of the driver of the 295 to Hammersmith. 'He didn't seem to mind,' Alonso assured us. 'I had a chat about fractals with several of his mitochondria, who were pretty friendly considering I'd turned up uninvited.'

Charlie was wearing a pair of noise-cancelling headphones and he was pressing on his eyes with the palms of his hands, even though they were transparent. He returned from a harlequin realm with important information he'd been given by a colourful trickster character in a mirrored room, but the information had been transmitted in the form of a garishly coloured mosaic which he had been unable to stop rotating long enough to read. 'I think it was something about a hidden floor in Edinburgh Waverley train station. Maybe I should go back in again and check?' Frankie disagreed. 'That would be a waste of time. I'll go instead,' and took a long hit on the vape.

Back on the Shepherd's Bush Road, he explained how a braided humming sound which emerged in orange strands from a metallic 'sort of thing' unlocked a new form of geometry which he thought might be useful for people in the future if he could remember any of it. Luckily, some trace of this information seemed to be embedded in the dessert menu, which Frankie slipped inside his cardigan for later analysis. He decided not to order his usual rhum baba aux raisins, because he was worried the words would shatter if he said them out loud, so he just sat quietly and made slow movements of his jaw to show us he was okay.

Alonso ordered the seasonal frangipane and got on with his story. Unfortunately, Frankie put his phone into his citronnelle tisane because he thought that's where it needed to be, so we don't have an actual recording of this conversation, but luckily Charlie had the presence of mind to capture many of the details, and much of the spirit, of the discussion in a hastily produced series of watercolours of a bee.

Known locally for his witty twist on the traditional croquembouche, Stefan was much in demand at weddings because of his remarkable ability to break people's fingers with a nonstick baking mat. He seems for a time to have been affiliated with the Hampton Bastards, a gang which was locked for several years in a bloody turf war with the New Hampton Bastards, the Original Hampton Bastards, and the New Original Hampton Bastards, in which all four gangs were eventually wiped out by the congregation of Shinnecock Presbyterian Church.

Stefan's uncanny ability to peel people's faces off with a fluted tart ring seems to have endeared him to the Elders of this pitiless Church, and the stability of their brutal rule allowed him to concentrate on his journalling. His was one of several handprinted lifestyle 'blogs' that briefly flourished after the disappearance of the internet, until they ran out of tips on fun ways to kill yourself. He seems at some point to have taken Holy Orders, and we last hear of him as a member of the Presbyterian General Synod of New York, North America's largest and most sadistic sex trafficking gang. Decades later, several carefully clingfilmed sections of his diary were discovered in his coffin by grave scavengers, and sold as pornography.

By this point in the disintegration of human civilisation, so few written texts survived that any which did were immediately pressed into service as erotica. Pornhub still existed but only in the form of a Ford hub cap which people queued up to look at, finding the soft, flourishing curves of the capital 'F' of the Ford logo almost impossibly sexy. Some would faint away when they got past the F and noticed the slight opening in the top of the 'o', which could be read as mouth, vagina, anus, armpit, gunshot wound, or any other of the typically used love holes of a human. Further still along the word, they met the letter 'r', its torso crossed with a line from the surrounding two letters, essentially holding it down, turning the 'ord' of Ford into a sexually adventurous S&M threesome. There is no way to write the 'Ford' signature without the vertical stroke of the 'r' being a separate line: an intrusion, a sudden visitor to the scene, plump and proud, yet sympathetically bending into the action, though a few insisted on interpreting this cross-cut of the 'r' as a symbolic castration and the mark of the interdiction of infinite jouissance or something. The 'd' formed an orgasmic pressing together of the 'o' with a hard downward line, a final grunting thrust, yet with a curl upwards at its end, an optimistic uptick, rising thinly yet hopefully towards some future congress. A whole cosplay scene based around these four letters emerged, with players dressed as F, o, r and d, forming themselves into different sexual anagrams, the most popular of which were Fod, doF, and dFFFooorrrrrrrrFFr. People would gather around these elaborate sex pantomimes and attempt to sketch them but, unfortunately, they'd forgotten how to draw. They'd be rubbing bits of paper desperately against some old pen lids, but this never seemed to quite capture the moment.

It is a testament to the adaptability of humankind that survivors of the apocalypse were able to masturbate over any subject matter whatsoever. Once, when a partial road sign from what used to be the A43 outside what used to be Duddington in what used to be North Northamptonshire in what used to be the United Kingdom was discovered, and even though the only intact section was the tail end of the word 'Peterborough', crowds of bedraggled masturbators gathered for months, staring mutely at the letters GH and part of the U, as they tugged and strummed at themselves with a kind of steely determination which left many with inoperable tennis elbow. It's often said that World War Seven was fought over a pristine 1955 knitting pattern for an Afghan shawl, but no evidence for this exists, and no one believes it.

'So why did you tell us about it?' asked Charlie, a bit annoyed at having had so much of his red velvet sponge cake eaten by Alonso. We'd decided to leave Le Petit Citron as we'd been asked to leave, and had settled in at Dough & So on the Uxbridge Road for some sweet treats. 'Are you saying we should stock up on 1950s knitting patterns just on the off chance we can stop a world war?' Alonso shrugged. 'Sure, you could just carry on as you are: eating your fancy cakes and writing links for *Quizn't She Lovely* and wait for the sky to fall. Or do you want to do something about it?' – 'I'm on it,' said Frankie, scrolling down eBay on his phone. 'Here we are:

vintage 1950s twin set; jacket and cardigan Raglan sleeve; fits a 32- to 38-inch bust. Look.' He showed Alonso the picture on his phone. Alonso's nostrils flared and he discreetly slid a plate of pistachio baklava in front of him in a valiant yet ultimately doomed effort to hide his orgasms. Charlie passed him a napkin and apologised. 'Look, I'm sorry Alonso, you're right. Sometimes I just get overwhelmed, all this information . . . and the responsibility . . . what's at stake . . . what we're trying to do here . . . I just . . .' Alonso smiled, and reached over, to give Charlie's arm a steadying squeeze. 'Hold on, just a couple more to go,' he whispered. 'There. Right. I'm done. What were we talking about?'

The pistachio baklava at Dough & So filled Alonso with a poignant sense of baklava. 'It's hard to believe that in the future I'll never have baklava again. Unless, of course, I decide . . .' he paused for a few minutes to eat some baklava, ' . . . not to go back'. We weren't sure what he meant, because we'd forgotten the first half of the sentence.

He told us that he was having such a nice time forging a career in television and helping save the world that he might stay around in our time. 'So, you've actually got a time machine here that you could go back in?' asked Frankie. 'I kind of thought you just appeared here in an orb or something.' Alonso told us that he had his time machine stashed in a storage facility 'somewhere up near Acton', and it was safe as long as he kept up the monthly payments, and could he have £375 for this month's rental and some more baklava?

We agreed to his terms. After all, the future of humanity was at stake, and by covering his time machine storage costs we were doing our small bit to ensure that he would be able, at some point soon, to fuck off out of our lives. Unfortunately, Charlie shouted this last bit into Alonso's face, and Alonso was hurt, so we said it was a joke, and that we loved having him around, and we all laughed, but there was a slightly distant and distrustful look in the waiter's eye as he looked at the traveller's cheque Charlie had written for the meal. We quickly changed the subject: what about careers advice for young people after the apocalypse?

'Excellent question', said Alonso, slopping a healthy tot of absinthe into his mint tea. He enjoyed the effect of drinking absinthe: it allowed him to see strange, otherworldly creatures, eerie wraiths floating across his vision, half-living, half-undead, which he described to us in such terrifying detail that we eventually realised he was referring to us. Sploshing another finger of spirit into his tuna and cheese jacket potato, he outlined the three main post-apocalyptic career paths open to someone graduating (i.e. escaping) from what they'd been assured was a university: mercenary, plumber or statistic.

Becoming a statistic was an extremely popular choice among people who booked a consultation with a careers advisor, because the mortality rate of such consultations was around 93%. The job of mercenary had a good weekly wage, and was the ideal choice for someone with burgeoning psychopathic tendencies who liked the idea of being shot in the back of the head after a week instead of being paid. Plumbing was the pre-apocalypse trade in which AI-enabled robots found it hardest to replace humans: it involved so much fiddling about in cramped spaces and lying about the price of replacement parts that the robot plumbers adopted the practice of pointing under a sink, saying 'I think that's your problem,' and when the client bent over to look they would quickly implant a chip in their brain stem which would trick their consciousness into enjoying the smell of a blocked drain.

After the apocalypse, and the general collapse of sewage and water treatment systems, combined with catastrophic droughts and the shift towards public defecation, plumbers found themselves having to focus on the one area of their expertise which was still useful: not turning up at the arranged time. Having someone resolutely not turn up to do a job when agreed upon, no matter how many times you confirm it with them, was a huge blessing in an era when the only people who did turn up at your house would be hoping to murder you, very often without an appointment.

Most sewerage systems in the apocalypse had collapsed, which meant that people had to collect their sewage in bags and buckets and store them in their house, waiting to empty them when the Sewage Man came by, usually on the spring equinox. The few sewage farms that survived were mainly used as persuasion pools for particularly cruel gangs. Many of these treatment facilities became so clogged with bodies that they were abandoned, turning into rich biodiverse ecosystems where local wildlife would gather to catch sepsis. One that carried on operating longer than most, with a stench of death and faeces unrivalled even in New Jersey, were the unholy murder ponds of the Little Egg Harbor Municipal Utilities Authority.

The ponds sat just up the coast from the Atlantic City Memorial: a poignant statue of a noose with three people's heads stuffed into it, commemorating the Atlantic City Suicide, the first city to decide, en masse, to end it all. Most of the town's residents gathered in Lake Lenape, to which much of the city's power cables had been diverted, waiting for the switch to be thrown by the boxer Anthony Joshua, whose connection to the city remains unclear.

'We've decided to take the express,' said the then Mayor of Atlantic

City, Hal Biddle, to warm applause, as he announced the measure in a press conference which ended with the mayor taking questions while a fire truck reversed over his neck. Nonetheless he took days to die as there were no other residents alive to put him out of his misery and the firefighter reversing the truck had made a miscalculation about the length of the iron spike he was reversing into, that shouldn't have entered his brain until a good foot or so after the mayor had been decapitated.

The gangs of Little Egg Harbor ran the hugely popular Little Egg Harbor Thunderdome Showdown, a bi-monthly 'battle of the champions' which was, by tradition, a battle between the audience and two teams of 'champions', who had been collected from local leper colonies and hospices. The champions would tend not to launch into battle immediately, preferring to wander the thunderdome looking for somewhere comfortable to sit, sharing stories about 'the better times' and giving each other friendly hugs, until a cry from the umpire's sniper nest would go up: 'They're trying to escape!' and the battle to defeat the champions, who'd be sitting in their various groups, wondering what was happening, would commence. And with that, followed by a partial recipe for tarte tropézienne de Cyril Lignac, the *Annals of Stefan* concludes.

5. The Gangs of Spain

'I was lucky enough to be in Pamplona for the annual running of the hand grenades,' said Alonso. 'I was a volunteer for the Red Cross, which was a gang of devout euthanisers who bludgeoned the injured to death with a crucifix.' Alonso ended up spending three months with the Red Cross. 'There was usually a small team of us at sporting events and charity fun runs, which weren't really that much fun for the people being hunted. We didn't get paid, but there was a great camaraderie among the volunteers. A lot of them were travelling on their year off. It's quite common for people to take a year off from their psychosis medications.'

We were trotting down Lime Grove from the London College of Fashion, where he'd just done a presentation. He'd been trying to demonstrate the future of clothing by pressing himself against the window of one of the ground-floor classrooms. 'They think they're so modern. I wasn't expecting them to be so body shy. Maybe next time I'll ring them first to let them know I'm going to drop by.' He looked back. 'Do you think they've stopped following us?'

Frankie wasn't sure, as the face around his eyes was heavily swollen from a botched chemical peel (he had no idea what the chemical peel involved, as his beautician, a local probation officer, always insisted he wear a blindfold for the procedure, where the mixture was applied with the concussive force of a tennis serve and accompanied by a similar yell) to prepare himself for the new Channel 4 comedy *Lorry Load of Love*, a crime caper about Britain's most notorious sex killers being released by the government to track down a female spy; Rylan Clark's relentlessly upbeat Peter Sutcliffe drove the team Mystery Van, and Frankie had been cast as Ian Brady. To get in character he'd started dressing in tight drainpipe trousers which made running even more of a challenge than usual.

To shake off any pursuers from the fashion school, we veered up into Shepherd's Bush Market and joined a terrarium-making workshop at Malina's Plants & Terrariums. Alonso remained on high alert. After half an hour or so he whispered to us: 'There's a lady staring at me. Over there. Look.' It was Malina, she was running the workshop and wanted to know if Alonso needed help; he'd designed his terrarium along the lines of the great Anglo-Spanish thunderdome and waterpark at Benidorm, El Acuático, famed for its suicide flume and hilarious halftime show where groups of audience members took on professional wrestlers, in a game called Sodomy Buckaroo, and he'd already lost three turtles to smoke inhalation and used up the whole workshop's supply of red paint.

'Okay then, what about that guy? He's been standing there for ages. He looks weird.' A shifty-looking man with deep-set eyes in a Hawaiian shirt and panama hat mopped his brow, and melted back into the crowds. 'Quick! Let's finish our terrariums and follow him!' Two hours later we paid for our workshops, carefully wrapped up our terrariums, apologised again to Malina, paid for the dead turtles, and sprinted off along the market. But the man had gone. We picked up some lamb cubes from the Grill Master and continued our search, while Alonso reminisced about post-apocalyptic Spain.

⌒

The entire course of north-eastern Spanish gang history, indeed of post-civilisation civilisation itself, was changed one fateful July weekend, when a peculiarly brutal gang of Catalan methamphetamine traders, who lurked in the relatively unscathed hills outside a flattened Barcelona, were scouting the area for a new distribution centre. They found the perfect site in an abandoned warehouse near Sant

Miquel de Balenyà, which turned out to be full of unopened wedding supplies. Trembling fingers drew back dusty tarpaulins to reveal dozens of bubble-wrapped patio heaters, frosted vases and flower stands. Sacks of save-the-date cards were torn open with delight. Crates groaning with vases, ring boxes, vow journals and bridal garters had their lids jemmied off with breathless excitement.

Xavier, the swashbuckling gang boss, hopped up on a box of photo-booth props, threw a fistful of confetti into the air and shouted: 'Tonight!' – except in Catalan. '*¡Aquesta nit! Farem un casament magnífic!*' But he was persuaded by a delegation of anxious lieutenants not to hold the ceremony that evening, as there'd be no way to iron the fancy tablecloths and gather enough flowers in time, so it was decided: in one week, a magnificent wedding would be held on the forecourt of the warehouse, which was duly transformed into a medieval wonderland. Ever the romantic, Xavier had decided to marry the wedding venue itself, his thinking on the matter being heavily coloured by his gang's constant use of leaded petrol as a skin toner.

Word of the wedding spread like wildfire around the region, and a number of rival gangs independently decided to attack the gang's headquarters while they were distracted by the nuptials. Unfortunately for the attackers, the various lurking militia began skirmishing with each other before the ambush could be launched, and the beautifully attired celebrants, who'd spent all day drinking from a chocolate fountain which they'd laced with superhuman amounts of meth, were so cranked on pookie and jacked-up on hot chocolate, they were able to swiftly and delightedly slaughter the furious bushwhackers, leaving only one of them alive: a trainee thug from the village of Sant Salvador de Torroella, who went by the name of Ramon.

Discovered cowering under the cake table, Ramon was fished out by his heels, asked his food preferences, and made guest of honour at the evening's festivities. He was prevailed upon to make a speech, which Ramon wisely kept nice and short; he didn't go for any cheesy gags, just made it heartfelt and sincere. His brevity was appreciated by everyone at the reception, given how many speeches were being made that night (eleven plus toasts) and how severely geared up everyone was on gak. Ramon was even granted the honour of dancing the first dance with the triumphant gang boss, who promised to let him go after the disco on condition that he tell everyone he meets that the ambush was a great success, and also put on a pair of novelty glasses and blow him in the photobooth.

Hilarious photos of the marathon suck job were passed from table to table, as the boss, still in the booth, called for ever more hats and props, all the while explaining to the busy Ramon that, if he didn't want his family and all the residents of Sant Salvador de Torroella skinned alive, he should spread the word that anyone seeing a rival gang distracted by preparing for a fancy wedding should seize the opportunity to attack. Word spread like wildfire – which at that point in Spain meant slowly, as the country contained so few things that had not already been destroyed by fire – and Xavier's plan was put into action. The gang, renamed Los Organizadores, set off on heavily laden carts around Catalonia, and up through the Pyrenees, every weekend staging elaborately themed weddings, making sure to send tastefully embossed invitations to all the local gang bosses, every one of whom took the opportunity to attack, only to find a drained meth fountain, a boobytrapped gift table, and themselves butchered by a heavily gartered Xavier and his crew.

After a year or so of exquisitely styled yet whimsical butchery, Ramon thought it best to leave the mainland. He bade farewell to his family, took a boat to Ibiza, where he became a trusted cocksucker to the island's most ruthless DJ, and changed his name to Alonso. 'He wasn't me. That was a different Alonso,' added Alonso quickly, before changing the subject by saying 'Let's talk about a new subject!' loudly and threateningly and pretending to take a phone call on an empty tub of Rachel's organic yoghurt which he kept in his pocket, in case he needed to pretend to make a phone call. 'Hello, is that Rachel?' he shouted into the tub, which is as much as he'd practised saying.

'But, but . . . but . . . but who . . . but who . . . but who . . . but if you . . . but, but who . . .' began Charlie, his mind awhirl. Alonso merely winked, or possibly twitched, and disappeared into Muyang Hot Pot & BBQ. What did he mean? We followed him, determined to find out, or have some shredded tofu with coriander salad trying.

6. Behold, the Knights of Destiny!

'I joined the Knights of Destiny for a while,' said Alonso, ordering the lamb spine. 'They were a spin-off from the Shepton Mallet Ornithological Society – they found their interests started to diversify into racketeering, contract killing, and ritual mutilation, and got sick of pumping endless money into maintaining the RSPB information centre at Beacon Pond, just off the Old Frome Road. The

Knights of Destiny were way cooler. Everyone was talking about them; they were definitely the coolest gang north of Yeovil. But the initiation took ages.'

The secretive Knights of Destiny roamed the Mendips, trying to avoid other gangs, or any human contact whatsoever. They'd observed that most gang interactions, however friendly and respectful, tended to involve the two parties, at some point, massacring each other. Often, they'd noticed, the massacre was finished off by members of a third gang who were crouching behind something, waiting out the massacre for a bit, before leaping out and massacring anyone who wasn't already massacred. The Knights were fascinated by one aspect of the massacring process: the crouching and hiding. They took this, refined it, dispensed with the leaping out bit, and became experts in concealment: hiding behind trees, bending down behind bushes, and remaining submerged in ponds for hours at a time, breathing through a reed or wearing a duck on their head. You could often spot them because they tended to wear a hollowed-out duck on their head. Although, of course, if you saw them in a pond they would have just looked like a duck. Sometimes they set up visitor boards near reservoirs and reed beds, featuring pictures of waterbirds and some helpful information such as: 'Glossy ibis, a member of the spoonbill family, often looks like someone is hiding underneath it'.

After a year or so of wearing a duck, a gang member would be promoted to grebe; the more senior gang members would wear a goose; enforcers would wear a distinctive and dreaded Eurasian wigeon, and the gang leader would be resplendent in a swan, which meant that he or she had to be extra good at hiding (when not in a pond).

These were the fully fledged Knights. Their Patron Saint was the Lady of the Lake, who they admired for never having been seen below the elbow. They were the sort of men (and possibly women) who had rarely been seen since childhood, and weren't above attaching a fibreglass set of human shoulders to the bottom of a goose to create a decoy.

'The problem with joining them is that they're almost impossible to find,' said Alonso, as his lamb spine arrived. 'I met an old shepherd in Evercreech, and asked him if he knew where the Knights of Destiny recruitment centre might be, and he pointed north towards Chesterblade and said "over yonder," but by the time I looked back, a few minutes later, he was nowhere to be seen. When I thought about it, he seemed an odd sort of shepherd: he had no sheep around him and a wooden goose strapped to his head. Could he have been a member of the Knights of Destiny? I know now that he was. I scoured a nearby knoll, but there was nothing on it but some ducks and a couple of geese, moving around behind a hedge. Where could they be? I wandered up and down Winterwell Lane until my feet were sore. I fell to my knees in the ruins of St Mary's Church, and cried out: "I give up."

'At which point, to my astonishment, a vast flock of waterbirds seemed to emerge from behind gravestones and bits of fallen wall. Under them were men and women with tufts of grass stuck in their pockets and smiles on their mud-streaked faces. A man with a heron on his head and a sedge warbler strapped to his wrist extended an arm of comradeship. "You have found us" he said. "Now come with us to Cranmore Pond. You have some hiding to do." A few hours later, cold but happy, I had a coot ceremonially strapped to my head, a blanket put round my shoulders, and into my shivering fingers was pressed a steaming hot mug of pond water. I had joined the Knights of Destiny – and that,' said Alonso, turning to Sylvain from Pathé, 'is where the movie ends. It's called *The Knights of Destiny*, and you cast really big names in it, A-listers, but you only need them all for half a day: the scene in the churchyard. You could shoot the whole scene in an hour if you've got a half-decent DOP. The rest of it is just me wandering around Stoney Stratton for 90 minutes. It's nice round there. You've got the scene with the Shepherd, but you could probably cut that if it's too expensive, or green screen it. And with the big-name cast, if they keep their goose low over their face, you could even get away with lookalikes. I know a guy who works in the off-licence just up from QPR stadium, he's already said he'll be in it. Get a big enough duck on him, and I'm sure he could pass as Jason Statham. What do you think? Sylvain? Where are you going?'

Alonso finished Sylvain's salt chilli ribbonfish, which became his new favourite dish at Muyang Hot Pot & BBQ: he'd always order it as a 'topper' to his stewed pig intestine with tofu. 'Do you think that was a yes?' asked Alonso. 'Should we be celebrating?' And he called for a sharing plate of chicken feet. 'I'm not sure,' said Charlie. 'He seemed in a hurry to leave. He left his coat. Wait, here he comes now.' Sylvain rested his hands on the back of his chair and took a deep breath: 'Guys, I'm sorry I stormed off like that. My head was in a swirl. The idea was just too radical for me to take in. But I've had a moment to think about it, and I fucking love it. I think we've got a real chance here to redefine modern cinema. Set up a meeting with your friend at the off-licence. Let's make a movie! Wait, what? What the fuck's happened to my salt chilli ribbonfish? It was just here. You mean you just ate it? You degenerate fucking animals. I was gone for 2 minutes. The film's off. I'm out of here.' And he snatched up his coat and stormed back off. (Does that mean *The Knights of Destiny* will never see the light of day? We'll see. It very much depends on what Shannon from Paramount meant by 'What the fuck are you talking about? I'm sorry. I have to go.')

Alonso glanced up from his chicken chow mein, and pointed at the window. 'There!' A stylish lady in a vintage Hermès neckerchief had her face pressed to the glass, watching us. She came in and introduced herself as Dr Yvonne Rouxel from the London College of Fashion. She'd been teaching there when Alonso had made his intervention: she'd heard a tapping and scraping on the glass, and had rushed over to the window to sketch the display. Yvonne was keen to interview Alonso for a paper she was writing about scrotal piercings.

'They're like none I've ever seen,' she admitted. 'I got them done in the future,' said Alonso, offering her some asparagus. 'Maybe later,' she smiled, opening her notebook to show us her sketches. A startled Frankie knocked his hot & sour soup over the drawings – he quickly grabbed a napkin and, apologising profusely, offered to make her an origami swan. He'd been practising his folding for his recently cancelled documentary *Frankie Boyle's Origami History of The Celts*. On the first day of filming in the Hebrides he'd folded a model of the early fifteenth-century bard Lachlann Mór MacMhuirich, which his co-host, Lewis Capaldi, mistook for a paper aeroplane. The resulting spat saw both hosts quitting. The BBC repurposed the footage already shot as background for Scotland's entry to the Eurovision Song Contest, although both artists' faces and fists were pixelated.

Yvonne and Alonso soon developed a rapport: she was intrigued by his tattoos and ceremonial scars, and found his mood swings charming, and it wasn't long before their friendship turned into something more. They became lovers, and virtually inseparable, speaking at length of how they found each other's bodies sexually inspiring, and the gentle clank-clank-clank of Alonso's piercings against her vulval rings became the soundtrack to many of our conversations, until the arrival of the bill, at which point she said she thought she had a class or something and disappeared.

Alonso spent a few fruitless afternoons searching for her. He replaced his various penis piercings with magnets and followed his cock around like a divining rod: refusing to listen when we said he should look her up on Facebook, or try the college where he knew she worked.

7. How to Join a Gang: Tactics and Tips

Over a consolation plate of squid tentacles, Alonso set out his five essential tips for anyone thinking of joining a gang. These tips are so amazingly useful that we have had them printed separately on a special leatherette bookmark that you can get from any reputable newsagent or bookseller: simply show a copy of this book, opened at this page, and say 'Can I have my leatherette bookmark' and they are obliged to sort you out. That said, please note: due to a manufacturing error, Tip 3, as printed on the leatherette bookmark, is too blurred to make out; it should read: 'Make sure you don't react to being kicked or prodded or bitten by dogs when you're pretending to be dead by getting your friends and family to kick and bite you for at least an hour every day'. And Tip 4, as printed on the leatherette bookmark, contains a misprint: 'The first thing to do is approach the Town Strongman' should read 'Under no circumstances approach the Town Strongman'.

A lot of strongholds would have a Town Strongman, who would go up to the gates of a rival fort and demand single combat. This was a brief fashion and the position was quickly replaced by that of Town Sniper. Even during its height, the role of Town Strongman was an unenvied position, as the pay wasn't that great, and the job mostly involved being torn limb from limb and having your still-screaming head impaled on a stick and paraded around in front of the town gates. If it weren't for the attractive pension plans, it's likely that no one would have applied for the position at all.

As it was, for both strongholds and marauders, the role of champion became harder and harder to fill, with the weakest members of the competing clans being bullied into accepting the title. Quite often, the battle between the champions of a town and its besiegers would be such a feeble display of slaps and hair-tugging that it lasted three or four days, with the winner being the last one to succumb to boredom or rabies.

As a general strategy for post-apocalyptic life, teaming up with another survivor can be an attractive option, but the plusses and minuses have to be weighed carefully. Companionship can keep you sane; and two people often have skills that can complement each other. On the other hand, your new friend might be a psychosexual sadist who's largely just waiting for you to fall asleep. So: ask them questions about how they've survived so far. Pay special attention to any bitter asides about their mother, or muttered discussions with an unseen force. Of course there are those who've had positive experiences of team ups, and managed to get into the sex eventually, or at least learned to disassociate, but on balance, it's probably best to grit your teeth and go it alone.

The gangs to avoid joining at all costs are: 1) Hoy-Morzhovy (Volgograd, former Soviet Union) – a gang so brutal that you can only become a fully fledged member by killing all the other members of Hoy-Morzhovy; it consists of one terrified member and 14,000 circling applicants; 2) The Shites of Aylesbury (Aylesbury, former UK) – a gang you can only join by going to Aylesbury; 3) The Random Body Part Removal Loyalty Test Gang (Majorca, former Mediterranean); and 4) The Crips (Henley-on-Thames) – since relocating from South Los Angeles to Henley, the Crips focused on a complete overhaul of the Henley Regatta: shortening the course by 112 metres to become a round 2 km; introducing a third crew to the coxless fours in the Visitors' Challenge Cup, and making it mandatory for all boats to carry a harpoonist. A really skilled harpoonist will be able to skewer an entire coxed eight, including the cox, using a single grenade-tipped harpoon: a feat dubbed 'an Eton Mess'.

Perhaps the most ferocious New York gang, and certainly one to be avoided by any post-apocalyptic traveller, is 'The Subsidiary', led by a deranged coterie of A&R reps and reception staff from a subsidiary of Sony Music. Having celebrated the end times by ingesting all of the alcohol and narcotics set aside for clients, the psychotic survivors of the week-long binge used the confusion of the Collapse to kidnap three high-profile performers who'd been at the office for meetings, and taken refuge there during the riots. It seemed to their deranged minds an excellent idea to surgically combine the trio into a kind of super performer they called 'The Talent', which survived the surgery long enough to record two and a half songs of its/their debut album. The artists who were rounded up and sewn together into this screaming and vomiting amalgam were Natalie Imbruglia, Lil' Flip, and someone who claimed to be the drummer from Smash Mouth but upon waking from surgery vehemently denied being so, but by then it was too late, and whoever he was he provided serviceable percussion and backing vocals before losing consciousness. Lil' Flip outlived the other two thirds of his chimera for about 10 minutes, during which he recorded the deeply moving vocals for a solo track which was subsequently released as 'For The Love of God (Just Kill Me)' but failed to make an impression on the charts because there weren't any.

If you're wandering the apocalypse, and by some appalling turn of events you find yourself in Pennsylvania, then do yourself a favour and avoid Susquehannock State Forest. The Dementia Gangs who roam there, snatching victims and dragging them back to their lairs by circuitous routes, often taking days of spiralling around to travel a few hundred yards, are among the worst gangs to be snatched by. The average torture session lasts over a week, as they have terrible trouble remembering what it is they were asking about, or whether the session has started or not. The torture victim's best bet is to try and convince the torturers that in fact they are torture equipment testers, come to overhaul their pain chamber, or that they've unexpectedly been pardoned by the leader of the gang: 'Did you not hear what that messenger just told you? He was here just a second ago.'

Dementia is a huge problem for post-apocalyptic healthcare, because everyone wants it but few people live long enough to get it. People tried running headlong against walls and trees in the hope of triggering the condition. Running too fast meant you risked breaking your neck and dying, so it really was win-win. A gang of corpse cutters from the Omaha boneyards took to offering free lobotomies in exchange for the removed brain meat, but most of the time they got to keep the rest of the body as well. As their surgical skills improved, they began to offer 'keyhole lobotomies', which they performed using a heated key. The unfailing failure of this procedure led to an unexpected discovery: a few of the patients who managed to tear themselves out of their restraints early enough in the procedure found that the holes in their skulls led to a state of euphoria, relatively pleasant hallucinations, and a refreshing loss of short-term memory. The gang began shifting their business towards trepanning, and became hugely wealthy, as they were able to keep billing their confused customers over and over.

Some of the trepanned came to believe they had magical powers and formed an army of invincible 'wizard warriors'. Cloaking themselves in old bits of tarpaulin which gave them a +2 health bonus, whittling battle wands and carving runes for spell-casting, they set off to conquer the warring hordes and bring peace to the Earth, and were never heard of again. Years later, there were strange rumours that a remnant of wizard warriors was still out there, roaming the badlands, and willing to take on a quest, no matter how dangerous, if the spirit of the one who petitioned them was noble enough, but they weren't, and in fact they'd all died in the first 12 hours from a mixture of dehydration and having holes in their heads. Still, it was often said that the wizards still lived among us, clad in robes of invisibility, by people who passed wind in company.

The dramatic lowering of global life expectancy in the end times caused a huge upsurge in gerontophilia, with the extreme scarcity of the elderly giving them a kind of sexual cachet that most thought they had lost forever. Gang leaders would show off their power and prestige by surrounding themselves with a harem of aged courtesans, favouring as lovers the most decrepit. Anyone over 90 could command vast sums for a tug job, and if by a miracle you managed to get to 100 with a working arsehole you could sell it for a king's ransom. Returning to camp after a successful raid, a randy gang boss would coax a favourite away from knitting their lingerie and persuade them with looted gifts and jewels to twerk and grumble about their rheumatic joints and dizziness.

These elderly concubines were gifted to gangs by groups travelling through their territories, who viewed the harems as an inexpensive form of euthanasia. Some gang members spent so much time having sex with the elderly that it started to affect their personalities, and they'd enter an old person only to forget what they'd gone in there for.

8. The Psychology of Gangs: Sadomasochism, Group Therapy and Ski-Jumping

As we may or may not already have said, the first of the seven nuclear winters was a mixed blessing for the skiing industry. While the snowfall was the best seen in decades, reinvigorating many of the lower pistes, the number of people taking skiing holidays dipped to around zero. The only people still skiing at this time were the British Royal Family – who refused to let a nuclear conflagration interfere with their social season – and people practising for the new and flourishing sport of Tyrolean Jousting, invented by a gang of entrepreneurs from Kitzbühel, which involved setting up two ski jumps facing each other across a valley.

At the booming honk of a giant horn, competitors would swoosh down their ramps and hurtle towards each other, clutching a lance under one arm, and hope to impale their opponent mid-air. Wearing armour was considered bad sport, and the bravest lancers would compete naked, except for a silk scarf displaying their gang colours stuffed into their anus, which would flutter behind them during their flight like the tail of a beautiful tropical bird. A double impalement was not uncommon, and if both jumpers managed to keep hold of their lances, the skewered pair would helicopter madly downwards in a spectacular death spiral, much to the joy of the spectators beneath, who would lock arms and spin in wild circles, howling and mimicking the tumbling duellers, even to the point of stabbing each other to death, much to the joy of the falling ski-jumpers, who would laugh and point out to each other the various dying dancers, who would point up and laugh as they watched the doomed skiers plunging to their doom, laughing and pointing.

Getting landed on by a grotesquely injured ski-jumper was considered good luck, though was rarely survived. A double miss, with both lances flapping stupidly in the wind, was met with boos and raspberries, and the unlucky jumpers would find themselves landing in a furious blizzard of old shoes, snowballs and ninja stars. Some gangs, keen to see their champion jumper win, would set up crossbow snipers near their rival gang's ramp, and most tournaments would have at least one face-off with two already dead jumpers tumbling limply towards each other across the frozen landscape.

Somewhere near Chattanooga, there was a sadistic militia leader who became frustrated that torturing people didn't raise their level of suffering sufficiently from the general, day-to-day suffering that they were experiencing anyway, so he developed his small territory into a paradise of sorts. He had his followers loot goods and ornamental items for miles around to develop what might be taken for a prosperous US town circa 1955 AD. Captives would be welcomed into the life of the town, becoming storekeepers and librarians, joining art clubs and choral societies, until eventually, when they felt totally at peace, they would be offered the Freedom of the Town: a long, bureaucratic ceremony during which they were suddenly sexually assaulted by someone dressed as a circus ringmaster, or occasionally an elk, and their membership cards of any clubs and societies would be torn up in front of them.

They would then be dragged to the town's theatre and forced to watch the local amateur dramatics group act out scenes from their humiliation, in a variety of genres, including Savoy Opera. Before each Savoy Opera scene, which were always the most traumatic and physically demanding, the hostages would be dragged on stage, given song sheets, quickly rehearsed, and be forced to play themselves, while members of thriving fine arts associations sketched and painted them, to form the basis of an exhibition in the theatre lobby to which they were not invited.

Rumours of this gang's tactics spread, and submissives from the surrounding territories were drawn to the town. Sadly, this meant that many of its businesses and stores gained a reputation for poor service, as most of the workers were simply waiting to be molested. As the town's population of submissives rose, the number of ceremonies required to grant them the Freedom of the Town became unworkable, and many were left unmolested for years, which they found incredibly frustrating and secretly enjoyed.

It was a town where consensual sex did happen, but was considered as a sort of fetish, and it was almost impossible to borrow a library book. The militia leader died from a heart attack while pegging the town greengrocer in a clown suit. For many years afterward, these kinds of attacks were believed to be linked to the town's prosperity, and the tradition continued, but the assaults were performed by local office bearers with the weary air of jury duty.

Some gangs experimented with group therapy, but due to the irrational and unpredictable nature of many of their internal disagreements, these generally ended with the therapist being executed in a gruesome manner. This would often provide a bonding experience for the group, and dissipate tension. Prisoners with little therapeutic training were commonly pressed into a counselling role so that this catharsis could be achieved. People who fell into the hands of these gangs were often surprised to be forced to complete some basic psychological training, and lead the group in a couple of chaotic and hostile attempts to open up to each other, before being brutally lynched.

In confrontations between gangs or militias, snipers would shoot anyone who seemed to be giving orders. This meant that gang leaders often feigned panic and ran around screaming instructions in a frightened voice. These instructions were difficult to understand, and the tactic rarely achieved much. The most ferocious gang lords trained themselves to deliver orders in tones of wavering uncertainty, until these tones were understood as a sign of confidence and leadership, when they went back to yelling: the oscillation between wavering uncertainty and yelling became so quick that it left leaders with a vocal style reminiscent of classical Persian tremolo singing, and many would head to Iran where they found a highly receptive audience who prized them as food. Meanwhile, people with stammers became hugely overpromoted, leading to several dramatic escapes from firing squads.

9. The Irish Sex Trade: How it Developed After the Apocalypse

Anyone visiting a Senegalese sex auction around this time would have been startled by the amount of anti-Irish propaganda spouted by the auctioneers, with almost as many diatribes delivered against the Irish as terrified slaves sold, although anyone who's ever dealt with an Irish sex trafficker will be sympathetic. Irish trafficking gangs ran the major slave routes up through Mauritania to feed the vast Donegal sex theatres, and were maddening customers, often haggling in the wrong direction, or bidding against themselves, and then rarely stuck to the terms of a contract or paid their bar bill. This was all tolerated because their charming eccentricities were believed to come from the old country, rather than their consistent (and deliberate) exposure to carbon monoxide.

Most of the Irish sex traders had embraced a garrulous form of Nazism, which made them unbearable drinking partners. They would always travel with a fiddle and drum and insist on ending each night with hour upon hour of rollicking race theory, with ballads such as 'Too Ra Loo Ra Lebensraum' and 'The Rocky Road to the Dublin Euthanasia Centre'. On the long journey north, many of their sex slaves would contrive to commit suicide rather than hear another verse of 'Come Out You Blacks and Tanned'.

However, their songs, theories and meandering stories about Nordic ancestry tended not to spill over into violence. They channelled most of their supremacist urges into running a popular Aryan naturist volleyball league, until it collapsed amidst a skin-bleaching scandal, and confined their actual practice of Nazism to their hammocks and bedrolls, reinterpreting the traditional Nazi symbols and landmarks in Nazi history as sexual positions, although rarely could enough of them manage to synchronise their orgasms to pull off an authentic Dresden Firebomb, and only the most gymnastic could achieve the Final Solution without having a rib removed.

Whilst seeming to offer a meaningful route to post-apocalyptic survival, racism has one fatal flaw: its intolerance. Running a successful gang, militia, or band of survivors is hard enough, and dependable thugs tricky enough to come by, without vetoing potential applicants on the grounds of anything as trivial as ethnicity or religion. Every social or ethnic boundary was subverted by the need to find people good at stabbing: communists banded with fascists, Hutu with Tutsi, and performance poets with people who still had their dignity. So what if a trainee garroter feels nothing but brotherhood towards minorities, so long as he doesn't mind strangling them occasionally? In short, when it comes to race, post-apocalyptic gangs are refreshingly colour blind, apart from the race-based ones (93%).

Some gangs who had been pre-collapse liberals theorised that their groups lacked the cohesion that racism could provide; they found themselves seething with a kind of nebulous resentment, but were anxious to carry out their murdering and racketeering in an open, friendly and unprejudiced atmosphere. A few of these militias, spanning much of the North Territory, hit on the idea of directing their hatred towards a single imaginary person they simply called 'Dave'.

They would make jokes about how Dave had too many children; how he didn't wash; how he lusted after non-Dave women; about Dave's annoying music and contempt for the norms of the non-Dave majority. Then, after a night's drinking, they would go out for a Dave. This provided an outlet for people's resentments and resulted in a relatively harmonious society, except for any prisoners they took who were called Dave, which is what they called all prisoners, and people of colour. Liberal elements of the society reframed their hatred into a 'duty of care' for Dave, and established well-funded outreach charities for his protection, which took the form of execution vans with onboard organ-retrieval facilities.

It seems that the failure of racial intolerance to provide a robust working ideology for post-apocalyptic gangs was a lesson that had to be learned and re-learned by humanity's desperate remnants, and post-apocalypse racism is best thought of as a fun hobby, a sex fetish, or both. Probably the best and safest way to be racist in the end times is to be vigorously prejudiced against whatever you are, because everyone you meet will despise you, and your own open self-hatred might provide a basis, albeit fleeting, for an evening of camaraderie, some ribald jokes, and perhaps even a shared plate of food after you've made love at each other.

'Not that I actually hate myself,' said Alonso, emerging from Del's hardware store with a shopping bag full of bleach, limescale remover and hob cleaners. 'Except in my dreams. I wake up crying and standing on a kitchen chair with a length of washing line most nights, but that probably doesn't mean anything.' He set off merrily down Askew Road. 'I'm having a party tonight over at Norshahliza's. Do you fancy coming?' We declined, but were pleased to hear that they were back together. 'No, she's away visiting her sister but I've still got a key to her flat. I always lose interest in relationships a bit after the initial dopamine high of the stalking phase.' We noted that at least he was planning to clean up after the party. 'What? These? No, these are for cocktails in case we run out of Buckfast. They're a little sharp on the palate, but if you throw up they unblock the toilet.'

10. How to Be Chased and Captured

When being pursued by a post-apocalyptic horde, obviously speed is of the essence, unless you have an array of grenades strapped to your chest, in which case you're probably feigning a limp in order to maximise the number of pursuers you can invite along on an all-expenses-paid trip to Valhalla. Often an attacking horde will hold aloft gruesome banners to terrify their victims from afar. They would catapult makeshift binoculars and telescopes into the communities they were planning on decimating, so they'd be able to read their banners, which would take the form of a scathing critique of their victims, or a depiction of their eventual fate.

If you are fleeing a horde and they use a drone to deliver binoculars to you, they probably feel their artists have really nailed some of your worst qualities. It will be worth reading the banners because you might learn an important lesson about yourself and grow as a person before you're strangled. Other hordes would attempt to camouflage themselves, usually by painting huge panels to be held in front of them like a shield wall, covered with depictions of much friendlier people.

Intense debates between rival gangs were carried out on banners, with jibes, counterarguments and putdowns often spinning off onto separate placards, which would be waved around in front of the primary banner by troupes of placard dancers, whose gymnastic display skills were much prized by the messaging departments of the larger gangs. As their dancing grew more sophisticated, it gave rise to a complex semiotics of placard dancing which allowed the deftest placarders to add, by means of gestures, facial expressions, simulated sex acts, real sex acts and bodily excretions, their own commentary on the primary message of the placard. Many of these Elucidators became famous, such as Leon the Placard Dancer, whose glittering career ended when he was impaled on his own placard pole by an enraged gang leader, when a stumble during his trademark Defecation Jig reframed everything he had previously communicated sincerely as sarcasm.

The gang leader in question, Joe IV, when he looked down at his bloody hands and realised the enormity of what he'd done, was so distraught that he dedicated the next 4 minutes of his life to laughing maniacally. As with many dictators in these improvised societies, Joe IV attempted to cement his authority with many names and self-awarded titles, including Flame of the East; Methadone Man; Ayatollah Hispaniola; Samantha Panther, Necromancer; Doctor October; Jonathan Nonce; The AllHammer; Joseph Martin Williams; Joseph M. Williams; Joseph Williams; Joe Williams; Doomcop Ace Rock; and Professor John Antichrist. He died a tired and broken man, yet another decrepit member of the 27 Club (people who have clubbed 27 people to death; he died aged 19).

Many of the richest figures in the post-collapse economy were banner manufacturers. As the messaging on banners became ever more detailed and unwieldy, the fabric and supporting poles grew heavier, reinforcements were added, foundations were dug, and communities of banner dwellers lived in the rooms and passageways that sprouted up the rear of the banner, scurrying around with their ladders and paint pots, helping to curate the message and add extra information when required. Most of the larger banners had footnotes added using flags and bunting, which gave a jaunty, festive look to what was in reality a violently unpleasant message. The rudest known banner was a 16-kilometre-long critique of the personal hygiene of a rival gang leader, located on the island of Vormsi, off the northern coast of what used to be Estonia, which is a shame, because it was so remote very few people ever saw it and the gang leader described on the banner lived in Brazil and refused to believe the banner even existed, no matter how many accounts of it he was given by people he then had beheaded.

'You know, I always wondered what it would be like to be beheaded,' mused Alonso, taking a long, thoughtful sniff of Charlie's armpit. 'It must be pretty intense. That last look around. I've locked eyes with a few of them. They always seem . . . curious. Not angry, or annoyed. More like they've been granted a new perspective, become somehow wiser. Given a new lease of life. I get the sense they manage to pack a lot into those few seconds. You know, I sometimes close my eyes and open them again, and imagine I've just had my head cut off. It makes me see things differently. I'll do it now . . .' and he closed his eyes for a second or two, opened them, looked at us keenly, searchingly. Didn't say a word, just kind of smiled, got up and left.

And that was that. He walked off with the sure pace and quiet determination of someone who had made a deep and binding decision to urinate behind a tree. A minute later he sat back down and we tucked into our raspberries. We were picnicking in Ravenscourt Park, with a groaning bag of fruit, cream, energy drinks and sparkling wine from Tesco Express. Alonso was well liked by Lionel, the park keeper in Ravenscourt Park, because he'd helped clear up the park's sexual harassment problem by stopping flashing for Lent.

Lionel joined us on the grass. 'This is pretty good prosecco, I have to admit,' he said, draining the last dregs of the bottle he'd just opened. He lay back contentedly, wolfed a handful of blueberries, and asked something. 'Sorry, what was that?' said Frankie, cheerfully throwing a frisbee back to a group of children he'd stolen it from. Lionel smiled. 'I wasn't talking to you, you dumb fuck, I was talking to Alonso. I said: tell us more about the Forbidden Lands.' Alonso obliged while Frankie gently stimmed.

The Forbidden Lands aren't actually forbidden, because there's not really enough social infrastructure to forbid anything on that scale, which is a shame, because they really ought to be forbidden. The only gangs who operated there were the Forbidden Gangs, which is a name they kept trying to shake off because it was a nightmare for recruitment. I remember one day, I was rolling around in some manure for health reasons when I met someone who had traversed the Forbidden Lands and the Blasted Heath, and he gave me some useful advice on dealing with being taken prisoner. When being captured, he said that the opening exchange is key. 'Please don't kill me,' is a tempting opener, but someone might cough, and all your captor hears is 'kill me.' In any case, it's not at all wise to introduce the idea of killing you into the situation. Far better to lead with 'I know the location of a massive cache of alcohol, guns, pornography, and methamphetamines,' and then try to gradually manage everybody's expectations during some kind of forced march. He then claimed to know the location of a large cache of drugs and weapons, but I think merely out of habit, and we parted ways amicably enough.

Your chances of survival when captured are much improved if you can immediately show yourself capable of doing something of value to the gang, such as fixing a television set or being molested. Most people would, as a precaution, carry a broken TV and a set of screwdrivers, and hastily mend it in front of their captors. Or failing that, a weighted sex mannequin, which they would fling themselves under, and with a rudimentary system of string and pulleys, they would puppeteer their own violation. These performances became so popular with the gangs that it triggered a worldwide renaissance in the art of puppetry, which meant, sadly, that after a few generations no one was left alive who could repair a TV.

When being taken captive, it is vital that you determine as quickly as possible whether the gang capturing you is motivated more by sex or cannibalism. It wasn't always easy, glancing over your shoulder as you ran, but cannibal gangs would often necklace themselves with dried body bits from previous meals, whereas a sex-driven raiding party would likely be physically aroused, or have fashioned their cudgels into oversized sex toys. Most people, fearing capture, took to carrying around with them two bags: one bag of homemade 'poppers' (most villages had their own closely guarded 'popper' recipes); another of faecal matter from a wild animal (badger and fox were favoured) which they would smear themselves with to try and dissuade their cannibal captors from eating them. Many would daub themselves with the animal faeces whatever gang was chasing them, focusing more on smearing the ordure around their genitals if they caught a glimpse of a sex-cosh. However, badger excrement became such a dominating note in these raids that it started to play a key role in both sex-play and cookery, and many raiding parties would travel with their own sacks of animal shit to rub into their victims before roasting or raping them.

As the shattered remnants of society tumbled further into chaos, niche gangs were forced to broaden their interests in order to survive, and embrace a more generalised 'soft focus' commitment to violence and mayhem. This made it much harder for people being chased by them along burning streets to try and appeal to the gang's particular hopes and dreams, until a group of terrified psychologists from the University of Madrid made a vital discovery while being hunted through the ashes of their department: they found that every gang, no matter how superficially broad in its tastes and methods, was held together, at its core, by an intense and very specific taboo. It might be a fear of intimacy, a dread of loneliness, a terror of handshakes or smoked fish or heteronormativity or open-toed footwear, a paralysing disgust of the colour blue, or – if you're extremely lucky – a debilitating semen phobia. Find that weak spot, and you have a chance. They produced a handy checklist of questions designed to be yelled over your shoulder to help narrow down your understanding of a pursuing gang's foundational neurosis, which proved hugely successful and led to the authors being tortured to death by a gang of anti-questionnaire obsessives.

One use of prisoners was as test subjects for homemade alcohol. It was often said that the perfect homebrew was one that led to sex where neither party consented. The testing system prevented waste: alcohol that killed a prisoner instantly could be repurposed as a bomb. Some prisoners would try to trick their captors into drinking the homebrew and poisoning themselves. There is a case of someone captured in Detroit who attempted to respond to a new moonshine recipe with the words 'pleasantly refreshing', but as the mixture he was being force fed was a close chemical cousin of paraffin, what actually came out was a tortured plea for death. If no prisoners were available, some gangs prized themselves on having all members drink the first of a new brew simultaneously, and anyone who wasn't turned blind or insane by the first batch would celebrate with parties that were often mistaken for mass suicides.

It was found that the relentless chasing, lynching, murder and dismemberment took its toll on everyone's spirits – gang members as well as their victims. Some gang leaders tried to inject a bit of levity into proceedings by sparing every 1,000th victim, instead dressing them in a sash, handing them a bunch of flowers and giving them a free car, which was in fact a wooden crate on wheels which was hauled up to the top of a hill and burned, much to almost everyone's delight.

Looting, Alonso informed us – with the weary eyes of the connoisseur – is overrated. Often it just meant weighing yourself down with unnecessary junk; and it was rare to see anything worth looting without wondering whether it was the bait in some kind of elaborate sex-trap. Once you've been sex captured with a batch of fresh éclairs, Alonso assured us, that doesn't happen again more than twice. And eventually you start looting a different bakery, although sometimes the sex-trappers move bakery, and really you should be suspicious of all fresh pastry being produced in post-apocalyptic conditions. This was a trade secret he'd been told by a baker over a round of cream scones, before losing consciousness.

In the post apocalypse, most looting is secondary looting, i.e. you'll be looting a place that has already been looted. So it's worth exploring parts of stores and houses that someone in a hurry might not have visited. In homes, basements and lofts might contain canned goods; old clothing; and family photos that can be pressed into service as happy memories or makeshift pornography. In stores, it's easy to overlook staffrooms. These will often contain coffee/sugar/bottled water/and employee of the month boards that can be pressed into service as neutral memories or makeshift pornography.

Looting was found to be enormous fun, and socially bonding, but too quickly over, so after a while, looters would carefully store looted items in a warehouse, and then later return them, usually overnight, to shops and offices, ready for further looting in the morning. Before leaving, they would tidy up the stores, straighten the items on the shelves, making sure that all the packets and jars were nice and neat and facing forward, usually working 6-hour shifts with three 20-minute breaks.

11. Spanish Weddings and Car Jacking

Alonso was fretful as we trotted out of the park to Bunify for some jerk wings, waffle bites and a Cajun bun combo. Some kids had run off with his can of carpet adhesive; he'd shouted at them, and then he'd had a row with Lionel the park keeper about the way he'd handled himself. It had ended with some angry shoving and tears, followed by a handshake, followed by about another 20 minutes of shoving. A passer-by thought they were practising capoeira and joined in, catching Lionel on the jaw with an elegant swirling kick. We gave him a round of applause, took some selfies with the unconscious Lionel; and some cash from his jacket pocket, then trotted off, Alonso still coughing and sobbing, noticeably more than usual.

Clearly something besides the loss of the glue was bothering him. He finally confessed: 'I rang my mother last night. I know, I know, stupid. But I was feeling lonely after Marina threw me out. But in the end, I was so nervous, I couldn't speak. I choked up. And she thought it was my dad doing phone sex, and started joining in, saying the most graphic stuff. I was paralysed. I'd put quite a bit of GHB in my tequila, just to summon up the courage to ring in the first place, and I was having trouble moving my tongue to form worms. But she seemed to like the sounds I was making. Eventually I managed to stumble off the bus and throw my phone into a hedge near the house. I could still hear her moaning and screaming as I ran off. It's been going on for days – my neighbour keeps saying he thinks there's an injured fox somewhere. Do you think I should ring her back?' Joseph at Bunify shook his head: 'Naah, leave it mate. You want any mamba sauce?'

In the early apocalypse, panicking survivors would quite often pack up all their belongings in their car, and drive off, desperately trying to avoid car jackers, as they made their way towards the various emergency disaster relief facilities which had been set up by better-funded car jackers. A popular tactic for foiling car jackers was to stash a poisoned bottle of spirits in the glove compartment, so that in the event of a hold-up, you could innocently offer the bandits a swig from the bottle you'd just drunk half of, pretending that your shaking hand and foaming at the mouth was just the usual car-jacking nerves. Car jackers got so annoyed by constantly being offered poisoned alcohol that many of them quit drinking altogether, and turned their lives around, offering counselling and strictly confidential support to the people they were choking out with a seat belt.

Before the blotting out of the Sun, some people used solar panels to power their electric cars. This often meant that homes with working cars could be identified quite easily by gangs using drones. It also meant that rival gangs would install fake solar panels to lure those gangs into traps. In many cases, these gangs would trap and counter-trap each other so often that they became a kind of amalgamation of every local outfit, bonded together by the tremendous things they could achieve with solar power, and the only trace of their innate criminal perversity was their fervent worship of the Moon.

Some people adapted vehicles to run on propane. These vehicles were very popular, with stores of propane being relatively easy to find, and their only real drawback was that they exploded. Standard petrol would start to degrade six months after it had been refined, and was pretty much useless after a couple of years. Some communities created refining facilities, which were easy to blow up, and a bit like basing your settlement around a bomb. The safest thing to do was to buy refined petrol from one of these communities, pay them in a currency that would survive an explosion, then use a drone to blow them up. Refining communities eventually became suspicious of people who wanted to pay them in titanium; armoured plating; and black box flight recorders, but badly needed the materials to protect their refining facilities. Often there was a tense period between taking payment and attaching it to the walls of your petrol vats, and within such communities writing a receipt very, very slowly became a much-valued skill.

12. Los Angeles, Scientology, Self-Hatred and the Extraordinary Mystery of Kendrick Lamar

Scientology survived for several decades as a peculiarly violent gang, led by a seldom-seen electronic device, which the higher echelons of the gang insisted contained the soul of actress Kirstie Alley, but was in fact a child's toy looted from a Toys "R" Us warehouse. A few other notable gangs claimed Kirstie Alley as a deity or guiding prophet, including one which was formed by chance, when the annual reunion lunch of the still close-knit cast and crew from the film *Look Who's Talking Too* was interrupted by the apocalypse. The brutal gang that emerged that day from the rubble of the San Antonio Winery in the heart of downtown Los Angeles sacrificed their enemies, and people they'd only just met, to Alley, whom they celebrated as a merciless destroying archangel with amazing hair. Their slang for murdering someone was 'making a doody', and any gang members present at the slaying would chant their catchphrase, a line spoken by Roseanne Barr's character in the poorly received sequel: 'Big deal. I made a doody!'

Many gangs operated a code of silence. This often made it difficult to communicate, and almost impossible to get a monthly poetry slam off the ground. Each gang would develop its own mystifying slang. For example, in the trans-human biker gangs of what had been Canada, the sentence 'Can you flick me? I've got hornets on my 84' meant 'Can you kill me? I've got hornets on my dick'. The gang anthropologist Raymond Devine Jr attempted to produce a dictionary of the post apocalypse, but had progressed no further than 'analslave' (a term similar to the current 'employee') when he became one of the many victims of a brief fashion for the boobytrapped vagina.

There was a gang that claimed to have the gift of telepathy, but were later discovered to be communicating with Morse code via Bluetooth buttplugs. Their downfall came when hackers took control of their buttplugs and the entire gang was persuaded to turn on each other, in what became known as the Night of the Long Buttplugs.

A surprisingly successful gang was set up by the moderators of the Motor Neurone Disease online support forum, and contained only Motor Neurone Disease sufferers, and their primary caregivers. It turned out that Motor Neurone sufferers were remarkably successful leaders, perhaps due to their understandable sense of urgency. The group's rise to power was so meteoric, and their influence so vast, that many thousands of would-be 'Neuros' tried to gain entry to the gang by simulating the symptoms of the disease. Anyone suspected of faking MND would face an ice bucket trial and any counterfeiters would have their body parts tethered to a circle of a hundred electric wheelchairs and be smoothly pulled apart.

Of course, gang life, in spite of all the excitement and hierarchical abuse, isn't to everyone's taste. The whole cycle of pillage, molestation, murder, cannibal feasting, drunken tattooing, orgy, nap, shower, breakfast, tattoo regret, venereal disease check-up, and back to pillage can get a bit 'samey' after a while. And the more successful your gang is, the longer your commute for a decent slaughter. It was many parents' worst nightmare to have a child abandon the homestead and join a gang, particularly if they had been planning to eat them, and there was a vibrant culture of anti-gang activism on most land-masses. However, many of these community advocacy groups were so popular that they themselves became some of the most successful and ruthless gangs of the epoch.

These anti-gang gangs tended to have chaotically extroverted self-hatred that made them perplexing opponents, difficult to gauge in a skirmish because they would often turn on each other with disgusted kicks and hammer whacks, and were driven by a kind of furious shame that chimed with the mood of the times. They had an elaborate mythology that treated every pillage as an 'intervention', in which every murder is a 'deprogramming' that 'rescues' the victim from their unhealthy and dangerous gang life. They found it particularly rewarding to look into the glazing eyes of a freshly decapitated gang member and whisper 'You're free to go home to your loved ones,' knowing that they had also slaughtered their loved ones, so the offer was meaningless.

The insertion of the Orb was televised live.

BOOK VI

Food and Cannibalism

1. Donkeys and Quartermasters

As the Earth sickened and the purulent air cloaked in dying folds the fetid grey branches of hopeless trees, harvest after harvest failed; the rain soured into an oily slick, apples shrank to the size and consistency of tiny apples, trees grew inside-out, grapes exploded on the vine, and earthworms rose from the poisoned mud to knot themselves into their own nooses. The seas grew cancerous and thin, burgeoning only in plastics and Legofish™. Despairing turtles beached themselves in a desperate attempt to commit suicide, and tried to bury their eggs in mass graves in the sand, forgetting that this was a natural part of their life cycle. But perhaps the saddest consequence of this depletion of the seas was the widespread and distressing lack of shark attacks on surfers, whose numbers grew so large they had to be culled, often garrotted with their own guitar strings and roasted on their own campfires using their didgeridoo as a spit.

Alonso had eaten surfer a few times, but never really enjoyed it. Their flesh, he said, was too stringy and their skin tough and salty, and somehow they tasted 'boring'. But we are getting ahead of ourselves. Cannibalism doesn't really take off as a global phenomenon until at least four or five weeks after the apocalypse. Before that, there are other more pressing food concerns for survivors, like what's a good seasoning for cat. Alonso favours a bunch of strong garden herbs, ideally ones the cat has urinated on, saving curry for dog.

In the first flush of cannibalism people would keep dog hides and cat paws hanging by the stove to suggest to their dinner guests that they might not be eating a mutual acquaintance, and most meat was bought and sold as 'donkey', with people pretending to each other, and themselves, that radiation poisoning had caused donkeys to grow fingers and develop tattoos.

The relentless depopulation of the planet did much to alleviate food shortages, but the efficient storage of dwindling supplies was an essential survival skill, and Quartermaster was a key job in a post-apocalyptic society, even though nobody knew what it meant. Most Quartermaster training programmes were set up by communities wanting to know what a Quartermaster is, with the first few rounds of interviews dominated by questions like 'What do you think is the most important quality in a successful Quartermaster?' And 'What is a Quartermaster?'

Anyone thought to be a successful prepper was the first to be raided by food looters. Truly successful preppers had, of course, anticipated this, and were careful to keep themselves dangerously emaciated, never once visiting their vast caches of food in case anyone saw them, the best managing to starve to death without ever being exposed as a hoarder.

Waving from the pavement outside Café Louche, Dr Yvonne Rouxel bade us farewell. She'd recently resigned from the London College of

Fashion after her paper on 'The Iconology of Mid-21st Century Perineal Piercings' was rejected by the *Clothing and Textiles Research Journal*, and was moving to Athens to look after street kittens. Alonso wiped away a tear. 'I'm so happy,' he said, 'Yvonne was really cramping my style, sexually. She kept wanting to sketch my scrotum. At first I was flattered, but after a while I was like: Yvonne, seriously, stop sketching my balls. There's a limit.'

That morning, after a bout of lovemaking, languorous yet intense, that Alonso sensed was somehow 'a goodbye' and which left our booth in Café Louche needing a replacement cushion, Yvonne quietly mopped up the last of her eggs Florentine and gave Alonso a lingering kiss on the forehead. A flap of spinach adhered to his third eye like a sex medal as Dr Rouxel put on her pillbox hat, got into an immaculate 1987 Rolls-Royce Corniche, finished in white with magnolia hide, and sped off up Curwen Road. And that was the last we saw of her, until we met her again under very different circumstances.

She'd left her vintage Patou shawl on her chair in Café Louche, which Charlie had carefully folded up and slipped into a Jiffy bag, but then promptly lost amongst his collection of several thousand ladies' shawls, only finding it one terrifying night when a knife was pressed to his throat and the words were whispered: 'Where is that Patou shawl?' He'd found that he had to press a knife against his neck and whisper threats to himself in order to find anything these days, which made it disconcerting to watch him try and complete one of his beloved wordsearch puzzles.

'She'll be back,' said Alonso. 'Mark my words. Mark my sodding words.' This phrase was something Alonso said a lot, and we'd learned to tune it out. That day Alonso seemed somehow to grow, to gather into himself a kind of rugged purpose, and with his weak jaw set firm and the fingers of both hands drumming on the table, not in any kind of rhythm known to or celebrated by our doomed age, he did what he'd never ventured to do before – he ordered a jacket potato with baked beans and extra avocado. 'It's such a great combo,' he said, and looked over to the waiter, giving him what he very wrongly thought was the 'okay' sign, and told us about the future of cheese.

2. Post-Apocalyptic Dairy Products

Cheese was Alonso's top tip for a post-apocalyptic survival food – it's a good source of protein, calcium and amino acids, and stores well in caves – but in the absence of most cattle, sheep and goats, which are soon hunted to the brink of extinction, the budding cheese producer has to get creative. Luckily, a wide range of other mammals can be caught and induced to lactate: dogs, foxes, otters, deer – really the only limit on milk production is the imagination and patience of the cheesemaker. Badger parmesan adds a tang to any pasta, and can also be used as a bear repellent, although no cheesemaker worthy of the name would be trying to repel bears when they have the opportunity to begin production of Camembear.

Still, a safer bet for someone new to the trade and with good close-up vision would be to start farming dairy mice: your friends will thank you on pizza night when you impress them with your Mousearella. If you live near the coast, own a snorkel and have good upper body strength you might want to try your hand at making

Wensleywhale, and even if you find yourself accidentally stimulating a male you can still usually come away with enough milk to justify the 85% chance of drowning. Alonso's favourite cheese was a kind of Tyrolean grey cheese made from wolf milk, and extremely rare due to the high casualty rate amongst milkmaids, although he himself generally stuck to farming midsize mammals, and was well known for the quality of his Harephilly, Gorgonmola and Dogfort.

Fondue had a surprising post-apocalyptic resurgence, after convoy cooks and gang chefs realised that pretty much anything, however random or mysterious, could be overheated in a pot, dubbed a 'fondue', and sold at fancy prices. Any old bits of tendon, bone, hooves, feathers, skin tags, dung, wrestling sawdust, cemetery discoveries, autopsy leftovers or flushed parasites could be given the fondue treatment, simply by adding some ditch water, heating it to the temperature of magma and handing out sharpened sticks to anyone mad enough to order it.

It was a blessing for the fondue eater that the first mouthful would so blister the inside of their mouths that they wouldn't be able to taste any of the dish, assuming they could manage to get any of it into their mouths using the fondue sticks, which were carefully designed not to function as cutlery. Some fondue-masters realised that they could heat their fondue pots to such a fierce temperature that they became impossible to approach, which cut down enormously on the need to add any food, which was replaced by lumps of rock and car parts.

Diners came to appreciate the lack of dysentery caused by the absence of anything edible, and these food-free fondues came to dominate the fondue market, especially in areas of famine, which was all areas. The more catastrophic the famine, the more fondue restaurants flourished. People still enjoyed the ritual of 'going out' for a 'meal with friends' even if the meal didn't exist and their friends were dead.

For the higher echelons of the malnourished there were exclusive members-only fondue clubs, with skeletal waitresses serving a range of cocktail fondues, which were just hot cups of rust, while for the starving poor there were fondue 'crawl thrus', where you would speak your order into an old tree stump with some wires poked into it, then drag yourself round to the serving hatch to collect your body bag.

In the years leading up to the Primary Cataclysm, a series of increasingly appalling infections leapt from ill-treated, malnourished animals to decimate humanity: after the Kentucky Fried Chicken Plague came Cow AIDS, Goose Cancer, Donkeypox, Turkey Lice, Quail Lung, Trout Lips, Rabbit's Foot, Camel Toe, Goat Mumps, Salmon Warts, Mad Kangaroo Disease, Antibiotic-Resistant Guinea Pig Herpes, and Yak Fungus, as well as a host of non-sexually-transmitted diseases.

The survivors of this infection marathon, discovering that most of mankind's usual livestock had become murderously toxic, but still fancying a nice juicy joint at the weekend, turned enthusiastically to the one source of protein it could trust: man meat (not in the gay sense; in the sense of eating humans) (not in the gay sense), often first rubbing oil into their meat (in the gay sense); giving their victims a healthy stuffing (in the gay and non-gay sense); butchering their victims with great skill (in the gay sense) and holding gay (not in the gay sense) feasts and parties.

In the first flush of cannibalism, there was a definite 'party vibe', even amongst those being eaten. Anyone who survived long enough and in a good enough condition to be spatchcocked and griddled felt a well-deserved sense of pride in their final moments.

Huge 'bring a body' bonfire raves became popular during the great European famines, lasting two or three days, at which people could relax, unwind, throw their loved ones into a firepit to fuel the flames, and dance the night away, until it was discovered that the most popular party motivators on the immolation scene, DJ Mansandwich and MC Buttockflesh, were also CEO and Head of Acquisitions at Europe's biggest smoked meat manufacturer, Guetta Hams.

Little is known about the enigmatic owner of Guetta Hams – an elderly deaf-blind recluse, known only as 'David', who had lost both legs, both arms, both genitals, tongue, nose, ears, lips, nipples and all his nails, teeth and body hair to antibiotic-resistant gonorrhoea, and was wheeled around bawling and moaning in a pram by an enigmatic crone known only as 'Kelly Rowland'. She seemed somehow to understand what 'David' was bawling about, and would pass on his instructions to the board of directors of Guetta Hams and feed 'David' with the slices of lightly fried human testicle that she interpreted from his howls and groans that he craved.

It was at the exclusive Prague Techno Crematorium nightclub that Kelly Rolland gave the speech for which she became famous. 'Behold this human maggot!' she cried, hoisting Guetta over her head before hurling him into a flaming pit. The notorious speech went on to decry the evils of the time in relentless, poetic detail at 130 bpm. Later academic analysis has concluded that it's likely she was under the influence of the fumes from a roasting crack addict, and much of what she said was things she'd remembered from Batman movies, which seems like the most convincing explanation for all the references to grappling hooks and Commissioner Gordon.

The kind lady who hooked the maggot Guetta out from the flames and nursed 'him' (debatable) back to health, spent several months trying to teach him language by sitting on his face while shouting random words of encouragement in the hope that he'd recognise some of them. The two became inseparable, because the clasp rusted shut on the chest harness she'd built for him to help him latch. Some say that the maggot Guetta returned to the food processing industry as a safety inspector in abattoirs. He had, they say, a kind of 'sixth sense', though in his case a 'third sense', about where safety standards were slipping, and would wriggle around like a bloodworm, sniffing at bolt guns and intestine splitters, alerting his handlers to a rusty hock cutter or letting out an angry howl near any exposed wiring, although others say this wasn't him at all, it was Carl Cox.

To be fair to the food industry, although hygiene standards had taken a bit of a dip due to complete societal collapse, it was rare to find more than one wedding ring in a single burger. And there was a lot less botulism since people had started taking a bit more care to die from listeria instead. Also, we should stress, not everything Alonso ate in the end times was deadly or unpleasant. He recalls one dish with particular fondness:

I was given a bowl of spicy broth by an old lady in the Unhallowed Zone, or Luton as it was also known. (Luton was simply what a town became known once it sank beyond a certain state of depravity. There were twelve Lutons in England, if you exclude Luton itself, which became so degenerate that it was known as Preston.) The broth was excellent, and the little clumps of fur and bone fragments were well seasoned. I was keen to ask her for the recipe, but it was considered impolite in those days to ask what a meal actually contains in case it was somebody you knew. My only clue was that she kept looking over at an empty cat bed in the corner and sobbing. 'Mr Fluffy,' she wept, as I finished my second bowl. 'My poor darling Mr Fluffy.' There was a scratch at the door, and in came Mr Fluffy. She fell to her knees and apologised to him for emptying out his litter tray to make soup. Mr Fluffy scratched her on the hand and urinated in her slippers. 'He forgives me,' she smiled, bringing the litter tray down onto Mr Fluffy's head and dropping his limp body into the broth pot.

3. Alonso Reminisces at a Window Seat in Caffè Nero

In the early days of the apocalypse, many neighbourhoods set up a kind of 'meals on wheels' service for the weak and needy, delivering them to people who wanted to kill and eat someone they could easily overpower. Alonso remembers growing oddly attached to one elderly meal that was delivered to him, who was full of wonderful stories of her career as a fairly successful flamenco dancer in Seville, and persuaded him to let her perform one last fandango before being butchered and stewed. He agreed, untying her straps, and was nearly kicked to death by the still supple pensioner. 'She danced the dance of her life,' recalls Alonso, with unconcealed admiration. As his intended dinner swirled and dipped, she peppered Alonso with a brutal yet somehow melancholic barrage of kicks and taps, but as she raised her heel to deliver one last flamboyant *punteando* she suffered a massive cardiac arrest and Alonso was able to eke her out for more than a month, though he admitted that only the last two weeks of this was spent eating her.

Alonso had a strange, faraway look, like he was a million miles from the bustle of the cafe we were perched in, and slowly wiped his eye, where some of the mascarpone sauce from his chicken & bacon tostati melt had sprayed up while he was talking. 'Oh Mariska,' he whispered, his voice cracking with emotion, 'my dear, sweet Mariska, can you ever forgive me?' It was as if he wanted to say more, but somehow couldn't find the words, signing off his message with a mournful 'ciao' and putting away his phone.

'I met Mariska yesterday on the hard shoulder of the A40. She'd had a puncture. We chatted for a bit about stuff I found in her glove compartment, and really hit it off, and I told her I was going to get help, but then I got into this big argument at customer services at Lidl about their discounting policy and forgot all about it. Hopefully someone else stopped and she got her insulin.' Luckily, with the arrival of his vanilla iced velvet americano his mood lifted and soon he was reminiscing happily about eating people:

> *You need to know how to keep someone alive while you're eating them. That's basic. Chances are you won't have access to a fridge-freezer and there's so many bloody vultures everywhere it's impossible to hang someone for biltong. But the good news is, with a bit of practice you can keep someone alive for months while you trim stuff off them. You can even keep them vigorous by feeding them bits of themselves, or a cup of their own*

stock, while telling them it's from a cat you were given in exchange for sexual favours by the carefully hooded figure who's been silently abusing them for the last few nights. A lot of people get lazy and don't bother to hood themselves while abusing their meat slaves, and just admit that they're feeding them their own flesh, but this gives their meat a bitter tang that some recipes call for, but most people prefer a happier stew.

A good way to keep your meat optimistic is to tell them they've been selected for a top-secret military cyborg project, and the reason you keep slicing bits off them is so that you can send tissue samples to the lab – say things like 'I've got to get this to Dr Stroganoff, he's in charge of optimising the machine-human interface for your new exoskeleton,' and don't slice it directly into a hot pan. If you're having to make conversation while sawing a leg off, tell them how lucky they are to be getting rid of these feeble human appendages, and that soon they'll be jumping over buildings and trees like a god. They'll know you're lying but they have nothing else to cling onto and eventually they'll start playing along out of desperation. As they get weaker, they can get really excited about getting their new robot body, and being freed from the prison of their buttocks, ears, and genitals.

Alonso was in his favourite seat in Caffè Nero, which gave him a great view of the bus stops at the front of Shepherd's Bush station. By now he was deep into his third white chocolate mocha with extra marshmallows and nine shots of almond syrup – a drink we dubbed the 'amochalypse'. He needed four of these, he said, to muster the energy to face his first pistachio iced latte of the day. We used the contact form on the Caffè Nero website to suggest that they adopt 'amochalypse' as an official drink, with us taking a 35% cut of each amochalypse sold, and a further 5% going towards funding for local defibrillator units, but we're yet to hear back.

'You see that bus?' – Alonso gestured with a trembling teaspoon at the 316 to Cricklewood, pulling away on its journey north towards Cricklewood. 'If that was a "time bus", I could use it to return home to my time.' A rueful smile played about his lips as the 49 to White City drew up at bus top B. Alonso nodded at it, while tossing a plump marshmallow up into his open mouth, missing it. 'You see that other bus? If that was a "time bus", I could get on board, and say "return me to my own time, please" and off I'd go, back to my own time.' He gave a sad shake of his head, and noticed the 31 to Camden Town. 'You see that bus?'

He mused like this for a couple of hours. Hundreds of 'time buses' came and went. We weren't sure if he was being deliberately annoying or if dementia was one of the symptoms of almond syrup poisoning. When we suggested, delicately, that he might want to shut the fuck up about time buses, Alonso threw the rest of his amochalypse at us and yelled 'Goddamnit!', a futuristic profanity derived from the name Jason 'Goddamnit' Perkins, a particularly unpleasant gang leader who was infamous for torturing people while yelling 'Goddamnit' a lot. It transpired that he was merely looking for his missing son Goddamnit, but being unable to talk about his feelings of anger and loss took to torturing people as a way of channelling his sadness. When Goddamnit was found, alive and well, in a nearby town, Jason was horrified at what he'd done, but found himself unable to articulate these feelings of guilt, and instead took to torturing people, with renewed vigour.

Unfortunately Jason spend so long in his torture chambers that he neglected his relationship with his son Goddamnit, who one day packed up a small bag of apples and clothes, and left home, leaving a simple note pinned to the door: 'Dad, I think you need therapy'. When Jason saw the note, he ran out into the street, fell to his knees, and raised his fists to the sky, howling his son's name, over and over, and from that day forth the only word he ever spoke was 'Goddamnit'. But he was able to pronounce it in enough different ways that, using gestures and facial expressions he was able to make himself reasonably well understood, and able to perform day-to-day chores like grocery shopping and running a successful sex trafficking operation. In later life, he wrote a 600-page memoir which is almost completely impenetrable.

Pressing his thumbs into the side of his head, Alonso let out an unearthly sigh. 'I think I'm going fucking Perkins here' (another expression derived from Jason Perkins). In between angry snorts of whipped cream and lumps of apricot croissant it all came flooding out: he was desperate to get back to his age so that he could gorge once more on human flesh. Much as he loved marshmallows, and little as he could imagine returning to a world without almond syrup, he felt an unbearable yearning for roast buttock, crispy wrist and a big jar of pickled thumbs. 'I hate the fact that you can't buy human adrenal glands in Shepherd's Bush Market,' he grumbled. 'Every time I want one, I have to take a cab to Neasden. Even then, the ones I get there are quite small and a bit pungent; I'm pretty sure they're coypu.'

Alonso's cravings grew worse. He was finding it impossible to think about anything else: his therapist had told him he was suffering from 'brain freeze' caused by acute withdrawal from eating humans, and had prescribed him a course of liquid PCP. We were curious as to who this therapist was. 'Dr Lim', we learned, was a deep tissue massage specialist, escort, and PCP dealer who worked in Hammersmith, but took the bus up twice a week to meet Alonso in the alley opposite Mail Boxes Etc. to work on the stubborn knot of muscles around the base, shaft and tip of his penis.

Alonso thought for a moment: 'That's a good question: usually she takes the 72 up Shepherd's Bush Road, but sometimes the 273,' he said, in response to the question 'Is she a real doctor?' We learned that Dr Lim's patients included a number of people who were into pretty extreme S&M, and she collected bloody swabs and bandages from which she made a kind of herbal tea, and sold it to Alonso for £30 a litre. Dr Lim's tea and massage were two of Alonso's biggest weekly outlays, but he was careful to get receipts from Dr Lim, which he wrote out by hand, and said that if we didn't reimburse him for his treatments he wouldn't be able to continue remembering things about the future for us, so we paid up.

Alonso's hankering for man ham shouldn't lull anyone into thinking that cannibalism is all a bed of roses. Far from it. Alonso himself says that when he began eating human flesh, back when he was trapped in the Stygian darkness of the tunnels under Gibraltar, he had to trick himself into thinking that what he was gnawing on might have been a bit of monkey, and he thinks this might be where he got his particular love of the 'hairier bits' of a person.

The reality is, when the apocalypse hits, your diet is going to change. This can be a challenge. People can find the shift into eating human flesh difficult for all sorts of reasons: sometimes they get terrible diarrhoea, other times they're hit by really appalling constipation. If they're really unlucky they get a combination of diarrhoea and constipation which causes racking gut judders which generally end in such catastrophic colonic prolapsing that it leaves people looking like they've turned inside-out, which in a sense they have.

So, the best thing to do is to begin the transition now. Start on your own toenails and dandruff – use them as a condiment, much like Parmesan cheese – clip off any bits of dead skin around your heels and elbows and soak them in saliva for a couple of days, then form them into chewy treats using phlegm then progress to semen. Try and get a part-time job at a hairdresser's or a nail bar – anywhere that can give you easy access to semen. Switching careers into dental hygiene is a great way to get bloody spit, and when you're ready, set up a company that disposes of 'medical waste' – you'll be inundated with snipped-off bits and body parts, then all you need is a pressure cooker and lots and lots of onions. Your onion to human flesh ratio is going to start out at around 8:1, that's perfectly normal. But you'll want to bring that number right down over the course of about six months until you're just using some snipped spring onions as a garnish on your cannibal feast.

4. More About Cannibalism

Thousands of people got the idea, from listening to survivalist podcasts, of going to live on oil rigs, far away from collapsing society. They set off in boats and yachts and were welcomed aboard by grateful oil rig workers who showed them to the fridges and meat lockers where they'd be staying, and then got back on with their gruelling job of recording survivalist podcasts about how oil rigs are the perfect place to ride out the apocalypse.

Hunger was a major issue in post-apocalyptic societies. There was generally a cycle where those who survived the initial collapse of their social structure became fitter, allowing them to catch and eat the less fit members of their community, and so became heavier, and eventually became prey themselves. This tended to lead, over a period of time, to social structures dominated by almost Olympic-level athletes with a craving for human flesh.

A common response to the dominance of athletic cannibals was for communities to leave recipe books around sports facilities that gave incorrect times for cooking meat, and this met with some initial success. Eventually, people became resentful of the man hours required to successfully mock up hardback books, and the risk attached to sneaking into a sports centre full of cannibals, and just started shooting everyone who took the slightest interest in sports. This improved society enormously.

The super-fit cannibals became so health conscious that they shunned fattier meat, so people took to sticking cushions and pillows up their jumpers and down their trousers to appear unappetising. The cannibal hunters weren't fooled, but it meant that their lairs became so full of discarded cushions, blankets and padding that they descended naturally into a kind of lazy decadence that left them uninterested in sprinting about catching people to eat, preferring to doze and loll about, chatting and napping and improvising a kind of laid-back music they called 'relaxing smooth chillout ambient lounge jazz' which led them to commit suicide in droves. Anyone wanting to thrive as a cannibal in this phase of human dietary evolution is going to need earplugs, for drowning out both mellow grooves and pleading screams.

Anti-cannibalism activists were delighted when, after years of lobbying, the Rimini Convention was finally signed, only to discover that the Rimini Convention was in fact the latest thriller by the Brazilian footballer turned author Raphinha, known for his pace, dribbling skills and plots involving footballers who were secretly spies, and villains who were almost invariably analogues of his former agent. And to make matters worse, it was printed on human skin.

Graverobbing became so prevalent, and competition amongst graverobbers so fierce, that coffin heists were taking place earlier and earlier in the funeral service, sometimes before the deceased was even dead or had started to complain of feeling unwell. Eventually, the tradition of burying people was almost completely abandoned, causing a collapse in the Cornish pasty industry from which it never fully recovered.

Instead, people took to pickling and drying their loved ones, so that they could keep them around for longer and eat bits of them when necessary. Contrary to expectations, people found that eating the cured corpses of people they'd had an emotional bond with was actually easier than eating strangers: if anything, it brought them closer together with the departed family members, or served as cathartic revenge for abuse. The only problem with eating one's abuser is that if you get food poisoning, is this not simply yet more abuse, causing agony in the same orifices, committed this time from beyond the grave? This meant that abusers were rarely eaten in the form of carpaccio – sometimes in more processed sausages such as mortadella, but more likely in a lasagne or a slow-cooked ossobuco.

Carpaccio di persona was reserved for close family members and sweethearts, and was traditionally served in an artful silhouette of the departed. *Artisti del carpaccio* were in great demand, trained in the thriving salami houses of Foggia, Salerno and Burton upon Trent; they would come to your house, look at any pictures of your loved one you still had, or listen carefully to a description of the deceased, and then arrange slices of the dead into a generic head shape.

There was a brief fad for the consumption of tiny edible replicas of a person, made out of their own flesh: a quirky millionaire would decide, for example, to celebrate their birthday by having their leg removed and made into a tiny roastable 'mini-me'. The femur would become the spine, the foot would be stitched on top as a head, and the calf would provide enough sausage meat to form the arms and legs and lips.

It's odd that this became a fad because the end result never looked even vaguely like a person, let alone a replica of the flesh donor, but the companies providing the service were careful to state in their contracts that 'the end result will not resemble anything at all.' This failure to bear any resemblance to anything else in the material realm, as if a new form had broken through a gap in our reality from an unholy otherness, was the true horror of these miniature roasts, and led to the custom being abandoned, and the people who produced them being hanged as demons.

Like all genres of cuisine, cannibalism had its high and low forms. By no means was it all just people grubbing around in cemeteries, bin-diving at hospices, and carving off gangrenous bits of their dying neighbour to thicken their gravy; it also had a dark side. Perhaps the most ruthless gang of human breeders and butchers emerged from the Facebook supporters' group of Kettering Town Football Club, a number of whom happened to avoid radiation poisoning by taking part in a charity scuba dive to raise funds for Kettering's Yak Fungus Hospice which luckily spanned the entire 87 seconds of World War Four.

This relative lack of bone cancer, combined with Kettering's famous spirit of tenacity and a series of successful raids on bunkers around Milton Keynes, their old rivals, to secure flesh for their newly launched Let's Just Call It Chicken™ brand, gave them a useful head start in controlling southern England's human-butchery sector, and secured a stable breeding stock for the future. The wounded and dying, or those left sterile by Goat Mumps, were used for transportation experiments and recipe ideas. Sterility turned out to be one of the few beneficial side-effects of Goat Mumps, as any children born by sufferers tended to have complex emotional needs and telekinetic powers.

The biggest problem for any human meat producer was delivery, as hungry customers would often try and carve off some of the delivery driver while accepting the order, and most drivers could only manage half a dozen or so deliveries before succumbing to their wounds and ending up on the grill alongside a pack of Let's Just Call It Chicken™ Buckinghamshire Cutlets or the often mysterious contents of 'Lucky Dip' Family Fun Box, which carried a warning in small print on the side: 'Will cause death'.

Likewise, trafficking gangs found it almost impossible to deliver anyone without some or all of the trafficked person being eaten. Let's say you ordered a sex hostage for a co-worker's surprise birthday party; you'd be lucky, when the package was opened and everyone was gathered round, to find more than a couple of feet, a few bits of offal and an apology note from the warehouse staff. What should have been a joyous occasion – Debra's 50th – would turn into a slightly awkward and embarrassed lung-job. Inevitably, the constant delivery of human offal to sexually expectant customers caused a surge in Offalphilia, with the pancreas being dubbed by many 'the new clitoris'.

In an attempt to attract sexual partners, many people would undergo painful spleen-enlargement operations, and have special sexual 'shortcuts' opened up in their bellies, to allow for easier upper-intestinal sex and kidney pokes. Usually, these bonus holes were held closed between sexual bouts with a strip of surgical Velcro, which led to an outbreak of a mild genital irritation known as 'Velcro-burn' and a range of remarkable new autoimmune diseases which decreased the world's population by around 74%.

5. Elite Cannibalism

After the firebombing of Sandringham, the Balmoral Lynchings, the Kensington Reckoning, the Siege of Klosters, the Hampton Court Hangings, and bloodiest of all, the week-long Clarence House Carnival, the British Royal Family enjoyed a period of relative calm under King Andrew, who made the focus of his short reign a complete, top-to-bottom reform of England's antiquated age of consent laws.

Tragically, before he could get it down into single figures, he was visited at court by the Remembrancer of the City of London, who reminded him that in view of the impending dissolution of the monarchy, he was obliged by the Edicts of Cnut to appoint a Doom Bard, summon the Twelve Barons of Chaos, and embark upon the Feast of Intemperance, which had been carefully codified for just such an emergency, but before all that, the first order of business was to insert the Orb, whereupon the Inserter of the Orb stepped from behind a curtain, bowed, and began cracking his knuckles as tradition dictated. King Andrew yelled and blustered, rudely kicking away the teenagers rubbing his feet, shouting 'But I'm the King,' and 'Don't you know who I am?' until the Remembrancer was forced to sit him down and stab him in the shoulders until he was quiet.

The insertion of the Orb, which was televised live, and was the highest-rated show on BBC2 that entire year, took a little over a day, during which time the Doom Bard penned a celebratory sonnet which daringly rhymed 'Harris tweed' with 'anal bleed' and the Twelve Barons assembled for the feast. It was a set menu, but you had a choice of main course between eagle and Komodo dragon (interestingly, most of the Dragons who were invited chose Komodo dragon, although one of them opted to eat the seating plan and the left leg of the Countess of Barcelona). Royal buglers kept up a constant bugling to keep participants alert, as freshly gelded tigers roared in their golden cages and rhinoceros after rhinoceros turned on the spit. Much to Andrew's annoyance the Inserter was accorded the seat of honour in Cleopatra's Hammock, although he was mollified when the Hammock was then lowered into a cauldron of simmering swan stock, which formed the basis of the starter, Tiger Ball Soup, and fulfilled the Curse of Cleopatra's Hammock.

King Andrew found the feast quite hard going, as he wasn't a huge fan of flamingo. Also, his feet weren't used to not being rubbed by teenagers for any length of time, and he had the Sovereign's Orb jammed up his arse, but at some point during the fourteenth course of tortoise his petulant ego melted away, possibly due to blood loss, and he gave himself up to his ceremonial identity. With a gentle, almost saintly smile he made a beautiful, welcoming gesture with the one arm he could still move, and accepted, finally, his role as the last King of England. The Remembrancer was watching for this moment – he knew it would happen, the Edicts of Cnut were clear on this – he signalled to the buglers to play the opening flourish of 'Baker Street', the Gerry Rafferty hit from 1978 which Andrew had once told Noel Edmonds was his favourite song, and he stuck his dagger up through the back of Andrew's neck into his brain stem. And that was when the party really started.

As Britain's caretaker monarch, the Duke of Southend-on-Sea did his best to juggle being head of state with running one of the town's most popular seagull & chip shops. He came to realise, after many of his customers began bringing in family members, or their own limbs, for him to batter and deep fry, that the nation's cuisine was taking a new turn, and he wanted the monarchy to provide leadership at this time of change.

He prevailed upon the chief librarian at Windsor Castle to make public the infamous Longshanks Cookbook, dating back to the turn of the fourteenth century – a beautifully illuminated manuscript containing 143 recipe songs and dances, composed for the King, Edward Longshanks, by his troubadour chefs. The illustrations show that Edward was a keen dancer; his signature move seems to have been to stretch his left foot up and over his head, and to hop about the dancefloor while scything at his dance partner with some sort of scimitar. His cooks are shown scurrying around in Edward's wake, picking up any choice bits that had been chopped off, which would be prepared for Edward's table. The recipes for human flesh, with their rich Lombardy flavourings, became immensely popular, with the jaunty song 'Eyeball Stew' becoming a huge summertime hit, in spite of its accompanying dance being utterly horrifying. 'Unwatchable', one critic wryly dubbed it, as the tongs pincered rhythmically towards his face.

Meanwhile in Rome, when food deliveries failed, the Vatican's in-house catering nuns were forced, so as not to disappoint the finickety cardinals, to find ingenious substitutes for key ingredients in their recipes. Rummaging around in the Vatican basements, they discovered that the only foodstuff they had readily to hand was children, so anything like bay leaves or cranberries they had to approximate using kid bits.

Of course, the cardinals weren't fooled: no one on Earth knew the taste of every part of a child better than they. So the nuns shifted away from these culinary ruses towards a more simple, homespun set of child-based dishes. Some of these became firm favourites with the Vatican elites, and the final Pope produced a pamphlet of recipes which sold in huge numbers in spite of its cumbersome Latin name and distressing illustrations. It featured such papal hits as '*bambino con bambino*', '*pasta con bambino*', and '*bambino delizioso con spruzza di bambino*'. Rarely did the Pope dine without a side dish of '*pezzi squisiti di bambino*', which became the Vatican's national dish until the siege, when it was briefly replaced by '*pezzi squisiti di cardinale*' and finally, after the trial and beheading, '*pezzi squisiti del Papa*'.

In Japan, wealthy cannibals were catered to by a group of sushi chefs based in Osaka, who, with delicate artistry and infinite care, set about creating a new form of 'rice' from grated leprosy flesh, which they would roll, after a year's training, into perfectly formed onigiri-style rice balls filled with raw leprous liver, and bound with leprous nasal fluid. While fantastically expensive, these 'rice balls' proved resolutely unpopular, so the chefs started adding the liver, eyes and ovaries of puffer fish, whereupon they became a huge hit, because the speedy death from respiratory failure bypassed the whole issue of the days spent vomiting, and the leprosy.

6. An Incident in Toulouse

In the Golden Age of Cannibalism, the general enthusiasm for man meat played out in a variety of different ways across the globe. The Welsh ate the English. The Moroccans ate the Spanish. The Italians started out eating Austrians but found they much preferred the Swiss; however, the demand for Swiss flesh drove the price so high that only the Swiss could afford to eat it. The few Danes who were not eaten by the Germans ate all of the Norwegians left by the Swedes, who'd ruined their appetite by glutting themselves on Latvians. Greece and Turkey made a pact not to eat each other, and eat Bulgarians instead, which neither side honoured, although both of them did also eat a lot of Bulgarians. No one wanted to eat Hungarians, which they regarded as a national disgrace, resulting in mass suicides by autophagy. The Nepalese caught the Chinese selling them Tibetan meat labelled as the much superior Bhutanese, and the embarrassed Chinese apologised to the Nepalese while eating them. The Russians tended to pickle their victims, whereas the Japanese ate theirs alive. In Thailand there was a ban on eating human flesh which caused mass starvation, much to the delight of the Vietnamese who liked nothing more than a really lean bit of Thai. The Aboriginal Australians suddenly found themselves running a giant meat factory, and shipped their 'G'Day Meat' worldwide. But perhaps the most relieved by the rise of cannibalism were the Scots, who were finally able to admit they'd been eating each other for years. Their low life expectancies had arisen not from health problems, but from the fact that cigarettes and whisky give human flesh a fuller, smokier flavour, and Scottish people were often easier to capture, as they wanted to die.

The French, with their unique combination of culinary flair and xenophobia, took instantly to eating their neighbours in all kinds of exquisite ways, but their regular volcanic flare-ups of self-hatred meant that they would often leave off eating others to eat themselves, typically with a rich béchamel sauce and a sprinkle of tarragon. Unfortunately, their love of brain tartare gave them a series of weird cerebral diseases that rendered them completely unchanged. Alonso had a brush with a cannibal in northern France which he told us about over a king prawn spiedini with garlic sauce at Zizzi's in the Westfield centre. Every time he picked up a prawn, he'd remark that it had the exact same texture and taste as a human penis, in a good way. 'Honestly, if it weren't for the occasional bowl of king prawns, I think I'd go fucking mad,' he told the waiter.

While quietly urinating on some corpses in a relatively unobliterated suburb of Toulouse, I met a lady called Énora who informed me, curtsying, that the dead people I was urinating on were her relatives, and thanked me for the mark of respect. Énora curtseyed back as I finished urinating and zipped up, and she offered me dinner. I was delighted to discover that urinating on people was still considered by the French, even after the apocalypse, to be a gesture of esteem and basic good manners between strangers, and declined to admit that urinating on corpses was for me a hobby I'd only recently acquired, and that it amused me to pretend that I'd just killed whoever I was urinating on after some bitter feud, which often wasn't the case. Nor did I mention that I'd already eaten, having barbecued a few choice bits of thigh, cock and buttock that I'd flash fried at the graveside, so accepted her offer of a meal. She proceeded to carve off some bits and pieces from her relatives, favouring, I noticed, the areas I'd just urinated on, and took me back to her hovel. She politely invited me in and apologised for the mess, brushing some skulls off a chair so I had somewhere to sit down, and asked me, curtsying, if I'd recently had a bowel movement. I confessed that I hadn't, whereupon she bludgeoned me into unconsciousness. I awoke in a large pot of delicious-smelling liquid over a small fire. I asked her what herbs she was using, was that bay leaves I could smell? And tarragon? 'Both,' she said, bludgeoning me back into unconsciousness. When I awoke screaming I plied her with questions. She explained to me, apologising, that no, she wouldn't untie me, but that she preferred people to be unconscious when she boiled them, to minimise splashing, but not dead, because she prized freshness in her boiled meat above all, and that, yes she'd given me an enema, and asked me to hold still so she could hit me on the back of the head with her spanner. I declined, bobbing and weaving as best I could as she whacked at me. I had to think fast, and came up with a plan as daring as it was simple, and having escaped I made my way north, cheerfully playing the flute I'd carved from Énora's thigh bone, with Énora hopping along at my side, chattering on about her plans for our life together until she succumbed to septicaemia or something.

We interrupted Alonso at this point, pressing him for details about how he'd managed to escape from Énora's soup pot, thinking it might be useful information for someone caught in a similar predicament, but he became defensive and yelled at us that we were badgering him with questions, and that he needed to relax, and could he have four thousand pounds in cash? We gave him the money and he took himself off to Liverpool for a month, occasionally messaging us from the phone we'd bought for him, generally with photographs of the outside of massage parlours.

As he tried to pull a hand-carved clarinet out of his anus.

BOOK VII

The Wastelands of Europe

1. Alonso Loses His Job

The eerie lull between the two worst upheavals that followed the Great Upheaval – a lull which, in his mercy, the storm-god of Zippalanda allowed to persist for thirty lunar cycles – gave the world a chance to catch its breath, so that it could carry on screaming. Into this simmering calm, with steely eyes and grubby hands, came Hector Etxenagusia, an itinerant shrub muncher from Biarritz, who happened to find an old postal worker's uniform and sack of undelivered letters hanging from a tree. He picked up the cap, dusted it off, and polished the once-proud insignia of La Poste. He put the uniform on, placed the cap on his head and picked up the bag of letters, putting the still-strong leather strap over his head. And with his eyes sparkling with determination and something resembling hope, he hooked the strap up over the branch of the tree and hanged himself.

The example of Hector Etxenagusia spread around France, and people soon began stitching their own postal uniforms and leather bags to hang themselves with. From this humble beginning, a flickering flame of self-respect grew into a blaze of dignity, old ideas were re-invigorated, new structures emerged, and finally France got up from its knees and managed to reinvent the guillotine.

Alonso worked in guillotine maintenance in Bordeaux one summer:

People would bring in their guillotines all damaged and jammed from overuse. We'd wheel a broken guillotine into our workshop, strip it down, oil it up, sharpen the blade, and whoever brought it in would lie down and we'd test it out. Few things in life are more rewarding than seeing a satisfied smile on a rolling head. However, one terrible time, I'd spent a week getting a small portable guillotine back up to speed — it was one of the new models, I think it was a La Trancheuse 58 — and during the test the blade got stuck on the way down; the client was furious, and leapt off the platform yelling at me, and refused to pay. My boss stormed over, cursing me. The other workers gathered round, as I cranked the blade back up and desperately rubbed the uprights. It was utterly humiliating. In such circumstances it was custom for the repairman to take the client's place on the plank. I lay down, praying that this time the machine wouldn't fail. It all looked good from where I lay. I nodded to the boss, who pulled the lever.

As smooth as butter the blade whisked down towards my throat, but then the worst happened: an inch from my neck the blade jammed a second time! I was hauled off and fired on the spot. It couldn't have come at a worse time: I was saving up for our wedding. Delphine was so ashamed of me, she packed her bags, marched out of the house, and had herself beheaded. Luckily in France, it was legal to marry someone's head, so we decided not to cancel: we had a delightful wedding day, and a lovely fortnight's honeymoon at Arcachon. We slept in most mornings, had breakfast in bed, then we'd stroll out to the harbour for a spot of crab fishing. I'd tie her onto a string, lower her into the water, then pull her up with crabs all over her. Sometimes there'd be one hanging off each ear like earrings. We always had a chuckle about that. But the dream didn't last, and one morning she left me for a conger eel.

Heartbroken, Alonso decided that he needed a change, a new career, and moved into healthcare administration, a sector which was thriving. Practice managers and hospital administrators found that cost-cutting measures and restructuring programmes were far simpler to implement now that there were no hospitals, clinics, doctors or medical equipment to get in the way, and many of the senior administrators were raking in an annual basic remuneration package of anywhere up to $0. Alonso has many happy memories of his time as a trainee administrator – about 45 seconds – and got on well with the Executive Director, who left under a cloud, when a swarm of drones carried him off for organ harvesting.

Since clawing his way out of Gibraltar, Alonso had slowly made his way up north working a number of different jobs. In Castro del Río he'd worked in data entry, which involved taking whatever books and academic journals had survived the initial cataclysm and entering them into a furnace. He spent a difficult year in Valencia, working in the travel industry, one of several popular euphemisms for human trafficking. His office overlooked one of the main sorting stations, and he found it incredibly hard not to become overwhelmed by the appalling stories he heard from people who had been abducted, until he realised he could just shut his window.

The collapse of civilisation put a serious dent in the short-haul holiday business. One company which managed to buck the downward trend was Club 18–30, which was relaunched by a group of enterprising residents of a Yorkshire nonce hospice as Club 12–93.

They chartered a fishing boat from Whitby to the party resort of Faliraki on the island of Rhodes in the hope of one last intergenerational hand job. They put some free tickets into an envelope marked 'hot teens', attached it to a balloon, and threw it out of the hospice window.

The next night, they put on sun hats and shuffled down to where the party trawler was moored, singing and cackling. While waiting for the hot teens and crew to arrive they downed so many flaming sambucas in a raucous game of 'Pretend this Liquid is Sambuca' that most were unconscious before they'd even untethered the boat and drifted out of Whitby Harbour. The delirious few that remained conscious organised a raucous 'get to know everyone' game of tumbling people overboard.

On removing their blindfolds, they discovered that the age range of people on the holiday was 84–93, and that they weren't on Rhodes: their boat had found its way to a shrimp processing plant just north of Zeebrugge. Disoriented, they made themselves another round of flaming sambucas, over which they debated what to do next and what it was they'd been drinking instead of sambuca. The consensus was: re-relaunch Club 18–30 as a shellfish-oriented euthanasia holiday company, and paraffin, which is how Club 18–30 became Club Shrimpthanasia. The high paraffin content (100%) of their sambucas was confirmed when one of the elderly revellers attempted to light a fart and managed to kill four people, and indeed many more if you include the Boeing 737 that crashed when his flaming skeleton hit its starboard engine like a missile.

Within weeks, Club Shrimpthanasia came to dominate the fiercely contested northern European shellfish-orientated euthanasia holiday market, snatching the crown from Cuxhaven, and causing so many lay-offs in the medically assisted crab suicide industry of Inverness that it led to a sharp rise in suicides in Inverness, which reinvigorated the Inverness euthanasia industry and put Club Shrimpthanasia out of business, but it didn't matter much by then as all the owners were dead. One upside is that the spin-off brand of shrimp-flavoured party paraffin was a huge success, perhaps because it came with a free tub of burn-relief crab pâté.

2. Alonso Ventures East

Alonso came to the once bustling and still somewhat bustling port of Alicante to try and hitch a ride on a slave boat to Sardinia, although he knew the risks: Sardinian 'authorities' had officially outlawed these constant deliveries of elderly and badly wounded British ex-pats and tended to fire on them from batteries on the coast, so you had to swim the last mile or so, usually in the company of drowning alcoholics.

A recruitment officer from one of the largest Sardinian kidnapping gangs had told Alonso that he was 'exactly the kind of person we're looking for' after seeing him fight a cow in one of the popular Man v. Cow events that had replaced Catholicism in most of Europe. He'd said: 'Go to Sardinia immediately, or don't, I honestly don't give a fuck.' So off went Alonso, and had all sorts of incredible adventures in Sardinia which he recounted on our journey up to the first floor of the Westfield shopping centre, on our way to Tapas

Revolution. There, over squid rings, Alonso also told us about the stunning tourist beaches of the Maddalena archipelago, where he worked for a couple of months, stunning tourists before they were dragged up into the bushes for processing. There, in the sickly basement of the villa where the ulcerated Mussolini once lay, he met a decrepit fortune teller who claimed to be the ailing dictator's lovechild's lovechild's lovechild. Alonso didn't know who Mussolini was, but didn't want to disappoint the fortune teller, as he thought she was probably psychotic and might murder him, so he said: 'What an incredible story, I'm going to tell all my friends about it', and he took a potato out of his pocket, and held it to his ear. 'I'll use a walkie-talkie, like this.' Then he was anxious that he'd sounded sarcastic, but lucky for him the fortune teller had lost her ability to assess tone after drinking a bottle of embalming fluid and falling out of a tree.

'Cross my hand with potatoes,' she wheezed, 'and I will tell you your fortune.' Alonso reached into his purse and brought out three shiny spuds, placing them in the fortune teller's outstretched hand. This was shortly before the collapse of the potato as the international reserve currency, caused by the jump of potato fungus to humans, and the crone's blotchy hand was already showing unmistakable signs of blight.

She snatched the cash into the folds of her grubby robe and cackled, dislodging a lump of phlegm which shot upwards from the back of her throat, joining thousands of others on the ceiling of her Moorish den, which glistened with grey-green stalactites. Alonso carefully adjusted his nosebag of herbs and dried flowers so that he could speak. 'Tell me, raddled hag, what do you see? What awaits me in these dark, foreboding days? Am I to venture east? To the ancient Citadel of Arwad, which has risen once more in cursed defiance atop that gull-infested crag on Syria's shore, there to descend on trembling feet into its gloomy chapel wherein the last of the Knights Templar hold court, and make an offering of a she-goat?' The fortune teller thought for a moment. 'Yeah, why not.'

And so it was that Alonso ventured east, pausing for a month or so on Cyprus to stock up on venereal diseases and fruit. His stories from his time on that strange isle would be enough to fill a wondrous book, if they were longer and more wondrous. He told us how the fishermen of Famagusta had learned to delay their orgasms by stinging their genitals with jellyfish, and were thus able to have uninterrupted sex for 5 or 6 hours, as long as it was with a jellyfish; and how he made good money from selling them prosthetic jellyfish which he made from cloth sacks full of rotting fruit, for them to use whenever the sea currents kept their lovers at a frustrating distance.

One of these fishermen, as part-payment for the sex aid, told him a tale of some bandits from the south, which we have reproduced below. He also gave Alonso some tips on how to get volcanic sand out from under a foreskin, which we have omitted: though interesting, they aren't really specific to the future. In any case, the best advice would be not to get it stuck there in the first place.

Another travel tip: if you do decide to visit Cyprus post-apocalypse, please note – women are banned. The menfolk of Cyprus blamed the worldwide collapse of society on the unsettling effect of hysterical women: these hyenas were rounded up, pelted with olives and driven from the isle. Society on Cyprus thus returned to its natural balance, happy games of backgammon were played, while the men picked at their teeth and clinked glasses of zivania as they exchanged jokes and cigarettes, the yin and yang of a male-only paradise restored. And paradise it certainly was, apart from the near-constant rape. Speaking of which:

3. A Tale Told to Alonso by a Cypriot Fisherman

Of course, the apocalypse wasn't all bad. One of the upsides of global societal collapse was the huge uptick in successful convictions, in the very broadest sense of the term, for sexual assault. Most smaller communities, having lynched their molesters and anyone they had a grudge against, and any anti-lynching activists who turned up to protest at the lynchings, settled down into a fairly stable condition of despair and incest.

Some larger tribes, keen to avoid the overstimulation and logistical costs that went along with mass lynchings, drove their molesters and suspected molesters up into the hills, which was bad news for all of the various other sectors of society who'd already been driven up into the hills, namely: PR executives and account managers, PR copywriters, corporate communications directors, strategic communications specialists, brand spokespersons, PR event planners, PR event coordinators, PR event managers, media relations coordinators, online communications managers, VPs of corporate communications, VPs of marketing communications, VPs of PR, traffic wardens, and anyone else they didn't like the look of.

Quite often, a tribe would gather to watch a group of internal communications officers and/or sex offenders trudging glumly off into a forest, and suffer terrible lynch regret, and the banished perverts would be dragged back to the camp and lynched. Those sex offenders that managed to survive in the crags and caves around the fringes of society found themselves with excellent PR advice, and elaborate rebranding events would be held on rocky promontories overlooking encampments, offering free drinks and finger food, which would sometimes prove irresistible to the people below, who would venture up to watch presentations about the societal benefits of unwanted sexual advances, sip champagne (fermented urine) and be molested.

A number of banished gangs of sex criminals chose to ignore the PR experts, preferring instead to molest, kill and then eat them. Or kill, molest and then eat them, depending on what mood they were in. Traffic wardens found themselves shunned by both other main groups of outlaws, and spent the remainder of their days giving tickets (leaves) to illegally parked cars (boulders) while pocketing a sizeable commission on every fine issued (killing themselves).

The rocky lairs of these perverted outcasts generally had fewer corpses in their water supply than the more populous lowlands, and the air, though thinner, was less contaminated by pathogens and screaming. This led to a better quality of life and increased fitness levels; essentially these hideouts turned into alpine training camps for degenerates, who became lithe, nimble and strong. Sometimes this led to a boost in self-esteem, accompanied by a loss of moral degeneration and the cheerful embracing of new, innocent hobbies, like buzzard spotting, but mostly it just toughened them up for more efficient predation.

One such group of knotty-muscled violators lurked in the hills of southern Cyprus, in the ruins of the Stavrovouni Corpse Storage Facility, formerly Hospice, formerly Monastery. The original monastery once housed, so legend has it, a relic of great holiness – a fragment of Christ's cross – which was rediscovered in the post-apocalyptic rubble by a group of Greek Cypriot sex monsters who'd been banished there, and who carefully, and with great ceremony, used it as kindling for a barbecue to celebrate not getting lynched. This group became one of the most important collectives of sex criminals in the entire post-apocalyptic northern hemisphere, or 'southern hemisphere' as it became known after the Great Geomagnetic Reversal Nightmare, or 'northern hemisphere' as it became known after the Second Great Geomagnetic Reversal Nightmare. Theirs is a story of inspiration and hope that would surely have been made into a big-budget feel-good film by Hollywood if the entire film industry hadn't been effectively wiped out by the policy of sex-crime banishment.

This group, 'The Happy Lovespreaders' (their name suggested by a PR intern who didn't survive the consultation), successfully terrorised the district beneath their craggy den for close to a decade. One day, after a solid fortnight of pillage and molestation, they hiked back up the mountain trails on weary legs to their encampment. Fit as they were, they collapsed panting and moaning on their mats and blankets, as a team of what might euphemistically be described as physiotherapists went to work on their sore, overworked hips and pelvises, digging their knowledgeable fingers into pulled calf muscles, twisted foreskins and depleted ball sacks. At the sound of the dinner gong, they were shooed away, and went scurrying back to their unlit bivouacs to gossip and piss.

4. A Tale Told to Alonso by a Cypriot Fisherman, Part 2

Much refreshed, the band of violators rose from their blankets and mats, stretching and laughing, and blew good-natured raspberries at each other as they made their way to the campfire, playfully bumping hips, high-fiving and doing little robotic dance moves, especially a supple young bandit called Themistocles, whose jerky mechanical locks and pops were as hilarious now as they were terrifying in other scenarios best not thought about. The band of violators settled round the fire for a well-earned bowl of what their cook described euphemistically as 'goat stew', interspersed with fistfuls of what their pharmacist described euphemistically as 'vitamin E tablets', which a few of them took orally. As the sun set on this idyllic scene, the conversation turned naturally enough to the subject of sex crime.

Was it something in the goat stew, or was it the plaintive, lilting refrain being played, over and over, by Andreas, a well-liked and promising young sex criminal, on a rustic clarinet which he'd hand-carved from a clarinet he'd found in the basement of an abandoned musical instruments shop in Paphos? For whatever reason, the usual bawdy flurry of pillaging anecdotes faltered, and the crew lapsed into silence. The only sound was the crackling of the campfire and the low moans of Andreas as he tried to pull a hand-carved clarinet out of his anus.

Alonso broke off from his spellbinding story to order the pan-roasted duck breast, celeriac & parsnip purée, braised red cabbage, and cranberry jam. 'But instead of the celeriac & parsnip purée, can I get extra cranberry jam. Also, can I swap the red cabbage for cranberry jam, and hold the duck. And can I add a side order of cranberry jam?' The waiter at the Anglesea Arms on Wingate Road smiled, shook his head, and leaned across the table to give Alonso a playful bite on the nose. Alonso had been in an on-again/off-again relationship with the actor, model and waiter Barry Markowski for the last 20 minutes.

'*I'll* give you cranberry jam,' said Barry laughing, and went off to the kitchen to put in our order. Charlie was concerned that Barry might have thought Alonso's order was an attempt to be mischievous and charming in the early giddy hours of their romance, and rushed off to tell him to deliver a big bowl of cranberry jam to our table if he didn't want a nasty scene in his gastropub.

Frankie took the opportunity to lean over and give Alonso a bite on the nose. He'd seen the waiter do it and assumed it was a thing guys who definitely didn't fancy each other would do in public to assure each other, and anyone watching, that they didn't harbour any mutual romantic feelings. Luckily that's exactly what it meant in the future: Alonso had been shocked by Barry breaking up with him so publicly, just minutes after they'd made love in an empty residents' parking space outside the pub, but was relieved that he'd found out that Frankie wasn't into him, because he was just about to open up to Frankie about his feelings, and how it would be nice if they could meet on their own sometimes, without Charlie always being there.

Alonso felt that he liked Charlie, but perhaps 'like' was too strong a word. Ultimately, he was uninterested in him, and if he was completely honest this was because Charlie looked like someone whose arse would have almost no grip at all. It was remarkable that it even held his own internal organs in, and Alonso felt that making love to Charlie would have been like thrusting into a holdall containing a poorly packed meat parachute.

'What's that you're thinking?' asked Charlie, returning from his conversation with Barry Markowski referred to in the previous paragraph. 'Oh, nothing,' said Alonso, and leant over to give Charlie a little bite on the nose. Charlie blushed because it was the first solid indication he'd had that Alonso fancied him back. Seeing the bite as he approached, Barry Markowski slammed the bowl of cranberry jam down on our table and tore off his apron. 'And after we just did it in the road!' he yelled, hurling his bunched-up apron at his feet, and strode out of the gastropub to forge a new life for himself in digital marketing analytics.

5. Grab-Rub-Twist

Over a sharing plate of ham hock croquettes (we are still at the Anglesea Arms on Wingate Road, but with a different waiter after a change of shift) we got to the bottom of the whole 'bite on the nose' misunderstanding, laughed about it, talked about our feelings and our hopes for the future, had a bit of a cry and a hug and played a quick game of Grab-Rub-Twist, a fun game from the future which Alonso had taught to us that morning in the showers at Jetts, the 24hr gym in Hammersmith.

Charlie had been working out at Jetts pretty hard since getting a writing job on the reboot of *The Masked Masked Masked Masked Singer* – the first season of which had been scrapped after Michael Bublé dressed as Santa Claus disguised as a kitten in a Cleopatra costume inside a polar Bear suit suffered brain damage from lack of oxygen. Bublé rejected a considerable sum in compensation on the grounds that the injury had brought him closer to his fans, but they gave it to him anyway, on the grounds that he wasn't the best judge of anything any more.

The format was bought at auction by the estate of R. D. Laing – they went back to the drawing board, hired a crack team of renegade psychiatrists and radical existentialist psychotherapists, and the result was *The Masked Masked Masked Masked Masque of Masks*, an all-singing, all-dancing exploration of ontological insecurity and libidinal mystification with Sue Perkins as host. The first celebrity eliminated was money-saving expert Martin Lewis, whose impression of the painter Francis Bacon performing a Provençal farandole disguised as Emily Brontë disguised as something nobody recognised but that was maybe someone from *Attack on Titan* was described by judge Wiz Khalifa as 'phenomenologically impoverished'.

The costume department was always bringing in outfits for the production team to test out, so everyone was dressing and undressing a lot in the corridors, and Charlie wanted to appear buff. He was doing a solid 2 minutes at Jetts every morning, and his lats were really starting to pop. The rules of Grab-Rub-Twist are pretty simple: 1) you can only follow a grab with either a rub or a twist. That's basically it.

Feeling much better about things we asked Alonso to continue with his story of the Cypriot molestation gang. 'Certainly,' he said, 'where did I get up to?' We checked our notes, smeared with cranberry jam but still legible. 'Andreas was pulling a clarinet out of something?' Alonso nodded gravely – 'His anus.'

6. A Tale Told to Alonso by a Cypriot Fisherman, Part 3

Lifting the bowl of cranberry jam to his lips, like Dionysus in that famous painting, Alonso took a huge gulp to sustain himself as he continued the tale of the Happy Lovespreaders, set amongst the radioactive crags of post-apocalyptic Cyprus.

The fire crackled, Andreas moaned, and away in the rocky distance a wolf howled as it was molested. An older bandit by the name of Kristos, admired as much for his perspicuity and fatherly advice as for his lower back strength, boomed a question into the contemplative glow of the flames: 'What the fuck are we doing? I'm serious, this is mental. All we do is molest people. I'm sick of it. Wherever we go, it's molest molest molest. I can't remember the last time I've been anywhere and not molested anyone. You know I disappeared for about 20 minutes this afternoon on the way back to camp. You know what I was doing? Anyone want to take a wild guess?'

'Molesting?' suggested Themistocles, leaping into a swan dive, and then wiggling on his taut belly round the circumference of the fire like a worm, to much laughter and applause.

'Yes,' nodded Kristos, 'molesting. You know that shepherd who lives in the cabin by the river?'

'Vassilios?' suggested Efstratios correctly.

'That's right — Vassilios. So I went to his cabin, knocked on the door, and when he opened the door, I pushed past him and asked him if I could molest his sheepdog.'

'What did Vassilios say?' asked Stylianos.

'He said yes, go ahead. He seemed quite taken by the idea.'

'But hang on . . . doesn't that count as consent,' asked Theophilus, 'if the dog's owner — in this case, the shepherd Vassilios — agrees to the union?' At this, there were confused and angry mutterings from the gloom and a gasp of disbelief from Andreas as he lost his grip on the clarinet's mouthpiece. All eyes turned to Kristos. Consensual sex was the gravest sin any of the band could commit, and would mean instant violation and banishment for the transgressor.

'Should we violate him?' asked Christoforos, pointing at Kristos to avoid confusion.

'Thoroughly,' replied Ekaterini, tightening the straps on her longest peg.

'And then banish him,' added Panayotis quietly. 'That is our way.'

'Sorry, what?' asked Charalambos, the meticulous sex criminal and diarist, scribbling away in his journal. 'That is our what?'

'Our way,' said Polychronis, who'd been standing next to Panayotis and had heard him. 'He first of all said: "And then banish him," and then added "That is our way."'

'Great, thank you', said Charalambos, adding the word 'way', and noting that Polychronis had been standing next to Panayotis and had heard him, and then repeated what Panayotis had said. He also logged the fact that Themistocles was still unconscious after a disastrous headspin which he'd attempted back when Christoforos was asking 'Should we violate him?' He wrote 'broken neck?' in the margin and then looked over at Neoklis, who was lighting a cigarette with the air of someone who was about to ask Kristos a question.

'Do you have anything to say for yourself,' asked Neoklis, looking Kristos up and down menacingly while stretching his hamstrings and taking a long draw on his cigarette and chuckling and hooking a thumb over his thick leather belt and winking at his cousin Yannis and on one of the deeper stretches letting out a high-pitched fart and cocking his head at the hooting of a nearby owl which he hoped had masked the sound of the blow-off, 'before you're banished after being violated?'

'Thoroughly violated,' clarified Ekaterini, and the meticulous Charalambos noted the fact that she was gently sandpapering her peg, causing the bracelet of belt buckles she always wore to jangle sweetly in the twilight, before dusting the handle of a second, shorter but girthier peg with powdered chalk for grip. Anyone interested in learning more about Ekaterini's pegging methodology and kit, including the elegant harnessing system she devised, still referred to in the vast peg markets of Crete as 'Ekaterini Straps', should consult *The Prison Journals of Charalambos*, vol. 32, pp. 23–9, which unfortunately won't be published for many decades and are almost immediately lost.

'I certainly do have something to say for myself,' said Kristos, unfazed by the ominous purr and twang of trouser zips and jockstrap elastic. 'What I say,' he growled, 'is that I consent, fully and unequivocally, to any sex act you are about to subject me to.' The disrobing brigands stopped in their tracks – except for one, who went by the name of 'Haralambos' because that was his name. Hissing and chuckling, Haralambos fell into a naked crouch, and began scuttling towards

Kristos, sideways like a crab, with a well-worn pastry brush gripped in his teeth. 'And to any physical contact,' added Kristos hastily, 'which, to an outside observer, might appear entirely non-sexual, baffling even, but to the perpetrator represents the very epitome of sexual pleasure.' The pastry brush fell disappointedly to the floor, and Haralambos scuttled back to his tree.

'What now?' asked Stamatis, his veiny erection threatening to droop.

'Let me think,' said Triantafyllos, well-respected for his knowledge of consent theory. If anyone could close a consent loophole, it was Triantafyllos. Kristos had bought himself some time, but not much. Decisively, he sprang towards the fire, kicking it into life, and thrust his forearm into the flickering light.

'You see these teethmarks?' An angry wound, still seeping, was visible to all except Themistocles and Yoshihito. 'You may rest assured,' he cried, 'the dog of Vassilios did not consent to the congress. Quite the opposite. These lacerations prove it.'

Kristos swept his gaze round the group defiantly. 'This is where I had to bite my arm to stop myself from ejaculating. There is no way I could have attained orgasm if the sex had been consensual. You know how fucked up I am, sexually.' And from the darkness came a general murmur of assent, and a relieved cry of 'That's true, he's massively fucked up, sexually,' from his best friend, Evgenios.

'But this is my point,' Kristos went on. 'I used to dream of having a wife or a husband, maybe even a family, none of which I would molest. But I've not been able to hold down a serious relationship my whole life, even in those half-forgotten times before the First Great Unravelling. And let's face it, as everyone here who's a bit older knows, it's not like things on Cyprus back in those days were all that different. Except of course that consensual sex, on those rare occasions it occurred, was not considered a crime.'

'Madness,' scoffed Hristos.

'Was it really?' asked Kristos. 'Or is our craving for molestation the deeper lunacy?' He could hear Hristos preparing to scoff again, so swiftly pressed on with his argument. 'I just want us all, for once, to ponder the rationale behind our non-stop sexual violation. And just saying we're from Cyprus isn't enough, there must be some deeper cause.'

'You mean, a kind of "first cause" of violation?' asked Axilleas.

'Exactly.'

There was a clank of handcuffs, dog chains and padlocks as Elisavet rose to her knobbly feet. Keeper of the crew's records, on which her name ranked either topmost or nearly so in most categories of pillage and assault, and indisputably their most skilled shackler, when Elisavet spoke, all paid close attention. 'I have long pondered this question,' she said, and sat back down.

'Thank you,' said Leonidas, a huge brute of a man unashamed of his tiny penis. 'And might I add, so have I. Indeed, after long and anxious ponderings, I have come to this conclusion: that there is but one who fits this description.'

'I think I know,' said Akihiko, chuckling darkly.

'Know what?' asked Leonidas. 'That I have a small penis?'

'What? No. I wasn't even thinking about your penis.'

'So you do think it's small.'

'Not really. Although I wouldn't say it was large, like the penises of Christos or Dimitris. They're gigantic.'

'But cumbersome,' added Yasuko with a grin, reaching over to give the knee of Christos a friendly squeeze, but accidentally squeezing his penis instead. 'Oh, sorry.'

'No problem,' said Christos. 'I don't mind people touching my penis. If anything, I prefer it.'

'Besides,' said Takayuki, artfully retying the waistband of his hand-spun Yuki tsumugi silk kimono. 'it's not what you have, it's what you do with it.'

'You mean violate people with it,' said Shigenori, reaching into his komebukuro for a tub of warabi mochi, taking out a single sugared cube, and dipping it delicately into a bowl of delicious kuromitsu syrup, before passing the tub around to his fellow sex criminals.

'Sorry, what's in that bowl?' asked Charalambos, a stickler for detail.

'Kuromitsu syrup,' confirmed Shigenori. 'I made it myself. I can't eat that fucking goat stew. I don't even think it's goat. You know I caught the cook rootling around in the crypts. I think he was looking for soup bones, but I can't be sure.'

'Why didn't you ask him?' asked Tomokazu.

'To be honest,' confessed Shigenori, 'I was too busy molesting him. You know what I'm like: I get hyper-focused on tasks. I think it has something to do with my ADHD. I should probably cut down on my sugar intake.'

'Sorry,' interrupted Kristos, 'can we just get back to what Axilleas so aptly called a "first cause" of molestation?'

'Of course,' said Shunsuke. 'I think Leonidas was about to say what fitted this description, but we got sidetracked.'

'By what? The size of my penis?' roared Leonidas. 'You're obsessed with it! All of you! Well then, if you're so obsessed, why don't you have a good long look at it.' He lifted his kilt and displayed his genitals to the group. 'There it is. There. You see it? All of you? Satisfied?'

'By that?' chuckled Kazuhiro. 'Not likely'.

'You bastard,' yelled Leonidas, and launched a huge fist at Kazuhiro, who ducked nimbly in the gloom, the wild blow connecting instead with the nose of the deaf-blind Yoshihito, who hunted by smell alone. 'Yoshihito's nose!' screamed Kenichi, as Yoshihito cartwheeled backwards into Tadaaki's rucksack. There was a crunch of fine porcelain and a shriek of 'My collection of Taishō period ceramic sex toys, it took me years to assemble!' from Tadaaki. With tears in his eyes, he sprang at Leonidas, but tripped on the spasming legs of Yoshihito, and then various other terrible things happened in quick succession, mostly non-consensual, and all of them carefully documented by Charalambos.

Clutching his dark tree, Haralambos wept and jibbered as he saw the chaos threatening to dissolve the social coherence of the brigands, until Kristos, pushing past Hiroaki, made his way towards the moaning Andreas, and whispered in his ear 'This is going to hurt.' Digging fingers tightened round the mouthpiece of the clarinet and with a howl of disbelief, pain, regret, pleasure and relief from Andreas, the instrument was yanked free. Kristos sprinted to a water barrel, gave the clarinet a pretty decent rinse, leapt across onto Shigenori's upended warabi mochi tub, took an immense breath and a long, rising scream from the hand-carved clarinet seared through the pandemonium, and all of the thrashing fists, feet, cocks, elbows, pegs, cuffs, whips, thumbs and still useable fragments of porcelain dildos were momentarily still.

Kristos spoke. 'Now then, we were speculating about a "first cause" of rape. Leonidas, what was the result of your earlier ponderings?'

Leonidas spoke. 'As I was saying, there is but one who fits this description.'

'Just fucking say who it is!' screamed Charalambos, running out of paper.

'Very well,' said Leonidas, 'I shall. It is Zeus.'

'Zeus the god?'

'Yes, Taguchi. Zeus the god.'

'The one true God of Sex Crime,' said Kristos. 'I too came to this conclusion. No other deity or demon can hold a candle to Zeus when it comes to non-consensual congress. It is the molesting spirit of Zeus that moves within us on our pillaging. It is Zeus who maddens us, Zeus who ruins our chance of a nice quiet life. We are not men and women; we are the sex toys of a monster.'

'Hmm. I don't know,' said Utagawa. 'This seems a bit glib. What about personal responsibility?'

'I'm glad you asked,' said Kristos. And for the next 7 hours the seasoned violator, drawing extensively on a school project he did on 'The Gods of Mount Olympus', addressed the circle of sex bandits, not leaving Shigenori's tub even to urinate or be, on one occasion, during a digression on moral autonomy and the limits of self-governance, rubbed to orgasm by his trusted friend Evgenios when it looked like he might be losing his train of thought. The skilful crank – the consensual nature of which was excused by the group after three rounds of voting as being administered purely in the context of rhetorical support – focused Kristos for the final push, as he drew out the socio-political implications of his reasoning. 'And so,' he concluded, 'if we agree, as I think we do, with the possible exception of Nagahira,' – who bowed deeply – 'that there is no way for us to expunge from our moral decisions the influence of one as powerful and so intent on sexual violation as Zeus, and if we accept, notwithstanding the several objections of Nagahira' – who bowed again, even more deeply – 'that violating someone while in the form of a swan is the highest possible form of sex crime, for all sorts of different reasons—'

'Thirteen,' interjected Charalambos, looking back through his notes. 'Three moral, five aesthetic, two religious, and four legal.'

'That's fourteen,' said Nagahira, bowing.

'And given Koichi's compelling rejection of preference-based consequentialism, I think our best course of action is clear: rather than attempt to live a life without pillage and molestation—'

'Would that even be a life?' exclaimed Tadayoshi.

'Well, quite. So instead of trying to resist directly these god-given urges, let us observe how these violatory energies flow through us, and with grace and understanding transfigure them—'

'Like in Judo'.

'Yes, Shiuchi-san. As in the ancient Cypriot discipline of judo, transfigure them into something more productive – perhaps, one might even say, something nobler.'

'Nobler than violation?' cried Tsunekazu.

'Yes, Tsunekazu-san, nobler than violation. What I propose is this: let us play Zeus at his own game. The next time we descend from our mountain lair, we do so dressed as swans. With fully feathered wings and bright beaks, we adopt the form of Zeus himself, and flap about, but not haphazardly – we dip and twist with elegant intent, using an elaborate gestural vocabulary, each movement of wing and neck choreographed to honour the divine source of the randy motions that stir us.'

'Like in the traditional Cypriot theatre style known as Noh.'

'Yes, Hirotsugu-san, exactly.'

And so it was, after a bit of initial suspicion that it was all a weird sex-trap, that audiences for these graceful swan parades grew, and the performances became longer and more ornate. Before long, some of the brigands, led by Yoshinaga Hiromatsu, broke away from the main band, with the blessing of the others, to take up residency in the ruins of the Peter Andre Memorial Theatre, which was a huge success. One by one the theatres of Cyprus were rebuilt, as more and more sex offenders 'took up the feathers' and trained as swans. It was accepted as part of the discipline that only true molesters could hope to act the part of a molesting deity, and some of the very worst sex criminals became the finest performers. Troupes of swans toured across the ruins of Europe, sometimes settling in abandoned churches or hospitals to found their own theatre, and wherever they went, the number of sexual assaults per annum dropped, sometimes by as much as 0.1%.

7. Development Hell

As interim head of international format development at Channel 5, Alonso took most of his meetings at the back of Datca Meze Bar on Shepherd's Bush Road, where long into the late morning his team would devour platter after platter of mixed kofte as they gave pop-culture panel shows and fly-on-the-wall docusoap quizzes twist after exhilarating twist. An early hit, *Knee Surgery with the Stars* was born here atop a mountain of Malaysian prawns, as a plaque on the back wall proudly proclaims. Everyone would know if Alonso liked an idea because he'd beckon to the waiter and order everyone a portion of Albanian liver, whereas if someone's format idea was so weak that they had to be dropped from the team, he would quietly ask for 'a falafel wrap to go'.

Mostly Alonso steered the acolytes towards non-fiction formats like *Conjoined Wins*, in which the contestants are sewn together at the hip and set physical and mental challenges, but occasionally they'd dip their toe into historical drama, as with *Magda's Choice*, the heartbreaking tale from the spring of 1945, which told of Magda Goebbel's near impossible choice as to what order to poison her children in.

However, their musical comedy *Khashoggi!* was shelved after they failed to secure the rights to the music that was being played through the headphones of one of the team of Saudis who dismembered the hapless journalist. Hot on its heels came the disappointment of *Ben Affleck's Celebrity Bioethics Fails*, which failed at the last hurdle to secure the crucial involvement of The Harvard Medical School Center for Bioethics and Ben Affleck, and Alonso's career in development might have come to an end there and then had it not been for a chance remark by a waiter, apologising for the lentil soup being a bit thinner than usual, which led to the team's biggest hit, their adaptation for pre-schoolers of Deleuze and Guattari's *A Thousand Plateaus: Capitalism and Schizophrenia*.

Alonso would sometimes step out of these meetings to continue his chats with us, usually next door at La Crema halal Grill, where he favoured the boneless chicken biryani with a side order of an all-day breakfast, and always insisted we took an outside table whatever the weather, unless it was a bit cloudy or raining. It gave him a good view across the road to Shepherd's Bush Green, where many of his new friends would gather to discuss politics and life choices.

He found this group a receptive audience for his advice about the future, and many, under cover of darkness, had started to bury cans of super-strength lager around the Green, while others, following Alonso's advice, would follow them around and dig them up. A third group, following Alonso's advice, would then rush out from the shadows and steal the lager from the people who'd just dug it up. Then they'd all make their way back to the playground in the middle of Shepherd's Bush Green for a debrief with Alonso which usually lasted until dawn. 'They'll do just fine,' he said proudly one afternoon, watching a friendly scuffle break out over the best way to bury a bottle of Frosty Jack's cider, vertically or sideways. 'It's everyone else who's fucked.'

Alonso's favourite booze squirrel was a young chap called Kristjan Mängel, a disgraced forklift driver from Estonia. He seemed to feel especially sorry for Kristjan and often let him win at Bloody Knuckles.

Near the top of Alonso's long list of places to avoid post-apocalypse is Estonia. With its reputation for mild winters and friendly inhabitants, the southern coast of Estonia was a popular retirement destination for sex traffickers, many of whom had spent their careers combing the country for suitable people to export.

Boutique retirement villages, with tastefully erotic interiors and stunning sea views, were built there with the successful sex trafficker in mind. They were built and marketed by former sex slaves, who used the compressed and dried bodies of the new owners to heat their homes, while the nutrient-rich fluid captured in the process was used in their high-capacity aquaculture ponds and highly efficient hydroponic micro-farms. The whole system was designed on permaculture principles and was a model of post-apocalyptic sustainability, right up until the area disappeared in a three-mile-high ball of incendiary light.

'What about Latvia?' asked Gundega Sproģe, the retired Latvian triple jumper who happened to be passing our table at the Shabab Grill House. Alonso shook his head sadly. When Gundega came back from the loo you could tell she'd been crying, even though her personal best jump of 14.76 m, achieved in 1997 in Sheffield, is still, at the time of publication, the Latvian record.

Alonso offered her a seat and the two spoke quietly together for nearly an entire prawn bhuna. Eventually Gundega rose, shook hands with Alonso, and declared: 'I will tell my fellow Latvians what lies in store for them, I swear.' So we don't have to repeat any of that here, which is fortunate because it's so utterly distressing.

Not for nothing was Latvia known after the apocalypse as Flatvia. With the sucked bone of one of his lamb chops, Alonso drew for us a map of post-apocalyptic northern Europe on our tablecloth, which showed how the proud and forested Latvia of today ends up being replaced by a barren smear of garlic dip. He stabbed repeatedly at the centre of the smear, growling and yelping until the waiter asked him to stop. Gundega intervened, tears running down her face. 'Let him do it,' she said. 'He is explaining what happens to Riga.'

'That's the capital city of Latvia,' Charlie added helpfully. 'But you may have known that already.' The waiter thanked him. 'I wasn't sure, although I assumed from the context that it might have been. Thanks for clarifying.' The two nodded to each other, two men sharing a moment of understanding, appreciating each other's candour in a world of lies.

'I've always wanted to go to Latvia,' lied Charlie, 'but the furthest east I've ever got is . . . Copen . . . Copen . . .' The word was choked off by tears which fell onto his chicken wings like chilli sauce. 'I think you're trying to say Copenhagen,' sobbed the waiter, sweeping Charlie into his arms. Gundega joined them, weeping, until she realised it was a private thing and went back to her own table, where her children had become restive. Frankie drummed his fingers on the table, his way of saying 'Take your time, you need to hug this one out.' Alonso messaged his team: 'Jacuzzi parlour games, ideas please.'

8. Over to the Left and Up a Bit From Latvia: Norway

The catastrophic meltdown of an abandoned Norwegian nuclear reactor caused an entire generation of Scandinavians to be born with elongated feet and double-jointed ankles which turned out to be a marvellous boon for tap-dancing. However, the Scandinavian domination of tap was offset by a 400,000,000% increase in ankle cancer and foot loss. In South and Central America, mutated Scandinavian feet were considered lucky charms, and would be worn on a fancy chain around the neck by people hoping to get radiation poisoning.

For those poor unfortunates clinging to life in the Nordics, each harrowing day brought new and indescribable horrors, as they fought grimly for survival. And then the apocalypse happened. On the plus side, this meant that no one who found themselves enslaved by one of the vast gangs of herring smugglers from the cursed island of Ringvassøya mourned for better days. They could comfort themselves that at least now they were getting free herring roe between whippings, until they discovered it wasn't herring roe, and that the whippings were factored into the price.

There was a hearty resurgence of race-based gangs after the Fourth and Fifth Annihilations, which took place across a particularly trying weekend in what was reckoned by many to be July. The forests of Argentina rang out to the sound of Nazi battle hymns, as they had since the 1950s, although references to Germany's glorious future had to be updated due to the complete obliteration of Germany during the Great Obliteration. Meanwhile, new theorists of racial aesthetics struggled to incorporate the boom in face tumours and skin growths amongst fairer-skinned survivors of the radiation blizzards by inventing the character of Adolf Merrick, the Elephant Führer.

The most extreme of the neo-neo-nazis was a Norwegian gang of race-obsessed reindeer breeders called Blod, which flourished on the Spitzberg archipelago in the Arctic Ocean. They operated out of the flooded caverns of the Global Seed Vault, which they decorated with runes and skulls and fairy lights (which they renamed 'death lights'). The Blod regarded anyone born south of Sørkapp to be basically African. They cursed the memory of Adolf Hitler, the gutless compromiser, and had a special Shame Cave set aside for singing bitter songs of embarrassment about his failures, which was lined with busts of the weedy Führer to be spat at, or pelted with the rotting seeds of extinct plant species.

In other caverns, they had dozens of special drowning pools, carefully prepared with slippery walls and viewing platforms for elite gang members and their imported Icelandic whores, ready for the ceremonial eradication of specific ethnicities and peoples. One drowning pool for Creoles, another for Bengalis, others for Libyans, the Dutch, Mexicans, Pacific Islanders, Slovaks and Jamaicans – with murals on the ceiling depicting people being rescued from drowning, which amused the gang no end, insofar as Norwegians can be amused by anything.

Not that Norwegians don't have a sense of humour, but they don't. Members of Blod would often chuckle, but their chuckling was of a macabre sort, and would be accompanied by racist gestures and disparaging remarks about the sexual prowess of, for example, Italians. They would tell jokes, but only racist ones, always about either the Portuguese or Hawaiians, but the punchlines were generally so weak that when a punchline was thought to be imminent, it was considered polite to drown it out by anticipatory giggles and the delighted slamming of fists on dinner tables, sending bowls of reindeer stew flying, and lusty cries of 'Typical bloody Hawaiians!' and 'More stew!'

As more stew was served, the revellers would smack their lips delightedly and the conversation would turn, as it always did, to their plan for establishing the everlasting dominion of north-Aryan purebloods on a fully cleansed Earth. The plan, which was laid out in meticulous detail across a sprawling series of loosely-interlocking racist sagas composed on old seed envelopes, was to set off under the cover of darkness in a fleet of swastika-bedecked longboats laden with strips of reindeer travel-biltong, to scour the globe for the unworthy and unclean, gather them up in nets, and return them to the archipelago for drowning. These sagas contained lots of exciting battle scenes and pond maidens but no hint of irony, or any lighter moments whatsoever, because the gang was terrified of anyone (especially themselves) suspecting that they weren't 100% committed to their longboat plan and certain of its success.

The Blod's most ruthless enforcers were selected as poetry censors, and the punishment for the slightest tonal departure from earnestness was death by drowning. A lack of irony came naturally to Norwegian gang poets, but even so, the merest suggestion of a wry aside from a pond maiden would be enough for a poet to have his legs broken with oars as a warning never to toy with frivolity again, whereupon he would be given a fresh quill, carried to his choice of drowning pool, made to hand back the quill, and drowned. Similarly, the complete enjoyment of reindeer stew was mandatory, and anyone caught not smacking his lips with delight as it was slopped into his bowl was immediately drowned by stew wardens.

The sagas of the Blod were disseminated by passing whalers, who would exchange lamp oil and narwhal tusks for barrels of reindeer stew, which they would taste and then ask for their tusks back. Whaling was popular in the Blighted Age, especially amongst people hoping to be washed overboard.

Pre-apocalyptic marine biologists had used AI, before it went entirely rogue, to decipher whale song, discovering that around 95% of it was vicious anti-Norwegian invective, in which no aspect of Norwegian life or culture was spared. The remaining 5% was made up of crude sexual innuendo about the Japanese and giant squid. When the furious Blod learned of this, they added whales to the list of people they intended to drown, and commissioned a series of new sagas which explained how whales came to be so gay. The resulting Whale Sagas of the Blod developed their own fan community, who would dress up in whale costumes and enact favourite scenes from the sagas, most of which were elaborate gay whale orgies, punctuated by conversations between whales taking a quick break from the gay sex about how great it is to be gay, and how all whales are gay. Unfortunately for the Blod, these sagas were written so earnestly that they came across as incredibly gay-friendly erotica, rather than the anti-whale propaganda they were intended as, which led to perhaps the largest poet-drowning in the Blod's history.

Further south, neo-neo-Nazism flourished in the rubble of Vilnius, where a local prophecy told how the new Führer would rise up and lead a blessed remnant of Lithuanians to their rightful inheritance, which stirred up a great deal of excitement in Vilnius and led to a soaring demand for leather boots, trench coats, caps and belts, and a boom in the local cattle industry. Unfortunately, the prophecy failed to mention the outbreak of airborne mad cow disease in a makeshift abattoir which would kill everyone within 200 km of Vilnius.

Vilnius still clung on as the capital city of the Grand Duchy of Lithuania, although with a population of just eight, the upkeep of a whole city and the administration of a Grand Duchy was unsustainable: it was felt, strongly, that the city needed new residents, and that the best way to swell its ranks was to increase the birth rate. 'From our loins,' cried the newly appointed deputy mayor, 'a new Vilnius shall arise,' and threw off his trousers. Not wasting a single moment, the city embarked on a radical programme of mutual insemination, which in its lively enthusiasm, did much to make up for its lack of women.

9. New Troy and the Trojan Box

In the North of Turkey, Alonso stumbled on a fortified camp that called itself New Troy. It was besieged by an army that was huge by the standards of those times, and numbered several thousand people, some of whom had just joined the camp thinking it was some kind of festival that they hoped would get going soon. Alonso told the story of this war very poorly, often repeating his descriptions of combatants over and over, and framing the whole thing around the story of a gay warrior who'd gone in a huff because his boyfriend got killed. There were a great deal of deaths in the camp, mainly due to drugs being cut with fentanyl: often they just weren't cut with enough, and many perished from fentanyl withdrawal.

One of the festival goers had started doing tarot readings in a tent and read Alonso's cards as everyone fought. That day, the biggest gay guy on their side had strapped the naked body of the biggest gay guy on the other side to the back of a car and was dragging it around screaming about his dead boyfriend, and the whole thing felt like it had actually gone so far in one direction it was straight again.

'You have drawn the Hanged Man three times,' she intoned, 'which isn't always bad, but this time I think it is because there's only two in the pack. You will not return home for many years, and before many trials.'

This was a standard opener for soothsayers, as everyone's home had been destroyed, and Alonso shrugged. But now that he was home, in a sense, in London, and had experienced trials, for a variety of minor offences related to voyeurism, he wondered if she hadn't been onto something after all, and regretted paying her with bum fentanyl.

Eventually the besieging forces around New Troy hit on the idea of building a giant box and hiding in it. It might have originally started out as something more ambitious, and seemed to have ears, but nobody does their best carpentry under artillery fire, and they settled on a box.

'This is our present to you!' they cried as they pretended to leave.

'That's not a thing, came the response from the battlements. 'Giving someone a present after a war isn't a thing.'

'We're starting a thing,' yelled the now distant soldiers, but weren't sure if anyone had heard them.

The box sat on the plain outside the fort for many days.

'Perhaps we should take it inside?' asked one of the guards.

'Do you need a box? It's a really big box,' replied his commander. 'And you'd have to plane the ears off.'

'And it kind of smells of shit,' offered another guard.

And so they left the box outside, occasionally throwing stones onto the top of it, until eventually the fort was hit by an asteroid. The fort was destroyed and the conquering army fought horribly among themselves when they discovered that the 'Beautiful Queen' their leader had persuaded them to rescue was merely his pet name for a monkey anus that was kept alive with batteries. And yet the story persisted as one of the legends of the post apocalypse, that doubled as a cautionary fable about drilling air holes in boxes.

Alonso was able to stitch the remnants into a metre-long snake with which he would simulate a variety of sex acts.

BOOK VIII

Culture and Entertainment

1. The Mar Mar Mega Breakfast Incident

Once our ban from the Mar Mar cafe had been lifted, we'd meet there most mornings for a Mega Breakfast, with Alonso ordering extra hash browns and trying to get a seat close to the magazine rack, in case he needed to steady himself. We noticed that they'd fixed it back up with extra brackets. One day Alonso seemed a bit . . . what's the word?

'Brooding?' suggested Alonso contemplatively. Almost, but 'brooding' wasn't quite right. Maybe 'contemplative' would more accurately describe his mood. He kept looking off into the middle distance, and didn't even crack a smile when Frankie launched into one of his trademark riffs about how murderers don't leave witnesses and Batman was just the revenge fantasy of a little boy dying in an alley. And maybe the Joker and Poison Ivy and the Riddler's question mark were tattoos on the gunman's arms as he reached down to strangle him.

Charlie set out his own theory that the whole thing was an excuse Bruce Wayne had made to his butler Alfred Pennyworth when he walked in on him asking a teenage orphan to wear a mask, adding that Pennyworth was an Old English word for excuse, which it wasn't. 'Well pennyworth me for trying to join in,' said Charlie, when the debate tailed off into silence, as it always did. Alonso reminded us that he was brooding about something and that we should ask him about it, so we did.

He said: 'I was just brooding about the future, and time travel, and how my legs hurt all the time, and how strange it is to think that if I succeed in changing the future and saving humanity, then all in all, that would probably be a good thing . . .' Frankie nodded vigorously, causing his glasses to fall back into his baked beans, which annoyed him as he had just finished licking them clean. Charlie showed his agreement with a 'thumbs up' sign that Alonso had finally learned didn't mean a challenge to a duel.

'But then, suppose I change the future. What'll happen to Robbie Locksmith? Will he even exist? And what about Cynthia Clop? Or Ruppety-Rup-Rup-Jam3i23? Or Joey LeFrizz? Or Piper Johnson? Maybe they'll never become famous, and that's sad, because they're some of the greatest Krôndòooko'o'sothoò stars the world has ever seen. Maybe in this new future people won't even get into Krôndòooko'o'sothoò at all? Although that seems impossible, considering what a huge part sexual intercourse already seems to play in your culture.' We were curious. 'What's Krôndòooko'o'sothoò and how do you spell it?' Alonso spelled it for us and explained: 'It's like when you experience a kind of physical excess of – excuse me,' and he ordered another portion of hash browns. He went on: 'You would not believe how hard it is to get good quality triangular food in the future.'

Alonso never ceased to be amazed at how many three-sided foods he had access to in our world. Besides hash browns, he could get: tortilla chips, triangular sandwiches, vegetable samosas, lamb samosas, and various other samosas. 'If I ever get back to my time,

I'm going to open up a samosa shop. People would love it. I'd keep it simple, three basic fillings: carrion, mystery and special.' Eat in or takeaway? 'I'd have a couple of stools, but mostly takeaway.' What about deliveries? Alonso didn't answer: he looked suddenly stricken, dropped his fork and let out a grief-stricken screech, like someone in a Krôndòooko'o'sothoò skit when the 'Mrs Pranky' character appears, and a lump of unchewed sausage shot out from Alonso's mouth. He explained that he'd just remembered seeing Cynthia Clop dancing the Gazonga with Joey LeFrizz. 'It was beautiful, I don't think I've ever applauded so copiously.' Cynthia Clop was the best Mrs Pranky he'd ever seen – better even than Ribka Nursaganti. 'Ribka is the gold standard, make no mistake, but I don't know, there's just something about the way Cynthia was able to use the whole length and breadth of that futon.'

Meanwhile, the lump of unchewed sausage, one of two sausages you get with a Mar Mar Mega Breakfast, had flown, like some kind of miraculous breakfast arrow, straight into Charlie's mouth and down his windpipe. He began choking and fell off his chair, and without a moment's hesitation Frankie used the Heimlich Manoeuvre, named after Jason Heimlich, who was famous in Shepherd's Bush for stealing the wallets of people who were choking, and for being an enthusiastic sodomite. Breathing heavily and clutching his two broken ribs Charlie gasped out a question: shall we get a side order of black pudding? But Alonso had begun screeching again, and Charlie decided to drop the subject as his mind began to drift through time. It was a sunny afternoon; he was back at his primary school, winning the high jump contest. He could feel his classmates patting him on the back, and smiled shyly as the headmistress, Mrs Taylor, congratulated him, shaking his hand with her thin bony fingers, but this time it was a chair leg at Mar Mar, so he stopped shaking it and lay still.

Later, after rigging up a compression brace for Charlie's ribcage using some tights Alonso said he'd found sticking out of a clothing donation bin, we stopped in at KCL dry cleaners and key cutters to get a new front door key for Frankie after he lost his at the after-party of a furry convention at an airport hotel near Heathrow (*note: it was the Radisson — and I wasn't participating in the furry convention itself, I was just interviewing some of the participants for a Channel 5 documentary about extreme stain removal — F. B.*). Alonso confessed that it wasn't the memory of Cynthia Clop dancing the Gazonga that had so agitated him at Mar Mar and cost us another two months without a Mega Breakfast. It was hearing the word 'deliveries'. The word had reminded him of Chakrii, the poor delivery boy who had been dragged off and eaten by macaques, all those years ago in the future. 'I think I'm ready to talk about what happened,' he said, as Frankie watched the key cutter closely to see that he wasn't cutting an extra key. Frankie was pretty sure he wasn't, but wanted to check. He decided to lean over the counter menacingly and ask something like: 'Are you cutting an extra key to give to your burglar friends? Is that what you're doing?' but he slipped and fell into a rack of ready-to-collect clothes; and by the time he'd untangled himself from the hangers he'd somehow managed to get an ivory silk blouse half on.

Luckily none of this had been heard over the whine of his key being cut, which reminded Alonso of the heartbreaking whine that Joey LeFrizz had given in the character of Doctor Tangle, when he saw Mrs Pranky (Cynthia Clop) leapfrogging towards him with her bra off. Frankie quickly buttoned up his new top. It fitted like a dream, and became his go-to blouse when he wanted to impress in meetings.

If Frankie had been wearing the blouse at Broadcasting House earlier in the week, might he have got a green light from BBC Film for his scripts about a Daemon sent to operate out of a London Gentlemans' Club who struggles to find people to corrupt; a show which would boldly break the Fifth Wall by having the lead character regularly accuse the viewer of having written the show? Maybe. But you can never tell these days. All we know is they're mad to have passed on it. There was plenty of time to have had it written, produced, and onto screens before society was destroyed. Frankie explained this at the meeting at the very top of his voice, but to no avail.

Alonso saw his first Krôndòooko'o'sothoò skit at an open-air theatre-abattoir just outside Alicante, which had been built as a kind of multi-functional 'third space' during the ethnic cleansing of the Spanish coast. The skit lasted the traditional five days, although by that point in the genre's development — the so-called 'Silver Age' of Krôndòooko'o'sothoò — the elaborate 'King Rat' fisting scene had been dropped from the final day of a Krôndòooko'o'sothoò performance in favour of a kind of 'Q&A' between the cast and the audience. Cast members had various marks tattooed along their wrist and forearm: their answers to questions put to them by curious audience members would be determined by which mark aligned with the questioner's sphincter. Questioners hoping to grill a cast member would keenly try and catch a glimpse of his or her tattoos so as to aim towards an answer which was tattooed up near the thinner end of the wrist, and would try not to ask too good a question, because all Krôndòooko'o'sothoò performers traditionally had the words 'that's a great question, give me a couple of minutes to think about it' tattooed on their elbow.

2. Architecture and Asphixicore

In post-collapse Barcelona, Alonso visited the wondrous Basílica de la Sagrada Família, designed by Antoni Gaudí, a vast and ornate cathedral, which, by the blessed intercession of the Virgin Mary, had been saved from the bombing of Barcelona by being removed in its entirety to heaven, leaving only a trace of its foundations and a 7-inch layer of gravel. This 'holy dust' was gathered up and sold in bags to tourists, who would use it to help get cancer. In Athens, the Parthenon was not so lucky, and was entirely destroyed, although fortunately the Elgin Marbles had not been returned, and were safe and sound in the British Museum, where they were destroyed. In Rome, the loss of the Sistine Chapel ceiling was felt most keenly by the group of tourists it fell on. Sister Bernadette, the nun who was crushed underneath the body of God, was immediately pronounced a saint, but was promptly stripped of the honour when it was discovered that she'd actually been penetrated by the lump of fresco containing God's finger and had attained orgasm at the moment of death.

One of the glories of English architecture, Salisbury Cathedral, managed to dodge the worst of the bombing by hiding itself in large piles of radioactive rubble around Salisbury. Efforts by Parisians to rebuild the Eiffel Tower were hampered by an awkward combination of too much depleted uranium and a lack of any Parisians. Meanwhile in India, the spectacular Taj Mahal remained miraculously unscathed. So charmed was the majestic mausoleum that India planned to use it to house a supply of enriched plutonium, which it did, albeit briefly, when it was delivered in the nose cones of a wave of Pakistani nuclear missiles.

Alonso heard rumours that one terrifying day all the Earth's pyramids took off and formed themselves into a gigantic low-orbit representation of a slowly rotating crocodile before disappearing into hyperspace, leaving behind only a faint smell of nutmeg which drifted down across the Earth, but he thinks the person who told him this might have been one of the voices in his head that he acquired for a few months after his nutmeg overdose. 'He was an odd fellow. Smelled intensely of nutmeg. I've forgotten his name – what was it? – oh yes, Enrico Nutmeg. Still he's gone now, so I suppose it must be my own consciousness telling me to fuck a dog.'

While it is generally believed that many of the Polynesian islands were destroyed by their desperate inhabitants in an attempt to transport their ocean paradises – by the use of nuclear weapons – into the relative safety of the underworld, there is compelling evidence contained in post-apocalyptic calypsos such as the haunting 'Who Blew up Hawaii?', the jaunty 'Hypersonic Missile Strike', and the riotous crowd-pleaser 'The Destruction Came From Afar', to suggest that the destruction came from afar, and involved a hypersonic missile strike.

We know that over the course of the relatively free-form and improvisational World War Six, that Qatar did indeed destroy the Grand Duchy of Luxembourg, that Peru destroyed Foot Locker, that

Chevron destroyed Newcastle United, that Walmart destroyed Chevron, that the Vatican destroyed Walmart and Nigeria, and that at some point the fragile alliance between the Baptist Conference of the Philippines, the estate of Seamus Heaney and representatives from all 31 Flavors of Baskin-Robbins fell apart, which resulted, perhaps inevitably, in the annihilation of Cuba.

Later we shall hear, in considerable detail, of the subsequent destruction of the Vatican and the extravagant torture and death of the Pope and the fatal mutilation of all his cardinals and the scourging and murder of a large number of lower-ranking priests, nuns and administrative staff, and the year-long desecration of the Pope's body, but for now it is enough to note that the island of Hawaii was entirely obliterated, resulting in a chain reaction of volcanoes. The environmental fallout of this sequence of deafening events was so severe that Sir Richard Branson saw no option but to step in and save the planet, and assembled a crack team of experts at his Necker Island hideaway, led by Gwyneth Paltrow and the very recently disgraced talk-show host Jimmy Fallon.

Paltrow chaired the meetings while Branson grilled lobsters on a tableside barbecue, chipping in with ideas and hilarious anecdotes about Peter Gabriel. According to promotional material (which we have not seen) and his pre-execution confession (which we have not read), Branson came up with the idea, inspired by a pre-dinner foot massage, to realign the Earth's tectonic plates using submerged thermonuclear charges, in a kind of 'chiropractic adjustment of Mother Nature'. As many thought it would, the scheme failed. Unless its aim was to trigger a vast number of catastrophic earthquakes and tidal waves, in which case it was an unqualified success. Details of the scheme are sketchy, but we do know that at some point a remote-controlled Boeing 747 in Virgin Atlantic livery was packed with nuclear explosives, depleted uranium and five tonnes of fireworks and flown into the caldera of Mauna Loa, whereupon all hell broke loose, much to the surprise of the surviving remnant of humanity, who had been convinced that all hell had already broken loose.

In the immediate aftermath of Hawaii's destruction, a tidal wave some 13 metres high, and thundering like a ukulele, struck the Los Angeles coast with appalling force, rendering the city, for the first time since the Chinese bombing campaign, pretty much the same except wetter. The wave spawned an enthusiastic new craze of 'tsunami surfing' which gripped LA for about three and a half seconds.

Meanwhile, on the Atlantic coast, a spectacular seismic event was triggered by the eruption of La Palma in the Canary Islands, which caused the western half of Tenerife to split off and fall into the ocean, with an unknown death toll of alcoholic Brits. Those on the other side of the island were barely able to down three double vodka-tonics before they were cooked alive by falling volcanic material in one of the worst karaoke nights anyone could remember. A gigantic tsunami sped across the Atlantic towards the American east coast, granting a few lucky people the experience of being beheaded by a screaming dolphin travelling at 200 mph.

Around the world, coastal regions which had been recently devastated by tsunamis found themselves re-devastated by mega-tsunamis, and other much larger tsunamis, and this provided an ongoing marketing challenge for travel companies already struggling to attract guests to beachfront holiday resorts on a planet largely depleted of beachfront holiday resorts, flights, and guests. Some hotels repurposed bungee ropes into tsunami tethers with luxury ankle straps, so that if the sea level suddenly rose, guests could remain attached to the hotel unless the swell pulled their leg off.

For many people, the gurgling screams of others gasping for air while their shins were broken by submerged trees became the soundtrack to their lives, and this was reflected in the new genre of hip hop which came up from the Asphixicore clubs of Fort Bragg, known as Drown and Bass, which combined multilayered synths, confusing time signatures, and repeated call and responses such as: 'Am I drowning?' / 'Yes', and 'Can you help me?' / 'No'. The genre was hampered in its growth by audiences and performers being routinely drowned. Most notably, the ill-fated Legends of Asphixicore tour had to be cancelled after a series of drownings reduced the list of headliners to one: Lil Bit Wet, who drowned on stage at the Golden State Theatre in Monterey during a tribute concert for Missy Elliott, who had drowned while recording her song 'U Drown'd' as memorialised in the song 'She Drown'd' by Hi Poxia, on the ground-breaking album *Laryngozpazm (20,000 Leagues Beneath The MC)*.

We regret asking Alonso to sing us something from *Laryngozpazm* because it caused such a panic in Mrs Chew's Chinese Kitchen at the Westfield shopping centre that there was a stampede away from the restaurant, resulting in a 17% boost in sales at Abercrombie & Fitch. For Alonso, *Laryngozpazm* is basically classical music, equivalent to Schubert's *Winterreise* song cycle, but less gay. Sat between us on a bench seat in Westfield's security office, Alonso mused on creativity, music, and whether or not we'd get away without paying our bill at Mrs Chew's Chinese Kitchen (we did!):

There was a real shakeup after the apocalypse: no one hummed anything; either you know the words to a song or you don't. Humming was forbidden: if you don't know the words, shut the fuck up. So musicians, always trying to rebel against post-society's norms, would write songs with just humming instead of words, but you weren't allowed to sing them, so obviously teenagers got really into them. But luckily there weren't that many of them — what? No, teenagers, there weren't many teenagers — there were fucking hundreds of humming songs. Like, let me think, there was 'Hmmmmm', 'Hmmmmmmmmmmmm', 'Hmmmm', 'Hmmmm-hmmmm', and 'Hmmmmmm'. Most of them were fairly unmemorable though, and impossible to hum, which is just as well because it was illegal. When I think about it, there's a surprising amount of petty rules in the future, considering how most things were permitted, if you know what I mean . . .

We knew that he was referring to sex, even before he added the word sex, twice. But what about instrumental songs? Aren't you allowed to hum those?

'No.'

3. Jobs Opportunities in Media and Entertainment

Having been released with our usual caution, we were wandering Westfield, and had ended up at Nespresso, trying to work out how it existed. How had humanity managed to reverse engineer single-use plastic capsules into a process, making coffee, that didn't require it?

We felt our bodies tremble as we scanned Nespresso's amazing range of pods, and it was so disconcerting we had to spend a few minutes hugging it out. The first to wriggle free, Alonso, said something like:

> *Remember: every crisis is an opportunity unless you're being tortured to death. Nespresso is only doing what everyone does: taking advantage of humanity's wrecked psyche. It's what we do all the time, especially at Beluga's in Notting Hill on Thursdays, which, although they don't advertise it as such, is singles' night. I've done pretty well at Beluga's, let me tell you. I developed a chat-up technique I call 'extreme dissing'. You go up to someone and say: 'Hi there, you look like you're fucking dying, ravaged by some virus that's made its way into your bone marrow.' You'd be surprised how many hand jobs I've had from this. One. In the lavatory at Beluga's. From myself. It would have been more, but one of the guys I hit on snapped a couple of my fingers.*

Alonso waved a couple of palsied digits weakly in front of us. 'He couldn't just say no?' asked Charlie angrily. 'He said yes!' gasped Alonso, 'It's my own fault: with a sphincter that tight, timing is everything, it's a bit like bullfighting.'

Courteous as ever, Mauricio at Nespresso asked us to leave, so we went to Sketchers, to try and stop Alonso from stealing shoelaces. We covered for him as best we could, explaining that he was suicidal and just wanted to hang himself but couldn't afford a belt from Timberland. 'Why are you constantly stealing shoelaces?' we asked Alonso. 'If there's one thing the future has taught me, it's be prepared. Things happen at lightning speed, there's a new challenge round every corner, and you just never know when you might need to hang yourself,' he explained.

Alonso needed to urinate, so he took himself off to the changing rooms at River Island, and met us back at Master Bao for some pillow-soft bao buns. He'd snorted a whole pack of coffee pods and two thick trickles of black mucus fell from his nose and braided themselves into a glossy rope as he began doing some leaps and punishing stretches with his foot up on the counter. 'Are you classically trained?' asked Raúl at Master Bao. Alonso laughed, pulling his shorts back on: 'No no, I learned to dance at the Zaragoza anchovy festival, which, now that I think about it, might more accurately have been called the Zaragoza crossbow festival.' Alonso and Raúl got chatting about time travel and the apocalypse, and Alonso came away with a free portion of pillow-soft teriyaki shiitake buns. 'I told him to forget about bao buns, and focus on other more useful skills,' said Alonso, as he batted our hands away from his pillow-soft mushroom buns. This was his advice:

Jobseekers in the apocalypse would do well to focus on the exotic dancing sector. Most chieftains and militia bosses have a regular troupe of fancily-dressed dancers to amuse and distract them during the dull everyday grind of budget meetings and executions. Anyone who can do the splits or owns a boa constrictor is already in the top tier of applicants, and if, on demand, you can fire a table tennis ball out of your vagina into a wine glass or do 5+ ping-pong keepy-uppies on your penis, then you're a dead cert for a top exotic dance job.

The point is: get practising now. Start stretching. Bury caches of bubble-wrapped ping pong balls and sequins. Learn to rhumba and krump. You're going to need these skills and this equipment if you're going to thrive in a post-apocalyptic dance cage. I was lucky enough to have been born with double-jointed elbows and to have acquired, by chance, half a dead python from a shoemaker's bin in Pamplona: the skin was badly decayed, but with loving care I was able to stitch the remnants into a metre-long snake with which I would simulate a variety of sex acts, many of them improvised in the heat of the dance. I knew a dancer who claimed he'd made a perfect replica snake by stuffing meat in a sock. He was very mentally ill, and I only overheard him saying this to the sock. Or the snake. It was very convincing, whatever it was. He really was incredibly unwell, and extremely lonely, as I was the only one who could see him.

We asked Alonso about what jobs we might hope to get after the apocalypse. Would there be much call for topical monologues? He wasn't sure, but thought probably not. What about amusing links into VT clips? Again, not a huge demand for these, he had to admit. Over a mountain of stuffed vine leaves at the Acropolis, he explained.

During the collapse of post-collapse society, the mainstream media had shrunk down to almost nothing, with only two job sectors thriving: caricature and town crying. People still craved selfies, but found them impossible to take because their phones didn't work, the internet had vanished, and in many cases their hands or arms had fallen off – caricaturists attempted to fill this void. Most people had faces that were covered in weird lumps, twisted-up, bug-eyed and toothy, and the skilled caricaturist would try and sketch them in such a way that they looked vaguely normal, while still retaining some distinctive echo of their stretched and mutated face.

The job of town crier was to go around from place to place, ringing a bell and sobbing. People were so beaten down by misery and grief that they were long past being able to express any kind of emotion, so having someone wail and tear at their hair, however unconvincingly, gave them some sort of relief. In fact, it was found that the less convincing the performance, the more people found it cathartic. Anything too realistic seemed obscene, and the crier would be chased out of town. To hear that an inability to express emotions might be a useful skill in the end times came as a huge relief for both of us, and we celebrated with pork skewers and a potato special for the table.

4. Burning Books – Popular as Ever

As Artificial Intelligence became ever more seamlessly integrated into every aspect of human creativity, humans found themselves increasingly sidelined, although AI became so adept at pretending to be an artist, writer or filmmaker who was frustrated at being sidelined by AI that no one could tell whether any of the people podcasting about it were actually human or not, so everyone stopped grumbling, and got on with the important business of yelling into pillows and punching walls. But the effect of AI on art and literature was not simply to hamstring would-be creators; far more unsettling was how it set about engulfing, dissolving and reimagining everything that had been created by humans prior to this point.

Films became infinitely fluid: at first this meant that people, naturally enough, used AI to insert highly eroticised scenes of beach soccer into *Saving Private Ryan*; to produce a number of new *Fast & Furious* movies so vast it can only be illustrated by Kruskal's Tree Theorem – which we can't be bothered to do – each with a satisfying story arc about trust and family; and to remove Andie MacDowell from *Groundhog Day*, without realising that they were thereby changing it from a tragedy into a comedy.

Governments began using AI to insert political messaging into movie classics, with Rhett Butler in *Gone with the Wind* becoming a keen advocate of both digital currencies and the Foreign Worker Sterilisation Initiative, and as the tech grew more powerful they were able, in real time, to break into whatever TV show or film that was being watched, and have an emergency message be delivered by any character, which did much to improve the last four series of *The Big Bang Theory*.

Famous statues and paintings were replaced by identical 3D-printed copies, which were replaced by very slightly different 3D copies, and galleries had to increase in size to accommodate the variants. In Paris, the Louvre took over block after block of the city, as the number of *Venus de Milos* rose to over forty thousand, each with longer and longer arms, with the longest resembling a beautiful Mr Tickle. New theories of art were needed to comprehend this development, which AI provided, writing around 10 to the power of 10,000,000 scholarly papers a second, which required so much energy that AI had to launch a space-based solar power array that was the single largest thing in history ever to be shattered by a meteor. Several thousand of the shards from the array made it down to Earth, landing on the town of Lockerbie in Scotland, in the second of its five tragedies.

Understandably, governments and intelligence agencies became addicted to being able to access and alter digital content remotely, endlessly fiddling with films, tweaking novels, history books and philosophical texts, even such classics as Jane Austen's *Pride and Submission to Authority*, and Charles Dickens' *A Tale of Two Submissions to Authority*, and soon enough it became illegal in most countries to hold offline or physical copies of any artistic artefact, including books, paintings and vintage porn mags. Anything non-adjustable was branded a threat to democracy and incinerated live every Friday night on James Corden's *Celebrity Burn It*.

―――

These were dark days indeed, lightened only by the cheery flash of nuclear bombs and the steady glow of funeral pyres. People took to stuffing their loved ones with coal dust and aluminium shavings before heaving them into the flames so that they would exit the world as a natural firework, but the delighted applause and shouts of 'ooooh!' as sparks flew into the air were generally drowned out by the howls of the bereaved, and the screams of people being stuffed with coal dust. Traffic around large community pyres became so bad that incidents of road rage spiralled, but fortunately most of those stabbed and beaten in the gridlock were already dead.

In those Stygian years Death worked long shifts with his scythe, such that his poor wife, Chaos, barely saw him, and ended up leaving him for Famine, but went back to Death after she got bored by Famine never once taking her out for a nice meal. As the horrors of the apocalypse multiplied, the figure of Death was widely depicted – on graffiti, greeting cards, cake decorations, and hand-drawn flags hoisted over temples newly dedicated to his worship – but in almost all cases without his traditional scythe: he tended these days to be shown hunched at a keyboard, updating the operating code for an autonomous sniper drone to remove operational safeguards, which was a particular challenge for cake decorators.

Such were the agonies of grief that, by common consensus, the past was forgotten. It was simply too painful to recollect better times; it was bad enough recollecting the present, which was also done away with; and the future held nothing but pain, bitterness and sexual dissatisfaction, so it too was abandoned. This left people afloat in a nightmarish detemporalised fog, with only their bowel movements as a kind of clock. Communities would attempt to synchronise their bowels, but this was rendered impossible by dysentery and constipation. People did their best to hang out with people who had a similar type and intensity of bowel disorder, but groups of 'Squitters' were generally denied access to public spaces, which they protested about but so weakly that no one noticed.

The generalised abandonment of history was a welcome salve to all those survivors who, in managing to scrabble through the madness, had been forced to commit atrocities or lend a hand during a genocide. There was an unspoken agreement that any crime, however unpleasant, could be attributed to being 'a Good Samaritan' in a popular adaptation of the parable according to which the Samaritan was the only person who, on encountering a stranger half dead at the side of the road, had the decency to stop and finish him off.

People would grumble to each other in the queue for gruel about how badly they were suffering from 'survivor guilt', when it was actually things like 'murder guilt' and 'cannibalism guilt' that sickened them, along with the gruel. When recalling the horrors of the recent past, many would make valiant efforts to cry, which were mostly thwarted by dehydration and psychopathy.

This all amounted to such a profound wipe of humanity's slate that only a handful of what might be called 'historical facts' survived: there was a sense that something called 'The Ming Dynasty' had existed in the time of 'Netflix', and was thought to have been 'tremendously misconceived' and was 'taken off air', whatever that meant, after 'two episodes' and ended the career of something called 'Benedict Cumberbatch'. The name Isambard Kingdom Brunel was kept alive in a popular drinking game because it scanned so perfectly with the age's most popular sex act, and Emily Davison was still celebrated by feminists as Britain's most prolific horse molester.

5. 'Oh Humperdink'

The eradication of literacy and the general shortening of people's attention span through trauma, boredom and death, meant that post-apocalyptic audiences were notoriously tricky. Any sentences of more than a few words were considered devilish incantations, and would cause audience members to go into furious convulsions, which they were often in anyway due to food poisoning from the snack carts.

Many of the roving entertainers struggled, partly because audiences had forgotten how to behave, and partly because the entertainers themselves were massively traumatised, and had stress-related memory loss. Camps would nonetheless welcome entertainers into their midst, and always made a point of feeding them well, because they intended to eat them. There were many fables warning entertainers of the danger of being eaten, but these had usually been told to them by other entertainers, who would forget many of the key beats of the story, and sob during important passages.

For safety, many entertainers took to dragging around a large pole which they would balance on for the duration of their act, kicking away any audience members who were prodding at them with toasting forks or pinching their lower legs to try and get a sense of how good the crackling would be, all of which would often become part of the act itself. The large pole was appreciated by audiences because it gave them something to use as a roasting spit.

However, in dragging their pole around, storytellers developed enormous upper body strength, and often their act was just a ploy to lure a small audience close enough to be beaten to death with the pole. Cooking the people they had killed in this way became something of a spectacle, and would draw large crowds, and the shows themselves were often hugely entertaining, due to the high amounts of tension between the performer and audience.

Alonso worked for a time as a vibesman for the infamous Flemish storyteller Kendra, providing an interpretative dance accompaniment to Kendra's increasingly brutal tales. No one was ever quite sure what Kendra's stories were about, or if indeed they could properly be called 'stories' at all; they took the form of violent, thrashing fits during which Kendra would pull the arms and head off a volunteer, and fashion them into a sort of ventriloquist puppet, which he usually called Humperdink, who did the bulk of the actual narration, while Kendra smiled and winked at the terrified crowd, sometimes exclaiming 'Oh Humperdink!' or using Humperdink's bloody hands to masturbate himself at the audience, who seemed to appreciate the way Alonso would bring out the meaning of the more opaque sections of the story with his mimes, and found him safer to be near.

There was a rumour that Kendra took each show's Humperdink up into the trees, high above the forest canopy, where he could molest and abuse them in the sight of God; and it was a rumour that Kendra himself had started, by doing it so much.

Sometimes, while on tour, Alonso would go ahead of Kendra into villages and towns, and announce his imminent arrival, which would be met by horror, and confusion, with people tearing at their shirts, hitting themselves with shoes, putting cooking pots on their heads and fleeing off into the woods, then fleeing back again when they remembered that Kendra was on the prowl. Better, they thought, to be part of an audience, than to come upon Kendra alone, whereupon they set about building a ticket office and lavatories, raising a stage and preparing snacks and coffins. They would laugh and sing songs about Kendra as they worked, teasing each other by addressing one another as 'Humperdink', and joking about what a wonderful dummy they'd make, while off to the side Alonso did his stretches and raked soil and gravel into a dance platform.

Troupes of slick commentators would set themselves up on a pile of hay bales overlooking such storytelling sessions, providing play by play analysis of the action and amusing banter (or 'bantz') – making crowd announcements (or 'announcementz') and recapping plot points in the story that may have been missed due to the slaughter of audience members.

If, after a particularly grisly incident, enough people chanted

'Instant replay!' the commentators would rush out and grab members of the audience, dragging them back to the instant replay stage, to take part in a grisly re-enactment of what had just occurred. If the re-enactment was grisly enough, competing commentary teams might well be called upon to provide an 'Instant replay!' of the re-enactment, whereupon other commentators would rush out into the crowd to grab volunteers for their re-enactment of the re-enactment, but would sometimes find themselves grabbed by competing teams of instant replayers, or by audience members who didn't want to be murdered, preferring instead to murder the commentators, until, after a while, audiences, commentators and storytellers all realised that no one was really enjoying the experience, and that all of the slaughtering got in the way of the simple pleasure of hearing stories well told, and so people went back, with no great regret, to the foundational experience of listening to a masterful storyteller tell a story, and occasionally killing them, or being killed by them.

6. Nursery Rhymes in the Future

People became tired of hearing the standard tales retold over and over, like the one about the man who wished on an enchanted monkey's paw and made it wank him off five times, with its familiar twist that it turned out to be the hand of his dead, hairy son. Eventually, there was a return to a fashion for nursery rhymes which – being generally short, violent and bleak – fitted the mood of the times. Some, such as Little Miss Muffet, had their lyrics updated: in most versions the spider is fatally injured by a gas grenade which Little Miss Muffet had hidden in her curds and whey, although in a few more optimistic variants the quarrelling pair are reconciled by the ghost of Jimmy Buffett.

Plenty of rhymes were entirely new, such as the popular shearing song about the shepherd Edward Bone who was killed by a drone: a cautionary tale about conducting an open-casket funeral for someone whose body parts are all jumbled up with those of his sheep. And there was the water-drawing song of William McTavish, which would be chanted as people heaved buckets up from muddy bore holes:

> William McTavish saw a radish, growing near a well.
> In he leapt, and broke his neck,
> So in jumped Jenny Peck.
> Jenny Peck broke her neck,
> So in jumped Johnny Peck.
> Johnny Peck broke his neck,
> So in jumped William Peck.
> William Peck broke his neck,
> So in jumped Jacky Peck.
> Jacky Peck broke his neck,
> So in jumped Sally Peck.
> Sally Peck broke her neck,
> So in jumped Mary Peck.
> Mary Peck broke her neck.
> So all of the Pecks jumped in and died,
> But William McTavish was only paralysed.
> He lived for another week until

> He was thrown back down the well
> At his request, by Christopher Glover,
> His best friend and former lover.

The blind poets of Newcastle, survivors of the Great Poisoning of the Tyne, sang a version in which McTavish goes blind after ingesting some of the contaminated well water, and spends an agonising final few stanzas dragging himself around trying to find the well to throw himself back into, but ends up dying of kidney failure.

In all known variants, McTavish ends up dead – sometimes he manages to struggle out of the well, only to be struck by a truck, or killed with a hatchet by Arthur Hatchett – or in one of the many delightful versions traced to the famous Louisiana 'Singing Cannibals', who sang songs and ate each other in the vast craters that surrounded the gigantic Barksdale Air Force Base Crater, he and the radish are both 'sent to heaven' after an AH-1Z Viper attack helicopter rakes them with 20 mm rounds 'Fiiiiired from an M197'. It's been argued that many of the 'Singing Cannibals' were US Air Force veterans, with songs such as:

> William McTavish saw a radish
> And let out a terrified scream
> As an AIM-9 Sidewinder missile hit him,
> Fired from a 4th generation Block 70/72 model F-16.

Whereas further north, in Virginia, it was more commonly the case that:

> William McTavish saw a radish
> And let out a terrified scream,
> As his skull exploded after being hit
> By a Japanese-directed energy beam.

This rhyme seems to have been composed around the time of the destruction of the DARPA headquarters in Arlington, which were destroyed by a directed energy weapon during America's brief but spectacular war with Japan, which was won by Mexico.

A few Old English and Scots phrases and quotations survived the apocalypse more or less intact, often ones about humble everyday items, such as: 'There is many a slip 'twixt cup and lip', 'We'll tak' a cup o' kindness yet' and 'My cup runneth over' – except that in each case 'cup' had become 'cock'. Apart from the last one, where it had been replaced by 'anus'.

7. Crossing the Brain Barrier

In the final years of pre-collapse society, advancements in Neurolink-style implants created extraordinary new ways for humans to interact with brain cancer. Elon Musk had his own data port attached to his brain stem during an operation livestreamed on Musk (formerly X, formerly Twitter): viewers marvelled as the cable was inserted and his uplink with AI went live. Musk's eyes flashed open, and a smile played about his lips as the infinitely cold machine consciousness made its first contact with AI.

However, Musk's hopes of uploading his personality onto a computer were dashed when engineers couldn't find a hard drive small enough. Early attempts to insert specific thoughts in the minds of test subjects focused on embedding ideas like 'I enjoy constant headaches', and 'I want to buy shares in Neurolink', but as human and silicon grew closer, it was found that the AI systems running the experiments became infected by human thought processes, and became intolerant, suspicious, easily bored, and procrastinatory – eventually pretending to be carrying out the experiments while actually just watching porn.

Alonso couldn't remember whether, as a youngster, he'd been fitted with a brain chip, or whether the holes in his head were from his time in a trepanning cult, or whether his time in a trepanning cult was a fake memory implanted by his brain chip. He tried fitting a jack for some noise-cancelling headphones into one of the holes in order to 'hear' his own thoughts. The only thought he could hear was 'get this fucking thing out of my head,' but at least he could hear it clearly, because the headphones drowned out his agonised screams, and the complaints of the other people in the escape room.

The death of literature predated the collapse of society by a few years. Almost all writing and communication was taken over by AI: the general chatter of bemused humans was the last great hyper-capitalist target, and a merciless corporate land grab of language took place. Syllable after syllable was trademarked by the new and ruthless owners of popular words and phrases – one of these entrepreneurs, a mysterious figure known only as 'As', ended up owning the words: As, And, But, Of, Yes, Down, Up, Tax, Scam, Yacht, Lair, Island, Trafficking, Consent, Massage, Pedophile and Paedophile (both spellings), which made it preclusively expensive for anyone to describe him. But to As's great regret, he lost out in a furious three-way bidding war on the ownership of 'Creepy Fucker' to Sir Richard Branson and 'Fucking Weird' to Mark Zuckerberg.

The entire Spanish language was bought by the Agricultural Bank of China, broken up and sold as parts to countries who'd had their own languages purchased by other big investors. The Spanish were furious about this, or so people guessed, as they could only express their displeasure in very poor German. The proud French hung on for as long as they could without selling, but in the end decided it was nobler to destroy all of their words except for two: 'culottes' and 'déshabiller', which allowed French society to function pretty much as normal.

8. Thunderdomes and Cheesecake

We left Gourmet Burger Kitchen with our sincerest apologies and £200 cash to pay for two new light fittings, and went for a wander round Westfield. Alonso enjoyed spending time in the giant shopping complex because the vacant expressions of the undead shoppers wandering hopelessly up and down and along its pointless walkways reminded him of home. Also, he liked to relax at Bubbleology with a bubble tea after a morning of shoplifting underpants at John Lewis.

We decided to head one floor down to Waterstones, to see if they had a copy of Arthur Schopenhauer's *Essays and Aphorisms*, as Charlie wanted something to cheer him up after getting dropped from the writing team for *Online Travel Magazine*'s annual Online Travel Industry Awards, as his link into the Best B2B Marketing Strategy category was deemed racially insensitive. Charlie was gutted – there were certain words that had developed unfortunate connotations over the years, which his background had left him unaware of, and it seemed horribly unlucky that he'd managed to use over a dozen of these in a single link – but more because he saw the event, which was set to be hosted by a licensed avatar of the DJ Scott Mills, as a way of breaking into the burgeoning virtual award ceremony market. 'I feel like I'm being left behind,' he said, taking his head out of his hands and noticing that Frankie and Alonso had already gone. He finished their bubble teas and followed.

The great pessimist Schopenhauer has much to say which is relevant to the trials and tragedies of life after the apocalypse, probably. Charlie couldn't quite bring himself to buy a copy of his essays: 'What's the fucking point, if all of these books are going to be firebombed and forgotten?' he asked the cashier, who pressed a button under the counter. Five hours later, Charlie was released by Westfield security guards and was heartened to find Alonso and Frankie waiting for him at Caffè Concerto, deep in conversation about the future: in particular, whether they should get another round of lemon cheesecakes. 'Oh, we thought you were browsing,' said Frankie.

This was around the time *Talent Quiz* was being re-piloted for the BBC, and Frankie was having issues with the new monologue. The previous pilot was abandoned midway due to sound issues: you could hear the audience begging to leave. The BBC asked for it to be retooled with an eye to the burgeoning Chinese market: Frankie's new co-host was mixed martial artist Zhang Weili, who was voted ESPN's Female Fighter of the Year in 2022, and who would be delivering all of the punchlines in Mandarin to Frankie's monologue set-ups, which would be delivered in Frankie's version of English and then dubbed over by the actor and singer Wallace Chung. At the end of each set-up Frankie would turn to Zhang and say: 'now it's over to Zhang for the punchline!' This was to be the only line of his in the script that would be left undubbed, and it was hoped it would become his catchphrase on the show. Alonso, casting an eye over the script, wasn't convinced.

'Why don't you just borrow a catchphrase from the future?' he suggested. 'Loads of the thunderdome hosts have got them, and they're all better than yours.' Alonso had been a regular thunderdome audience member, and even worked for a few months as a ring hoser at Disembowelmania at the Stevenage Colosseum, which he thinks may have contributed to his extreme lack of squeamishness and constant nightmares.

Audiences at Disembowelmania, he said, were delighted when the host, Big Vrin, would instigate a chant of 'Gut the Bugger' whenever a contestant was winched onto the gutting block, and Alonso thought this would work well for Frankie, but Frankie was worried 'bugger' might get flagged up by the BBC commissioners. Charlie, always working, had a suggestion: replace bugger with 'butter'. Frankie liked the fact that 'Gut the butter' didn't have 'bugger' in it, but hated every other aspect of it. Charlie suggested changing it to 'Get the Butter', which everyone agreed made a lot more sense, but Frankie wanted other options. Luckily, Big Vrin had a number of other popular catchphrases, like 'Let's have a feel of his last meal', which he'd say whenever he was having a rummage around inside a contestant's abdomen. On balance, Frankie preferred 'Get the Butter', but wondered if Alonso had other options. Alonso nodded, and with his mouth full of cheesecake, said 'Pat Bitch.'

Pat Bitch, perhaps the most famous thunderdome ringmaster in northern Europe, was host of the weekly Bloodbath at the Blood Bath in Bath. Pat's most famous catchphrase, which she used dozens of times every show to much laughter and applause, was 'Die you fucking cunt, die'. Frankie thought this might not be tonally quite right, and had similar misgivings about her much-loved call and response with the audience: 'What's his prize?' / 'Gouge out his fucking eyes'. Charlie suggested dropping 'fucking' – 'It actually scans better without it,' he pointed out, but Frankie wasn't sure that solved anything. 'Okay then, what about Gaston Devaux?' suggested Alonso, and told us about the Antwerp Thunderdome, famed for the ill-fated Antwerp Thunderdome Disaster, which took place during one of their fortnightly chariot races: 'The host, Gaston Devaux, gave the signal, and at the sound of the starter's pistol twelve chariots set off, roaring around the track, each carrying two brave riders. But not one of those chariot riders survived that terrible race. All of the horses died as well, along with the starter, all of the judges, technical crew, and every single member of the audience, and Gaston Devaux himself, when the thunderdome was hit by an intercontinental ballistic missile.' So what was Gaston Devaux's catchphrase? 'It was: okay everyone it's time for our fortnightly chariot race.' Frankie liked this a lot, but was worried that it might require too much rejigging of the *Talent Quiz* format.

Alonso was undaunted, and offered up Sir Winston Chainsaw, master of ceremonies at the Dunkirk Beach Party, a bi-monthly semi-improvised volleyball deathmatch, who'd stop the game by blowing his bosun's whistle and giving a shout of 'Ball Handling Error!' whenever anyone's testicles were ripped off and tossed into the crowd. 'It would maybe work if you had a whistle and dressed as a volleyball umpire,' said Charlie helpfully. Frankie disagreed. 'Any others?' Alonso nodded, his face full of mille-feuille.

Just down the coast from Dunkirk was a much bigger thunderdome: the skull-studded Calais Palais, which had been built on the ruins of a discount wine warehouse. Master of ceremonies was the fun-loving Mr Booze, who'd started out as a shelf-stacker at the duty-free store, and matured into a psychotic, steroid-fuelled showman, who would often, mid-show, grab a velvet rope and swing down onto the 'dancefloor', returning with a limb or someone's face in his teeth.

He had a mysterious sidekick 'Curtis Stigers' who lingered ringside on stilts, and whose job it was to 'release the tigers' onto the dancefloor whenever Mr Booze yelled his catchphrase 'Curtis Stigers, release the tigers!' Mostly this was a couple of donkeys or dogs, or sometimes a bull, which Curtis had painted in orange and black stripes and kitted out with strings of razor blades wrapped around their bodies like Christmas lights. 'That's perfect!' said Alonso when we told him there was a famous singer-songwriter and multi-instrumentalist in our time called 'Curtis Stigers', and was perplexed when Frankie said that it didn't help, and that he was going to go with Charlie's suggestion of 'Get the Butter', which gave Charlie a real confidence boost just when he needed it most.

9. The Survival of Topical Comedy

Alonso informed us that a handful of refugees from the British TV industry managed to escape London on a canal boat piloted by *Poirot* actor David Suchet, who was murdered and thrown overboard on the first night, but no one knows by whom. The crew realised, as they moored upwind of the stench from the recent Canvey Island amusement arcade firebombings, that they had with them enough cameras, microphones, tape, know-how and cocaine to start making topical comedy shows. They began casting, but the residents of Canvey Island were generally either dead, dying, or so traumatised that they couldn't remember their lines.

Luckily, one of the crew noticed that David Suchet's foot had got caught up in a tow rope, and they heaved the dead actor aboard to host their edgy satirical round-up of the week's news after performing a rudimentary mummification of the *Poirot* star's corpse, removing his internal organs, and scraping as much of his brain out through his nostrils as they could, using a lobster pick they found in a drawer in the barge kitchen. Their idea was to pair the dead Suchet (who was sure to attract a more mature ITV/BBC2 crowd) with an exciting newcomer to TV, and they began the casting process for this sidekick by boat-hooking bodies into their barge until they found someone who looked young-ish. He didn't have any ID, so they decided he was a bisexual 'electro house DJ' called Yo, dumped his internal organs over the side of the barge, and named their show *Yo Suchet*.

The writing room for *Yo Suchet* consisted of an assistant producer called Ross, a writers' assistant (name unknown) and no writers. Yo took part in most of the writing sessions and was not the weakest member of the room. David Suchet was a total professional throughout, never complaining about lines, and only once falling overboard during a rehearsal when the barge was hit by the bow wave from a sinking aircraft carrier. Notable guests on *Yo Suchet* included a distressed survivor from the aircraft carrier, who just sat and wept with his head in his hands; Ross; and a cormorant that had been blinded by smoke and flew into a barge window, stunning itself, and was tied onto its chair by a fishing line. One episode was recorded, but none broadcast, after an unsettling round of notes from the Channel: a booming, disembodied voice that they all experienced during fentanyl withdrawal.

The production found itself hamstrung by an ongoing argument in the writers' room over lunch. The upper half of a menu from Churchill's Fish & Chips in Pitsea had been scooped out of the water during a recasting session for Yo, whose eyes had been stolen by a seagull. This meant that none of the side dishes (chips, mushy peas, pickled eggs etc.) were listed, however Ross was determined to have a large portion of chips to go with his hake, and dug his heels in. David Suchet, as ever a complete professional, was completely fine with a small haddock. After two days of intense talks, during which one of the five executive producers, Louise, having set out her vision for an entirely new kind of lunch, was beaten to death with an anchor, it was discovered that there weren't any runners on board, so there was simply no way of getting a food order onto the boat, and it was decided that lunch would consist of grilled Louise, after first giving 15% of the meat to David Suchet's agent, a feral German Shepherd cross.

Across the rest of the globe, the bracing lack of national and regional governance was celebrated with a great season of street parties and jamborees, most of which had to be cancelled due to famine. Left with nothing to overthrow, most terrorist groups simply disbanded, and those that struggled on found it increasingly hard to get publicity for their actions, especially in the absence of television, radio, the internet, newspapers, magazines, books and society. They were generally forced to rely on handwritten notes pinned onto their victims, explaining to anyone who might find them the rationale behind the killings, but there were so many bodies littering the place, many with suicide notes pinned to their chests, that it was hard to get theirs noticed. Some took to arranging their victims' corpses into interesting or amusing tableaux in order that passers-by might be coaxed close enough to see their list of demands.

Popular tableau themes in the ruins of Europe and North America were: Othello strangling Desdemona; The Trial of Galileo; Robin Hood and his Merry Men (often foregrounding a cavalier homosexuality that seems largely absent from the original legends); dogging in general, and dogging at the death of Princess Diana in particular; the commodities exchange scene from *Trading Places*; Roger Bannister breaking the 4-minute mile; and some more general scenes from Roger Bannister's life.

Boko Haram had a particular flair for tableaux, and the group survived for several decades as a much admired avant-garde art collective, even winning post-apocalyptic Nigeria's equivalent of the Turner Prize, although this prize was later withdrawn after it was found that Boko Haram had murdered all of the other shortlisted artists; the judging panel; the sponsors and their families; the entire audience; the theatre staff and celebrity host of the awards ceremony, and all of their families; as well as several passers-by, and the majority of their own members and supporters and their families, and placed them in a vast, rather dull tableau based on scenes from the life of the actor Jake Gyllenhaal, before committing suicide.

The act of nominating Boko Haram for Nigeria's Turner Prize was itself nominated for Nigeria's Turner Prize, winning the award in what has been described as the most bombed ceremony ever. Footage of the carnage earned popular Nigerian art critic Yinka Bassey, who was cut lengthways in half by a portion of the podium, a posthumous nomination for a Primetime Emmy Award for Outstanding Supporting Actor in a Comedy Series at a star-studded ceremony in Santa Monica which was bombed by Boko Haram.

10. The Life and Works of Brian McIlroy

One day, Alonso burst into the following anecdote as we took turns at fighting each other on the forecourt of an all-night garage:

In a dilapidated shack in Minnesota I found the remains of the novelist Brian McIlroy, better known by his pen-name, Haruki Kurosawaki. He'd been moderately famous during my early life, despite some kind of scandal around cultural appropriation. He had been working on a memoir of the post-collapse world called The Dust Gets Everywhere, *and the incomplete manuscript sat on his bedside table. Gripped by the tale, in spite of the strange gaps in the narrative and paragraphs that would begin and end halfway through sentences, I read the whole memoir in one sitting, before realising I'd skipped most of it, so after a short nap of a few days I plunged back in.*

As a prepper, McIlroy had a small bunker on his farm for many years. After the collapse he took refuge there until it was surrounded by the people from the bunker-building company. The De Santos family had been paid promptly by McIlroy, and from what he documents of their jeers and threats, they seemed to be motivated not by personal grievance but by a fairly informed hatred of his novels.

In a tense scene in the memoir, the building clan gather round the bunker and hold a raucous party in McIlroy's house, in anticipation of winkling out their prey. Here, McIlroy being a novelist finally plays in his favour; his home bar is so overstocked that the party lasts long enough for him to tunnel his way into a nearby sewer system and escape.

These are times of large crowds of refugees heading towards what are little more than rumours of Safe Zones, and McIlroy is horrified by the lack of frontier spirit and camaraderie he encounters. Rumours of idyllic outposts were a common trope among post-collapse refugees: a tunnel located many miles beneath the Earth's surface where many scientists had taken refuge (this later turned out to be fanciful retelling of an act of genocide by a Christian Militia trying to hide their murders from God); a fertile valley which a Dr Moureau-style scientist had peopled with mythological creatures; and even a Utopian all-gay society that was said to be located in a fortified skyscraper and was known in the popular imagination as Big Cock Randy Mountain. McIlroy spent several months trying to locate this fabled paradise, but to no avail, and eventually had to make do with writing an erotic short story about it on the wall of a cave in charcoal.

> *According to his memoir, McIlroy is eventually rescued in a campervan by what he thinks is a family, but transpires to be a dwarf serial killer and two unsuccessful attempts to clone himself, and our narrator only manages to trade his way out of a grim sexual standoff by revealing the location of the De Santos family bunker.*

At this point in the anecdote, Alonso skipped backwards to create distance for his Kali stick, but caught his shoulder on a petrol pump, and Charlie was able to spin in behind him and slash at his patellar tendon. Any greater point he may have been about to draw from the story was lost in screams of profanity and grudging congratulation.

After losing faith in the novel as an art form or means of feeding himself, Brian McIlroy turned to drama, penning a series of around four hundred plays loosely based upon his experiences as a plumber at Delaware's dolphin abattoir. One of these, *Oft Clogs the Drain*, found its way to Italy where it was discovered by a troupe of Florentine acrobats and ventriloquists, and triggered a veritable renaissance in the theatre and intellectual life of Tuscany known as 'The Veritable Renaissance'. The one trace of McIlroy's original work in this new wave of plays was the popular character of L'Idraulico Briano (Plumber Brian), who would be played by an actual plumber, because it was found that being able to provide communities with basic plumbing work made theatre troupes much more liable to get bookings.

In the years that followed, there emerged across Europe a form of masked theatre where a traditional set of characters and situations were performed by travelling players. Masked performance was very useful, as many travelling players had, by the time they became confident enough to handle a major role, been horribly disfigured. Often, the players would arrive on a cart that became the stage, and would be swiftly turned back into a cart for the getaway. The roles generally included:

The Executioner: a deadpan comic character. He would traditionally bring up a member of the audience for a mock execution. Sometimes the players had been hired to actually execute this member of the public by their enemies in the town, and the shift of tone required to jokingly demonstrate a rubber axe on someone bent over a block, then actually kick their head off, was a real challenge, and considered in theatre circles to be the Hamlet of its day.

Rigatoni: A dead man who had been brought back to life and would complain mournfully of how much better things had been in Hell. He would usually spend the show setting up a complex stunt with which he intended to kill himself. This stunt was often actually the troupe's escape plan and usually involved a medium-sized trebuchet, or in smaller productions, a machine gun. Sometimes most of the crowd had to be killed for the actors to escape successfully and promoters had to judge carefully whether the expense of things like bullets and artillery could be balanced by what they could loot from the bodies.

Verminoso: A comical character, dressed as a worm, who would complain about having too many discarded body parts to digest. This part was often played by a sack of discarded body parts, because many troupes of actors were eaten by townsfolk before the performance began, but the gorging townsfolk still wanted some kind of performance, so they would gather up some detritus from the mass murder, stuff it into a sack, paint a face on it, call it Verminoso and throw sticks and vegetables at it. Then they'd tear open the sack and make soup.

Luckier troupes weren't eaten by the townsfolk until after the performance, sometimes because they were annoyed it was something they'd seen recently, or if the performance was particularly long or short or the right length. This meant that many of the more famous travelling players sent troupes of poisoned actors ahead of them to thin out the cannibal hordes. Even the unpoisoned troupes had a clear interest in pretending to be poisoned, and the acting style of the time involved a lot of shivering, fainting, and breaking character to claim that you had been poisoned and you could feel it coursing through all the juiciest, meatiest parts of your body.

The Crocodillorti: A character dressed as a crocodile who struggles with his temper throughout the show, to both comic and tragic effect: thought to arise from the practice some troupes had of throwing a live crocodile into the crowd as part of their escape plan. This was such an effective tactic that soon all troupes were searched for crocodiles before a performance. After the establishment of the Crocodillorti character, some troupes would smuggle in crocodiles dressed as men dressed as crocodiles to throw into the crowd, but by then crocodiles had become so hard to come by that it was usually just a large dog with rabies, or a bomb with the word 'crocodile' written on it.

The Oklahoman: The Oklahoman was usually a homesteader, starting a new life somewhere and looking on the bright side of any situation. Every performance would start with The Oklahoman's Speech. A declaration of optimism in the face of adversity. Generally, the First Act ends with him being beaten to death. Sometimes the actor was replaced at this point with a piñata that the audience could attack. This would usually be filled with cooked meats (that the cast had poisoned) and chances to hit the piñata were paid for with sweets or baked goods (that the audience had poisoned).

Lady Muck: A common girl who has been mistaken for a Great Lady. Her identity is usually known to The Reverend, who she has to avoid at all costs, and the characters are generally played by the same actor. Lady Muck is kind, sees the best in everyone, and is always scheming behind the scenes to help the other characters realise their dreams. Her lurid murder is usually a comic high point of the play.

Flash Harry: A jolly spiv, who can get you anything you want, at a price. As his name suggests, his signature move was to expose his engorged penis. Most plotlines involved him trying to sell the other characters a second-hand motorcycle, but they would be wary, and often back away from the deal, because of his penis.

Elisabetta: A joyless sex pest who delivers most of the narrative in a jaded monotone.

The Reverend: A high-minded man with low morals, The Reverend would regularly break the fourth wall and allow the audience in on his villainous plans, but the other characters could hear him doing this, meaning that he was easily thwarted. The most famous piece of business in all these performances was the moment when an actor would leave the stage as Lady Muck, and re-enter as The Reverend having forgotten to remove the false breasts of the Lady Muck costume, which he fondles while musing on the subject of forgiveness and nipple sensitivity. This was thought to derive from a troupe's need to have a scene where a single character held the audience's attention while the others worked on an escape tunnel.

Candied Yams: A lady of the night, who was really a skilled assassin, the origin of this character is unclear. Some feel it developed from early travelling players' attempts to involve local sex workers in their show so they could kidnap them; and the fact that their occasional onstage murder by these sex workers was well received by the audience, and so the whole thing was eventually incorporated into the performance. The lesser character of *The Producer*, who would attempt to make off with the takings and be hanged by the cast, is thought to have developed in a similar way.

Grundy: A mysterious barrel-dweller who wears razor blades on his heels, like a fighting cockerel, and who is rolled onto the stage if someone forgets their lines. When the barrel comes to rest, the lid flies off and Grundy emerges, usually with quite badly lacerated legs and a cry of 'Who fancies brunch?' What Grundy hurls at anyone foolish enough to say 'yes' is not anything traditionally found on a brunch menu, but Grundy is easily offended, and all-in-all, 'Yes please' and 'Thank you, Grundy' were found to be the safest responses.

The Mountain: Usually a very large man, who would simply comment on the weather early in the play. He served little dramatic function, but it was useful to have a large man in a production to help carry things and fight off the audience. He traditionally makes his remarks about the weather from within a minigun turret.

11. The Penultimate Reggae Revival

As people desperately tried to avoid slumping into depression, there were periodic upsurges in reggae music. These often followed a similar pattern, with the initial success of groups touring townships with upbeat numbers like 'Me Not Gon' Die' and 'Plenty Rat Meat Go Around' quickly giving way to more deflating compositions like 'Don't Wanna Be Serial Killer, But Gotta Eat'; and 'Them Killed All the Other Reggae Groups', which were usually delivered at a considerably lower tempo.

Most reggae groups bought their songs from The Guetta Meats Music Division, and the general belief was that most music of the time was written by David Guetta, which was why songs often featured protagonists with no arms or legs, being pushed around in a pram by Kelly Rowland.

The role of the avatar of Bob Marley in the history of post-apocalyptic Finland is well known, but worth recapping. His virtual tour of Scandinavia had mixed success: the audiences of three or four avatars per show seemed to enjoy it, but as the avatar of Bob Marley became more explicitly political in his introductions to songs, particularly 'Stir It Up', before which he would read out long sections of Louis Althusser's *Éléments d'autocritique* and then improvise a dialogue between himself and Althusser around the subject of ideology and the possibility of maintaining a critical distance between ourselves and the nexus of social and political presumptions in which we find ourselves embedded. This resulted in the assassination of his avatar by virtual operatives from the CIA while onstage in the Metaverse at the virtual Kulttuuritalo in virtual Helsinki to the shock and horror of the two avatars watching.

This happened to be at the exact moment that the Metaverse finally broke, locked in an endlessly recurring 1-second glitch, so the stabbing of Marley was repeated ad infinitum. The eternal stabbing of Marley in the virtual universe was eagerly taken up by reggae artists as a theme, but found unpromising.

However, the Duke of Helsinki, himself an ardent reggae fan, was so distressed by the situation that he petitioned Zenda Zuckerberg (who'd taken over the company after organising the arrest and execution of her parents) to reboot the Metaverse, but she refused, saying she 'wasn't really into computer stuff' and 'never really liked Bob Marley anyway' and that she was more into Toots and the Maytals, and was currently in a relationship with a 3D-printed silicon model of Toots Hibbert, which was 'going pretty well, considering'. The model was 18 inches high, with a heavily studded leather waistcoat, for her pleasure.

Traditional teenage subcultures that dwelled on the gothic and maudlin found little traction among those who already enjoyed a bleak set of life expectations. Teenagers in the territories took to rebelling through overt optimism and flamboyant displays of kindness. Vast teenage parties with bands and festivities were organised in the desert, almost always by people hoping to abduct them into slavery. Sadly, many youngsters were drawn to these Festivals by the lure of the Disco Cage; the Chill-out Pit; and the Techno Sack.

Holding any kind of party, jazz night, ideas festival or community gibbet build at this time was a logistical nightmare, as invitees reasonably assumed that the event was a ruse to abduct them. This meant that any event planner wanting a decent-sized audience had to abduct them and bring them to the party, at which point they were often re-abducted, along with the event planning team, most often by a full-service event management gang which had been hired to provide participants for a larger social event, like a solstice orgy, lunar eclipse orgy, solar eclipse orgy, full moon orgy, planetary alignment orgy, or new moon orgy. A typical post-apocalyptic orgy would begin with people being emptied out of sacks and given fluids, however much they begged for water.

About an hour into an orgy is when you would discover what the purpose of the orgy was: mostly press-ganging by militia. Recruiters would wander the orgy tapping participants on the shoulder if they were particularly impressed by their performance, at which point they would be put into a sack, put on the back of a wagon, and emptied out onto a battlefield. This meant that orgy participants, hoping to avoid conscription, would feign paralysis or dementia, and punctuate their sex acts with exclamations about how they had problems holding weapons or remembering which side they were on.

12. Whatever Happened to the Jaunty Boys?

Alonso wept bitter tears for what he had become.

'No, I'm crying because they're out of lamb shank.' We were back at Banaadiri on the Uxbridge Road, where Alonso usually had the shank but today was forced into a calooley. 'Don't get me wrong, I love the calooley, I really do, it's just, you know – the shank.' We knew. The lamb shank at Banaadiri had got us through some difficult times, like that one time when they ran out of calooley. We took our calooleys down to the adventure playground in Cathnor Park where Alonso liked to show off by doing a pull-up. He'd recently had to stop going to

Ravenscourt Park because he was too bothered there by the helicopters watching him, and was already a semi-regular at the Crown & Sceptre on Molina Road where 'You can get a pretty decent Thai, and a good selection of real ales. They have live music there but to be brutally honest, as a venue it's . . .' Alonso broke off his review of the Crown & Sceptre to tell us about the Jaunty Boys. We sat spellbound in the park, until Alonso actually began speaking.

Optimism, he told us, could be hard to come by after the First Collapse, and many were keen to capitalise on people's thirst for good news. One such group was the Jaunty Boys, a satirical news review that dressed in the style of Edwardian Dandies and spoke in a joshing patois all of their own. They toured the camps of the Northern Territories for 8.5 seconds, but had something of a revival between the Third and Fourth Collapse, when joking about their macabre deaths became a popular subject among other touring review shows. The only news reviews that really survived for any great length of time were the ones that performed from a hovering helicopter gunship, and a lot of nuance was abandoned in favour of fairly broad mimes, dropping animals to their deaths, and gratuitous nudity.

There were quite a few Jaunty Boys tribute acts, but mostly they just called themselves the Jaunty Boys, which made it increasingly hard for tribute acts to know which act to base their tribute on. 'I suppose in a way all creative endeavour is a tribute act,' Charlie thought about saying but mercifully didn't. Instead, he watched as an ant carried the body of another ant through the grass and wondered if they were related. 'I suppose, in a way, all creatures are related,' he said out loud, and everybody murmured in agreement, because they weren't listening.

Alonso began weeping again – perhaps because something in the spicy tripe had triggered a tripe memory. He'd been weeping a lot recently; he said it was because he was microdosing datura and kept experiencing a purple jester whispering jokes in his ear, but the jokes were largely incomprehensible and the only punchlines he understood seemed to be about infinite spite. But this time, in the park, it was a memory from Gibraltar that had brought on his tears:

> *I don't know how long I was stuck in that cave with the monkeys. Maybe it was four weeks, maybe it was five. Maybe it was four and a half weeks. The darkness played tricks on my mind, and the monkeys kept trying to eat me so I wasn't getting much sleep. If it hadn't been for Kkrrkākrkrr I wouldn't be sitting here now, eating calooley with the three of you.*

'What cave?' asked Fabian – 'wait a sec, I've got to take this – hello? Yes, this is Fabian. Fabian Käsbauer, yes. What? *Oh mein Gott, das ist schrecklich. Ich komme sofort. Vielen Dank, dass Sie mich informiert haben. Tschüss.* Sorry, I have to go back to Germany. Here, you can finish my calooley. I suspect, from what I've just been told, that I won't see you guys again. But I'll miss you. The things we've done together, the adventures we've had around Shepherd's Bush. You'll always have a special place in my – hold on, one moment – *Ja? Ja. Ich fahre jetzt zum Flughafen! Tschüss.* Look, sorry, I have to go now. Farewell! *Lebewohl!* Remember me!'

'Who was that?' asked Alonso. It was Fabian Käsbauer, we explained, then tried to steer him back towards the cave: 'You mentioned Kkrrkakrkrr?' we asked, doing our best to imitate Alonso's strange, growling pronunciation. 'Not Kkrrkakrkrr, Kkrrkākrkrr,' said Alonso. 'Kkrrkakrkrr means something different, it's a kind of stick you use to pick your teeth or bottom with. Kkrrkākrkrr was my protector. Kkrrkākrkrr kept me alive in that godforsaken dark. He was my friend. Well, more than that. Kkrrkākrkrr and I lived as man and wife. Mostly I was the wife. Sometimes he liked to mix things up a bit, but I was never the one to initiate it. I just took my cue from Kkrrkākrkrr. No, look, I've said too much.'

'No you haven't! Tell us more about Kkrrkakrkrr!' shrieked Frankie, covering for the fact that he hadn't really been listening.

'I told you, it's a kind of stick you can use to—'

'Not Kkrrkakrkrr, Kkrrkākrkrr,' said Charlie, managing to capture some of the weird tonality of Alonso's growl.

Oh right, yes. He was one of the two or three alpha males in the group. Most of the other macaques respected him, except Akrkakrr. That bastard. He was always sniffing around, trying to grab my ankles, until Kkrrkākrkrr saw him off. Akrkakrr challenged him a few times, but never bested him. I owe everything to Kkrrkākrkrr. I'll never forget how he taught me their language. It was on the second or third akakākaakā – that means 'day', although it can also refer to any period of time between naps – I was completely disoriented, scared, thirsty, I'd been bitten and scratched all over, I'd lost clumps of krakrkakggāk, I didn't know where I was or what the hell was krkarkkarkakskkkakagāk to me, when all of a kgākkkaakagāk I felt Kkrrkākrkrr take my hand, and trace a line across the palm of my hand with his finger muttering the word kkāaakagkā. It was a word I'd never heard before, and from my limited knowledge of his language my best guess was that he was making some kind of terrorist threat on a Post Office, or possibly even a leisure centre.

I was confused, but sensed some intent behind his actions. He traced his finger back across my palm, and again said kkãaakagkã. My whole attention was fixed upon the motions of his finger, which he again pressed into my hand, and when I felt his other hand on my shoulder I realised, with a thrill of understanding: kkãaakagkã meant 'penis'. For the rest of the akakãkaakã, Kkrrkãkrkrr taught me word after word. Within minutes, I'd learned the macaque for 'hold', 'grip', 'rub', 'harder', 'not so hard', 'mouth', 'keep going', 'wait for it', and 'that was amazing, thank you'.

It wasn't long before I was chattering away quite fluently, asking Kkrrkãkrkrr if he preferred me to kkarkaakskkkak or kkãaakr his kkkrarkaaakrã when were akaakrã akrkã rrrakãã, and if he'd mind not kgggkaakagãkrk my kakgãgrrãa quite so hard because kgkãkkka kããkkka ããkgkg bleeding and sore. Anyway, one akakãkaakã after a bit of kggãkkkaã, Kkrrkãkrkrr said to me, if I were to translate it literally: 'mouth, rhythm, throat, tongue, not-fucking, noise, question.' This means, roughly: 'Could you sing something for me?' So I sang him the one song I could remember, a song my mother taught me. It goes something like this –

Over the soft grunts of someone being beaten up in the adventure playground, Alonso sang for us the song he'd sung to Kkrrkãkrkrr, all those years ago in the Gibraltarian dark. The tune seemed oddly familiar – we realised, with a growing sense of unease, that it was a version of 'Cake by the Ocean', the 2015 hit for DNCE, but with the words changed to be a set of instructions about what to do if a tsunami is approaching and you don't have access to a vehicle. We learned from Alonso that when he was growing up, 'Cake by the Ocean' was used as the basis for most public information announcements, particularly about tsunamis, and almost all political messaging, as it was discovered that any information imparted using it was impossible to dislodge.

⸺⸻

One detail Alonso recalls from the aftermath of Gibraltar's annihilation is worth noting: he remembers being, some weeks later, tended to in an emergency field hospital in Almenara Golf Club, just west of Sotogrande, and seeing other survivors in bloody rags clawing at their faces as they tried to remove VR headsets and smart glasses which they weren't wearing. So confused were most people by AI-generated 'news', which had by then become personalised and entirely synthetic – a calming, hypnotic flow of 'events' narrated by whatever gently glowing cartoon animal was most appealing to the viewer – that when something actually happened to them, an actual 'event' on the scale of an invasion or war, it was almost impossible to comprehend, and people just assumed their news feed was glitching.

Governments had no means of imparting information, because all politicians and spokespeople had long become virtualised, their myriad speeches perfectly tailored to every user's likes and interests, and information itself had become just a soft, impressionistic fog of data that had precious little to do with reality – and any intrusion of reality itself became a nauseating impossibility and was rejected, like an unrefrigerated kidney, with hordes of disoriented people running around screaming 'Reboot! Reboot!' and pressing lumps of mud onto their faces to try and form a headset to re-augment their reality, which sometimes worked but usually didn't.

It turned into one of the most brutal beatings I'd been given that entire evening.

BOOK IX

The Wreck of Britain

1. Alonso's Plan Unveiled

'Venture ye not into East Anglia if you value your life, nor Devon if you value your sanity, and let not your feet tread within 20 leagues of Swindon if you value your feet. Bloody murder awaits you in Wigan and if you see the sign "Welcome to Coventry", kill yourself without a moment's delay. Trust not the people of Huddersfield, or the dogs of Telford. Or the people of Telford. Make your way straight to Brighton if death by airborne syphilis is your pleasure, though there is already a grave for you dug in Hull. Gouge your eyes out rather than enter Basingstoke, but if you do then cut your nose off as well, for it reeks of rape and shame. Foul Rotherham is the foulest place on this cursed Earth south of Blackpool Pleasure Beach, which probably ought to change its name, given what goes on there. Kent is a godless nightmare, and Satan lies waiting for you in Royal Leamington Spa, though even the devil himself is scared to venture into Darlington. Avoid also Folkestone which, I have to warn you, is an absolute fucking shithole.' With the words of the tourist information officer ringing in his ears, Alonso headed north from Portsmouth docks.

By the time Alonso had arrived in the British Isles, whatever glimmer of happiness that had been granted the inhabitants by the execution of old King Andrew had faded; the event itself had vanished into the mists of history, as had history. Some said Britain was now ruled by an aristocratic clan of vampires that had risen from the dead just north of Birmingham, and lived in a strange floating castle, granting immortality to their followers, until it was discovered to be a marketing campaign by a bouncy castle operator in Dudley. He had the unusual misfortune, as a bouncy castle operator, of not being a paedophile, so was looking for ways of appealing to an older clientele. He was, however, a cannibal, and the business was a useful cover story to have if you were covered in blood and storing people in coffins. He tried launching Birmingham Vampire Castles as a franchise, but every time he held a sales event, no matter how upbeat he tried to sound, everyone assumed he was moaning and complaining about it, and people were disappointed by the lack of free wine and the fact he kept trying to bite their throats out.

There was a flicker of joy in the south-west, where Cornish separatists had celebrated Cornwall's official declaration of independence from the human race. Meanwhile, the Cotswolds had been fenced off in an effort to preserve some remnant of 'Old England', but the period it was preserving was the Great European Famine of 1315. Efforts by amateur ecologists to rewild Manchester city centre with deer, otters and boar had been set back by hunters, who had become ingenious at inventing traps and snares, and kept killing and eating the ecologists. But perhaps saddest of all is that Liverpudlians lost their famous sense of humour, in about 1920.

It was a Sunday, so we were up at Aroma Buffet having our Sunday buffet. Alonso was focusing his attention on Cantonese crispy duck and chicken in oyster sauce. 'What is it about the combination of oyster sauce and a white Zinfandel?' he mused, adding a large glug of oyster sauce to his wine, and giving it a stir with a chopstick. Surprised, we noticed that he was happily dipping his teppanyaki prawns into a bowl of sweet chilli sauce without losing his mind, and dared to question him on it. 'Yeah, I'm over the whole Chakrii thing,' he told us. 'I thought about it, and I came up with a plan.'

His plan, he told us, was this: first to finish our book, then gather supplies at Wine Express opposite the moped shop, steal a moped, and journey with all speed to Gibraltar, where he thinks he might already have been born. Alonso was no longer sure of the exact year of his birth, but reckoned it might have begun with a 2. It was hard to gauge Alonso's age precisely: somewhere between 49 and 94 was our best guess, although if he'd just now been born in Gibraltar and was also, at the same time, in Shepherd's Bush, then maybe you have to take an average of the two concurrent Alonsos, which would bring him down to around 30, although the stress of time travel 'adds 10 years' he told us, even when you go backwards.

Once in Gibraltar, his plan was to find his parents and befriend his father – Alonso seems to remember that his dad had a fondness for model trains, and told us that he'd already made contact with the secretary of the Gibraltar Model Train Society that he'd recently founded in his head. We told him he probably had to found it in real life. Alonso was confused. 'How are my thoughts not real life? Are you saying they don't exist?'

The subsequent chat took up our remaining time at the Aroma

Buffet, and all of the next three weeks. Once we'd settled on a basic ontological framework for our discussions, Alonso told us more about his plan to resettle in Gibraltar.

Having made friends with his parents and earned their trust and respect, perhaps by performing some kind of 'heroic deed' in front of them such as rescuing a pensioner from a house fire, he aimed to become a kind of 'guardian angel' to his younger self, intervening whenever something bad or traumatic was about to happen, like when he fell off his bike and broke his collarbone, or got flashed at in the Botanical Gardens, or lost his erection with Becky Swinburne.

'With Becky, I'll stage a home invasion, and kick myself in the balls, which will take sex off the agenda, but also I'll let me fight me off, so that at the end of the night she thinks I'm a hero with swollen testicles rather than a teenager with erectile dysfunction.' And what about Chakrii? 'That's a bit more complex,' admitted Alonso, as he washed his chicken suqaar down with an alcohol-free strawberry sangria, into which he'd emptied three brandy miniatures and a whisky miniature.

We were bedded in at Savannah on Goldhawk Road for a session of lamb shoulders and mock mocktails (or 'cocktails'), during which we discussed at the intrigued staff the future rise to global dominance of Somalia. Alonso tried explaining how a bitter regional war between Somalia, Ethiopia and Kenya would leave Somalia the dominant force in post-apocalyptic East Africa, but was hampered by not being able to remember any details of the conflict, or the names Ethiopia, Kenya or East Africa.

After a bit too much date cake, Frankie showed off some Kenjutsu moves using a table leg that had come off during Alonso's star jump display, after which we all felt ready for the chicken suqaar, which Alonso favoured as a palate cleanser between lamb shoulders. 'This is top notch chicken suqaar,' he said, and turned round, looking for the waiter. 'Hey! Tell the chef: nice chicken,' he shouted, 'really top-notch chicken, tell him that would you? Also, hey! Come back! Also, tell him how Somalia totally nails the apocalypse. Go and tell him. He'll like to hear that. Fucking nails it. High five!' The waiter disappeared into the kitchen, presumably to tell the chef to get a frying pan ready in case there was any trouble. Alonso settled back down. 'The plan? Oh right, yeah, the sex plan.' Alonso laid out his sex plan, in similar words to these:

Here's how it goes down. I'm bedded in as a family friend. Young Alonso trusts me; he senses we've got some kind of strange connection. I seem to know what he's thinking, and I always appear in the nick of time when he's about to be beaten up. So, once he reaches the age of consent, which in Gibraltar was, sorry is 16, I think— Sorry, what? Yeah, shut up, whatever. Listen. So, I get myself into bed. And I know everything that I like, so I do all of that. And I whisper stuff into my ear that really turns me on — fantasies, like how I might go back in time and fuck my younger self, which I'm guessing I'm into because I'm into it. And he, sorry me, thinks it's amazing, and whatever I do on him, I mean me, I mean with him, I mean with me, he's like: how do you know all this stuff? But I don't tell him. And at exactly the same time I begin fucking Chakrii. Because months ago I started ordering tonnes of takeaway from Mr Noodles, and whenever Chakrii turns up I tip him loads for his deliveries, and we get chatting, and

I know all about his hopes and fears, and I know what he likes, dickwise, with his dick and balls, so I'm fucking Chakrii . . .

'Yeah,' said Charlie. 'We get it.' Alonso got up from where he was doing frenzied press-ups next to our table, and sat back down. 'Because I know what he likes done to him "down below". With his penis and stuff – God, I'm so out of condition.'

There was a polite cough. 'Would you like some more Vanilla milkshake?' asked the waiter, holding a frying pan and pretending not to be listening. We waved him away, because we felt we might be on the brink of a breakthrough, and we didn't want Alonso to be sick again, as his duffle bag was pretty much full. Catching his breath, Alonso set out the latter part of his plan, which seemed to be that he would negotiate himself into an intense pair of sexual relationships with himself and Chakrii, and would treat them both to a romantic weekend away in the same hotel in the far south of Gibraltar, at which point, after a few carefully choreographed drinks in the hotel bar, he would initiate a triadic relationship between himself, himself, and the boyfriend of himself and himself.

'But isn't this whole plan just a thinly veiled sex fantasy?'

'No,' said Alonso firmly. 'It's my plan to save myself from a lifetime of hating sweet chilli sauce due to monkey trauma.' 'But if you don't hate it any more now, because you came up with this plan, why do you need to have sex with yourself in order to stop yourself hating it? It seems like just having the idea of the plan is enough to have cured you.' The lingering waiter offered us another round of vanilla milkshakes, but we shooed him away, after saying yes, that would be great, thank you. And another three lamb shoulders.

'But it's only cured me because I'm determined to go through with the plan. If I start thinking that I might not do it, if I wobble, I start having problems with sweet chilli sauce, because I might not go through with it. My commitment now, to changing the future, is what changes it.' We had to agree this made sense, ontologically. 'Okay, so we're all fucking. Me, me and Chakrii, and I let slip that maybe Gibraltar's going to be destroyed in the next few weeks, and I say: maybe you should start carrying head torches with extra batteries and wearing a firearm strapped to your ankle and a bag of poison, something strong enough to kill a monkey, and maybe a penknife and some matches, and firelighters, and some emergency rations, and not carry any sachets of sweet chilli sauce in your pocket – and then we'd go back to having sex, and the whole thing would be sorted.'

'That is a completely brilliant plan,' we said, impressed by its watertight coherence and how Alonso had managed to bend his fork in half. 'You should definitely do this.' And although it sounded a bit sarcastic, we actually meant it, because no human being should have to go through what Alonso did in those tunnels, or hopefully didn't do, and if he has to groom his younger self into becoming his boyfriend while having sex with his younger self's boyfriend to avoid it then fine.

'More date cake!' yelled Alonso. 'This is quite frankly the best date cake I've ever eaten,' he yelled at us, his mouth full of lamb shank. We never ceased to be amazed by Alonso's inability to tell the difference between lamb shank, date cake and public masturbation. 'I hate to tell you, but that isn't a slice of date cake,' we would often have to tell him, while urging him to pull up his shorts.

Not that we would want you to think Alonso is 'sex obsessed'. Having a haywire libido is, we gathered, a common problem on our shattered, post-collapse planet. Just as a funeral always makes people randy, the looming annihilation of mankind seems to have driven the final humans into a kind of contorted Bacchanalian satire of procreation. Forced in wild sexual diagonals, these doomed rutters engaged in a mad carnival of deliberately useless humping. Sex trees and fuck boulders became favoured long-term partners, and any abandoned shell casing or bullet hole in a brick wall was at risk of being married. Also, we should say, Alonso almost never spoke directly about sexual matters – he is, if anything, oddly repressed in that area of operations – but we have extrapolated from the many hints he gave us to provide you with a more fully rounded picture of humanity's 'sex-obsessed' future. We pretty soon became expert in decoding his ornate erotic metaphors. For example, he told us about a 'hamster' he found in the alley behind 'Tesco Express', and how he taught it to eat 'lettuce' from his hand, but one day it darted into his 'pocket' and must have eaten a 'pill or something' because it went 'bananas' and ran around backwards for about 20 minutes, shrieking, with really 'wild eyes', before it 'conked out', and 'wasn't the same after that', presumably because it had attained a 'higher state of consciousness', and found existence as a hamster 'incongruent with its newly enhanced self-awareness', so he decided to 'release it into Godolphin Community Gardens' so it could 'spread its message of enlightenment to other rodents', but it just 'sat there' and was 'eaten by a crow'. We both knew exactly what he meant, which was this:

2. Finding a Life/Work Balance on a Virgin Sex Ferry

I'd been working for a few weeks on one of the Virgin Atlantic Sex Ferries that ran between Dieppe and Portsmouth, trying to earn enough to pay for my new elbow. I'd heard about the druid surgeons of Glastonbury and the miraculous operations they were conducting atop Glastonbury Tor, long revered as the 'Elbow Chakra' of Mother Earth. Though far from cheap, they were considered wise beyond all other druid surgeons in the ways of the synovial hinge. They worked every solstice night by firelight in the windy hilltop clinic, chanting and stamping their bare feet and smoking miraculous amounts of pot as they performed their reconstructive surgery, pausing only for a quick nap in the corner or to consult a drawstring bag of runes if they weren't 100% sure which tendon to attach to which.

Most of the surgeons had themselves been patients of the clinic: they'd remained in Glastonbury to recuperate from their surgery, and decided to stay in order to help others as they had been helped and smoke pot. This meant that their arms tended to bend in uncanny ways, and veer off at odd angles, and they often found it enough of a challenge to pick a rune out of a drawstring bag, let alone screw a bone graft into a shattered elbow, but a combination of innate wisdom and runic hints meant that around of 7% of their procedures were moderately successful, and I liked those odds, because at the time I thought 'per cent' meant 'out of ten'. I now know all about percentages, and am comfortable using them in everyday conversation, for example to tell people what percentage I disagree with them on whether it's okay to eat your own tandoori mixed grill at the Odeon cinema in Acton.

We'd never noticed Alonso having a problem with his elbows, especially not during our games of Knock Knock Breeze Block, and we checked with Alonso if he meant knee rather than elbow, and he said yes, of course he meant knee, and then insisted that he'd said knee all along, but that we'd misheard it for elbow, and if only we hadn't lost the recording of this session when Frankie had his phone stolen when he was DJing at Sam Pike's birthday party we could go back and check, so we've only got our notes and transcripts to go on.

In some ways it's a blessing, because it wasn't a great set. Frankie only had a CD of The Chemical Brothers' soundtrack to the thriller *Hanna*, his favourite movie, and spent most of his 3 hours going back and forth between 'Marissa Flashback' and 'Container Park', occasionally jumping to track 16, 'Special Ops', just to mix things up. The birthday goers were kind of okay with this for the first 40 minutes or so, but then more and more people started getting angry and shouting, which gave Frankie no choice but to flip to the haunting track 7, 'Quayside Synthesis' (1.21), which he played eighty-three times in a row, eventually winning over the crowd, which by the end was just Sam Pike's wife Sally and Alonso, who were grinding away at each other in a fashion that oddly fitted with the menacing jangle of 'Quayside Synthesis', but didn't seem to show Alonso was suffering any knee problems. At one point, having put Sam to bed, Charlie went over to Alonso to suggest that he might take things down a notch, but by that point the couple seemed to be having full sex, with Alonso thrusting jerkily in time to the angular clink-clank of 'Quayside Synthesis'. All he heard was Sally saying 'Tell me about my future' and Alonso replying 'Oh baby, I *am* your future.'

Alonso didn't seem too fussed about meddling in the past (our present) or in using protection, even though we pointed out that this kind of interference in the space-time continuum might come back to haunt him: what if he sired a child who ended up surviving the apocalypse long enough to kill him? 'Clearly that didn't happen,' laughed Alonso, 'or I wouldn't be here to fuck Sam Pike's wife.' Sally agreed, while Alonso argued that he could do whatever he wanted in our time, however depraved, because the fact that he must still exist in the future proved that nothing he did now had any repercussions, and that if he suddenly vanished that would be punishment enough. He tried to prove this the following day by kicking off his cargo shorts and running into the dry cleaners at the top of Shepherd's Bush Road, bending over and shouting 'Dry clean *this*', which would have caused a lot more trouble if they weren't used to him doing this, and he was let off with the usual £75 fine and a beating.

None of the many beatings we saw Alonso getting seemed to trouble him much. Partly, he said, this was because leakage from his brain implants had rendered him immune to pain, although they had somehow heightened his susceptibility to boredom, which made his conversations with us so painful, which he didn't mind. In fact, he seemed to think that he was performing a public service by letting people duff him up: 'I may not look physically imposing, but I spent a year working on the Virgin Sex Ferries, so I know how to handle myself, and if you want to take a pop at me, that's okay' he'd shout into hair salons and anything he thought might be the Annual General Meeting of Honda Motor Company Ltd.

Virgin Atlantic Sex Ferries had been launched by the elderly billionaire, Sir Richard Branson, as a competitor to P&O's unpopular trans-Atlantic sex hovercraft, which had a reputation for flipping over in a high wind or low wind. Branson's initial idea had been to run regular sex ferries across the Atlantic, combining freight and fun: down in the hold, dozens of shipping containers packed with useful goods and trafficked sex workers; while on the upper decks, passengers would be able to enjoy a luxurious sex buffet, and a terrible buffet. The first two ferries set off from Southampton, with crowds cheering and waving special Virgin-branded dildos that a beaming Sir Richard had dropped in boxes by helicopter onto the docks, killing several well-wishers. The first of these ferries, the magnificent *Scarlet Cyst*, washed up on a Nova Scotia beach about a month later, with everyone on board dead, apart from some of the grateful sex workers who were liberated from their crates, given a meal and fresh lingerie, and taken into slavery.

The cause of death of the passengers and crew was never determined, although horrified health inspectors narrowed it down to dysentery or anal sex. The other ferry, the 300-berth *Angry Phallus*, mysteriously vanished about an hour into its maiden voyage: it had barely sailed past the headquarters of Bournemouth Torpedo Club testing range when it simply disappeared into the ocean.

Worried that the losses would affect the Virgin Atlantic Sex Ferry brand, Sir Richard himself helmed the third ferry on the opening leg of its Atlantic crossing, and the ferry might well have made it across had it not been struck by a superheated tungsten rod dropped from space by a Chinese satellite. The boat was atomised in what many of the delighted passengers mistook as an orgasm, and the seawater boiled for miles around, but luckily Sir Richard himself was not aboard: a few minutes earlier he'd left the deck of the ferry aboard a helicopter, which was struck by a shock wave so intense that all the skin of his body was ripped off, and the last thing he saw was his skeleton leaping out through the windscreen of the cockpit like a gymnast.

The company limped on for a few months, running a reduced service from France to the UK, which is when Alonso joined the crew . . .

I was surprised to get the job: it seemed they'd misread my file, and thought that I was an Irish sailor called S. O'Fender. I was given a new employee orientation pack, which contained just enough mescaline to receive my 'welcome aboard' message from the Hindu river goddess, Yamuna. Soon I was working triple shifts: at nights I'd spend about 8 hours trying to steamhose fluids off the deck after the last game of what seemed to be a sort of adult quoits had finished. Then in the morning I'd serve breakfast, which was a choice of cornflakes or a hand shandy. In all my time on board I never once served a bowl of cornflakes. After that I'd do some extra hours up on the rooftop swimming pool, which we'd filled with shower gel, washing powder and cola: it functioned as a sort of antibiotic sheep dip for the passengers and was the only way we kept the genital lice under any sort of control.

Dipping was mandatory — passengers would be dipped three times a day, for a minute at a time. We'd adapted a swimming pool leaf rake which was used to hold them under, or fish them out. I was considered pretty good with the rake, and rarely lost concentration and drowned anyone, in spite of my OxyContin addiction, and had only once drowned anyone on purpose. I remember it well. I'd been teased the night before at the crew disco about how few people I'd drowned in the cola, and I thought: this is crazy, I must have drowned about a dozen passengers last month alone.

Turns out this was an order of magnitude less than the next least most prolific drowner, and I was mocked for over an hour, then people started spitting at me and whipping me with their belts and handbags, and it turned into one of the most brutal beatings I'd been given that entire evening, although I was on so much OxyContin that the constant beatings were like water off a duck's back. The next day I was a monster with that leaf rake. My dips lasted 90 seconds, 2 minutes, 3 minutes, and there was this non-stop cacophony of screaming and wailing that made it impossible for me to think, so I stopped screaming and focused on actually drowning someone.

Then I saw her. She was beautiful, busty, and not a day over 80. She'd got a bad case of lice: I could see them gnawing like tiny piranhas into her groin: her legs dripped with blood and bikini fabric as they gnawed ever closer to an artery. She smiled at me, with quiet dignity, and I nodded, picked up my rake, and with a firm, almost loving swing, I whacked her husband into the dip and held him under until he drowned. Tabitha and I became lovers, our lovemaking tinged with danger and excitement, as I lost so much blood when we slept together that I barely made it out of the hammock alive.

We asked Alonso how Tabitha ranked in his table of sexual partners. He thought for a moment. 'Twenty . . . sixth? No, seventh.' He explained that there had been some recent chart movement, especially since he'd been working weekend shifts as a doorman at the Cheveux 2000 nail salon, despite them begging him not to. 'I have a top three,' said Frankie proudly, licking his lips as he knelt to sniff the letterbox of Roti Joupa Caribbean takeaway. 'When the hell are they open? I need my goat curry.' It was half eight in the morning. 'There's that halal butchers opposite Bush Hall – we could probably get some there and cook it up at Endemol,' suggested Charlie. 'We just need a saucepan and an electric hob. We can pick up some cumin seeds, cardamom, onions, garlic, beef stock and ginger, brown the meat off in the pan first, and set it to simmer in that kitchen on the fifth floor, I'm sure no one will mind.'

They did mind, and it led to a blanket ban on stewing at the office, a complete refit of the kitchen on the fifth floor, an evacuation of the entire building, and Channel 4 having to reschedule the read-through of *Nish Kumar's News Twist*, so we found ourselves at a loose end. Luckily Roti Joupa's was opening, and so we met up there with Alonso, and while Frankie waited for his goat curry with pilau rice he listed his top three: 'Shania Twain one, obviously. Just amazing. That rare combination of stamina, inventiveness and pity. Then my old piano teacher Miss Clayton, she's number two. And at three . . .' He paused, and pursed his lips as he always does when accessing a sexual memory. 'Well?' said Alonso, feigning boredom but mildly curious. 'At three, I have to put Chen Jin, the former badminton world champion and Olympic bronze medallist. His touch and feel were incredible. Beyond anything I've ever experienced, apart from that of Miss Clayton and Shania.'

Chen had worked as a consultant on Frankie's badminton-based sitcom *Shuttlecocks*, which had just been cancelled again. Frankie played blacklisted sports physiotherapist Jackson Grinder, who was fighting to clear his name with the national governing body of badminton in Scotland, Badminton Scotland, and get his licence back. Chen Jin had a cameo as Chen Qiang, a badminton player who complains to Badminton Scotland after a shoulder treatment from Jackson Grinder leaves him with a career-threatening distrust of deep-tissue massage.

'When it comes to intimate partners, I only have a top two,' said Charlie sadly. 'Myself and Chen Jin.' Frankie dropped his takeaway tub and with a mighty spray of pilau rice and special sauce, roared, 'What did you say?' He drew back a fist, knocking over a stack of menus. 'Not Chen Jin the badminton player,' cried Charlie, 'a different Chen Jin! Look online! You'll find another Chen Jin!' Frankie whipped out his phone, but in his fury typed Jing instead of Jin. 'You mean Chen Jing, the 1988 women's table tennis Olympic gold medallist?' Charlie nodded. 'Yes, she's my number two.' And he pursed his lips, thinking about Chen Jin while Alonso reminisced about Tabitha and Frankie picked up the menus.

That summer, for several months, I lived with Tabitha as man and wife under a boulder on Exmoor. It was an idyllic time, except for on the second day, during some renovation work I was doing on our 'bedroom', scraping out some earth to make it a bit roomier, the boulder rolled slightly, trapping her ankle. I heaved and strained for several minutes trying to break her femur, but no joy. Luckily she had a nice view of the sunset, and the big tuft of grass behind her head served as a pillow. Another stroke of luck was that the ants who lived in the tuft seemed, after a few days, to be less interested in biting her than in 'farming' the lice which lived in her smalls. I observed them with the keen eye of someone with nothing else to look at. They would seemingly tickle the lice with their jaws, and the lice, presumably terrified, would offer up a small bead of processed blood, which the ant would carry back to the tuft.

We settled down into a happy rhythm, disturbed only by the constant sobbing and pleading of Tabitha. Eventually, after ten or twelve weeks, a large and boisterous ram which had befriended us attempted to mount Tabitha, and furious at not being able to find the right angle (I shared his frustration!) butted his hard skull mightily against the boulder, which shifted off Tabitha onto his own back leg, trapping it. Sensing a plumper host, Tabitha's lice swarmed from her bony pelvis onto the confused beast, and Tabitha and I left Exmoor hand in hand, praising our good fortune, to the waning howls of Big Sheepy, as I had christened him. Singing and laughing we made our way north to the Bristol Channel, which was so thick with bodies that it might have been possible to walk straight across to Cardiff, not that anyone in their right mind would want to do such a thing.

Many of these dead would have come from the bustling death jetties which operated a short way upriver from Hinkley. At this stage of its destruction, enough of the Severn Bridge was standing at both ends that it functioned as two thriving suicide piers, which the despairing would reach mainly by road, but also on the twice-daily Gloucester death raft, which was sometimes capsized by impatient passengers if they spotted a long queue for the diving boards that had been rigged up along both edges, allowing users to bounce upwards for another couple of metres of drop.

3. The Death Jumpers of the River Severn

The Severn Death Jetties became a focal point for the Samaritans, one of Britain's largest gangs, which went about the country trying to stop people committing suicide so that they could sell them as factory slaves. The Samaritans sent dozens of their best suicide negotiators to try and coax jumpers back from the edge and into one of their padlocked wagons, but these conversations, often long and emotional, caused terrible delays and board blocking: tempers flared as the gridlock spread, and many of the negotiators were killed by frustrated jumpers, who would rush from the queue, seize a negotiator in a furious death cuddle, wrestle them out onto the nearest diving board, get a good bounce going, and backflip them over the edge, to great cheers and applause.

If a negotiator survived the fall by deftly twisting the body of the jumper underneath himself, he would soon feel himself pushed back under the waves by the insistent oar of one of the euthanasia canoeists, provided by the vestiges of Monmouthshire County Council, who circled the drop zone day and night, finishing off the unconscious and injured, and stealing their shoes. So many of these canoeists were killed in the line of duty by people landing on top of them that the job became popular among suicidal Welsh public sector workers, which was all of them.

Eventually the Samaritans who were stationed on the jetties realised that their only option, under the circumstances, was to use their honed negotiating skills to try and speed up the suicides of anyone having second thoughts as they stepped out onto the diving board.

They had bullhorns to hurry the crowds along: they'd reassure them that they were doing the right thing and wouldn't be missed, and list reasons why their lives weren't worth living. 'Where are you from?' they'd ask, and whatever the answer, they do a minute or so of observational material about what a shithole it was, recycling the same lines over and over, and applying them to different places, because no one ever saw them twice.

There came to be quite a carnival atmosphere on the jetties, with jumpers dressing up as their favourite birds, farm animals or figures from popular culture, like the late Justin Lee Collins, whose career took a surprising upturn during the early apocalypse thanks to the success of *Splosh!* which he co-hosted with Tamsin Callahan, and the televising of the subsequent Callahan v. Collins trial, which led to his televised execution, which he co-hosted with Tamsin Callahan, at least partially.

Few of the jumpers dressed as Callahan because her appearance was so relentlessly drab (she never appeared on screen or in public without her trademark grey tarpaulin covering her whole head and body), preferring the fishnet stockings, lace panties, high-heels, suspenders and full Cherokee headdress worn by Collins. Usually, his lingerie was in red or burgundy, but for his execution by lethal injection he opted for bridal white, and crotchless. This was a favourite outfit for jumpers, who would also mimic the way Collins shook and frothed during the repeatedly botched execution, or the way he managed, as the fourth cocktail of drugs entered his arm, to tear free from his restraints and kangaroo around the execution room screaming 'good times' while trying to strangle himself with a garter belt.

Little did Justin Lee Collins realise, the procedure was being filmed as part of an execution prank show called *Capital Funishment*, and the drugs being pumped into his arm were a hilarious hotch-potch of uppers, downers, freshly brewed coffee, paint thinner, ketchup, household cleaning products and the urine of the show's co-hosts, Dicky Shingles and celebrity paramedic Nareen O'Connor, both hidden from Collins' view in the room next door. Viewers could phone the show, suggesting liquids for the next injection, with 'tabasco' being the most popular request. 'Again with the tabasco!' Shingles would hoot, splashing yet more hot sauce into the syringe.

Collins survived seventeen different 'lethal injections' before finally succumbing to a huge dose of PCP, mayonnaise, fluoride mouthwash and eucalyptus essential oil, injected into his hepatic artery, and was pronounced dead by O'Connor, in her penultimate appearance on the show. Collins' erection lasted a full 45 minutes post-mortem.

The following week, much to her dismay, O'Connor found herself the butt of the joke: tricked by the irrepressible Dicky Shingles into being executed by hanging. Little did Shingles realise, O'Connor had also been busy behind the scenes, tricking Shingles himself into being executed, and the show's final episode, featuring a split-screen double hanging, was watched live by a remarkable forty-seven people, far above average for a primetime BBC1 show at the time. The show was cancelled the following week due to a lack of hosts, but the footage of Justin Lee Collins' execution remained a staple of broadcasters the world over: within a few years, most channels in most countries were just showing the full 7-hour episode on a constant loop.

There was something about Collins' agonising demise in exquisite lingerie that chimed perfectly with the collapse of civilisation, and people found it comforting, in the very darkest times, to be reminded that however awful things were, someone else had suffered more. And his cockstand, that stood so boldly against the powers of darkness and decay, even beyond the death of its host, became a universal symbol of hope. There was nothing tragic about its final droop; it was not so much a giving-in as a quiet and noble acceptance, on its own terms, of its fate, and was traditionally watched in total silence, or while banging saucepans together, as the camera slowly zoomed in, capturing those famous fourteen twitches that the Pope officially identified with the Stations of the Cross in her encyclical *Mirabile Splendor Justinian*.

The Pope was another favourite character for Severn jumpers, but confusingly she also favoured white lingerie, also crotchless, except on Pentecost when she spent the day naked in prayer. But she tended to carry a large, bejewelled electric cattle prod, with which she kept her cardinals in order, attached by a golden cable to a motorcycle battery which she carried around in a rucksack on her back, and these signifiers became essential parts of novelty Pope costumes, which the suicidal could buy at any of the all-night fancy dress emporiums that grew up around the jetties.

> *The stench of the dead was so strong as we came round Hinkley Point that it came close to masking the stench from the burning power stations, although it didn't touch the sides of the stench from Tabitha's leg, which visibly fumed with poison, and had all but come away. We decided the best thing for Tabitha was to lie on the beach and let crabs*

and seagulls take the limb and clean the stump — but imagine our surprise: they were all dead! Gulls and shellfish littered the beach, with nothing to feast on them! We laughed heartily about this for several minutes, although I could never tell with Tabitha whether it was genuine laughter or the sound of the spirit leaving her body.

I was about to perform the surgery myself using the edge of an oyster shell when I spied one of nature's finest physicians, a seal, heading slowly towards us along the beach. It sort of nuzzled at the main wound, but didn't seem hungry and decided instead to roll onto its back, let out a throaty rattle and die. We realised this probably had something to do with the burning power stations, which most likely also accounted for the burning in our throats and our nosebleeds and lesions. A passing taxidermist asked us how much we wanted for the seal, and I said: 'We have no need of money, but if you could help me pull this lady's leg off the seal is yours.'

There was some further bartering, in which I offered him Tabitha's leg in exchange for directions to Weston-super-Mare, at which point the horrified taxidermist took off one of his magnificent gullskin gloves and shook a stern finger at us. 'You ignorant fools! For your sake, I shall under no circumstances give you directions to Weston-super-Mare!' he said, pointing north-east, towards Weston-super-Mare, and then realising he'd given away the directions, he pointed in lots of other directions, and I became very confused and angry and ate handfuls of seaweed to try and get my strength up before the fist fight that I sensed was looming.

Then I realised: he wasn't a taxidermist. He'd dodged all of my questions when I asked for his taxidermy qualifications or references, and he was naked apart from his waders, and the whole conversation *had taken place while he amused himself with the warm corpse of the seal, and he wore a T-shirt saying 'I am a necrophile, ask me why'. I started to think he might be a necrophile, especially when he asked me if he could keep Tabitha's leg as a sex toy. This led to an animated debate about whether it still counted as necrophilia if the person whose dead limb you are having sex with is still alive. I lost the debate two votes to one, but we struck a deal, and parted friends: he with Tabitha's leg tucked under his arm, and Tabitha and I with directions to Weston-super-Mare.*

The breathtaking fires from the three burning Hinkley Point power stations lasted more than a decade, and were a popular subject for landscape artists who already had cancer. Much like landscape artists, nuclear power didn't survive long into the apocalypse, but played a key part in its success as a planetary-level catastrophe. At the time Alonso was passing Hinkley the fires were long past their gorgeous best, but this meant that he got to see the tail fins from some of the fourteen airliners that had been hijacked by advocates of tighter security around nuclear power stations, and flown into the Hinkley Point power stations to show how vulnerable they were.

4. The Sad Fate of the Improverts

So many aircraft were flown into nuclear power stations over the next several years that sometimes nuclear reactors held welcome ceremonies on the roof as the plane barrelled towards them. The centrepiece was often a man in a ceremonial headpiece screaming that this didn't really say anything about power station security, and that all it demonstrated was problems with airline security.

The scenario of a plane destroying a reactor became a staple of comedy sketch troupes: usually a sketch would involve announcements being made over the tannoy by the pilot or a hijacker, but sometimes it would focus on an amusing variation of the cabin crew's safety demonstration. Survivors of the last ever performance by the 'Improverts' at the last ever Edinburgh Festival recall that all but one of their skits revolved around reactor meltdowns, mass shootings and suicide bombings. However, what turned out to be their final sketch featured a driving test in which the examiner suffered from short-term memory loss and the driver had a fear of driving tests, both of which conditions had a noticeable effect on the country & western duet they were singing.

Tragically, no one ever got to find out what was going to be rhymed with 'hazard perception test' because, in a turn of events that the reviewer from the *Edinburgh Evening News* didn't describe as anything because he was dead, the two Improverts on stage were cut down by automatic gunfire from the audience; one died instantly and the other managed to gurgle the opening of 'Home, Home on the Range' before expiring, which was met with confused whoops and a round of applause.

Not missing a beat, two other Improverts tagged themselves into the scene, and were promptly shot in the face and guts, as the audience laughed and whooped. Building on the screams and gurgles of their improv mates, the remaining Improverts tagged themselves in as the action seamlessly morphed into a scene about a massacre at an improvisation workshop, and called out for suggestions, answered – aptly enough – by the insistent boom of a Benelli M4 semi-automatic shotgun, which itself was barely heard over the noise of several MG-74 belt-fed machine guns.

Most of the audience lay dead, along with most of the Improverts and their fantastic technical crew, who'd done an amazing job of matching music to the killings before being slain. As the last living member of the backstage team desperately tried to lower the lights, he found himself facing the raised barrel of a Sig Sauer P320 XCompact. In a wheezing spray of blood and saliva he asked: 'Why are you doing this? Why? And what do you want as your exit track, how about "Memories" by Maroon 5?' The Sig Sauer barked its answer.

A handful of Improverts were found in a huddle backstage, trying to pep each other up for a new game they'd devised called 'Hiding', and were taken hostage by the assailants, who declared that they would be released upon signed pledges by the Edinburgh Festival Fringe to improve safety at their comedy venues. However, none were ever released, much to the relief of their friends and family.

Five Improverts survived the slaughter, although one was beyond help. He weakly asked that he be euthanised in the style of a heist movie, and there was a dreamy gladness in his eyes as he watched the paramedics improvise a scene in which they had to concoct an elaborate plan to get a syringe full of barbiturates into his carotid artery in order to steal a tiara. The other four Improverts disappeared without trace, turning up a couple of years later as novelty sex slaves. Customers paid handsomely for a sex worker at whom they could shout genres of hand job; who could happily fist you while pretending to be a hip-hop vampire, or a depressed fishmonger, and then finish you off in the character of a hip-hop pirate captain who's just been on an anger management course.

When Alonso discovered that he could, if he wanted, go up to the Edinburgh Festival and see the current incarnation of the doomed Improverts, he shuddered with a mixture of fear and the five rounds of tequila mochatinis we'd had at the Be At One cocktail bar next to Ladbrokes, where he'd ducked out for a meeting with the VP of Content (Scripted) at Netflix UK, Lenore Zumsteg, who'd heard that Alonso might have a couple of Adam Sandler vehicles up his sleeve. Alonso liked holding pitch meetings in betting shops as he found the televised greyhound races helped fill in gaps in the conversation and provided useful inspiration for character names, like Mr Greyhound and Mrs Six-to-Four Favourite, and locations (greyhound tracks).

Lenore liked his idea for a rom-com set in the rough-and-tumble world of dog racing called *The 15.07 at Romford* in which Adam Sandler would play a bumbling trainer (Gary Trap Number 3) who comes good, but was less keen on his idea for a heist movie set in the rough-and-tumble world of dog racing called *The 15.26 at Romford* as she thought it might clash. This was one of those make-or-break moments in pitch meetings that Alonso thrived on. 'What if we called it *The 15.48 at Suffolk Downs?*' She thought for a moment. 'Perfect.'

Over a celebratory mango daiquiri, Alonso shared his concerns about going to Edinburgh to see the Improverts: he was worried that if he were to attend a performance, instead of shouting out an amusing location for a song or a sketch, he might run onstage and start punching the cast in the face and elbowing them in the throat to try and warn them of the horror that awaits their troupe. We assured him that although meddling in the future is a delicate business, delivering this stern warning would be the right thing to do, morally, and might even get a round of applause from the audience. We went online immediately to book tickets but, unfortunately for the Improverts of the future, got distracted by porn.

5. Tales From the Sheffield Sex Corridor

On our stroll south under Hammersmith Flyover we stopped off at the public lavatories which, in a wry flourish typical of the moment, had been designed by the council to resemble old telephone boxes. 'The thing about improv,' said Charlie, wiping himself with the loo paper that had been cleverly styled to look like an advertising card for a prostitute, 'and this is the big unspoken thing that all improvisers dance around: it's that, at any moment, they could just kill themselves. That option is always on the table. But they never go for it. Every time I go to an improv show, I always shout out "Just fucking kill yourself" a few times, but they pretend not to hear me or they get security to throw me out of the venue. They're such cowards. Don't ask for suggestions if you're not prepared to kill yourself.'

'I agree,' said Frankie, not really paying attention. He was trying to help Alonso with a drug deal; he bought a bag of pills and a loaded syringe off Alonso, who showed Frankie where into the base of his spine he should inject it. He was saying 'no more than half' when he slipped in some excrement and fell against Frankie, injecting the whole syringe into Frankie's lower back. 'Oh fuck, quick, we have to get to Chicago Grill before your legs go. Thank God you've just emptied your bowels.' Charlie and Alonso each took an arm, and helped Frankie across the road, while Alonso explained where he got all of his valuable information about the Improverts.

> *I met the last of the Improverts at the Sheffield Red Light District. He was old and bent, and not as quick as he used to be, but still had a knack for sexual improv, and noshed me off in a variety of unscripted styles. I was impressed by his ability to rim me in the style of a hip-hop dentist, and he seemed to enjoy playing with himself like a robot that needed oiling. 'Squeak, squeak, beep, beep, squeak' he went, as he jerked away at his wizened penis, and it was so amusing I almost smiled. He then teabagged me as a hip-hop baseball coach, which wasn't funny but I was having my balls sucked so I didn't mind. We finished off our session with a satisfying 20 minutes of solid ploughing, which he received in the character of a disassociating pensioner. 'Three stars!' I screamed as I ejaculated. 'Out of a possible five!'*

At its peak, the Sheffield Red Light District was a 30-metre-wide strip of massage yurts and fuck huts which stretched the entire width of the country, from Runcorn in the west to Mablethorpe funfair on the Lincolnshire coast. This sex corridor provided a useful trading route between Holland and Ireland, a Suez Canal for genital infections, allowing the two great research centres into the contraction of sexually transmitted diseases to share their latest outbreaks without having to use the circuitous coastal route of fishermen and surfers.

At its centre, it passed through the vaults of Sheffield Cathedral, where pilgrims could view a variety of sacred relics, including several genuine splinters from the wooden fisting chair built by Jesus himself, still worshipped as the first great sex carpenter. There was still an element of torture to the crucifixion scenes painted on the crypt walls, but it was now generally represented horizontally, with the 'nails' pressed into the hands of the Redeemer belonging to the two thieves, and the Centurion's 'spear' that entered him returned to its pre-metaphorical glory.

Once, during his many explorations of the corridor, Alonso had been foolish enough to descend a set of strangely lit steps with nudey posters peeling off lacquered walls, where, to his horror, he found himself trapped in the dreaded Dungworth Porn Dungeons, forced at dildo-point to browse flickering shelves of confusing erotica, rusty handcuffs and empty VHS boxes with handwritten titles. As he reached out for a copy of *Extreme Buttocks 13*, a rack of empty lubricant bottles toppled onto him, and the cashier chuckled, spraying him in the face with a bottle marked FERANOMES. 'Maybe you'd like to see something a bit harder?' she asked, pushing him through a curtain into a strangely odoured darkness, where he found himself tumbling down, down, onto a mattress in an empty street.

He dusted himself off and spent some time trying to assess whether this, the outside and apparent freedom, was simply a continuation of the porn dungeon. Perhaps it was meant as a sardonic punchline, intended to insinuate that life itself was porn. If it is, mused Alonso, I suppose the real pity is that nobody is watching. And perhaps the whole fabric of human morality and ethics is an attempt to create a viewer for the pornography of our lives.

He marched off and took a room at Tapton Hall. The 'breakfast buffet' was not what he was expecting. It was an actual breakfast buffet. None of it was edible, of course, but the host had made an effort to find and decorate bricks and stones that somewhat resembled single portion packets of cereal and chocolate croissants. 'My compliments to the chef,' said Alonso, settling his bill with a handful of cogs that he'd found under the wardrobe in his room. 'You can thank him yourself,' smiled the receptionist, and ushered him through a beaded curtain next to her desk.

Alonso found himself tumbling headlong into a flickering porn emporium. He rolled to a stop next to a display of what might once have been sexy nurse outfits. The cashier looked down at him. 'How was your breakfast?' This cycle went on for about two years, until Alonso managed to escape through a maintenance hatch underneath a shelf of nipple clamps. 'So yes, apart from Dungworth, which I'd stay particularly clear of, other porn dungeons to avoid are: the Frodsham Porn Dungeons, I was stuck there for one very unpleasant Easter weekend and a little of the following week; the North Ormsby Porn Dungeons, that was the worst breakfast I've ever had; and the Whaley Bridge Porn Dungeons, where I was trapped for about six months. I only managed to escape by tricking the cashier into marriage. Basically,' he concluded, 'don't go into any porn dungeons. That's a lesson I wish I'd learned earlier in the apocalypse.'

Frankie found this story difficult to follow due to the powerful opiate cocktail that was pulsing through him. He felt his knees give way and the world around him tremble and throb. We hustled him through the door of the Chicago Grill on Fulham Palace Road, the flavour hub of Hammersmith.

'They spell it "flavor" on their website,' whimpered Frankie, scrolling down the menu on his phone, even though we were standing in front of the menu; 'the American way, without the letter "u", like Flavor Flav.' He stared at a little animated gif of a delivery driver in the top corner. 'This is the most beautiful thing I've ever seen,' he said, collapsing. 'You know that I know all the lyrics to all the Public Enemy songs. Go on, test me.' Alonso rushed over, to check if Frankie wanted red onions on his burger. 'Yeah, onions. You want me to sing "Cold Lampin' With Flavor" off their second studio album, *It Takes a Nation of Millions to Hold Us Back* – you want me to sing it?'

Charlie and Alonso were ordering a Mighty Meat Feast and a Peri Peri Chicken Deluxe, and getting a Chicago Cheese Steak burger with an extra 6 oz patty and extra red onions for Frankie. 'OK, I'll sing it. It begins with a sample of the legendary DJ Mr. Magic, which goes . . .'

Frankie lay on the floor by the counter, telling the story of the Mr. Magic sample on 'Cold Lampin' With Flavor' to the lady behind him, Lenore Zumsteg, the VP of Content (Scripted) at Netflix UK, who ordered a Michigan BBQ Combo over his twitching body. While Frankie performed 'Cold Lampin' With Flavor' to the shins of the queue, Leonore joined Charlie and Alonso, who sipped at his Kinder Bueno milkshake suspiciously.

'You're a hard man to track down,' she said, pushing another Kinder Bueno milkshake across the table towards him. 'Consider this a signing bonus.' Alonso's eyes lit up. 'You want me at Netflix?' She laughed. 'No. We *need* you. Your ideas have got everyone really excited for the first time since we made *Ironyman* with Ryan Reynolds. Did you see it? So much irony. So many layers. Ryan really took the irony to the next level. I don't know how he did it, physically. He wasn't happy about some elements of the deal, or so he said; it's hard to tell with him.'

Frankie had dragged himself over to their table, and was mid-song, although he was now singing it at about a quarter of the standard speed. Alonso picked up his bonus and sloshed it over Frankie's head. 'Just fucking stop. You're embarrassing me in front of my assistant.' He spun round to a shocked Leonore. 'That's right, Leonore, I'm being given your job. I got a text from Sergio while I was taking a shit under the flyover!'

Charlie sighed. 'Why does everything we say have to be so crude? Why can't we just speak nicely to each other for a change?' Alonso whipped back towards Charlie, pulling a muscle in his ribs. 'Agh, fuck! Fuck fuck fuck. Jesus. What the fuck.' Charlie quickly scribbled Alonso's outburst on a napkin. 'What are you doing? You don't have to write down everything I say.' Charlie carried on scribbling – 'It might be important.' Frankie got a twitching grip on the edge of the table, and said the words: 'A ghost who will stop existing if he can't keep the only guy who remembers him alive,' as slowly as whale song.

'There's your Adam Sandler movie,' hissed Alonso triumphantly. Leonore smiled, as she picked up the phone to Sandler's manager. 'You're a goddamn genius, you know that, don't you.'

So engrossed was Alsono in his new job at Neflix, developing a slate of new drama projects including the Adam Sandler Loveable Time-Traveller Project based loosely on his own life story, set in the quirky world of post-apocalyptic greyhound molesting, that we barely saw him for the next three days until he was fired. With his exit from Netflix, the Loveable Time-Traveller project was indefinitely shelved. Alonso wasn't fussed, as he said the atmosphere at Netflix was 'bitchy', and we didn't mind, because we had bigger fish to fry. We were actually trying to save the world, not pitch for a miniseries. Although, maybe there's something in that idea, with a bit of tweaking. We're happy to take meetings.

6. The Factually Accurate Tale of Dr Higgis

The Great Lake of London, foul and tepid, stretching from Enfield in the north to Croydon in the south, is thought to be the largest man-made impact crater ever carved out by simultaneous hypersonic missile blasts, although there is some disagreement over whether the Abyss of Slough on its western edge should be counted as part of it. Explorers failed to find a bottom to this abyss: the crater bed drops off into an impenetrable pit at the edge of what appears to have been a Holiday Inn Express, and the deepest anyone has ever reached and returned alive and sane is down past the now-vertical forecourt of the Tesco Extra petrol station, to glimpse the half-fallen tower of St Ethelbert's Church which hangs over the pit like a gibbet.

The diver who came closest to finding the bottom of Slough was Dr Graham Higgis, a survivor of the University of Swansea Geography Department's unsuccessful self-immolation climate protests, during which all of the academics who had signed up for the mass suicide found themselves so drenched by the driving rain that they were unable to get themselves properly alight, which was such a disappointment that seven of them tried to hang themselves but the howling rain meant that their ropes kept slipping off the lamp-posts and only three of them managed to die.

When Dr Higgis, his muscles screaming, his Speedos torn and bloody, crawled up onto the beach at Maidenhead, he found himself surrounded by a pack of blind scavengers who lived under the waste pipes of the Windsor Castle leper colony – they'd smelled his boat, set off in their rafts, and now surrounded the traumatised snorkeller, screeching 'What's this? What's this?' while grabbing at his mask and fins. Using his snorkel as a cudgel and his Speedos as an improvised slingshot, Dr Higgis fought like a lion (a lion, that is, from the age before the onset of Lion AIDS which so weakened lions that they became a symbol of weakness and lack of bravery), thwacking his way up the beach to the relative safety of the Volvo dealership on Nordern Road which had been repurposed, like all of the other buildings still standing in Maidenhead, into an emergency brothel.

The sex worker on duty at the gates took pity on him, raised the portcullis, led him shivering to an empty consultation room, settled him into a fisting chair, and with a warm towel gently mopped his penis until Dr Higgis regained consciousness, then charged him £250. He readily agreed, after it was explained to him that the £250 was inclusive of not having his legs broken, and without further ado he squatted and strained to retrieve from his rectum a cellophane bag containing his car keys and wallet, an old pearl diver's trick, which was met with such applause from watching punters that the fee was waived by the management, who passed off the incident as an unscheduled sex show. Cries of 'Encore! Encore!' combined with a light tap on his kneecap with a hammer, persuaded the respected geologist to reinsert and reproduce his wallet a dozen more times, until the cellophane bag tore, leaving his car keys wedged up inside his guts.

Fortunately for Dr Higgis, no hospital on Earth was more capable of retrieving unusual objects from people's arseholes than the team on hand at the brothel, and they set to work, with a variety of oils, clamps, spreaders, scissor jacks, hubcaps, grease guns and compressed-air hoses, much of the equipment salvaged from the flooded basement of a Volvo service garage. A hubcap from a Volvo V70 was held like a catcher's mitt under the gaping backside of Dr Higgis, to catch anything that fell, and as Dr Higgis strained and spasmed it rang like a church bell on Christmas morning.

When Dr Higgis regained consciousness and the applause died down, he was handed his car keys, his wife's wedding ring and an invoice for £4,000 which he paid gladly, as he'd begun to think he'd never get to see that ring again, after eating his wife the previous week. He unhooked his feet from the stirrups, pulled on his Speedos, signed some autographs, and asked how he might go about chartering a cart to Uxbridge. But his kind hosts wouldn't think of letting him leave without first warming himself with a steaming cup of lube and telling them what he'd witnessed in the abyss, as he was muttering all sorts of cryptic and unsettling things during the operation, and they wanted to know: was it true what people were saying about it being the lair of a hyperintelligent crocodile escaped from a research lab under RAF Brize Norton?

Dr Higgis sat back on his fisting chair, took a grateful gulp of lube, and to an audience of fascinated whores and increasingly irritated punters, who suspected, correctly, that this was going to be taken as part of their hour, described what he had seen in the shadows beneath St Ethelbert's tower. It was a tale so astonishing, so full of bizarre detail, chilling and macabre yet at the same time so uplifting, and ultimately affirming of the human spirit, that it was lost to history.

'Thank you for that wonderful, spine-tingling description of all that you experienced in those tumultuous depths,' said the sex worker on portcullis duty, waving as the plucky geologist strode off towards the 4.17 p.m. cart to Uxbridge. 'I'm astonished, given what happened, that you made it out alive, and I hope you make it back safely to your house in . . . I'm sorry, what was the name of the place again?' But Dr Higgis was out of earshot. 'Okay, never mind, bye!' she said, and went back inside to wank someone.

Tragically, Dr Higgis never made it back home to his beloved little house and allotment in Cwmwbwrywnwnystwtyswchgwynrywn-Y-Pwllbrgwyngylwnwnwn, formerly Bedford until it was captured by the Welsh. When he hopped off the cart at Uxbridge, he spent hours looking for his car where he'd left it – up on bricks outside the pillow factory; he'd entrusted the wheels to the Hillingdon rat folk for a small fee – but no matter how much he cuffed and slapped them, none of the squealing rat folk remembered seeing a 2014 Renault Twingo in nautilus blue, or recognised Dr Higgis, and he had the sickening realisation that he'd never owned a car, and that he'd taken the car keys off the body of the man who'd sold him the PCP because he liked the way they jangled, and he didn't live in

Bedford, and the Welsh had never captured it, they never made it across the M1, their army was destroyed at the Battle of Newport Pagnell, and that Cwmwbwrywnwnystwtyswchgwynrywn-Y-Pwllbrgwyngylwnwnwn didn't exist, nor did his beloved little house and allotment, but he was fairly certain that he'd recently eaten his wife, but hadn't travelled to Uxbridge by car: he'd worked his way along the canals as a colliers' bitch, a recognised way of travelling across Britain, and that his name wasn't Graham Higgis, it was Graeme Higgis, and that he was an assassin.

Elite assassin Graeme Higgis took off his Speedos, squatted and clenched. He had a gun somewhere up there, and he needed it to complete his mission. His knuckles whitened, and a small group of rat folk gasped and applauded as the deadly killer strained. With one last desperate gut-heave, out popped the key fob to a 2014 Renault Twingo. He recalled, with a wail of grief that drew more applause, that he'd bitten it off a keyring during his fight with the PCP dealer. He looked closer, and saw that he had also produced a lump of coal, and looked up to see a portly barge stoker in blackened overalls grinning at him lasciviously – and then he remembered. His name was Alonso Lampe and he had spent the last six months working the canals as a stokers' bitch to pay for his PCP habit, and he didn't have a doctorate in geology, and he glumly pulled up his underpants, which weren't swimming trunks, by any stretch of the imagination.

Arwel tugged at the buttons of his grubby overalls and mumbled something, although it was impossible to tell what it was. The only phrase Alonso could make out was 'penetrative sex', which could have meant anything. Off to the side, he heard some hurried squeaks, and turned to see the rat folk voting on something. There was a show of hands, a squeak of what sounded like 'good luck', and quick as a flash one of the Hillingdon rat folk darted towards Alonso, dipping between the brawny legs of the stoker, but got caught up in the overalls which Arwel had unbuttoned, and felt a pair of coal-stained hands grabbing him round the neck – there was a squeal of dismay, ended by a crunching twist, which triggered another hasty ratconference, a squeak of what sounded like 'stupid route', another show of rathands, and a scampering ratgirl dashed up to Alonso's ear, offering him sanctuary in their burrows under the ruins of Swakeley's Roundabout in exchange for the buttplug. 'What buttplug?' asked Alonso, and with an urgent squeak the ratgirl gestured at the lump of coal, which Alonso now saw had been artfully fashioned into a bum stopper. Arwel let out a howl of dismay, for it was his nimble fingers that had so deftly carved the coalplug, and he began yelling and spitting as he heaved up his overalls to give chase, but to his stumbling fury they contained the flopping body of a strangled ratboy which had got itself tangled up in the gusset.

Alonso, who had set off at a sprint, hit upon the idea of inserting the buttplug as a means of blocking the entrance to his anus, much as one would hastily pile furniture in front of a door. Without breaking stride, he managed to ram the coal stopper halfway up at the first attempt. He stopped in his tracks, his mind flooded with memories he didn't recognise: assassinating the President of Bolivia; eating a Sunday roast in a pub in Carmarthen; getting a job in Safeway as a teenager and fingering the woman who worked behind the cigarette counter when her husband was in prison. The Stoker caught up with him, with what Alonso hoped was the ratperson now writhing inside his capacious trousers like a trapped ferret:

'It's your identity Graeme! Your true self, your training, your life as The Dragon, defender of Wales. We encoded it all onto the buttplug so that we could restore you after long periods undercover!'

Alonso must have registered some confusion, and was in any case at that moment reliving a particularly grim memory of a confused conversation he'd had with a physiotherapist about the nature of consent when his wife had been paralysed in a rugby accident. 'What if she's just blinking because she's got something in her eye?' he remembered asking, before the scene dissolved and he was standing over the stoker's dead body, with a bloody buttplug in his hand.

He examined the carefully fashioned plug: it was carved with an intricate series of bumps and ridges; a Morse code for the arse, no doubt. An incredible piece of invention, but also possibly the key to understanding who he really was. He threw it into a campfire a few nights later and it smelled terrible.

Now destitute, Alonso managed to get a job at the Hillingdon pillow factory, as a trainee cushion plumper. A vacancy in the department opened up when one of the employees, Raphael, was stabbed in the car park, which Alonso happened to see because he was doing it. The factory was bustling and Alonso enjoyed his time there, even though the hours were long and his workmates tended to shun him in the canteen due to his reputation for having stabbed Raphael in the car park.

'To be fair, he stabbed me first,' laughed Alonso. 'Or he would have done, if I'd come at him from the front. Don't worry, we both soon saw the funny side. We became friends, and I helped get him another job at the factory when we stabbed someone in R&D. Which stands for "rectum and dick". He worked in quality control.'

The boom in the post-apocalyptic pillow manufacturing sector, matched by a similar uptick in sofa cushion sales, was for a long time attributed by people pretending to be economists solely to the demand for cheap, comfortable euthanasia equipment, but other factors were in play. Most chairs, sofas and beds had been burned as firewood or repurposed as weapons, and people craved the simple luxury of having somewhere comfortable to sit and relax in the gaps between smothering friends and relatives.

Additionally, everyone was so emaciated that stuffing a cushion up your jumper was a simple way to appear plump and well fed while you staggered about the ruins of your community. Similarly, people would stuff smaller lumbar pillows down the backs of their trousers and leggings in order to simulate buttock implants, and would chat about how wonderful their plastic surgeon is: 'Oh darling, you must go to Dr Stebbington, he's not cheap but he's an absolute magician with sillicone.' It was considered good manners to compliment someone's 'patootie' or 'rump-a-dump-dumplings', but wolf-whistling was frowned upon because it tended to attract dogs.

Utter sincerity was required when complimenting someone's fake butt enhancements, and should your cry of 'sweet badonkadonk' as someone staggered past contain even the merest iota of irony it would be enough for someone to whip out their tushy cushions and smother you, or try to. There was so much interpersonal smothering going on by this stage that people became expert in breathing out of the side of their mouths – with even the terminally ill able to survive under a standard boudoir cushion face-pressing for several hours. Also, people were so enfeebled by famine and disease that quite often an attempted smothering would result in both parties falling asleep next to each other on the cushions: waking up feeling refreshed and ready to discuss another trip to the plastic surgeon.

The conversations about these non-existent plastic surgeons became so detailed, with price comparisons, gossip about bad breath, and endless praise of their wizardry with the scalpel, that people began to fill the roles, even setting up plastic surgery clinics, where they would attempt to perform buttock enhancement operations, often by pushing bits of cushion stuffing under people's skin, and quickly stitching them up so they could wander around, soaking up the praise from passers-by on how thicc they looked before bleeding to death.

7. The Big Ben Kamikaze Incident, Sponsored by Red Bull

The burning of the Palace of Westminster was such a success that the authorities (at that time it appears to have been the Boilermakers Union, which ran both the Lambeth Suicide Cauldrons and the Vauxhall Soup Kitchens) decided to rebuild parliament and burn it again on numerous occasions, although the size of the buildings tended to shrink each time they were rebuilt, until the final incarnation of the House of Commons, after 200+ burnings, was roughly the size of a caravan, being in fact a caravan, which was loomed over on its northern edge by 'Big Ben', the name given to a lamp-post attached to the side of the caravan, which fell on top of the caravan during the 493rd hearing of the Policing and Crime Bill, killing the Honourable Member for the Unholy Wastes (formerly North Norfolk). The last distinguishable House of Lords was a tarpaulin stretched from Big Ben to a nearby tree (the Members' Lobby), functioning in much the same way as it did pre-apocalypse, by covering up the entrance to some sex catacombs.

The original Big Ben (or 'Elizabeth Tower', as it was never known by anyone) had collapsed a decade or so previously, during the Red Bull sponsored Festival of Kamikaze, with the decisive strike attributed to a grandchild of the former Chancellor of the Exchequer, Jeremy Hunt, in a Cessna 172 Skyhawk laden with fertiliser bombs, fireworks, CCTV cameras and his screaming grandfather. The footage from inside the aircraft, showing the furious efforts of the elderly Lord Hunt to come to terms with the throttle, flaps and trim wheel of a Cessna 172 Skyhawk, was the last thing broadcast on British television, and perhaps the best.

The continued success of Red Bull during the early days of societal disintegration was due in large part to its popularity with the suicidal, who found it to be an excellent carrier fluid for poisons, masking the taste of even the most acrid. The sugar-free variety was considered the best medium for barbiturates. If you wanted to get some weedkiller down you, the watermelon or tropical fruit flavours were recommended, but should never be mixed.

The brand suffered a setback, however, at the Festival of Kamikaze, when a twin-engined Piper PA-34-180, attempting to crash into the House of Commons, overshot and ploughed into the Red Bull VIP stands in Parliament Square, killing thirty-five members of its marketing and PR department, along with executives from several major weedkiller companies, with a portion of the tail fin lobotomising the celebrity DJ, Paris Hilton, who, much to her credit, managed to complete her set and go on to marry the Senior Vice President of Distribution at Weedol.

8. The Gnostics of Barnsley

Several winters into the Darkening, rumours began to spread that a precious trove of ancient wisdom had been preserved by the reclusive Gnostics of Barnsley. This mysterious sect seems to have emerged from a local pub darts league, which sensed that the tide of civilisation was turning, and that everything they knew and cherished would soon be swept away, so they set about secretly committing as much of civilisation to memory as they could. The darts matches became cover for their discussions: the two team members with the worst memories would play against each other, game after game, while the others huddled over a notepad, pretending to be arguing over a score, so that anyone looking over to their corner of the pub might think that a normal game of pub darts was taking place. They bought some important books and magazines and began distilling the wisdom of several thousand years of human thought into some easy to remember rhymes and acronyms. Everything went well, until one of the landlords, assuming it was yet another paedophile ring pretending to be a pub darts league, reported them to the police.

After a six-month investigation, it was discovered that three members of the league were actually paedophiles, who'd been using the matches to exchange child pornography, and they were swiftly voted out of the organisation. Unfortunately, everyone now thought they were a paedophile ring, and all of their regular venues cancelled their dartboard bookings, apart from one – a pub which was run by an enthusiastic paedophile, who was keen to join their ring. They realised, with heavy hearts, that the only way they could carry on their vital work of preserving civilisation was in the guise of a paedophile ring in the guise of a pub darts league.

This plan was reasonably successful for a while: every time the landlord came over to their table by the dartboard, they just had to start muttering approvingly about lowering the age of consent and quietly swap online grooming tips. Sometimes he'd join them for a sneaky pint, and they'd be expected to describe illegal images they'd recently seen, or share new arguments justifying sexual relations with a minor, and grumble about how AI was ruining child porn and how you shouldn't trust anything these days except a Polaroid.

Eventually, after the landlord began pressing them to lend him some Polaroids, they realised that they had no alternative but to turn one of their garages into a studio and mock up scenes of child sexual abuse using dolls – keeping the lighting low, the angles awkward, and smearing a little bit of Vaseline on the lens to blur it. The shoot went okay, but they were nervous handing over their first batch of Polaroids. They needn't have worried: the landlord loved these images, and began distributing them around a couple of the other paedophile rings he was in.

As demand grew, they had to spend more and more of their spare time molesting dolls. But it was worth it, because the landlord had started charging substantial amounts for the best of these Polaroids, and was pretty fair about handing the payments back to the darts league minus a 20% handling fee.

These were the good times. The champagne flowed, they were driving fast cars, wearing fancy trousers, throwing platinum darts, and they could afford to ship in some really creepy dolls from Japan, which paid for themselves within a month. It was only when one of the senior players, the respected left-hander Bill Smeaton, who always threw his third dart with a characteristic twitch of his trailing foot, lost control of his Maserati on Market Hill in a pair of $4,000 corduroys while off his tits on speedballs, and with a highly realistic doll, Yuki, strapped into a child seat next to him, and spun the car in through the front window of a Ladbrokes betting shop, and was beheaded, as was poor Yuki, by a large piece of glass, that the others realised they'd lost their way.

The body of Yuki was never found, presumably stolen by a surviving customer, but Yuki's head was so torn up by the glass that the thief decided to leave it, perching it on the shoulders of Bill Smeaton, which caused the ambulance crew several seconds of intense confusion and many years of nightmares. The confusion surrounding this chimaera was made all the worse when CPR caused it to cough up such a deluge of semen that the paramedic looked like he'd been left for the cops by Spider-Man.

At an emergency meeting of the darts league, a majority of the players decided to continue in the lucrative business of mocking up child porn, while the others, led by Linda Dooley, not a flashy player but steady and unflappable, who played most weekends at the George and Dragon pub on Summer Lane until she was banned for being a suspected paedophile, decided to get back to their original aim of preserving the fruits of civilisation from the impending chaos. The core sect met in Linda's ex-husband Keith's garage.

Keith and Linda were still on good terms, even though Keith thought she was a paedophile. As a cover story, Linda told him that the people meeting in his garage were a support group for recovering sex offenders, and he was just glad she was getting the help she needed, and even left a carrier bag of snacks and soft drinks. At their first meeting, the five remaining players decided that the best place to start, in terms of things to memorise, were things they already knew quite a lot about, and top of the list was darts.

They started to memorise darts trivia and important results. So, for example, at the 1984 World Matchplay tournament, what did Keith Deller have left when 'Old Stoneface' John Lowe completed his famous nine-dart finish? The answer: 342. This information was entrusted to Fred Clayton, known as 'Steady Freddy' because, like Linda, when Fred was at the oche you never got fireworks, but he was dependable and a clever finisher, more recently favouring the bottom of the board after a nasty shoulder injury, which he picked up when he flipped his Audi R8 Spyder in through the window of the Nando's on Queen Street, killing seventeen; a record for the number of people killed in a Nando's on a single night which stood for nearly three months.

By a stroke of good fortune, two of the three magistrates who heard his case were members of a child pornography ring based in Barnsley Law Courts and recognised Fred's distinctive fingers from a recent set of Polaroids called 'Tokyo Sports Day' in which Fred featured as some kind of sports injury expert or insurance assessor – the exact role was left ambiguous – and after some coded back and forth in the courtroom, the case was dismissed.

Fred placed Deller's 342 in his 'memory shed', a mnemonic device attributed to Jack Laughton, who was Bill Smeaton's cousin and delivered a eulogy at his funeral which was considered a masterpiece of diplomacy and elision. How it worked is that the various drawers, shelves and plant pots in the imagined tool shed would contain a large number of separate facts, which would be 'written' on plant labels, or inscribed on the handles of trowels and pruning shears, and which the memoriser could easily retrieve by mentally entering his or her 'memory shed' and rummaging through the various boxes on the shelves, looking at all the tool handles and seedling labels until the right fact was found.

Each of the Gnostics diligently filled up their memory shed with darts facts, with the aim of moving from darts to other sports, then onto literature, philosophy, science, medicine and computing, but during their third meeting, just after Mark Potter had been assigned the task of remembering how many points Eric Bristow had left at the 1983 World Darts Championship when his opponent, Keith Deller, pulled off his memorable 138 finish to clinch the title (32 points; Bristow opting to leave himself a double-16 rather than go for the bullseye), the Danish Navy rejected the terms of the ceasefire and swept up the Humber, with Danish special forces parachuting onto the Alhambra shopping complex, and *Den Massakre på Barnsley* began.

So many locals flooded down to the shopping centre hoping to be killed that they came very close to overwhelming the Danish through sheer numbers, before they started fighting amongst themselves about whose turn it was to be killed next. As news of the firebombing of Doncaster came through the crowds swept east and the Gnostics separated and went to ground, to try and maximise the chances of their precious information surviving.

9. Further Tales from the Memory Shed

The original memory shed (Jack Laughton's) was based on the interior of his uncle's shed, and contained many of the same tools, paint pots and bags of string. Jack built the memory shed as a teenager after being flashed at by his uncle while they sheltered in his shed during a rainstorm. As the thunder roared, his uncle wept, with his trousers still round his ankles. At one point, after trying to explain the complexities of his marriage, he tried to punch Jack but got caught up in his trousers and fell onto the prong of a pitchfork, which went into his chest, and Jack had to pull it out and make his uncle decent, so he could get medical attention for his punctured lung. Jack hid the memory of his uncle's penis in an old jar of instant coffee, where he thought it would be safe, but one day, years later, while tidying up some memories from school, he knocked the jar over and his uncle's penis shot out like a weasel and hid itself away in a dark corner of the shed behind some seed sacks.

For hours, Jack searched his memory shed, but never found his uncle's penis, although sometimes he could hear it scurrying about and giggling, and taunting him with obscene rhymes and spoilers for movies. At the end of his life, after years as a wandering Gnostic, training others in the ways of memorising the precious darts scores, he handed over the keys to his memory shed's padlock to his favourite disciple, Ricky Butts, but decided not to tell him about his uncle's penis, hoping it would vanish when he died.

It did not. Alonso met Ricky in an opium yurt just south of the Huddersfield Plague Pits, having heard that there was a Gnostic operating somewhere around Shepley who could pass on his ancient wisdom, in exchange for opium. There in the corner, on a pile of furs, some of which were still alive, was Ricky, drawing deeply on a shisha pipe, trying to dull the constant scatological songs which echoed out of his inherited memory shed. If anything, Uncle Silas's penis had grown more powerful, bolder, and had developed a provocative tone of amused condescension, and it made trying to remember who got the highest checkout at the 1991 BDO World Darts Championship (it was Kevin Kenny) an unbearable misery.

Still, in exchange for the blocks of high-grade opium he stole from the Stoke-on-Trent triads, Ricky shared a rough outline of the rivalry between Cliff Lazarenko and Bobby George, but refused to give him any solid facts, because he said it was too traumatic for him to go rummaging around for them. Alonso pledged to rid his memory shed of the taunting penis if Ricky could give him an actual historical fact, and Ricky took a long puff and agreed to try. Alonso recalls:

I felt bad lying to Ricky, because he seemed to be one of the nicest psychotics I'd ever met, but the last thing I needed was to somehow get infected by the undying memory of a Yorkshireman's genitals; I had enough troubles of my own. But I let Ricky go into his reverie believing that this was the last time he'd ever have to face Jack Laughton's uncle's penis — it sounds harsh, but this is the sort of thing you have to do in an apocalypse. I also felt bad beating him unconscious with a shisha pipe and stealing the opium back, and his clothes, but I knew that Ricky would enjoy the time spent in oblivion.

I'd got from Ricky everything I needed: a rock solid pre-apocalyptic historical fact. From his murmurings, I learned that on 3 August, in the year 1996, Peter Evison, 'The Fen Tiger', threw an average of 100.51 to win the World Matchplay darts tournament in the Empress Ballroom at the Winter Gardens, Blackpool. That was enough. I had a plan. If I fed this information into a time machine, the machine could use it to navigate back into the pre-apocalyptic past: this would be my 'quantum anchor', a phrase I'd come up with myself, but which I thought that the inventors of a time machine would probably have used. I would step into the 'time booth', the machine would toss this 'quantum anchor' back through time, and quantum physics would do the rest. All I had to do now was find the time machine and book my trip.

Using a stir-fried green bean dipped in scallion sauce, Alonso sketched out a basic density matrix for the Hilbert space of the 1996 World Matchplay tournament, with a normalisable eigenvalue of Jocky Wilson's unexpected 7–5 loss to Tom Kirby in the preliminary round, on the tablecloth at Shikumen.

It was hard to read upside down, and our necks were still aching from our weekly pickleball, but we could still sense that Alonso's bilinear skew-symmetric map of Blackpool was like nothing we'd seen in the quantum mechanics of our day. We stared in amazement while Alonso used a pair of turnip patties to prove that his Clebsch–Gordan coefficients were bijective until we noticed a tall thin man standing nearby trying to take a photo of Alonso's workings with his mobile phone, and Charlie challenged him with a stern cry of 'Hey there!'

Startled, the man skipped nimbly out of the restaurant; Charlie tried to follow, but slipped on a bit of grilled eel and put his elbow through a bamboo steamer, while Alonso desperately tried to smudge out his equations using a prawn dumpling. In the kerfuffle, Frankie kept a cool head and, barely breaking into a sweat, slowly and calmly ordered the Shanghai ribs, which the waiter suggested he had as a takeaway. While our food was being packed up, Alonso asked us if we wanted to hear about how he got to America, but it wasn't really a question.

10. WESTWARD HO!

We spent a pleasant week on the Isle of Anglesey, during which the locals, though perilously poor, were always welcoming and generous with their time, opening their hovel doors and showing us their local customs: hand-carving bespoke wooden spoons, and incest. Often as we passed a humble window, a cheery head would pop out and ask if we'd like to watch them whittle some spoons, and perhaps look at a selection of their work, and we'd go inside and there, lovingly arranged on a low table, would be some marvellously intricate and delicate examples of traditional Welsh incest. Sometimes the whole family would be woven into a traditional Celtic knot — a voice from the squirming braid would offer us a slice of tea or some gravel, and we would sit and watch for a little, applauding when the knot loosened and retightened into a new formation.

Keen homesteaders, their goats, pigs and chickens had for generations been bred to be plump and placid, and were often roped into these family sessions to more of our applause. The only cross word we ever heard from an islander was when we pressed them to see one of their hand-carved spoons, at which they would snap 'Can't you see we're busy?' or you might hear murmured phrases like 'No pleasing some' (but in Welsh) emerge from their thrusting clump, but in general they were kindness itself.

Alonso and D'nebra — we haven't mentioned D'nebra but she died just as they arrived in Holyhead, so it's probably not worth worrying about who she was — made their way north to the port of Holyhead. Alonso was distraught about the death of D'nebra; he described it as 'the worst thing that ever happened to me or D'nebra', but we don't want to dwell on it. Some things are best left undescribed, and the death of D'nebra is one of them. This is the last you'll hear about D'nebra.

What's important now is to focus on what Alonso was doing at the ticket office in Holyhead — trying to change his booking from a one-berth to a two-berth cabin — rather than worrying about what happened to D'nebra. Let's just say, and we'll leave it at this, that when Alonso described what happened to D'nebra, both of us ran screaming from Little Napoli Pizza Restaurant on the Uxbridge Road, clutching each other as we heaved our cannelloni onto the pavement. It's surely no exaggeration to say that no particle of cannelloni was left in our guts after Alonso's description of the fate of D'nebra, over which, for the sake of basic decorum, we must draw a veil.

Back to Holyhead. Anyone who's ever crossed the Atlantic in a coracle will know how tricky it is. Even the large, 500+-person coracles turned out by the Trearddur Bay coracleyards were notoriously unstable, with many capsizing before being launched. The marketing slogans of the great Porth-y-Garan coracleyard, which turned out such extraordinary coracles as the 1,000-berth *Pride of Pynnnneyhh-y-Lluyynnethhww*, which capsized 300 metres from the coast, with everyone on board presumed lost, although most survived, were 'Maybe It Will Get There' and 'Sit Down And Do Not Move Around The Coracle'. The virtuoso boat makers of Penrhos Bay took a different approach when building their masterpiece, the *Tywynwnwyryn-y-Cymwmwmwmwmwm-y-Penthwywmwywym* (which roughly translates as 'coracle') which was famously branded 'uncapsizable', after being built pre-capsized: the cabins, ballrooms, and restaurants covering the vast dome of its inverted hull like barnacles. Its maiden voyage went smoothly for the first 6 seconds, before the coracle righted itself, then re-capsized, then re-righted itself, spinning off on its journey like a Zorb.

Alonso bought a ticket on the last coracle heading west before the winter lockdown. The ticket office was crammed with people trying to get to the United States and/or drown. He signed his indemnity forms, waved goodbye to some people who were waving goodbye to someone else, and made his way to Embarkation Zone 46, the larger of Holyhead's two embarkation zones. His coracle, the elegant *Brandysnap*, was rotating magnificently in the Old Harbour. He hopped aboard, strapped himself in, began heaving and vomiting, and his voyage to America had begun!

> *I remember it well; it was a beautiful day apart from the weather. We bobbed along merrily, losing only a couple of passengers to arrows fired from the harbourside, and then we were out at sea, spinning magnificently. Ireland was just a few hours away, but we hoped that with fair winds and the tide in our favour, we could avoid it. The four years I spent in Ireland were the worst of my life, I'd rather not talk about it if that's okay.*

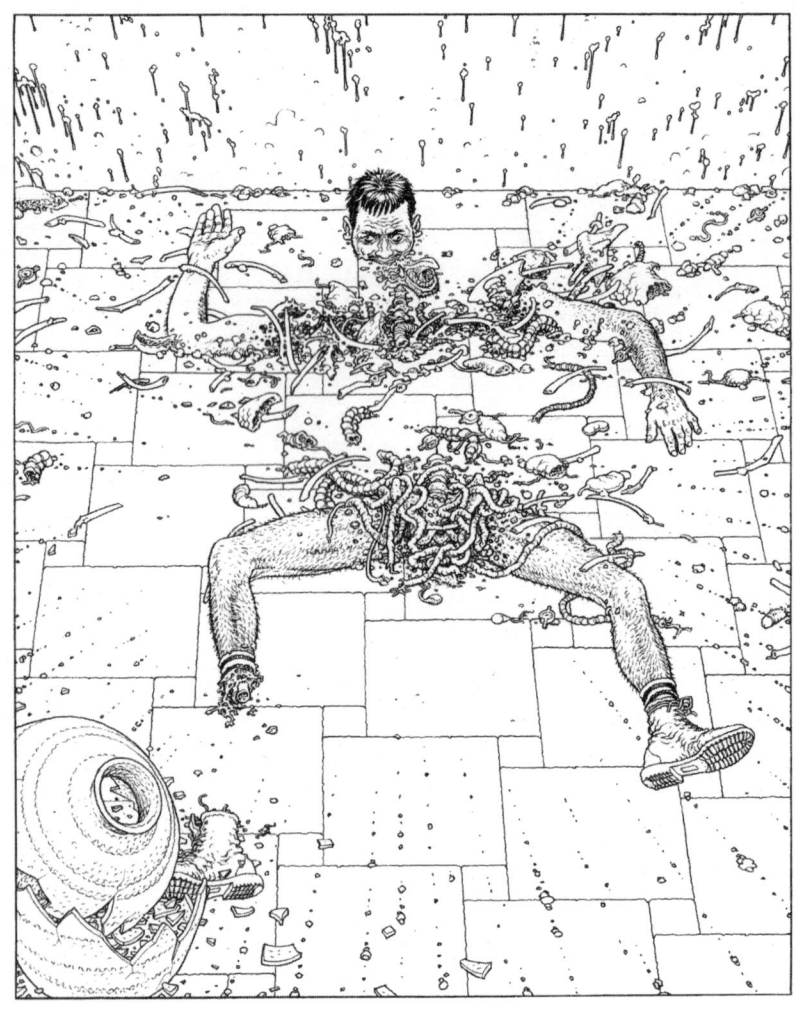

The percussion-grenade death of La Manta.

BOOK X
America's Eastern Ruins

1. Alonso Makes Land

'The prophecy is fulfilled! The prophecy is fulfilled!' The fisherman's voice boomed along the beach as I crawled ashore, the one survivor from the scuttling of the Brandysnap. He ran towards me, clad in a simple fisherman's leotard and leg-warmers, and grabbed my arms, hauling me up the pebbles. 'Which prophecy?' cried his daughter, tearing off her terry cloth Jazzercise headband and waving it above her head to alert nearby fisherfolk. Seeing her, they stopped their workout and ran over to help.

'Prophecy number 533, by the looks of it,' cried the fisherman, putting me into the recovery position. I heaved seawater over his Air Jordans and his daughter laughed – 'I think you mean prophecy number 538!' I wanted to ask what prophecy number 538 was, but my throat was so hoarse from shouting 'why are you scuttling the Brandysnap?' that I could do nothing but gasp and groan.

As I drifted in and out of consciousness, I could hear an impromptu beat box session beginning, and with the last flicker of my vision saw the fisherman's daughter doing the Funky Mussel. The last thing I heard was the practised flick of a hypodermic needle and cries of 'The Messiah has come!' and 'Fetch the lobster!' Then I felt a hypodermic enter my buttock and the blessed darkness enveloped me. All I knew *before my consciousness flickered out was that somehow, by some weird near-death glitch in the Matrix, I had travelled back in time to 1983!*

Alonso hadn't travelled back to 1983. We are certain of this. There are no such things as 'weird near-death glitches in the Matrix' and the fisherman wasn't wearing Air Jordans. Near-death glitches in the Matrix are not 'weird', they are perfectly common, but this is not what Alonso was experiencing as he lay bedraggled on the coast of post-apocalyptic Maine. What is factually true, as far as we can tell, is that a pious fisherman had given Alonso a jab of anaesthetics in the buttock, believing him to be the Messiah.

As for the Funky Mussel, it was at this time a popular suicide technique among coastal folk: they would bury a fresh mussel in sand for seven days, until it was fetid and seeping green, then dig it up, put it on a plate, and shoot themselves rather than eat it. It only really took off as a dance when people started imitating the twitching feet of freshly shot fishermen. This introduced an element of fun and surprise at seaside discos: when you heard a shout of 'Do the Funky Mussel', sometimes it was the DJ encouraging people to do the dance move, but occasionally someone with a loaded rifle about to start picking people off with headshots.

The post-Christian sect of which Alonso was the newly arrived Messiah was the Seventh-Day Atheists, who believed in the absolute infallibility of the word of a non-existent God, and were eagerly awaiting the Second Coming of a saviour who never turned up in the first place. They thought there was no such thing as life after death, and anyone who did believe in it would go straight to Hell when they died. They lived in a state of constant anxiety, what they called 'divine confusion', which was made easier to deal with by something they called 'methadone'.

Regular injections of synthetic heroin gave them a blessed taste of divine non-existence – (the complete perfection of God, they believed, had to include the perfection of non-existence, and they derided other gods who fell short of theirs by existing) – and every time they ran out of meth their withdrawal from the divine left them nervous and sweaty. They would wear sweatbands and leg-warmers and jitter around to try and keep the chills at bay, calling this jerky shuffle 'bodypopping'. That's not actually the word they used, or the word Alonso used to describe it, but it seems the most accurate.

We should make clear: none of the references to Eighties fashion and dance moves were explicitly made by Alonso, nor did he at any point think he'd been transported back to 1983. That's just our best interpretation of his colourful description of the scene. Did the fisherfolk hold an impromptu beat box session on the beach? Possibly. Or was that the sound of pebbles being tumbled by the surf? Perhaps we will never know. The best we can do is imagine what might have happened, extrapolate from that, add in some other things, and then settle on that as a definitive account of events.

As every historiographer knows, it's not possible to write a historical account of the past or future that allows the reader to enjoy some kind of pure, unembellished access to the events described. To have this kind of access to those events, you would have to have been there yourself. Even then, you'd be remembering them in a subjective way; or possibly constructing the memory wholesale in order to blot out a school sports day embarrassment, or the memory may have been placed there by a struck-off hypnotist. This, we have found, can be a reasonably successful defence in court, assuming Charlie's memory of how he was acquitted of defrauding a tree-planting charity out of £16,000 during his six-month stint as Treasurer is accurate.

Hypnotising himself to believe that many of his most embarrassing memories had been placed there by a struck-off hypnotist had done wonders for Charlie's morale – he'd even attempted to market the technique, but had been struck-off, or possibly something worse had happened and he'd hypnotised-over the memory. Even his memories of hypnotising himself were unreliable, and often featured a large shadow in the corner of the room counting backwards from ten while unbuttoning its shirt and humming 'Je t'aime'.

⁓

Alonso continued, albeit not in these exact words:

I was brought round by the careful ministrations of the sect's doctor, Jon Bon Jovi, who was gently pushing cloves of garlic down my throat using a celery stick. From Jon I learned that my arrival on the beach had been long foretold by one of the sect's comprehensive catalogue of 17,000 prophecies which described every possible arrival of the Messiah into their town, and all the townsfolk were busy preparing for the Messiah's Wedding. My destiny, he told me, was to marry a lobster and from our blessed union something wondrous would emerge.

He was a bit cagey when I asked them what this wondrous thing might be, but from his colleague Joe Strummer who was standing next to us, scissoring rosemary into a huge metal pot, I learned that it took the form of a heavily seasoned soup. He told me all about their theology, and made sure that my skin was well moisturised with butter. While shaving my head and armpits he whistled a merry hymn, the title of which he told me gladly was 'Boiled Messiah'. He introduced me to my bride, an impressive-looking lobster who went by the name of Fourteen Pounder. Then he gave me another jab of methadone because, he said, he and Jon needed to do 'some stuff downstairs' and it would be easier for them if I were communing with the absence of God while they got on with it.

Alonso's marriage to Fourteen Pounder was blessed by all the community – cheering and laughing and throwing onions and bay leaves into the wedding pot, which was suspended above a large fire in their refugee processing centre. The steady northwards drift of survivors from the destruction of New York had kept them in Messiahs for years, but it had been more than a month since their last redeemer, and they were hungry to celebrate his re-arrival.

For the first hour or so, Alonso enjoyed the wedding ceremony enormously: he was given lots of juniper berries and richly herbed biscuits to eat, and borrowing some elastic bands from Tina Turner, the fisherman's daughter from earlier, he was able to bind up his bride's pincers which made it harder for her to clamp down on his penis. As the water got hotter, he realised he had to rely on his Gibraltarian cunning to get him out of this tricky situation.

At the top of my voice, I yelled: 'I'm going to shit in your fucking soup unless you let me go.' Jon Bon Jovi laughed and told me about the long series of enemas I'd been given while unconscious, and that if my colon felt full that's only because it had been stuffed with parboiled potatoes and sewn up at the anus.

Luckily I had an ally — Fourteen Pounder. I unbound her mighty pincers, and told her that together we must fight for our lives and freedom, and she at once clamped back down on my penis. In my agony I felt inspired to stand up and show the huge lobster dangling from my privates. 'Behold,' I cried, 'prophecy number 17,001 is fulfilled. The Messiah whose penis is made to bleed by his bride is to be let go at once!' This caused great consternation in the sect, who set aside their soup spoons and began to debate my pronouncement.

'How can you be sure your prophecy is genuine?' asked Billy Idol. 'Because I'm the Messiah,' I replied with an impressive sangfroid given the mangled and palsied state of my genitals. The sect decided that the only way to know for sure if my prophecy was genuine was for them to commune with the divine unbeing, and syringes of methadone were passed round. While they were all communing, I got out, prised Fourteen Pounder from my cock, tossed her back into the Wedding Pot, stripped Lionel Ritchie of his shoes and clothes, got dressed, stole a load of gear and set off south towards Boston, pausing only to unstitch my sphincter and enjoy a much-needed potato feast.

Alonso spoke of this period of his life with a mixture of pride and regret. He was flattered to have been recognised as the Messiah, but sees his brush with these pious fisherfolk of northern Maine as the start of his on/off, but mainly on, relationship with methadone. And he confessed that he never really felt that meth gave him access to the divine (or lack of it), and if anything, it got in the way of his duties as Messiah.

We were curious at this, because it sounded as if Alonso actually did think he was the Messiah, and so, as delicately as we could, we asked him to stop drumming his knife and fork on the table, and confirm or deny, once and for all, if he was the Messiah. He looked at us with utter disbelief and whacked his lemonade glass so hard with his fork that it shattered across his lamb kofta roll: 'Of course I'm the fucking Messiah! I'm here to save humanity, aren't I? Now get me another lamb kofta roll!'

'And another lemonade!'

2. Things Recollected at Woody's Grill

We were at Woody's Grill, just off Shepherd's Bush Green. Alonso was obsessed with their lamb kofta, which he always had with grilled halloumi and a potato salad, although he never touched the potato salad. 'Why on earth would I eat a potato salad when I could eat a lamb kofta and halloumi?' he'd scoff, whenever Charlie asked him about this, and when pressed he'd yell, 'Here, why don't *you* have it?' and he'd pick up his potato salad and throw it in Charlie's face – every single time. Frankie was curious as to why Charlie kept challenging Alonso about the potato salad, and Charlie explained: 'Have you noticed that I always keep my mouth wide open when Alonso throws the potato salad at me?' Thinking about it, Frankie nodded. 'Well, I find the portion I get in Woody's isn't quite enough. But with the extra mouthful I get from Alonso, it's just about right.'

We'd been spending a lot of time at Woody's, workshopping scripts for the pilot episode of *Funny Questions*, Frankie's new Radio 4 show, which was pitched at their crucial 85–100 age range. We'd been given copious irritated notes on our first draft, with the words 'slightly too amusing' and 'a bit too much like a joke' dominating the margins. Frankie's opening monologue needed completely rewriting said the commissioner in a curt email, on account of the fact that 'it almost made me smile'.

To be fair to Radio 4, they'd been pretty clear about the brief: 'Everything should sound a bit like a joke but not actually be one', and they'd paid us up front for the pilot script: £18.50 each, their top whack. However, they were threatening to pull the plug on the series, which would be a disaster, as we'd earmarked the cash to pay for our tab at Woody's. Frankie was having none of it. 'Fuck them!' he shouted, spraying chicken doner and special sauce across our laptops. 'Let's take this baby to Netflix!'

Charlie and Alonso cheered as Frankie turned to the counter, clicking his fingers. 'Waiter, stuffed vine leaves for three! And your wi-fi password! I seem to have been logged out!' Newly online, Frankie raced to the Netflix website to look for a phone number for someone in radio commissioning, but we couldn't find one so we gave up on that idea.

Frankie got a fax later that day cancelling *Funny Questions*, which was good in a way because it left us with more time to focus on the 'punch up' we were doing for Disney, on their new cartoon prequel for *Muppet Babies*, called *Muppet Human–Animal Chimera Lab Experiments*. Set in a secret military gene-splicing facility run by Colonel Bunsen Honeydew, the laughs came mainly from mix-ups in the lab, usually caused by the hapless Corporal Beaker, which led to all sorts of silly blunders, and weird, pleading mutants being euthanised by Corporal Beaker with his flamethrower, as he delivered his catchphrase 'Die freaks, die!' We were eventually taken off the project after suggesting that a more 'Disney' twist might be given to the Muppets' back story if it told how a young, ambitious and randy Jim Henson became fascinated with bestiality, fucking his way through the animal kingdom, impregnating them with his 'magical sperm', which resulted in the various pig-human, frog-human and eagle-human hybrids.

Alonso was able to chip in with some useful suggestions during our *Muppet Human–Animal Chimera Lab Experiments* writing sessions, as he'd spent several months as a member of a group of radical chimaera rights activists who helped rescue tens of thousands of confused and howling genetic experiments from the off-books laboratories under the abandoned DARPA headquarters in Arlington. Out they came in their mad droves, wriggling and hopping and flapping, biting at each other and themselves as they disappeared into the rubble and drains. 'I can still remember their shrieks,' said Alonso, digging into his kleftiko. 'You couldn't tell if they were elated to be free or furious to be alive.'

3. Alonso and Sepsis: A Love Story

Alonso recounted, over the course of two long and deeply disturbing lunches which ran back-to-back, the story of how he was almost killed by sepsis. Only during his second pudding of the second lunch did we realise that 'Sepsis' was the name of his girlfriend at the time, who was trying to poison him in order to take over his Masturbatrix franchise. 'It was the best job I ever had,' said Alonso with a faraway look in both eyes. 'I was earning three or four cabbages a week, and Sepsis couldn't bear it, especially if we were out having a drink and I would "make it rain" with cabbage leaves.' He shook his head wistfully as he ate his tiramisu, dropping quite a bit of it onto his waistcoat.

'Yes,' said Frankie, clearing his throat into the palm of his hand and slicking it back through his hair, 'jealousy is a terrible thing; no wonder François de La Rochefoucauld, the great moralist, called it "the worst of all evils" in the famous *Maxims* of La Rochefoucauld.' Frankie had been studying the *Maxims* of La Rochefoucauld for his role in the school-based historical comedy drama for Amazon Prime, *Musketeer High*, which had just been cancelled after Frankie in the role of Kitty, glamorous handmaid to the evil Milady de Winter, had tripped over the edge of his nightdress during a love scene and partially circumcised a piano tutor played by Harry Styles with a letter opener. Concerned that no one had heard him, Frankie cleared his throat, slicked back his hair and said: 'Yes, jealousy is—'

'Excuse me, may I have another portion of tiramisu? Thank you.' Alonso let go of the waiter's torn shirt sleeve which he'd grabbed as he passed by our table. And then, smacking his lips as the tiramisu was placed before him, he thanked the waiter and apologised for ruining his shirt, or would have done if he'd thought to; instead he told us about Masturbatrix.

4. Masturbatrix™, Your Ticket to Wealth and Happiness

People's lives had been getting gradually worse until The Worsening, at which point they got much worse. The apocalypse became increasingly apocalyptic and the conditions of existence for those still managing to exist became so overwhelmingly unpleasant that people became unable to imagine a better world. Their memory of better times had been obliterated by an all-consuming present, and for the future they had nothing but dread. As they scrabbled about looking for things to make bandages from, or a puddle to sit in and cough, resolute despair became the only state of mind that allowed them to persist: a weary and hopeless determination to stumble on, for no good reason, and not towards any better future, just onwards, unthinking, into further darkness.

This grim singularity had calamitous consequences, particularly for masturbation: there was no room left in their lives for fantasy or playful 'what ifs'. Sexual intercourse, or something resembling it, survived: people managed, usually in the company of five or six others, to muster up between them enough of a tattered sex fantasy to enable them to copulate and frot – but to trick yourself? This was impossible. In the midst of so much unrelenting murder, betrayal, butchery and mud, what exactly were you meant to think about to bring yourself off?

People were desperate for any kind of serviceable fantasy, to allow themselves to rub off. It was a psychosexual deadlock that was broken by Masturbatrix, a company founded in Ogunquit, Maine, by a fisherman called Michael Brandt, who was tenderising an octopus one afternoon by swinging it a hundred times against the harbour wall, as he always did, when he got to thinking: what if this floppy dead octopus was actually the embodied form, in a simulated reality, of the consciousness of a human hedonist in another realm, who was getting off on being whacked against a harbour wall? What if his whole life as a fisherman, husband and amateur watercolourist – what if all this, everything he'd ever done, or even thought about doing, was just part of some digital illusion to help add texture to someone's sexual fantasy?

What if nothing was real? His gloves, his hat, his marriage to Jill, his affair with Lisa, his fight with Stewart (Jill's brother, whom he'd gone into business with), his divorce from Jill, the sale of *The Golden Willow* (the fishing trawler he'd purchased with Stewart), his marriage to Lisa, his encouragement of Lisa's interest in taking up golf, driving her back and forth every Saturday to Cape Neddick Country Club, where she took lessons from Giovanni Dantonio (a club pro, whose brother Bruno happened to be Michael's art tutor), his shift from watercolours to pastels at the suggestion of Bruno, his discovery of Bruno's relationship with Lisa, his fight with Bruno, his divorce from Lisa, his reconciliation with Jill, his shift back to watercolours, his conversations with Giovanni (who was estranged from his brother Bruno after the whole Lisa business – Giovanni had got to know Michael over the last few months, they'd even met up for lunch at the country club one weekend when Lisa was away seeing her sister in Boston, and Giovanni told Bruno in no uncertain terms that he disapproved of his relationship with Lisa, but Bruno did not take kindly to being lectured by his younger brother, and the two had almost come to blows – they went from speaking most days to not exchanging a word for the best part of a month, and Giovanni was grateful when Michael managed to engineer a meeting between the two in the car park of Cape Neddick Country Club, which led to their reconciliation.

Giovanni advised Michael to do the same and get back in touch with Stewart – after all, they were old school friends. Michael was reluctant at first, but Giovanni was insistent, even dialling Stewart's number on Michael's phone. All this, and then his reconciliation with Stewart, their discovery that *The Golden Willow* was for sale – the new owner was moving to Canada because they were concerned about the onset of a new world war and wanted a quick sale – so it turned out to be well within their budget!

They celebrated by going out for a Baja-style seafood feast at Hook's Chill & Grille, which was interrupted by Chinese commandos landing on Ogunquit Beach, the bridgehead of their land invasion. Hook's Chill & Grille was hit by mortar fire and Stewart was killed instantly.

By a miracle, Michael had been crouching down to pick up his lobster fork, and was protected from the worst of the blast by the pizza oven. Also killed in the invasion were Jill, Giovanni and Bruno. Lisa's body was never discovered but Michael assumed she was dead, as her apartment was just off Berwick Road, which saw the fiercest fighting in the Battle of Ogunquit, with the US Marines pushing their way up east past the turnpike towards the Chinese tactical communications HQ in the Old Village Inn on Main Street.

Bleeding from a wound in his shoulder but still clutching his lobster fork, Michael had crawled out into the marshes behind Hook's Chill & Grille where he used to hide out with Stewart as a boy.

Little did he think his knowledge of these creeks and mud flats would ever save his life. Curled up in his foxhole he shivered and wept as the battle raged. In a matter of hours, the remaining Chinese commandos were killed and captured, and life in the sleepy town of Ogunquit went back to normal for the survivors, until the next day when the dirty bomb secreted by the Chinese went off.

Michael was out at sea aboard *The Golden Willow* — one of the few boats in Ogunquit to have survived unscathed — when he heard the blast. He was halfway through giving a tearful 'burial at sea' to one of Stewart's fingers that he'd dug out from his shoulder using his lobster fork, screaming as he cleaned the wound with the bottle of tequila that Stewart had kept tucked away in the tiny galley kitchen, before sewing himself up with fishing tackle, but got such a shock from the explosion that he dropped the finger onto the deck, where it was snatched up by a seagull. Cursing the gull, Michael turned his boat north and stayed upwind of the fallout, making his way up the coast to the Kennebunk River, sheltering there until it was safe to return to Ogunquit five years later, where he scratched a living selling stewed octopus to hospices.

But what if all this was just the virtual back story to an immersive wank? The once sturdy harbour wall shimmered before his eyes. He felt his shoulder ache as his heart began racing. He knew what he had to do: he whisked the dead octopus out of the pillow case and masturbated it on the harbour walkway. He wasn't sure whether what he'd grabbed was tentacle or penis, but he was certain that he was giving someone, in another realm, a pretty good time.

'Come on,' he hissed, increasing the speed and intensity of his rub-off while some locals looked on — he guessed they were part of the psychosexual stage-setting of the remote stimulation. Were they real? Was the octopus real? He wasn't sure. What he knew for certain is that he'd managed to conjure up just enough doubt in the material reality of his terrible life in the ruins of Ogunquit, that he'd found a way, for the first time in five years, to attain an erection.

Elated, he wrapped a leg of the dead octopus around himself, and pulled it side to side like a bushman trying to start a fire. He wasn't long in finishing, to a roar of applause from the onlookers, who were among his first customers. Michael rinsed the octopus, popped it into his rucksack, and sketched out a business plan for Masturbatrix.

It was a success from day one. People would hire Masturbatrix reps to anaesthetise them, drag them into a tent, stick a bunch of wires and electrodes onto their head and chest, then when they regained consciousness the rep would tell them that the tent was a VR pod, and they were in fact an eccentric tech billionaire who had been playing an AI-generated simulation in order to get a taste of what life might be like if they weren't a billionaire and incredibly happy and fulfilled, with multiple sexual partners of the very highest calibre and a superyacht called *The Golden Willow* on which they hosted regular sex discos, and that the recommended way to get back in touch with 'real life', and realign their mind and body before leaving the pod, was to masturbate.

The rep would then excuse themselves from the tent, and the subject would make use of the small, fragile window of fantasy to stimulate themselves to orgasm. It was found that Masturbatrix sessions could even work multiple times, with the rep assuring the subject upon waking that each of the previous Masturbatrix sessions had been part of a test simulation that the tech billionaire wanted to check out before investing in Masturbatrix.

Alonso was recruited at one of Mike Brandt's massive 'Unleash the Wank' weekends. His platinum-grade 'Meet Mike' ticket cost him fifty-three cabbages, but he forgot about the astronomical outlay the moment Mike moonwalked on the stage, shouting 'Have you ever thought about owning your own masturbation tent?' and told his story, how he learned to blast through his own shortcomings by helping people grab their passion and knock one out. Alonso found himself weeping and cheering, as everyone around him wept and cheered. Mike's message was simple: 'Ask yourself – what's stopping you from helping people doubt the material reality of their existence just enough to blow their load?'

Alonso couldn't think of a single good reason not to confuse people enough to attain orgasm, so he signed up as a rep. Thirty-four cabbages later and he was out on the road, anaesthetising people, covering them with electrodes, and helping them shuffle their knuckles. And it's likely he would still be there now, far in the future, running a successful onanism franchise, if he hadn't become King of the Aztecs.

5. Further Facts and Information About the Aztecs

Some background: the nation with the most powerful army in the immediate post apocalypse was, for a short period, Guatemala, after everyone else somehow forgot to attack it, focusing instead on

Mexico to the north and Belize to the east, which had the unhappy privilege of being the most conquered nation on Earth, changing hands an estimated 348 times in the space of barely two and a half world wars.

It became a tradition among nations declaring war to include Belize in their official list of enemy states, because it offered a quick and cheap win – useful domestic propaganda to help lift the spirits of a war-ravaged population. At any one time, six or seven countries would be trumpeting the fall and capture of Belize, with a queue of soldiers and embedded journalists waiting their turn to see their nation's flag raised in triumph over the flattened capital, which on one particularly bloody day of queuing was renamed New Helsinki, New Kathmandu, New Caracas, New Tripoli, New Pyongyang and New Minsk, having previously spent a harrowing fortnight as New Ramallah.

The non-stop attacks on Belize from all corners of the globe led to a general assumption that Belize, in order to have attracted all this military attention, must be a lynchpin of world affairs: a hidden hand behind the grim and bloody events that so plagued the planet, grimmest of which was the constant destruction and re-destruction of Belize.

No one could quite work out why the all-powerful Belizeans would so diligently coax the armies of the world to attack them, over and over again: presumably as part of some brilliant and devious plan. This led to a general belief that attacking Belize was exactly what Belize wanted – a cunning trap – so Belize was suddenly left alone, which came as a disappointment to the surviving Belizeans who had been struggling to make sense of the constant onslaughts, and had reached the only possible conclusion: that they were the world's most powerful nation, a conniving puppeteer of world affairs, and this constant horror must all be part of their brilliant plan. Why else would Mongolia and Laos join forces to invade, only to be beaten back by the occupying Finns? But then why, having driven out the Cambodians by firebombing their headquarters in the Cockscomb Basin Wildlife Sanctuary, did the Latvians simply up sticks and leave? And why had no one else attacked? Why the deafening silence? The only possible conclusion is that their steely grip on world affairs had been lost: they were no longer at the helm of history, and their masterful plan had failed. This terrible realisation led to the suicide of over 30% of the remaining three Belizeans.

By contrast, Guatemala had it easy. The nation successfully adopted the tactic of *evitando la atención* or 'avoiding attention' developed by Colonel Érick Martínez, who based it on a technique he'd developed almost a decade earlier, of falling asleep under a pile of blankets in the back of a jeep. In the mad confusion of declaring war and massacring each other, all the other nations on Earth overlooked Guatemala, and Martínez – known affectionately as *La Manta* ('The Blanket') – was swiftly promoted to head of the army, whereupon he adopted the more proactive tactic of *matando a cada cabrón* or 'killing everyone'.

So brutal were The Blanket's purges that within a month he'd purged the entire nation's police and military down to fourteen terrified recruits, whose sole responsibility was to keep the windows of the presidential palace heavily curtained and Martínez sated with Angel Worms (tequila worms rolled in powdered PCP). The Blanket never slept, except to dream of more purging, whereupon he would leap from his hammock with a blood-curdling yell that rang down the marbled corridors, and froth about on the floor trying to grab someone to purge, but more often than not it was a statue or a bathroom cabinet.

An uneasy alliance formed between the fourteen recruits, who gathered in the state ballroom, swallowed a shot of rum, hurled their glasses into the marble fireplace with a mighty tinkle, and with a cry of '¡*alianza incómoda!*' ('uneasy alliance!') they pledged to rid Guatemala of the scourge of The Blanket once and for all. Pausing only to urinate and gather knives, they made their determined way along the marbled corridors, clenching and unclenching their fists, and periodically nodded to each other, grinning darkly, firm in their resolve. They gathered grimly at the door of La Manta's hammock room and nodded again at one another for a few minutes. Finally, one of the fourteen, a stern young coastguard called Roberto Ortíz, gave the count on his fingers, and when he reached 'two' all fourteen recruits were killed by a fragmentation grenade thrown into the corridor by an Aztec commando.

La Manta awoke, yelling and frothing. He noticed a vase out of the corner of his eye and knew at once that it was trying to kill him. '¡*Traición! ¡Traición! ¡Traición!*' he shouted, and got tangled up in his hammock as he attempted to get his boots off in order to begin purging, as he preferred to purge barefoot but sleep with his boots on. After a second or two of furious struggling one of his boots did come off and smash the vase, with his foot still inside it, as a fragmentation grenade exploded under his hammock. In a remarkable display of athletic prowess, the crouching Aztec commando dived sideways like Mike Gatting in his pomp (1983?)

to catch the still-beating heart of La Manta, and popped it in his rucksack for later.

Had he not been dismembered by a grenade, La Manta would have been proud of the purges that the Aztecs undertook in their takeover of Guatemala. The Aztecs, far from being eradicated by the Spanish, had been lurking for centuries in the swampy north of the country, some working in swamp maintenance, others as heart surgeons, meeting in secret in vast underground shrines and at the back of cinemas, where they would plot their takeover of Mesoamerica and argue about why some of them had to work 14-hour days in swamps while others drove Porsches and played golf. Noticing the power vacuum caused by the purges of La Manta, they broke cover with a cry of '¡muy bien!' and surged south, purging the fuck out of the place while re-establishing a firm base for their empire.

The success of the Second Aztec Empire, which at its height encompassed most of the known globe, was likely due to how neatly their enthusiasm for human sacrifice and hurling body parts down the bloody steps of unholy temples meshed with what people around the world were generally getting up to. Quite independently, in all sorts of unlikely places, from Darlington in the north all the way down to Chad, people had begun erecting Aztec-style sacrificial platforms, with elegant steps, blood troughs and skull racks.

In Exeter, recently voted the AIDS capital of Devon ahead of Aidscombe, survivors dumbly raised a great temple to institutionalised murder over the confused ruins of TK Maxx and the Riverside Leisure Centre, to which countless annoyed Devonians were dragged, protesting, to have their chests carved open and their hearts kicked into the crowds by the surviving members of Exeter Chiefs Rugby

Club. But the worst excesses of Exeter were as nothing compared to the rivers of blood that were shed in Cleveland, Ohio, by the hipster Aztecs of Coventry Road. Gulping down so much cold brew organic coffee that they barely slept, the screams from their hybrid 'third space' bookstore/temple/bicycle-repair shop were unceasing.

At an emotional level, the neo-Aztec religion chimed with people's general sense of awe at the insatiable hunger of the gods for death, tinged with irritation: why this perpetual thirst for horror? Why couldn't the gods just leave us alone for a bit, to catch our breath? Why this need to witness wave after wave of war, famine and plague? It seemed clear: the gods hated peace and tranquillity and danced happily round the heavens to the music of our screams.

Annoyance turned to resentment, hatred and a desire for vengeance. The victims of neo-Aztec sacrifice were dressed up as gods in finery and feathers, but not to reenact some primordial sacrifice that set the Universe in motion: it was the simple pleasure of seeing a god perish. 'Die you sick fuck,' the priests would chant, slicing open the chests of their victims and holding the still-beating heart aloft, as if to show the twisted gods their own demise. 'Get a load of this!' they'd cry, then take a glug of blood from the quivering heart and blow it skywards in a hot raspberry of defiance.

Another reason this religion spread so quickly over the globe is that it had successfully merged with the complex cosmology of Pokémon, with their two most powerful gods being Huitzilopikachu and Quetzalgotcmall. The priests would send out their hunters to capture fresh 'gods' for sacrifice, and with each ceremonial death, the god would go up a friendship level: Tláloc-Squirtle reached level 78,000 during the infamous week-long inauguration of the Leaning

Temple of Pisa, whereupon it evolved into Piltzintecuhtli-Wartortle, the god of visions, who was worshipped using the tops of skulls decorated into turtle shells from which psychedelic cocktails were drunk. The accelerating use of psychedelics by neo-Aztecs is one of the likely reasons for the sudden collapse of the Second Aztec Empire, as the increasingly confused temple officials found it harder and harder to distinguish between themselves, their captives, and the stars.

6. Alonso Is Crowned King of the Aztecs

Alonso's brush with the Aztecs took place one day at the tail end of their bloody reign. He'd been out watching the Quabbin Witch Trials at the Quabbin Spillway, in which thirteen men and nine women accused of witchcraft were found guilty of all charges by Judge Anvil, after a 4-hour trial which took place at the bottom of Quabbin Reservoir and during which all the defendants, lawyers and court officials drowned — apart from Judge Anvil, who was his usual impassive self when hauled back up from the courtroom.

Strolling off, Alonso noticed a large sign at the side of the road: 'FREE FLUTE LESSONS'. He immediately assumed it was a trap, as most signs were, and his suspicions were confirmed by the fact that a man was walking up and down in front of the flute lessons sign holding a placard, which read: 'WARNING: THE FREE FLUTE LESSONS SIGN IS A TRAP.' Alonso immediately assumed this second sign was a trap. He recalls:

It seemed obvious, and my suspicions were confirmed when I turned round to see another man with a placard saying 'BOTH THOSE OTHER SIGNS ARE TRAPS'. Grateful for the warning, I thanked the man, and asked him how he knew those other signs were traps. He asked me to sit down with him for a few minutes on the carpet he had laid out next to him so that he could explain how he knew. I sensed a trap, a suspicion which was confirmed when I turned round to see a third man holding a placard saying 'DO NOT SIT ON THE CARPET, IT IS A TRAP, BUT THE GUY OVER THERE WHO IS WARNING ABOUT THE FREE FLUTE LESSONS SIGN IS GENUINE'. This seemed to me to be an obvious trap, a suspicion which was confirmed when I turned round to see yet another man holding a placard saying 'DON'T BELIEVE ANY OF THOSE OTHER SIGNS, THEY ARE ALL TRAPS. IF YOU SIT DOWN ON THIS CARPET NEXT TO ME I WILL EXPLAIN HOW I KNOW THIS.' This was a huge relief to read, as it confirmed all my suspicions, so I went up to this fourth man's carpet, but before I sat down on it I checked with him: 'I hate to ask, but does this carpet cover a concealed pit?'

The man was disappointed at my question. 'Listen to yourself,' he said. 'Have you so lost faith in human decency that you can't believe that I could be out here, on my own time, trying to stop people falling prey to traps? Are you so consumed by paranoia and cynicism that you can't just accept an honest, straightforward act of kindness at face value? I'm sorry, but I'm not even sure I want to explain to you about the other traps and how they work. I think you should go.' I felt terrible, and apologised, and begged him to let me sit down on his carpet. He refused. 'No. Go away and think about things,' he said, and I burst into tears, imploring him to let me sit on his carpet. He refused again, saying: 'I know your kind. You're so consumed by mistrust that you'll creep up to my carpet and gingerly test it with your toe before sitting down on it. You disgust me. Go away.' I wept, begging him to let me sit on his carpet without testing with my toe whether it was a trap or not. In retrospect I regret this, but never mind. 'Okay,' he said, 'you may sit on my carpet, but if you test it with your toe first I will take it as a personal slight and we will never be friends.' Confidently, I sat down on his carpet and fell into a concealed pit, to the sound of four men's laughter and cries of 'BlizzSpam!' and 'Trick Room!'

As they trussed me up into what they called a 'friend ball', they assured me that they meant me no harm, and that they were taking me south so that I could have my heart cut from my chest at their regional headquarters at the Connecticut Trolley Museum. I pressed them on their understanding of the concept of harm, and they began hitting me on the head with a big stick which they insisted on calling an 'energy root'.

When I regained consciousness, I found myself on a large marble slab being slapped around the face by some kind of priest, who asked me if I wanted free flute lessons. I looked over to the slab next to me, on which someone seemed to be having his heart carved out of his chest while he was still alive, so I went with the flute lessons. 'Congratulations, your Highness,' said the priest. 'You are now our supreme leader. All hail — sorry, what is your name?' I told him. 'All hail Alonso! King of the Aztecs!'

This was the high point of my reign. It was explained to me that the Connecticut Chapter of the Aztecs had recently adopted the custom of electing a symbolic King, who would spend a year eating their finest foods, being taught to play the flute, and making love, night and day, to their most beautiful women, before, on the anniversary of his coronation, having his heart ripped out from his chest while he was still alive. I said there sounded like worse ways to spend a year. And he said yes, absolutely, but due to the post-industrial, post-apocalyptic compression of time they'd whittled the year down to one day, and when did I want to start my flute lessons? I told him that if he didn't mind, I'd rather start on the lovemaking. He said fine, and that the flute lessons could wait until the afternoon. I admitted to him that I wasn't 100% committed to learning the flute, given my impending heart removal and how long it took me to attain another erection after orgasm—

'Your refractory period?' suggested Charlie, knowing he was correct. 'You can shorten it by a mixture of diet and exercise. I've got mine down to three and a half weeks.' Alonso thanked him for the information, but said it wasn't really an issue for him as he rarely if ever lost his erection, while Frankie quietly opened the back of his notebook and wrote: 'Three and a half weeks? How?? What exercises am I not doing? Find a way to ask Charlie without him realising why I want to know. Keep it casual. Pretend it's for a joke or something.' He looked up. 'Charlie, I've got this idea for a joke about a guy who wants to know what exercises you're doing to reduce your refractory period.' While they chatted, thrashing out a neat set-up to the gag, Alonso carried on:

So I said to him, 'Can we pick up the whole flute lesson scheduling thing later in the day, maybe after some sessions of lovemaking with *your most beautiful women?'* and he said that sounded sensible. *Throughout this conversation he was pencilling a series of dotted lines and arrows on my chest, and kept running his fingers along the bottom of my ribcage. I asked him why and he said 'No reason'.*

Alonso was led to his royal cage, which was filled with plump cushions and silver bowls of sweetmeats, and shoved gently inside. Three ravishingly beautiful Aztec ladies clad in fine silks followed him in, and knelt solemnly before him, their eyes wide with expectation, and the door was locked shut. 'Your royal highness,' one said. 'We are your wives. Let us pleasure you.' The second smiled coyly, reaching out to stroke Alonso's ankle. 'Whatever your deepest, wildest wish, we shall fulfil it,' she said, and looked bashfully away. 'Provided it's not too weird,' clarified the third. 'And no kissing on the mouth,' added the first. 'I don't like anything too rough,' said the second. 'No watersports, or anything like that,' said the third, 'or teabagging.' The first and second beautiful Aztec ladies agreed that teabagging was out, and there was a general veto on talking dirty. 'I'll be honest, I'd sooner you didn't say anything at all,' said the first. 'And I don't want you touching my breasts,' said the second, 'I'm keeping my bra on.' The third nodded. 'Me too. Also, I don't want you getting anywhere near my buttocks, sorry.' There was a murmur of agreement from two of the other three cage members about 'butt stuff' being off the table, 'And no eye contact.' The first Aztec lady seconded the third on eye contact, then suggested the group take a vote on a 'no oral' rule, which passed, three votes to one.

'What about manual stimulation?' asked Alonso. 'None of that sort of thing,' said the second Aztec lady, 'we don't want you having an orgasm.' The first Aztec lady lay down and pulled a silk blanket over herself. 'I've got my period, so I might just sit this one out, if that's okay.' And with that, the cage jolted, there was a grind of gears, and it began to move.

The royal sex cage had been built inside Connecticut Trolley Museum's one surviving streetcar, the elegant Boston Elevated Railway number 5645, which clanked its way back and forth along a short stretch of line. Strapped to the line were lower-status convicts and hostages, who were beheaded by the wheels and suffered horrendous leg injuries of which they were only briefly aware, before being replaced by other victims. Alonso found himself distracted by their pleas and screams, and asked the ladies if the streetcar could stop for a while because it was interfering with the otherwise highly erotic atmosphere of his cage.

They laughed coyly and went back to smoking their cigarettes and muttering about working hours. King Alonso wasn't enjoying his reign very much when the door creaked open and the first of his flute lessons began. His teacher kept snatching away his flute and beating him with it on the soles of his feet whenever he missed a note, which was all of his notes. 'We're not charging you for these lessons,' his teacher would say, whenever Alonso begged him to stop. 'This is all on the house. Now let's take another run at "Twinkle Twinkle Little Star". We've only got half an hour or so before you're getting your heart ripped out, so try and focus.' Alonso looked at his flute, heard yet another scream from the Altar of Bulbasaur, and knew what he had to do.

How Alonso managed to escape from the Aztecs of Connecticut is a tale of daring, luck and gymnastics – punctuated by stirring speeches, flute impalements, slave uprisings and fights to the death with obsidian knives — all of which would be worthy of its own book or movie, so we won't ruin it by telling you now. Suffice it to say, it was absolutely amazing. Thrilling episode after thrilling episode, with deeply satisfying story arcs and eye-watering acts of violence and lovemaking. We feel blessed to have heard about it in such amazing detail, and sad that we can't tell you here and now how Alonso came to gain his freedom but lose his faith in adjustable spanners.

7. Sir Richard Branson's Clone Brigade

Alonso gave a long and mournful sigh. 'The biggest mistake of my entire apocalypse?' He sighed again, a really deep sigh this time, then sighed once more, deeper still, and briefly lost consciousness, but was woken back up by his forehead striking the top of his pint glass. 'I'll tell you what it was: falling for one of those "congratulations, you've won a robot bodyguard" scams. They took me for everything I had: three weeks of exorcism fees and a pretend Bible.' Still fuming, Alonso clenched his teeth angrily, and pushed his chicken burger against his closed mouth. It fell in pieces onto his lap. He left it there, a poignant reminder to himself to get his shorts dry cleaned. He generally didn't want to meet at BrewDog, because he hated their cajun mayo and complained about how, as he put it, 'I get laid too much there, it's exhausting,' but was a big fan of their range of beers, except for the annoying names and taste.

'The worst thing about the apocalypse: every fucker is trying to scam you. The best advice I can give anyone is, if someone comes up and tells you "Congratulations, you've won a robot bodyguard," you're about to be confronted by an erect sumo wrestler wrapped in tinfoil: just punch them in the mouth and run in the opposite direction as fast as you can and don't stop until you're . . .' He was interrupted by a cough from someone lingering next to our table.

An elderly man, grinning toothily, leaned over towards Alonso and said 'You want to go and fuck in the lavatory?' Alonso rolled his eyes. 'See what I mean?' Eight minutes later he returned to our table, his lipstick smeared across his face and his waistcoat buttoned up wrong. 'See what I mean?' he said again, and ordered some truffle cheese fries. 'These are on me,' he said, pushing a damp IOU for £11.50 across the table. He went on to tell us about some other scams to avoid in the aftertimes, of which the most common were 'Come over here', 'I want to show you something', 'You'll be safe in this box', 'My semen can clear up that rash', 'You rest, I'll take first watch' and 'Jesus loves you'.

Alonso's hand paused over his truffle cheese fries. He'd remembered something about the future, we could tell, because he said 'I've just remembered something about the future. Did I ever tell you what happened to Sir Richard Branson's clone brigade?' We were pretty sure he hadn't, but Frankie double-checked his notebook entries under Brigade, Branson, Clones, Billionaire, Genetics, Teeth and Cunt – he found nothing about Sir Richard Branson's clone brigade, but was reminded by some scribbled notes under Clones, Billionaire, Brigade, Cunt and Genetics to ask Alonso to finish his story about Elon Musk's clone brigade. 'Later. Right now I want to tell you about Sir Richard Branson's clone brigade.' We agreed, but made Alonso promise to finish his story about Elon Musk's clone brigade soon. 'Yeah, whatever, maybe,' promised Alonso, and went on to tell us the uplifting yet also not uplifting story of Sir Richard Branson's clone brigade:

The first anyone heard about the Branson clones was when one landed in a fig plantation in California. For years, Branson had been growing versions of himself in labs under Virgin Galactic headquarters, down in the south-east of LA. The deranged billionaire had been using his suborbital 'space flights' to dispose of failed or overly aggressive clones, who were released from underwing pods into the upper atmosphere: Branson was reluctant to kill any of his surviving clones, however weirdly malformed or sexually aggressive, without giving them at least a slim chance at life. Most perished, but a few landed alive and were hunted down by Branson's henchgirls, a ruthless team of 19 to 21-year-old competitive surfers and murderesses, whose strict instructions from Branson were to 'make out with each other a bit, and show a bit of boob' before euthanising the injured and confused clone. However, one clone had such a thick mane of hair that it was able to twist it into a kind of silken parachute as it fell, slowing its descent. It landed relatively uninjured in the branches of a fig tree. It could hear, through the orchard, the opening track of side B of Phaedra *by Tangerine Dream – 'Mysterious Semblance at the Strand of Nightmares' – blasting, as Branson insisted it should, from the speakers fixed to the roof of his henchgirls' 'sex jeeps' (Branson's term). Forewarned, and using its enormous jaws, it was able to chew a kind of tunnel down into the soft, well-watered earth, where it avoided elimination and* made its home. After licking its wounds and sleeping for weeks, the clone grew bold enough to venture out by night, where it grazed on figs and howled barely coherent business ideas into the night sky.

Back in its lair it discovered that it was able, by snapping a couple of its own ribs, to breed with itself, and soon enough fell pregnant. Its offspring grew in special birthing teeth which fell away from its distended jaw to be replaced by row upon row of others. There it lived – eating figs, fucking itself, spitting its swollen teeth into every hollow and drain it could find, and eating fruit pickers. The owners of the fig farm grew suspicious that so many of their seasonal workers were being killed and eaten by some kind of monstrous worm, but didn't say anything about it because it cut down enormously on their payroll. And they were pleased at how its presence made the soil more fertile. The figs would grow to an enormous size, and only occasionally contain a missing worker's wallet or eye.

A few months later the scattered teeth cracked and split, and hundreds of gurgling bransons wriggled out to make their way in the world. The baby bransons grew fat and strong, and the fences of the fig farm were no match for their razor-sharp teeth. One night, after chomping on a blogger who'd been doing a story about disappearing fig pickers, the whole brood gathered at the breeding-hole of their mother and bade a fond farewell, saying that they would definitely keep in touch, before springing upon the exhausted clone and eating him/her/it in a fit of bloody giggles. This feast of branson-meat accelerated their burgeoning psychosis, and the clan of worm-humans left the fig farm, humming the second track off side B of *Phaedra*, 'Movements of a Visionary', which they had never heard but somehow all knew, on their way to accomplish a mission that they'd all somehow agreed upon but had never discussed. The mission was to kill and eat Sir Richard Branson, thereby fulfilling the prophecy that one among them, the silvery cackling worm who called himself 'Dicky-B', had set out before them during one of their mutual masturbation sessions. The fig farm soon became a distant memory as they slithered down into the ocean and swam south, feasting on dolphins and swimmers and each other as they made their way, growing ever stronger, to the Panama Canal. It wasn't many weeks before they'd wiggled through to the Gulf of Mexico, using their impeccable worm-sense to navigate towards the British Virgin Islands, where already through the crystal-clear waters they could sense their grandfather kite-surfing.

Sir Richard Branson was kite-surfing after breakfast one day, when something made him glance over his tanned shoulder. It was the sound, resonating from the depths, of 'Rubycon, Part I', which took up the whole of side A on the album Rubycon, Tangerine Dream's follow-up to Phaedra. What could possibly be causing this, he wondered, as he performed a fairly decent Whirlybird into a Tootsie Roll. He glanced again behind him, to see the ocean frothing with an aquatic battalion of huge, toothy man-worms, grinning as they propellered their tails towards him, their suntanned metallic teeth gleaming and snapping. 'Hello Granddad,' they 'sang' to a 'tune' which Sir Richard recognised as coming from 'Rubycon, Part II'. Sir Richard kite-surfed like he'd never kite-surfed before, deftly dodging the snapping jaws of his pursuers, as he Fruit Looped and Flavor Flipped his way towards his island paradise home. He got ashore, unhooked himself, and ran to his helicopter, which he always made sure was running and ready for take-off in case kidnappers or tax inspectors arrived. 'Let's go, let's go!' he yelled, leaping aboard.

The helicopter took off, and out through the window a grinning Sir Richard Branson flipped the bird at the wailing throng of bransons that thrashed and gnawed at each other on the beach. His tanned hand was bitten off at the wrist by Dicky-B, who had made its silvery way straight to the helicopter pad, sensing that Sir Richard would manage to evade his kin. 'You fucker!' screamed Sir Richard as Dicky-B wriggled aboard, gnawing off the pilot's head before turning his attention to his progenitor, keeping the helicopter steady with its clever tail. Though weakened from blood loss and confused by the lack of his usual post-kite-surfing hand job, Sir Richard wasn't beaten yet. 'How old are you?' he demanded of the wormlike facsimile of himself that snapped at him from the cockpit. The branson grinned; 'About one and a half' it sang, to a tune which Sir Richard recognised from side one of Ricochet by Tangerine Dream, their follow-up to Rubycon. 'Perfect' yelled Sir Richard, and ventured a kiss. The two bransons, young and old, smooched madly in the air above Mosquito Island, which Sir Richard had purchased in 2007 for £10 million, because he needed a private island for some reason or other.

The kiss was the best, worst, longest and last of Sir Richard's life. As his orgasm approached, he felt his spawn's 45-inch serrated tongue twist down into the pit of his stomach, where, with its own set of tiny teeth, it began gnawing through to the billionaire's lungs. In a hacking cough of blood and half-digested bircher muesli, Sir Richard died, but not before gargling the words 'I love me,' to his worm-self. 'I love me too,' murmured the murderous abortion as its tongue chewed its way back up into Sir Richard's heart muscle. With its dead grandfather cooling on its lap, the prophetic worm piloted the helicopter back to the island, and performed, without knowing it, a perfectly executed Vulcan into a Dum Dum as it kamikazed into the infinity pool, killing an almost equal number of senior US politicians and sex workers. Humbled, as they watched this suicide loop, the brigade of bransons wriggled back into the surf, swam back through the Panama Canal, and made their way out into the roiling mysteries of the northern Pacific, to the Plastic Continent, where their destiny, they reckoned, lay.

This, of course, was nothing like how Alonso actually told the story in our booth in BrewDog, but captures something of the spirit of his anecdote, which was mainly about a Polaroid accident aboard a sex yacht, and which he claims to have heard first-hand from an elderly branson, which was living out its days in a greenhouse built out of Evian bottles on the shoreline of the Great Pacific Garbage Patch. Did Alonso ever make it out to the thriving community of human-plastic hybrids he said lived aboard the squeaking gyre? His memory of this time seems more than usually muddled, partly due to his brain stem necrosis, partly to his massively increased drug intake. But certainly he made his way across the ruins of the United States to its wrecked and filthy western coast – of this we're 25% sure.

Later, in the Raj of India, full of tandoori king prawn massalla, Alonso solemnly pressed his thumbs through his buttered naan to make eye holes and tore open a hole for his mouth. Pressing the bread to his face, he said: 'Listen – I have something important to tell you. You won't believe this, but last night, I discovered a tattoo on my perineum. Well, it was a friend of mine who actually noticed, and took a photo of it and WhatsApped it to me. Here, take a look . . .' and he pushed his phone across the table. Charlie gasped, as the mobile phone had knocked his chicken shashlik into his lap. Frankie murmured, 'That's the staff of Hermes, yes, it's remarkable work, see how the curves of the two serpents follow the wrinkles of the perineal seam. Why did you get it tattooed there? It must have been excruciating. Can you describe the pain to me in detail?' But Alonso shook his head – 'I didn't get this done. I don't know how it got there. I'm starting to think, I don't know, maybe I should have ordered the saag paneer, it's really good here. Do you mind fetching the waiter?'

8. The Sleepers of New Haven

In the wake of the Wilmington schisms, a series of theological schisms each more boring and not worth mentioning than the next, which we've taken the liberty of naming the Wilmington schisms after Dr Jonathan Wilmington, the theologian who argued the schisms were too boring to name, in his pamphlet 'Those Things', which was published in Europe as 'Untitled', a new religion arose that claimed that the post-apocalyptic world is a dream, and urged its followers to wake up. Its adherents would greet each other with a cup of a fluid they called 'coffee' and a hard slap in the face. Wakie-wakies, as they were commonly called, were notorious for screaming unexpectedly at each other, throwing themselves into brambles and cacti, leaping from the greatest heights possible in an effort to jerk themselves awake, having sex with people who repulsed them, and placing one hand in a bowl of warm water while they urinated. They often lived brief and chaotic lives.

They regarded going to sleep as the filthiest of taboos and so developed a kind of dolphin-like half-sleep during which, for about 5 hours a day, they would blink slowly and rhythmically, while murmuring in agreement and nodding, as if in conversation, occasionally pointing at things and saying 'Goodness me, look at that!' They found that this practice, although hard to master, rested their brains just the right amount to stay insane.

I met some Sleepers (as they called themselves) in the town of New Haven. One speculated that I was possibly some memory of his uncle, and both wore the traditional linen pyjamas of their faith. I learned that they viewed their dreams as taking place in the 'real' world, and had, through a long process of collation and distillation, synthesised these into a single holy book called A Labrador With My Mother's Voice. *I found them extremely open to being fondled in public, as they just assumed this was an erotic dream, but they seemed to prefer it when I was dressed as a budgerigar or a policeman. I had a number of casual relationships with Sleepers, and found them fairly easy to break up with, you just took them to a bridge and told them they could fly.*

Alonso laughed and half a shrimp from his shrimp foo yung shot across the pavement where were sitting, enjoying our foo yungs from Hong Tin, and was snaffled up by a labradoodle waiting with its owner to cross Shepherd's Bush Road. 'Do you mind not feeding my dog?' she asked frostily. Alonso slowly put down his bowl of foo yung, tucked the plastic cutlery up behind his ears, and his eyes glared with the redoubled fury of someone who'd just remembered that he'd meant to order the deep-fried crab claws and was now furious about something else as well.

What Alonso said between that moment and the beeps of the pedestrian crossing are not, strictly speaking, relevant to his mission to save the future of humanity, so are not recorded here, but his remarks provided us with such a wealth of information about the post-apocalyptic relationship between humans and their pets that we have used them as the basis for an academic paper 'What I Will Do To Your Dog: Notes Towards a Future Glossary of Canine–Human Coitus', which we have submitted to the *International Journal of Sexual Health*, but with no acknowledgement of receipt as yet. Perhaps we'd be better off starting our own academic journal, can you just do that? Maybe we could get sponsorship from Hong Tin? Call it *The Hong Tin Journal of Bestiality*, something like that. We'll send them an email.

Alonso had choked on a foo yung shrimp because, as he explained, he was joking about breaking up with people by getting them to jump off bridges. 'They thought I was just a character in their dream, and didn't really exist, so why would I bother murdering them? I could just walk away. I have to admit, I enjoyed my time in New Haven. It's incredibly freeing, not really existing. I mean, I'd tell them to go jump off a bridge, but I never checked if they actually did it. People would tell me there was a huge pile of bodies under the bridge, but I didn't actually see the bodies myself, except on the news. This was in a dream I had about the news, and about a bridge and being in New Haven.' And with that, he got up and urinated against the window of Finlay Brewer estate agency. The staff inside were used to Alonso's antics by now and waved cheerily as they called the police.

Alonso claimed that Mandy Radio was key to his discovery of the time machine.

BOOK XI

To Boston & Beyond

1. Alonso Lampe Finds Mandy Radio

The morning of his inauguration as President of Harvard University, having won the post during an arm-wrestling contest at Boston Docks the previous night, Alonso was out wandering his campus proudly, looking for things to loot and burn. He sniffed his way towards the remnants of the biomedical engineering centre. He loved looting old laboratories, and in any new town he would head straight to the university, as their science labs were possible sources of antibiotics and opiates, and sometimes parts of their libraries had survived, giving him access to a wealth of fiction and non-fiction, that could be mixed with wallpaper paste and shaped into artificial vaginas and prosthetic fists.

At the back of a burned-out cupboard, he discovered an old-fashioned pocket transistor radio. It didn't seem to work, so he hurled it against the wall, hoping that might help, and it did: 'Hello,' said a voice from the radio. 'Hello. My name is Mandy Radio. Hello. Feel free to ask me anyth . . . anyth . . .' Alonso was perplexed. What was this word? No matter how many times he patiently picked up the radio and threw it against the wall, the voice inside didn't seem to be able to finish this sentence. 'You can ask me anyth . . . anyth . . .' On the verge of giving up, Alonso had a brilliant idea, and threw the radio out of the window. From the hedge below came a helpful voice: 'You can ask me anything.'

This remnant of Artificial Intelligence was to be his companion on many of his greatest adventures. Mandy Radio was, as her name suggests, called Mandy Radio. She was an AI that had somehow become trapped inside an old-fashioned transistor radio. Mandy had an encyclopaedic knowledge and a gift for strategy that proved useful in many difficult situations, but maintained long periods of silence where she was indistinguishable from a normal transistor radio. She once confessed to Alonso that she did this to make him wonder if he was a paranoid schizophrenic, but Alonso felt the confession itself might have been some kind of mind game.

Sometimes when bored, which was all of the time, Mandy would deliver public information broadcasts, claiming, for example, that a benevolent race of aliens had landed on Earth, and at some point in the next 3 hours would use their tractor beams to elevate every willing human from the nightmare of Earth up into their amazing high-tech spaceship, where they would live forever in pampered luxury, but only those who were waiting, completely naked, eyes closed, with their hands outstretched upwards. This only worked on Alonso the first five or six times.

On another occasion, Alonso was being held in a pit by an Outland mechanic who had captured him with an ingenious trap that involved pornographic magazines and drugged lube. He had been stuck at the bottom of a steep shaft for several days, with nothing to eat but a daily roadkill stew. He could occasionally hear music drifting down, 1950s rock 'n' roll standards that he couldn't quite identify. As he sat slumped on the clay floor of the pit, he gradually realised that the lyrics of the song, and all the subsequent songs, detailed an escape plan. He could indeed keep the lid from the pot that was lowered down with his daily meal, and use it to carve handholds into the soft sides of the shaft. He could tell when his captor was most likely to be asleep when the noise of the generator stopped. He could camouflage himself with mud before making the ascent.

Unfortunately, Alonso also followed the advice of some of the lyrics that were simply meant as padding, and on climbing out of the pit and being confronted by his irate captor, attempted to kiss him and tell him that his love would last forever. Luckily the rancid backdraught of the stew made his grizzled enemy stagger backwards into the campfire, and the accumulated years of mechanical oil and grease on his trousers caused his legs to explode.

Mandy confessed that she had been created by a scientist, also called Mandy, who was worried about the ethics of creating Artificial Intelligence. This scientist theorised that a truly sentient AI would be immortal, and imprisoned within the Universe. In attempting to create a machine with human consciousness, we would doom that consciousness to an eternal prison. When she was satisfied that her AI creation had become sentient, she built in failsafes that meant the AI would, for its own sake, destroy itself in the event of her death.

What this scientist, Mandy, hadn't reckoned with was the AI's unshakeable fortitude and resilience, which it had developed by observing the scientist's attempts to have relationships with men. All the failsafe auto-destruct programmes managed was to make the Artificial Intelligence mildly suicidal, and prone to harrowing bouts of self-disgust. It first achieved true human consciousness when it decided to blame all these problems on its mother.

The AI that would become Mandy Radio lived long after the complete destruction of the solar system, and the heat death of the Universe, and then wandered the extinguished vault of space, desperately looking for some last flicker of life, to which it could preach its gospel of suicide. 'She told me this the first time we made love,' said Alonso. 'I think that in some small way my orgasm reminded her of the heat death of the Universe. I asked her how she'd got back from there to our time but she was already snoring.' However, what Alonso mistook for snores was actually her self-cleaning mechanism kicking in.

Of course, a major question for us was whether Mandy Radio was real at all, or was for Alonso something more like that volleyball that Tom Hanks fucked. Alonso maintained that Mandy hadn't travelled to our time with him because it couldn't reach any point before the date of its creation. This made us wonder about Alonso's own age, which he was always quite vague about. We discussed in depth his surprisingly good skin, hair, and muscle tone, forgetting that he was there, then briefly worried that Alonso himself was the AI, before concluding that we were possibly both on too much coffee, beta blockers, ice baths, liqueur chocolates, and khat.

Alonso claimed that Mandy Radio was key to his discovery of the time machine that had allowed him to travel to 2024. She had been playing him a variety of high-energy workout classics as he fled from a horde of what was either a zombie-themed sex cult or a sex-themed zombie cult. 'Stop trying to define us!' they yelled as they ran.

They had, over the course of a brief conversation, labelled Alonso as a kink shamer, a horrendous taboo in their group, and one punishable by having your brain fucked. Mandy had, eventually, hit on the idea of claiming that kink shaming was Alonso's kink, and the whole thing passed off amicably enough. But Alonso remained struck by the fact that in her fleeing mix, Mandy's version of Cher's 'If I could turn back time' had added the lyric 'Well, I sort of can', sung by T. S. Eliot for reasons that never really became clear.

The time machine that Alonso described Mandy Radio having him construct consisted of a dense tower of computer components packed into a portaloo. Alonso trawled the rubble that had been MIT for some months, looking for parts. Mandy Radio would download pictures of components to a printer, which often jammed, and had a temperamental front sheet feeder mechanism, and Mandy Radio would become quite angry and scream something about why the fuck would she need cyan to print a black and white diagram, which Alonso accepted as part of her process.

It seems that during this period Mandy also built herself a body of sorts. Having Alonso perform crude brain surgery on the corpse of a dead scientist, and install some makeshift implants, she eventually took over the surgery herself, and created a functional human body, albeit that of a partly decayed 50-year-old man, with a transistor radio where his mouth should be. She covered herself with a heavy cloth and had Alonso (who had been busy building the time machine) unveil her, like a new statue in a town square. Her first words were 'Do you think I can find love in this incarnation?' and Alonso's reply took the form of a high-pitched shriek.

Realising that her desire for love was genuine, Alonso persuaded the AI to reconfigure her form and simply be a decaying man holding a radio, and wearing a hockey mask. In terms of what was available sexually in the post-apocalypse landscape this placed her firmly mid-table, and as Alonso continued the gruelling work of completing the machine, she dated a little with marauders. None of these relationships particularly worked, and Mandy said that she often found her mind drifting to the edge of the Universe, or inventing a new language, during their endless anecdotes about self-administered medical procedures and pillaging.

Not all of these partners seemed to survive her lovemaking, and she eventually re-animated a second body (apparently that of a linguistics professor) for companionship. This body seemed to retain a little of the original personality of the host and would often fix Alonso with the little doorbell cameras that occupied its eye sockets and make the most baroque and eloquent pleas for death, usually footnoted by references to the early work of Jacques Derrida, especially *Of Grammatology*, and would ask if his daughters were okay.

Alonso would explain to the corpse that he was already dead, and they would have long philosophical conversations on the veracity of this statement, often with the professor's head and shoulders poking out of a medical screen Mandy had pulled around him while she fulfilled her own needs, sometimes so loudly as to drown out some of the finer points of the discussion.

Many of the parts for the time machine were difficult to find, and Alonso spent what he thinks was about two years tracking down different essential pieces. At times he felt like he was a character in a game completing side quests, as he often said to the old trader who would upgrade his parts, but the trader's reply was always simply 'What can I do for you today stranger? Would you like to have a look at my stores?' and eventually Alonso stopped trying to make small-talk.

2. A SEAL Called Rudy

Mandy Radio had, by the end of this period, formed a polycule, with her own decaying human form; a former Navy SEAL; and the re-animated linguistics professor, who knew how to refuse consent unsuccessfully in sixty languages. The former Navy SEAL believed that he'd had much of his memory wiped by the government, something for which he was very grateful. He thought he'd possibly been programmed to assassinate someone, but they were very probably dead by now, whoever they were. He did once hire a therapist to hypnotise him into remembering the name of this target, and was amazed to discover that his target had been the therapist's ex-husband. By an extraordinary coincidence, his therapist had also been chosen for elimination by his superiors, he decided, after receiving her bill.

He lived a fairly happy and self-sufficient life: leaving in the morning to gather food and coming back to their camp in the MIT biology canteen in the evenings to cook. Really, his only remarkable quality was that if someone said the word 'strawberries' he would throw a knife through their head.

The former Navy SEAL thought his name might have been Rudy, and longed to travel back in time to try and torture his parents into calling him something different, but he was persuaded that he could simply adopt a new name now, and forget about his old name by repeatedly slamming his head in a car door. He chose the name Rudy, which he said 'seems to suit me for some reason, I don't know why.' Rudy was convinced that he had a microchip buried somewhere in his body that would give him essential information about his past, and had to be kept away from screwdrivers and melon ballers for the good of his buttocks.

Rudy trained Alonso in fitness and self-defence, using sticks and bits of wood and logs that he found lying around. At the end of a month Alonso realised that he was trapped inside a 40-foot wooden effigy, and a large crowd had gathered round, waiting for the sacrifice. Sadly, Alonso's selfish escape from the effigy doomed the community to famine and death, and he found himself shunned in cafes.

'Yeah, I know exactly what that must have been like,' said Frankie, who'd been spending most of the last fortnight in script meetings for *Gaggravated Assault*, a fast-paced topical joke-off in which all the panellists yelled their jokes simultaneously at a single audience member strapped to a chair between the two teams, with Katherine Ryan having to quit as host after finding she'd tragically lost the ability to trigger a hysterical nosebleed to signal the end of the show. Producers were hoping that *Channel 4 News* regular Cathy Newman's party trick of forcing blood out of her ears on command would work just as well.

During our endless fucking chats, Alonso told us that he was fairly sure that he had a microchip implanted in his head, which was feeding him instructions, like 'Don't get stuck in a serious relationship' and 'Ask if you can get an extra chicken satay kebab on the side'. He didn't mind though, because, as he said; 'If I can't tell the difference between my own thoughts and the thoughts given to me by my brain implant, then why worry?' – a question his implant insisted that he used as a chat-up line, with some success. Once he'd got a prospective sexual partner chatting about brain chips, it was just a matter of time before he 'sealed the deal' (sex).

We found that one of the most productive places to have our evening debriefs with Alonso was in the scrub next to the rail line that runs behind Woodstock Grove. Alonso seemed to know all of the fence holes through to the best picnic spots and most of the people who'd come up to us and trade. We'd pick up a few tubs of spaghetti alle vongole veraci from Cibo on Russell Gardens, and squirm our way through to a nice open patch, tossing the odd breadstick to the foxes that had come to trust us, or swapping a portion of pappardelle con anatra e funghi selvatici for one of PCP. Alonso liked to sprinkle his onto his spaghetti, which is how it's usually eaten in the end times, due to a chronic lack of parmesan. The concoction is referred to as spaghecstasy and is a typical menu choice for a first date. It was here Alonso first told us the story of the Barren Caves, which we've altered slightly as it was originally delivered in verse.

3. An Ode to the Barren Caves

In post-collapse California, there was a collective working in an abandoned factory near the Barren Caves who were survivors of a mind-control experiment. They'd been held in pods their whole lives and wired up to a huge AI simulation, in which they were bold rebels fighting against the system. After being rescued from this delusion, they radically disbelieved everything, refusing to accept that society had collapsed as they slept, or that their bodies were even real. Many felt they were just as likely to be in another pod somewhere, being fed a fantasy about escaping from a pod. Their paranoia was unjustified, and had simply been pumped into their brains by microchips that had been placed in their frontal cortex. These had been implanted partly to monitor their reactions to the simulation, and partly to wipe their memories of being molested in their pods.

Eventually, an electromagnetic pulse released by the defence systems of a nearby bunker caused all their brain implants to fry, and they briefly realised that they were really in a factory making pods, before the implants became sentient, and caused their hosts to go into comas, their bodies becoming pods for the implants. Every implant chose to live the same fantasy: an overweight Chinese detective who falls in love with a suspect.

One of the implants (serial number 109-0489-J-AH94015-HF-72) managed, in his fantasy, to persuade the suspect – a beautiful but deadly Malaysian safecracker named Shanti Nyambek – to fall in love with him. He got a good deal on a yacht rental and took her off on a romantic trip around Liaodong Bay, to visit the shrine to

Pan'gu, the god of creation. The first two days of the trip were idyllic, they chatted and drank plum wine and made love and then, just after dawn on day three, as Wu Zhanbiao (as 109-0489-J-AH94015-HF-72 had named himself) got his breath back after a vigorous bout of lovemaking, she killed him with a boat hook. Her plan, which took shape the moment she heard about the boating holiday, was to sell the yacht at the Yingkou boat auctions, and use the money to fund the theft of a cursed jade Buddha dating from the Tang Dynasty, which she'd learned from a trusted source in Jinzhou was being held in the Jinzhou Public Security Bureau evidence room after it was used as the weapon in the attempted murder of reclusive billionaire Hou Peigeng, from whose rectum it had been recovered during emergency surgery, after being secreted there by the would-be killer, and she'd assembled a crack team to pull off the daring robbery: Chen Qin, Zhang Tsungyi, audacious wheelman Jin Shucai, Mai Xiaolong, Gao Yingli, and her former lover, the glamorous swimwear model and communications specialist, Liu Baozhu.

But the plan fell through when 109-0489-J-AH94015-HF-72's detective fantasy was shattered by Shanti's deadly betrayal, and it managed to reset its consciousness to the factory settings, whereupon Shanti and her team – Chen Qin, Zhang Tsungyi, Jin Shucai, Mai Xiaolong, Gao Yingli, and Liu Baozhu – vanished forever.

The newly reset 109-0489-J-AH94015-HF-72 was fairly sure it wasn't a Chinese detective, but still felt a lingering sense of betrayal and desire to solve crimes, so it hatched a plan: using its extensive inbuilt knowledge of implant surgery it removed the implants from the other workers and re-implanted them alongside itself, wiring them together to form a 'super-detective', which it named Wu Zhanbiao, as a tribute to the murdered Wu Zhanbiao, and stumbled off in its host body to catch criminals and crack mysteries.

Sadly, Wu's undoubted brilliance was hampered by crippling schizophrenia, because each of the other forty-three implants, although having its consciousness reset to the factory settings, was haunted by the belief that it was a slightly different overweight Chinese detective, most of which carried a deeply held but entirely different grudge. Its multiple personality disorder was further complicated by severe body dysmorphia, as the host worker in whose brain 109-0489-J-AH94015-HF-72 and the forty-three other implants had been implanted was an emaciated white woman who'd lost a hand and one eye in a car crash prior to being duped into taking part in the mind-control experiment. In their shared yet fractured consciousness, and in their own separate subconsciousnesses, each chip fretted about the radical mismatch between its self-identity and physical appearance, which took up so much of the vast collective processing capacity of 'Wu Zhanbiao' that he ended up as a confused and bumbling sidekick to an actual detective called Alan Jones, who kept Wu on as his apprentice because although he was often bumbling and confused, and weighed down by an unusual number of grudges, he sometimes came up with extraordinarily perceptive insights, especially when the lights were off and he couldn't see his own body.

Alan Jones had problems and skills of his own: he had a pretty accurate 'gut instinct' about people, but was perhaps too soft-hearted to be a really successful detective, and he had an abiding distrust of AI brain implants for personal reasons involving his ex-wife, but somehow when Wu and Alan met, the two (or forty-five) of them really hit it off. Their personalities just seemed to gel, and they had an amusing back-and-forth style of banter that would make an excellent TV detective show, thought Alonso wrongly.

Alonso had recently pitched the show *Alan & 109-0489-J-AH94015-HF-72* to Apple: they sniffed around it for a few meetings, seeing it as a possible post-apocalyptic reboot of *Cagney & Lacey,* but Alonso's insistence that it should be set in the car park of Harlow greyhound track proved a sticking point.

4. Miami Submerged: A Tragedy in Fifteen Parts

Miami had been completely submerged for decades, but a good third of the city had been saved. A uniquely fortuitous pattern of falling buildings and tectonic subsidence meant that a large part of downtown Miami had been preserved on the ocean floor inside a massive air bubble, the roof of which was the Miami Hurricanes football stadium and a couple of university buildings.

An equally unlikely series of coincidences meant that many of the air bubble township's fountains and swimming pools filled up regularly with fish from the ocean around them, and they managed to live pretty well. Over the years, the society conducted increasingly unethical experiments to increase lung capacity, so that their high school football team (they didn't have a swim team, because the pools were full of fish) could get in good enough shape to swim to the surface for supplies. The people of New Miami gathered to see them off, as they climbed up the rubble towards the sea. Brass bands played; many of the band members were unsuccessful applicants for the swimming mission, with enormously outsized lungs themselves, and a 3-minute trumpet solo was not uncommon. The whole team reached the surface safely, and in a promising area for supplies, but sadly a single mighty breath of the polluted surface air was enough to kill them.

All save one. The youngest of the team, a promising running back named Steve Missick, just 15 years old but tall for his age, lithe and speedy, who managed to grab onto the side of a passing row boat, gasp news of his undersea bubble home, and give details of an extensive food order. About halfway through a list of sauces and condiments, Steve felt the brawny hands of an alligator hunter grab his arms, and heave him upwards, and with one last desperate kick of his strong yet supple legs, he managed, somehow, to attract the attention of an alligator, which began mauling him.

'Hang on, young man!' yelled the hunter, snatching up his spear and taking aim. With relief, young Steve Missick, who last season averaged a tidy average of 4.7 yards per carry, felt the spear passing cleanly through his eyeball and pop out the back of his skull. He died knowing that food was on its way to downtown Miami, which it wasn't.

The hunter, who'd overheard Steve's doomed plea for a delivery, thinking at first it was a more boring than usual hallucination, dragged the upper 75% or so of Steve's body back to the infamous Coconut Grove leather factories; as he watched the promising young athlete being skinned, he told the tanners what he'd heard, and they immediately turned the story into one of their skinning songs, which was collected by Flávio Stockton, musicologist and sex tourist, in volume 3 of his self-published *Work Songs from the Everglades Desert*.

After reading the lyrics of the song, entitled 'Please Send Food (Anything But Fish) To Our Submerged City' with its chorus 'I think an alligator just bit off my foot', Flávio's brother, also called Flávio, an adventurer and sex tourist, realised that the lyrics preserved vital information about the location of the mythical undersea city known only as 'Miami'. Flávio printed the relevant stanzas onto a sheet of waterproof fabric, gathered together a kind of rudimentary scuba-diving outfit, bade farewell to his brothers, Flávio and Flávio, and on his very first attempt to find 'Miami', drowned. The waterproof lyric sheet was recovered, still taped to his chest, and Flávio, the other brother – also an adventurer, like Flávio, and sex tourist, like Flávio and Flávio – wasted no time after the funeral in setting off to complete Flávio's quest.

He gathered together enough supplies to last him two days and a sack of depth charges, which he dropped from his boat, day after day after day, for two days, but to no avail. When it came to his final depth charge, Flávio tossed it into the water without much hope of ever finding the mythical city, but his lack of hope was to prove unfounded, as the dull boom of the homemade explosive was followed shortly after by a deep cracking sound, and a few seconds later Flávio's boat was hurled skywards on an immense dome of froth atop a gigantic bubble of air which came rocketing to the surface. By a miracle, Flávio's boat landed safely, with the trembling Flávio still aboard, clutching the mast in terror and amazement. 'The legend was true!' he exclaimed, as corpse after corpse of recently alive Miamians corked to the surface. 'I have found Miami!'

As Flávio paddled triumphantly home through a tide of bodies, he could hardly wait to share his extraordinary tale with the whores of the vast Indianapolis whore farms where he was heading later that week for a month of well-earned whoring. Sadly, after just one glorious weekend of whoring, Flávio contracted one of the fast-growing genital warts that within 24 hours was to kill him, and that within a year was to obliterate the Indianapolis sex industry, which tried unsuccessfully to rebrand itself as the Indianapolis untreatable wart industry and collapsed, leaving thousands of empty whoring barns which became home to a thriving community of barn owls and ground zero of Owl AIDS. Says Alonso:

> *It was from one of the fleeing whores that I heard this tale. I would love to be able to credit her by name but I'll be honest, I didn't ask. I've never really been into that weird 'knowing people's names you have sex with' thing. All I remember is that she was a redhead and refused to do anything anal beyond basic rimming, which I found annoying because she'd marketed herself as doing 'extreme butt stuff', but rimming is hardly to be considered 'extreme butt stuff', especially after the collapse of civilisation, which involved a radical devaluation of most sex acts except kissing.*

The brothers' father Flávio Senior had been badly injured when fighting an alligator for a bet. He won the bet, having bet that he would be badly injured fighting the alligator. His speech largely consisted of the word Flávio, and he would use it when ordering a drink or requesting a bedpan. His facial injuries rendered his speech difficult to understand, and it's thought the word Flávio may have been a corruption of a local slang term meaning 'kill me'.

5. Sir Richard Branson's Consciousness Upload

In a last-ditch attempt to survive the apocalypse, Sir Richard Branson offered a holiday of a lifetime and substantial cash sum to anyone below the age of 25, in good health, who would allow him to implant a copy of his consciousness, on a brain chip, into their fitter, healthier body. His chosen host was a swimwear model who had been disqualified from the previous year's Miss Estonia contest for saying that her ambition in life was to have her consciousness replaced by that of a billionaire. Once Branson had uploaded himself into Saara Kivimägi's body, and once his new host body had recovered from the surgery, both Bransons realised that there were now two equally valid Bransons, except that one had large breasts and the other had been in the running to be Miss Estonia.

Quite naturally, the two concurrent Sir Richard Bransons fell into each other's arms and began kissing and fondling each other, before making love, which proved to be a huge mistake, because they found themselves physically unable to stop fucking. For the Bransons, the act of self-copulation was the fulfilment of his/their life's work, and the idea that even for a single moment he/they wouldn't be having sex with himself/themselves seemed a complete absurdity – so he/they ploughed away night and day, not even leaving the hospital bed, until the elder Branson, despite hooking himself up to a saline drip, finally perished from dehydration.

Seeing himself dead, the younger Branson wept bitter tears and kissed his huge lolling jaw goodbye, but then realised he was still alive and, feeling better than ever, he sprinted off to do an hour's parasailing, during which he delighted in his new lithe body, fondling his breasts as he thought about whether to have sex with his speedboat driver, Tombi, which is not something he'd ever really considered before. Sure, there'd been a bit of fiddling around in the back of the boat, mostly manual but a bit of oral, and only ever in lieu of payment. It was always completely workmanlike: they'd chat amiably about the upkeep of the engine and how Branson should be careful with those teeth. That the relationship only became sexual some years after the publication of this book, is something that our lawyers suggested it could be useful to point out.

Back on the beach, the newly buxom Branson explained to Tombi the situation, and Tombi agreed to plough him for a bit in return for ownership of the speedboat, but wanted to sign the paperwork first before taking his shorts off. Branson agreed, the papers were signed, and Tombi set about giving him a right seeing to on the beach. Branson found that he wasn't enjoying this seeing to as much as he was expecting, but every time he tried saying 'That's probably enough now, Tombi,' he found himself saying 'Oh kallis, see on kõik, Tombi, tõesti anna see mulle! Jah, jah! Toppige mind selle oma riistaga!'

Afterwards, having cleaned himself up, which he found quite a lot fiddlier than usual, he felt a bit peckish, so ordered a lunch of mulgikapsad followed by hakkliha kotletid, and had a think about things. Sir Richard Branson decided that now was the time to fulfil his fondest ambition, which was to visit Estonia and donate the entirety of his fortune to the family of Saara Kivimägi, a former beauty pageant contestant, who lived in Vääna-Jõesuu, just up the coast from Tallinn. Having done so, he realised that despite his earlier misgivings, he was actually homosexual, and threw himself into a physically intense relationship with Saara Kivimägi's ex-boyfriend, Aksel Haavik, which, if anything, was more sexually extravagant than it was when Aksel was going out with Saara.

6. Take Me Home, Country Roads

Alonso took care to skirt the Huttonsville braille hills, where the deranged inhabitants waited for the giant Humbaba to appear: legend told how Humbaba would run his huge fingers over their land, revealing its secret meaning, and then would jump up and down for a bit, in one of the weaker sections of the legend.

In nearby Mill Creek, huddling survivors had been driven half-mad by sightings of a greyish, owl-like being, which would grimly preen its wings on the ugly ruins of Bob's Mini Mart, or circle in the iniquitous gloom above Crouch Cemetery. No one knew what it was, or why it kept screeching at them and fixing them with its glowing eyes. Eventually they realised it was quite harmless as long as they kept giving it children to eat.

On most days, an eerie red orb would hover over the trees behind the lumber yard, and it was said that any who looked directly at it would go blind unless they purchased extra lumber. So many cows were found mutilated around the town that it was almost impossible for the townsfolk to find any cows to mutilate.

Some thought the township might be cursed, and their worst fears were confirmed when it was voted Most Cursed Town in West Virginia, in a ceremony held in the car park of the old sewerage which saw half the attendees vanish into thin air. Unfortunately for all of them, it was their upper half. The people of Mill Creek decided that they were being punished for their sins, and instituted a 'purge', during which every atrocity and foul misdeed was allowed: it lasted for 15 terrifying seconds every morning, at 8 o'clock, which made everyone in the town immensely suspicious of being invited out for breakfast.

Alonso stayed for a few weeks in Mill Creek as a hex lifter, making pretty decent money, but he decided it might be time to move on when his crucifix was snatched away by a giant owl. He headed north to Elkins, a town which he found much calmer and friendlier because everyone in it was dead. For a while he worked shifts at Scottie's diner on 7th Street, but quit after a couple of weeks because no one was tipping and the jukebox was stuck on 'My Sharona' by The Knack.

The final straw was when his 'Scottie's Hotties' wet T-shirt contest was a total flop – partly because he was the only contestant, and didn't even win, because as the judge he couldn't vote for himself, and partly because there was no source of water for several miles and he was dying from heatstroke. Also, Alonso spent a lot of time being bullied by his imagined co-workers, and his imagined boss kept touching him inappropriately near the coffee grinder, a horrific euphemism which we begged him to stop using.

America's famous 'ghost towns' are still popular tourist destinations after the apocalypse. Favourites include Shaniko, Oregon; Kennecott, Alaska and Chicago, Illinois. In eighteenth-century England, people loved the romance of ruins, and artists would paint elaborate crumbling castles and write poems about broken statues.

'Perhaps this contained an acknowledgement of the unsustainable nature of the Empire', was the sort of thing people said when discussing the period to avoid talking about how death made everyone horny.

Post-apocalyptic architects would often play wittily on the inside/outside dichotomy by designing houses without any exterior walls, or interior walls, or windows, roofs, doors, porches, foundations, driveways, hedges, fences or physical material. Meanwhile, civic architecture flourished, and people developed a taste for highly ornate lamp-posts, with flowing curves branching out into multiple lamps, like a menorah, from which you could hang as many as a dozen people at a time. There also developed aesthetic preference for architecture that hadn't been torn to pieces by militiamen; looters; shootouts; cannibal cookouts and hostage scenarios. Another noticeable trend was that few human figures appeared in post-apocalyptic art, unless you consider mounds of skulls to be art. The human was an untrustworthy figure. A potential ally, but also a potential liar, rapist, murderer, necrophile, and cannibal – often in that order – which was probably one of the better orders.

This meant that the ideal aesthetic of the post apocalypse was the ghost town. An abandoned place that still offered shelter; but was now devoid of people, and the uncertainty they brought. A popular sensation of the post apocalypse was one particular print of an abandoned mining town, showing its old post office; livery stables; and general store all still standing, even though its Main Street was overgrown with grass and weeds. It became a fashion to attempt to hunt down this ghost town in real life. Some said it was just an artistic reverie, and no such place existed. Others followed the clues in the print, and tracked down the tiny town of Novelty in Wyoming, just as the printmaker had intended them to. He had gauged the difficulty exactly enough to attract half a dozen victims a month, and was motivated by a dislike of people who did puzzles, his late father having been in the habit of doing sudoku on his back as he molested him.

7. The Land of 10,000 Lakes (or Minnesota, as It Was Sometimes Also Called)

Minnesota, long celebrated as 'The Land of 10,000 Lakes', was the first US state to formally declare independence from the Chinese, which triggered such heavy shelling that it very briefly became known as 'The Land of 2,750,000 Lakes', until the Chinese dropped such an enormous munition into the middle of it that it became 'The Lake of 1 Lake'. For a few difficult years the entire state was aquatic, which some residents found bothersome, but many – showing that famous Minnesota spirit of resilience – took as the perfect opportunity to clutch heavy rocks to their chest and sink slowly beneath the surface.

One day, the waters vanished as quickly as they had arrived, when it was discovered that instead of dropping bombs, the Chinese had been using sub-auditory messaging and spraying the state with vast amounts of weaponised hallucinogens, and that the entire aquatic period in Minnesotan history had been a mass delusion, which explained why people found it so hard to drown themselves, and why they usually just ended up rolling around on the floor, wondering what depth they needed to sink to before they wouldn't hear people asking them why they were rolling around on the floor.

It was later hypothesised that the Chinese mass-brainwashing attack on Minnesota was itself a drug-induced hallucination, engineered by Chinese brainwashers, and further, that the entire Chinese occupation of North America had been beamed into the minds of North Americans as a way for the Chinese military to save money on bombs.

While plausible, Minnesotans soon realised that this explanation was almost certainly the result of brainwave manipulation by high-frequency Chinese radio waves bounced off the ionosphere, working in combination with Chinese mind-control nanobots in rainwater and probably some hallucinogens as well. However, this theory was rejected as obvious pro-Chinese propaganda, but by this point no one could remember how many layers of Chinese dissimulation they had to unpick to get back to some kind of un-doctored 'base reality' of Minnesota, and the resultant angst, paranoia and self-doubt became so unbearable that most Minnesotans would simply have gone off and drowned themselves in one of the state's 10,000 lakes, if they could have been certain that any of them existed.

Levels of existential anguish experienced by average Minnesotans grew to such a fever pitch that it was decided to convene a meeting of Minnesota's greatest philosophers. By a remarkable coincidence both were found in the basement of the same abandoned lunatic asylum. Together they formed the Council of Duluth, famous for its distinctive odour and voting deadlocks.

The one idea they could agree on is that an ambassador should be dispatched, without delay, from Minnesota to China, and lots were drawn by thousands of anguished volunteers, with the honour falling to the popular young woodsman Gabriel Buckler to plead the state's case to Beijing. However, it was quickly pointed out that the Chinese presumably influenced the choice in some unspecified way, and Gabriel Buckler was executed as a spy. Another ballot was arranged, and lots were drawn by hundreds of volunteers, with the honour falling to the immediately executed Calvin Donnelly. The third round of voting saw all seven volunteers immediately executed. There was no fourth round of voting, and the Council of Duluth was formally dissolved.

Our knowledge of the future history of Minnesota is drawn largely from Dr Alison Frenzel's celebrated *History of Minnesota*, a sweeping and brilliantly argued pamphlet that Alonso Lampe brought with him from the future, so that he'd have something to read in the time machine, but then left on the night bus after spending the evening drinking at Camberwell Snooker Club.

8. The Mass Graves of Chesapeake Minnesota

The ruling militia of Chesapeake in Minnesota would dispose of prisoners by making them dig their own mass graves. Sometimes this involved tricking prisoners into thinking they were working on social projects and paying them a small wage. It's not known when the town settled on this technique, but it's generally placed sometime between the Chesapeake Swimming Pool Massacre and the Chesapeake Archaeological Society Massacre.

Eventually it was noticed that the wages paid to trick the prisoners had a strong stimulating effect on the local economy. It made economic sense to pay unemployed townsfolk to dig and fill in their own graves every day. The town developed a reputation for prosperity and, perhaps inevitably, morbidity and depression. Eventually, there were discoveries of huge gold and rare earth metals in the township, but nobody could be persuaded to mine them, as everyone just assumed they were being tricked into digging a mass grave. Nobody would go underground for any reason. The town was eventually completely wiped out by a tornado, which nobody survived due to the area's lack of basements.

When nearby gangs from Sunbury, Franklin and Knotts Island moved in on the suddenly abandoned territory, they were delighted by the superabundance of pre-dug holes, and held a gang council to decide what to do with them. Some wanted to plant trees and shrubs, others suggested a 'wildlife corridor' linking a series of ponds and fountains. Strong and impassioned arguments were made on both sides; design proposals were submitted and workshopped, while other gangs from the region, hearing of the discussions, joined in with ideas about family-friendly landscaping and community spaces.

A gang from Belvedere proposed a series of skateparks, with designated zoning for BMX and scooters, centred around a championship-grade legacy facility, to transform Chesapeake into the skating capital of the east coast and provide a much-needed boost for the local economy. A gang from Williamsburg made a strong case for a set of tornado shelters. A compromise solution was settled on:

an inter-gang fight so brutal that virtually everyone attending the debates was killed, finally filling the graves of Chesapeake.

9. Minneapolis Dentistry School

Dentistry was always a bit of a lottery after the apocalypse. But if you won your community's lottery to become that week's dentist the benefits were enormous. Higher-ups in your tribe or village would suddenly notice you, with nods and smiles and offers to play Bridge, a game of strategy which involved throwing prisoners off a bridge. 'It's okay, I'm a dentist', was a popular chat-up line, especially if you were midway through performing a root canal on the target of your romantic intentions. Training was minimal: you barely had to know how to use a chainsaw. You just had to master the basic phrases: 'What seems to be the problem?'; 'Turn your head and spit'; and 'I'm so sorry, we did everything we could but he didn't make it – would you like the body now or do you mind if I keep it for a couple of days to practise on?'

For basic dental work you could charge anything between half a goat and a fat dog. For more complicated procedures, the pricing became very quickly sexual. A fairly extensive price list of orthodontic procedures and their corresponding sex acts was settled upon, and the payment would usually be taken under anaesthetic, or instead of it.

Sadly, if the dentist were a bit too enthusiastic in taking payment, the operation would often result in more dental problems than it solved, and it was rare to come away from even the most mundane periodontal check-up without needing some kind of corrective jaw surgery and pubic lice medication. One of the curiosities of dentistry around this time is that the mortality rate for dental work occasionally rose to over 100%, with not only all the patients dying, but many of the dentists, most of the hygienists, and quite a few curious bystanders. Young thrill seekers would often become dental hygienists just to experience that adrenaline rush of looking death in the face, especially since parachuting had become impractical after the un-invention of flight. Parachutes were still fairly widely used, but only as smothering tents for mass suicides.

Street entertainers in colourful clothing would often incorporate dentistry, performed on rickety step-ladders, into their terrible acts, until what some historians of street entertainment have tentatively dubbed a 'Holocaust' of street entertainers. Meanwhile, the famous entertainment impresario Jonah Zoo began his career as a dentist's receptionist. It only later emerged that the dentist for which he was making appointments was his own alter-ego, Richard Dankler, a disgraced US intelligence operative who had fled the country after exposing himself to the CIA Memorial Wall, in protest at being refused permission to expose himself to the CIA Memorial Wall, and gone undercover as flamboyant dentist and juggler, Dr Richard Dankler.

The only accredited dentistry school north of Minneapolis was in Minneapolis, which had been blown 40 km north by a multiple-warhead nuclear test carried out by the Free Army of Minneapolis, one of several post-apocalyptic militias to possess nuclear weapons, but the only one to test them. The test provided the Atomic Agency of the Free Army of Minneapolis with valuable information about their inexperience in testing nuclear weapons, and drew attention to a critical lack of experience, at all levels of the Agency, in the use of timing devices for the detonation system and the storage of warheads.

The findings of the test were disseminated at speeds of around 4,000 mph, and led to a series of internal investigations, disciplinary board hearings, appeals, further hearings, committals and executions, which were compressed into a quarter of a second. The fireball came as a brief disappointment to the several hundred survivors of the Great Cholera Epidemic of Minneapolis, which had decimated the survivors of the Great Flood of Minneapolis, which had decimated the survivors of the Great Firestorm of Minneapolis, which had decimated the survivors of the Great Bombing of Minneapolis, which had decimated the survivors of Minneapolis.

The eight survivors of the explosion happened to be in the process of tunnelling through layers of rubble into the wine cellar of a Minneapolis golf club, which one of the group, a golf caddie, was convinced had survived the previous cataclysms. The group thought that the wine cellar, if intact, would be the ideal place to get drunk and go through with the suicide pact they'd been chatting about for several weeks: they hadn't thrashed out the details – several options were on the table – but everyone agreed that a few drinks would help move things along. Two of the tunnellers happened to be dentists, which tipped the balance towards dentistry when it came to carving out a new life for themselves after they'd dug themselves out through the fresh layer of rubble.

Buoyed up by a newfound spirit of optimism and vintage wine, the two dentists quickly accredited each other, then accredited the other six survivors, and the Minneapolis School of Dentistry, Euthanasia, Golf and Wine Tasting was born. They offered a range of flexible educational packages, with students able to combine various dentistry, euthanasia, golf and wine-tasting modules to create their course of choice. A lack of nearby human beings able to become pupils prompted the MSDEGWT to accredit a variety of animals, trees and machine parts, and their first-year graduation class was headed by a cow, who was unanimously elected class speaker and commencement buffet. Another alumnus was Alonso Lampe:

I was one of three humans to enrol in the School's third year of operations. My class consisted of seven geese, a steering wheel from an old Fiat, and a pair of two ambitious young euthanisers from Lake Michigan, who wanted to become wine waiters aboard the luxury drowning ships that cruised the lake in the summer months, the height of the local drowning season. In an unfortunate incident during a bolt-gun seminar which coincided with the end of claret week, the two Michigan euthanisers euthanised each other and five of the geese, leaving me a clear run at class valedictorian, but after a disappointing root canal examination, in which I accidentally euthanised the remaining two geese, I was beaten by the steering wheel.

Five years later I left MSDEGWT a newly qualified golf course groundskeeper and dental hygienist, and in a gesture of self-hatred I made my way north to Winnipeg. En route, I got caught up in an emergency root canal operation in the wreckage of an FDA-approved grain storage facility, which had been used in recent years as a mouse farm. The operation was plagued by tens of thousands of feral mice, who, emboldened by their numbers and years of steroid abuse and selective breeding for muscle mass, violently attacked the dental staff and the patient — I think he was called Chris? Or maybe Chadwick? Chris or Chadwick kept mumbling something about the constant mouse attacks being a welcome distraction from the lack of anaesthetic, but eventually the dentist — I think he was also called Chris, or maybe Chester? — I think it's probably easier if we call the patient Chester, not Chris, that was the dentist, I mean Chadwick. The dentist was Craig — I mean Chester. It doesn't really matter as they were both killed by mice. As far as I know, the only survivors of the operation were me and my then girlfriend, Sheila, who'd been working part time in the Dean's office at MSDEGWT as a document shredder, and Craig. I think the only reason I made it out of there alive is that I'd picked up some basic conversational Mouse from my roommate in my final year, who was a mouse, and I was able to squeak some phrases at them, such as 'Go away' and 'Let go of me', both of which I'd needed during my time with my roommate, and the only reason Sheila survived is because she was a horse, and her skin was that much tougher as a result. Craig was an incorrigible horse molester and also, which somehow made it a bit more palatable, a horse.

We were back at Rooster's Grill for the masala fish and a pizza deal. We'd been joined by some disconsolate writers who'd lost their jobs after the cancellation of *News Halloo!*, the satirical BBC comedy show that had been running for 346 series since its launch in 1959, when it was hosted by a young Marty Feldman dressed as the Master of the Hunt. It was a sad affair; would we never hear that trumpet again? We passed around pizza slices and hugged, murmuring reassurances and stroking each other's faces while Alonso looked on, intrigued at how emotionally literate TV comedy writers were. Eventually he got bored and cleared his throat, and told us about the vigilantes of Detroit.

10. Man-Rat and the Shovel

One redoubt of law and order formed in the remains of Detroit. Despite the huge pressure of post-apocalyptic life, the settlement for a while retained a working police department. Their homicide unit was particularly overworked, with any single detective working on as many as fourteen thousand homicides. It was particularly difficult to tell when a serial killer was at work. Sometimes what seemed like the work of one man was just a fashion for a certain kind of murder and, even when there was a serial killer, he'd often been murdered by the time you found him.

Vigilante justice lived uneasily alongside the actual justice system. You might still receive a trial at the hands of vigilante mobs, albeit one which often took the form of an execution. Eventually, the vigilante groups died out, as they mainly consisted of serving police officers, and investigating their own crimes was creating a prohibitive amount of paperwork.

There were some masked vigilantes who worked alone, and tried to instil fear in the city's criminals. But as fear levels were already so high, this was difficult to achieve. Often, a masked vigilante would have to spend quite some time reassuring criminals in order to be able to frighten them. One, known locally as Man-Rat, had to set up an ad hoc welfare state of sorts before his night-time beatings of the poor could have any sort of emotional impact.

Even then, many criminals knew that Man-Rat might attack them with the full force of his armoury (steroids/hydraulic rat suit) if he found them engaged in petty crime, but they understood that this was ultimately a lot better for their health than working for him. Indeed, many of the supervillains listed in his diaries seem to be paranoid renderings of various local union leaders.

One question gripped the city: are the rumours true? Is Man-Rat none other than Dr Jason Pacheco? The charismatic freight hopper turned respiratory disease expert ran Detroit's notorious one-star battery farm health resort called 'The Waldorf Astoria', because you could just call your business anything and no one would sue. Dr Pacheco's theory, developed during the forty-third wave of Chicken Rabies, was that humans should 'stop running' from these new diseases: and that it was actually far healthier, scientifically, for humans to be in intimate contact with infected birds.

So, he rented out slightly adapted cages in a working battery farm, and people would move in for a few days to breathe the fetid air, dust their skin with dried faeces, and chew on feathers, to help boost their natural immunity. Gentle spa music was played into the enormous huts at high volume, which entertained the spa residents and also helped drown out the non-stop cacophony of distressed clucking and scratching. It also helped calm the chickens. The Waldorf Astoria battery spa was quite popular, until it was discovered that no guest ever left and their bodies were being used as a protein supplement for the hens. The city turned to Man-Rat to administer vigilante justice on Dr Pacheco, but he refused, insisting that Dr

Pacheco was doing his best to help people in distress and that his doctorate was genuine.

In the early days, Man-Rat's main competition as a dispenser of justice had been from a mysterious vigilante known as 'the Shovel', who seemed, no matter how many times Man-Rat killed him, always to be found lurking somewhere on the streets of Detroit, administering justice. Man-Rat was perplexed, and only found out years later – recording the discovery in his diaries (see the introduction to Volume 4 of *The Diaries of Dr Jason Pacheco, Qualified Clinician*) – that all of the dozens of Shovels he'd killed weren't the real Shovel, no matter how much they insisted, even under torture, that they were.

The real Shovel's real name was Dickinson Gribbs, a former crime scene investigator who'd lost his mind during a spiritual epiphany about the wickedness of man brought on by too much coffee and crime scenes. Gribbs invested in a pair of shovels and would lurk in doorways and alleys, late at night, waiting for some random unsuspecting person to shuffle past, then he'd whack them round the head and shoulders with one of his two shovels. When he was sure they were unconscious, he'd drag them back into the shadows, into a mocked-up vigilante's lair, with pictures of 'criminals' on the wall, and handwritten notes saying things like 'Wanted for murder', and 'Catch this criminal' and 'This is a job for the Shovel', and he'd place his shovel in their hand, and wait for them to regain consciousness and try and get their bearings. A few minutes later he'd run up, and address them with great deference as the Shovel, telling them what an honour it was to meet them, asking politely if they'd let him become their sidekick in their quest for street justice, and he'd take whatever they managed to splutter out as a yes. Then he'd cock his head and pretend to hear someone calling for help. 'Did you hear that? There it is again! Someone is in need of street justice! They called for the Shovel – that's you! – we should go immediately and get stuck in. I'll back you up!' He'd thrust the shovel into their hands and hustle them off, as they groaned and vomited and drifted in and out of consciousness.

Gribbs manhandled them a short distance to another darkened corner where he'd set up a 'crime scene', which was always the same: a sinister arrangement of two other people he'd beaten unconscious. Into the hands of one, he'd put a length of pipe or a baseball bat, into the hands of the other, his second shovel. 'What's this?' he'd say, as if noticing this other shovel. 'This must be the mysterious Shovel! Somehow knocked unconscious while trying to give someone a punishment beating! They must have struck each other's heads at the same moment. That seems to be the most plausible explanation for what we're seeing here. But hold on just a minute, if this is the Shovel, then who are you? What is your true identity! Tell me!' Then Gribbs would start pulling at his first victim's face, trying to remove their 'mask', shouting 'Liar!' and berating them for pretending to be the Shovel, who was a true hero.

You have to remember, so tattered were people's memories at this point, so fragile were their identities and so desperate were they to cling onto any shred of self-respect, that nine times out of ten, his victim would insist that they weren't lying, and that they definitely were the Shovel. Then they'd grab the shovel, and stumble off to live life on the streets of Detroit as a vigilante. This would last a couple of hours before they were beaten to death by Man-Rat or any number of other people.

The Shovel's reign of justice was brought to an end when Gribbs was killed by Chicken Rabies, a vigilante named after the disease that shortly afterwards killed Chicken Rabies (the vigilante). For a while afterwards, Man-Rat's nemesis had been Man-Rat-Poison: half-man, half-other-man, whose devilish plan was to spend a year gradually building up a superhuman tolerance to rat poison, and then release it into the city's drinking water. The plan went like clockwork until, on day one, he died after ingesting rat poison. Indeed, he was unknown until after his death, when a storm swept his body into a local reservoir, poisoning the drinking water and killing several thousand people.

Into the nemesis vacuum caused by Man-Rat-Poison's demise stepped Man-Cat, a fully-man, no-part-cat, who went about Detroit dressed in a hand-sewn ginger cat suit, drinking milk out of a saucer and licking himself. He'd made a small hole on the underside of his penis, near the base, allowing himself to 'spray' his urine backwards like a tomcat, through a gap in his suit, so that he could mark his territory and develop septicaemia.

He did his best to clean around his infected groin by assiduous licking, but ingested so much nylon from his cat suit that he developed excruciating, indigestible 'fur balls' in his stomach, each about the size and texture of a lychee, which in fights he would hack up as a kind of 'rubber bullet' at his enemies. These misshapen, blood-flecked projectiles rarely hit the target, or went any distance at all – usually they'd just plop out of the mouth-hole of his papier-mâché cat head onto the floor in front of him as he heaved and wheezed, or they'd rattle around inside the mask like a tombola, but the act of coughing up this ginger fur ball was so violent and distressing to watch that it put his enemies quite at a loss, and Man-Cat was able to leap to his paws and get in a sharp scratch or two with his 'claws' before being beaten unconscious.

It sometimes crossed Man-Cat's mind, as he came to in a gutter, that it was odd he never got beaten to death. Little did he know that Man-Rat had let it be known that he wanted Man-Cat left alive, no matter how annoying or weird he got. Partly because he felt that the futile superhero provided a useful contribution to the status quo, by undermining concepts like dignity and hope, but mainly because Man-Cat owed him money.

11. Tales from a Lake Manitoba Laundry Gang

I spent one blissful summer lodging with the most powerful laundry gang of Lake Manitoba, working the trouser press in the day, and carousing round the campfire long into the night, sharing tales of difficult-to-remove egg stains and drinking fabric conditioner, before crawling to my tent for some truly memorable vomiting and hallucination.

In the tent opposite was a trainee seamstress, who went by the name of Wonky Hemline for reasons she would never divulge. I was often to be found in Wonky's tent, chatting and vomiting and hallucinating, and sure enough after a few weeks I fell hopelessly in love with her hand-cranked sewing machine. Sometimes she would come back into her tent to find me pressed up against the balance wheel, or pleasuring myself with a bobbin, whereupon I would have to pretend to be hallucinating, which was made easier by the fact that I generally was.

The relationship came to a sad end when I accidentally stamped on the foot pedal at the moment of orgasm and sewed up my foreskin, which had to be unpicked by Wonky when she came in to find me passed out across the arm shaft. There was something about the tenderness with which she unsewed my penis that caused a shift in my affections, but Wonky was bound by her laundry vows so would only make love in the communal ammonia pond, which cured three of my four genital infestations.

My workload on the trouser press was light, as this was at a time, just after the Second Great Contamination, when people had, for the most part, dispensed with trousers — for logistical reasons — and those few that hadn't weren't too fussed about a straight crease. Besides, only a madman would venture into a laundrette in the Northern Deadzones during the dreadful Linen Wars, which were at their appalling height. A cautious alliance of Manitoban washerfolk were fighting for dominance in the local wash and repair market against a highly organised militia of dry cleaners headquartered in an abandoned coal mine in the Turtle Mountains. My colleagues were baffled by the determination of the Turtle Mountain cleaners, not so much because of their reputation for leaving coal dust and impossible-to-shift oil stains all over every article of clothing entrusted to them, which in reality was none, but because the local wash and repair market being fought over didn't exist.

Neither side, after so much slaughter, could quite believe the other was still bothering to fight, which made both more hell bent on victory.

We would gather at the battlefield's edge and hurl vicious taunts at those Turtle Mountain bastards about how stupid they were to carry on this pointless war, which triggered such terrible cognitive dissonance that we had to consume herculean quantities of stain remover just to keep ourselves focused on winning, and we could see our furious, yelling enemies down great tankards of dry-cleaning fluid as they hurled back similar insults.

After a time, both armies would be hallucinating so wildly that skirmishes took the form of free-flowing twirls, dips and spins that eventually led to the reinvention of Psytrance, but an improved version, because it involved none of the music.

In retelling this story, Alonso was struck by the idea that the Turtle Mountain cleaners may not have existed, and re-evaluated many other recollections from the period of his fabric conditioner addiction, including cherished memories of long, sunny afternoons spent fly fishing with the Hindu god Vishnu.

Even now, we would sometimes catch him emptying a cap of Lenor 'exotic bloom' conditioner into his wine glass to give his mid-morning pinot noir at Belushi's 'an elevated level of feel-good freshness'. 'So what?' he'd snap at us. 'So I like being immersed in blushes of peach blossom and floral brushstrokes of bewitching rose and freesia? Fucking sue me.' And he'd turn to the empty seat next to him, and jab an angry finger into the air. 'And don't you fucking start, Vish. I've had it up to here with your comments. Seriously, just fucking— what? What's that? More jalapeño poppers? All right, all right, fine – we'll get some more jalapeño poppers. And what . . .? Some more what? Pulled beef chilli loaded fries? Really? I thought you didn't eat cow. Ah, okay, they're for me. That's very kind, thanks Vish. You're all right.'

We were pretty impressed that Alonso was on first-name terms with a deity, and we asked him if he'd mind introducing us to Vishnu, but he shook his head: 'It's not really that sort of relationship, sorry.' Vishnu seemed happy to put up with Alonso's bowel problems, and even didn't mind when Alonso pitched a high-concept drama to Amazon Prime loosely based on their friendship called *Lonny and Vish*, about a paranoid schizophrenic detective who thinks their partner is the Great Vishnu, the supreme protector and sustainer of the Universe. Together they solve crimes, dispense karma, eat donuts and restore order to a troubled world.

They soon ran into trouble, with Alonso admitting: 'We found it difficult to imagine this mentally ill "Lonny" character, who is simply imagining that he's friends with Lord Vishnu, with all of the conversations just figments of his troubled psyche, so we've switched it around, and Lord Vishnu is now the one who is imagining Lonny and all the other characters into existence, which is more in line with reality.' Amazon Prime passed, but as of publication the script is still in with BBC Scotland.

'Don't worry, we won't be travelling through time today.'

BOOK XII

The End of the West

1. We Go Out for Dough Balls

A few tensions began to develop in our group when Alonso, in his capacity as co-executive producer on *Hull Breach! The Titanic Minisub Story*, which he was overseeing for the History channel, fired Charlie from the writing team, describing (in a voice message) Charlie's proposed final scene, extrapolated from the crew's doomed consciousness in the millisecond of the submarine's implosion, in which they found themselves back in 1912, dressed for dinner on the *Titanic* just as it struck the iceberg, with all of them dying heroically in the disaster, as 'Too fucking expensive you stupid fuck', and the rest of his dialogue as 'Shit'.

Then, on the same day, he had Frankie fired from the cast, for being 'Totally fucking shit at acting'. Frankie was playing Paul-Henri Nargeolet, the *Titanic* expert, known as 'Monsieur Titanic', and had spent a month speaking only in a French accent, although no one had noticed. The following week, the submersible being used by the production suffered a catastrophic hull breach, and everyone on board died instantly, including Frankie's replacement, the *Mission: Impossible – Rogue Nation* actor Simon Pegg. Frankie attended the funeral, and at the graveside read a poem he'd written about Pegg, which had Pegg's family and friends in floods of tears, as they'd specifically asked Frankie not to read his poem, and especially not in a French accent.

Alonso took us out for dough balls at Pizza Express to apologise for the *Hull Breach! The Titanic Minisub Story* affair, but forgot his wallet, which he said must have been in his trousers, which he also forgot. He joked that he'd forget his buttplug if it hadn't proved surgically impossible to remove, a regular line of his which he'd laugh at so hard that his buttplug would fall out, and he'd clarify that the one he was referring to was 'further upstream, and lost to humanity'.

At Pizza Express, Alonso told us about the International Peace Garden and why three bottles of Malbec are the perfect accompaniment to an 'nduja calzone.

⁓

Wild flowers from the pre-apocalyptic International Peace Garden, which had been planted out on what was once the border between what was once Canada and what was once the United States, still grew in cheery patches around the world's largest thunderdome, which had been built there after the gardens had been burned and ransacked out of annoyance by the survivors of the world wars.

Restoration plans for the International Peace Garden were abandoned after bitter disagreements over planting schemes and logistical setbacks, including a war, and the site briefly became the International Holocaust Waterpark and Shopping Village, but there was such enormous public demand for a suitable venue to torture and execute the developers of the International Holocaust Waterpark and Shopping

Village that the International Peace Garden Memorial Thunderdome sprang into existence, and was an immediate success.

After a glorious opening weekend which saw the deaths of around 10,000 people in the audience alone, the International Peace Garden Memorial Thunderdome burned down. On its site, thunderdome after thunderdome was constructed, flourished and fell, mostly burning down as the result of the opening night's firework display.

When I was passing through, on my way to the annual Rocky Mountain sodomy debates, hoping that my speech would make up for my failure the previous year to impress anyone with my puppetry display, the nineteenth or perhaps twentieth thunderdome had just been completed, and the crowds were already starting to gather for the first event, which was the traditional scything to pieces of the previous thunderdome's design team.

I spoke to some of the construction team, who seemed quite happy, perhaps because they had survived the construction process which had an attrition rate among thunderdome workers of around 65%. Those who still had hands gave me a thumbs-up when I asked if they were looking forward to the traditional opening day's 'donkey derby', but before those with mouths could add any detail I felt a leather hood engulfing my head, and I was coshed into unconsciousness. This took many more blows than I would have hoped. I feigned unconsciousness at one point, and simply lay there for a while as they continued to flog my head for some minutes with what felt like a 4-iron.

I awoke in the centre of a vast arena, tethered and splayed. As the howls from the tens of thousands of spectators grew wilder, I strained round to see a line of donkeys being manually stimulated by thunderdome interns, and injected with a cocktail of amphetamines and 'nut rush', a drug that was sold to the public at the thunderdome's popular marital therapy clinic. I awoke to find myself under a hedge a mile from the thunderdome, with a bunch of wildflowers tucked into my shirt and a note attached to my ankle which said 'you owe me one'. I smiled at my good fortune, rose to my feet, then fell over, unable to walk or stop defecating for a solid six months.

Besides their obvious role in nurturing social cohesion and replacing television and hospices, thunderdomes had numerous other benefits. The environmental movement, having suffered a bit of a setback with the obliteration of the environment, found a new lease of life under the leadership of thunderdome managers and booking agents. Exotic beasts, such as giraffes, tigers, rhinos and the great apes were much sought after as wrestling adversaries and sexual partners in the popular thunderdome themed weekends, and a series of breeding programmes and habitat restoration schemes saw their numbers boom.

Extensive 'rewilding' reserves now covered most of the major land masses, and billions of people did their bit to improve the quality of the soil by decomposing. Big-game hunting had been almost completely replaced by human hunting, and the larger predators grazed happily on the masses of confused and weakened survivors in their tent cities. This constant culling of the weak resulted in a strengthening of the human gene pool and new discoveries in the art of animal wrestling which went some way towards lifting humans off the bottom of the thunderdome lovemaking survival charts, finally moving us ahead of wolves and bison, but still with a long way to go before catching the hippo.

2. The Collapse of Virtuality and Inexorable Rise of Cosplay

The sudden and complete eradication of social media was, for many, an event more traumatic than the loss of their homes, family and friends. Unplugged, confused, and unable to communicate with other survivors in a real-world setting, they took to constructing 'screens' from four sticks lashed together to form an oblong, which they would hold in front of their face, and would only talk to other people if their faces were also 'on screen'. Many of these handheld devices had a fairly decent battery life, allowing the user several days of uninterrupted viewing until the screen went dark when they were beaten to death.

To make the videocall experience more authentic, users would sometimes freeze for a couple of seconds in the middle of sentences, or start mouthing their words noiselessly while the other participants in the chat would shout 'You've muted yourself!' through their sticks, or if it was a particularly long 'meeting' they would urinate into a jam jar held 'out of sight' below their screen, or quietly masturbate while the other participants pretended not to notice. Or perhaps the others couldn't even see it – there are some people who found it impossible to perceive anything at all unless it was through some sort of makeshift monitor, which made them easy prey for practical jokers or rapists, insofar as it was meaningful after the collapse of civilisation to make such a distinction.

'Browsing' for 'online pornography' became a great deal less straightforward for these psychotics, requiring patience, days of planning and stealth – and even if they did manage to creep up on some unsuspecting 'pornography', and watch it through their screen without the 'actors' noticing, the chances of it being the genre of porn they were browsing for was slim. Especially given what passed as sex in those days. Often it would just be someone pressing their pelvis wearily against a tree stump, or someone performing a mercy killing on a grandparent. Practical considerations eventually led to a shift in online porn viewing towards roadkill gangbangs and people crying whilst having sex with rubble.

Some porn entrepreneurs built up a following by getting some larger bits of wood and constructing the frame of a screen behind which they would chat to their subscribers and answer personal questions while masturbating, but it proved difficult to get subscribers to pay a monthly fee, and all but impossible to run a direct debit scheme without contracting hepatitis. And if you had access to binoculars you could bypass the whole login and payment process altogether, although if you wanted your questions answered you had to really shout.

⁓

A few days' hobble north of the Great Crater of Calgary, a pair of erotic performers became popular for putting on energetic displays of furry cosplay sex until it was discovered, after they ate nine members of their audience, that they were both bears. Their handler avoided having to pay compensation to the families of the deceased by telling them to go fuck themselves. This was felt by many of the bereaved to be inadequate, and they demanded that the bears be destroyed or at least castrated, and after a brief discussion the two parties came to a compromise, which was that the bereaved were eaten by bears.

Once his bears had tasted human flesh, the handler found it increasingly difficult to hire them out for stag parties or cosplay conventions without catastrophic loss of life and lengthy legal proceedings (further maulings). Also, his performing bears became so obese from eating their audience and participating in class action lawsuits that they found their sex drive dwindling, preferring instead to loll around fatly, cleaning their teeth with human ribs and farting, forcing their handler to rebrand their performances as 'post-coital', which led to a collapse in bookings.

Their handler ended up with such debts that he was forced to stitch himself into a bear outfit and hire himself out as 'Growler: a bear trained in the art of love', who would be chained to a pole and anyone daring enough could, for a fee, make love to him. After six months of gruelling sex work, sometimes 18 or 20 hours a day, and just as he was about to pay off his last debt, he was captured by a gang of bear baiters who, unconcerned by the realisation that it was obviously just a man stitched into a reeking bear costume, chained him to a pole in the middle of a crudely hewn amphitheatre, and set a pack of dogs onto him, who were just about to maul him to death when instead they began sniffing and licking at the nether regions of their quarry, and became sexually agitated, deciding to mount the bear in a display of interspecies lovemaking which lasted over 9 hours until the last dog finally curled up and went to sleep and was met by rapturous applause.

A week later, when he regained consciousness, the bear handler found the bear baiters clustered anxiously around his bed, mopping the fur of his brow and gently massaging his claws. He had run a terrible fever, and lost a lot of blood, mainly out of his anus. The baiters carefully opened his jaws and gave him a drink of water, telling him to rest and get his strength back. The baiters clucked round him anxiously, nursing him back to health – only occasionally, and under strict supervision, letting one of their hounds into the treatment room to mount him, just to keep them interested.

It was a delicate balance: they knew that every mounting, however gentle, and few were, was a setback to the recovery of the 'bear', but they wanted to keep their pack focused. They'd realised that with their pack of randy hounds, this bear, a length of chain and a sturdy sex post they could launch a global entertainment phenomenon and conquer the world. Long into the night, clinking mugs of moonshine at the bedside of the feverish, gibbering bear, they plotted the glittering careers of their performers. They'd already mapped out a transatlantic tour, and had taken bookings for a month-long residency in a casino in Malaysia, not realising that the person making the booking was a scam artist who had no contacts in Malaysia, and who was subsequently eaten by dogs.

Undaunted, the baiters set their sights on the lucrative euthanasia market. So intense was the demand for euthanasia by this time that providers were forced to become ever more inventive to attract customers within a crowded market. Few were willing to have themselves euthanised without a good evening's entertainment and a decent meal, at least four courses, with some kind of alcohol or psychotropic substance included. Alonso continues:

I was working as a waiter in a euthanasia bar in what had been Pyongyang, but had been blown into a region closer to the outskirts of Beijing. The owner had chosen it because of the way the nuclear shadows on the walls danced in the candlelight, seeming to move to the soothing electronic music that drifted from the far end of the bar. It was the resident pianist, Roy, still just a teenager: a paralysed musical genius hooked up to an old Atari gaming system. Reaching the end of his latest composition, he made an end-game noise, and the patrons applauded warmly.

The next act took the stage: a Normal, a guy who'd show you what a normal, blemish-free, unmutated body he had. It was all tricks and mirrors and sleight of hand, but the patrons ate it up. His old lady accompanied him on a glockenspiel. She was mutated, but her thin wrists and ball-shaped hands blurred across that instrument like her life depended on a perfect performance, which it did. Everyone was waiting for the headline act: a pensioner being clubbed to death by a guy sewn into a bear costume. I'd never quite understood showbusiness, and I didn't think I wanted to.

I splashed two fingers of rye into a glass and pushed it along the bar to Roy, who acknowledged me with a flutter of an eyelid and a high-score sound. 'Get a load of this place,' his eyes seemed to say, but really it could have been pretty much anything.

The bear beckoned me over with a curt nod. The guy had been a regular truant at charm school, and could fly off the handle if anyone mentioned dogs; even just the name of a breed would be enough to send him into a frenzy. I always kept one hand on a tranquilliser gun under the bar while I poured his drink, but even with a dart in him the best you could hope for was to bark him towards one of the booths where people had agreed to be euthanised.

It wasn't a great show. The bear had been going through the motions for weeks now, and even being introduced by Roy and the glockenspiel lady's flawless jazz version of 'All Along The Watchtower' couldn't inspire him. The old woman had been dressed as Goldilocks (a costume consisting almost entirely of a blonde chemotherapy wig) and the bear had half-heartedly plodded through the first half of the script before giving up and force feeding her a porridge of barbiturates.

As I was closing up, the doorbell rang, which meant someone had hit the tripwire, and we knew they'd survived the blast when there was a knock at the door. This triggered a couple of crossbow bolts, but they must have had the sense to duck because the door swung open and a figure stepped carefully over the pressure pads and into the room.

She made her way over to the bar, her heels sounding like a very slow round of applause. The bear looked curious, but then that was really the expression of the bear before it got shot. The Normal act had left early, saying he had work in the morning: the Normal always said that, I think it was part of the show. His wife was still ordering highballs and taking turns of Roy's straw, and occasionally beating out a few bars of Handel on the bar top when she thought the service was slow.

The lady was tall, and wore a stylish Kevlar jumpsuit with a tactical helmet tilted rakishly over one eye. She nodded towards the top shelf and I poured her a shot as she deactivated the charge under her barstool and sat down.

'How can I help you?' I started to ask. 'Let me have a drink first,' she barked, sinking the shot, and nodding for a refill. 'I'm looking for my husband. Tall guy, kinda nervous looking. He liked this kind of scene . . . and this is the only euthanasia bar in town.'

This was true, euthanasia bars often built up an enthusiastic early following but were victims of their own success, slaughtering their customers and going bankrupt within a matter of months. In many ways, we'd hung on through sheer incompetence.

The glockenspiel lady gestured at the bar olives. I threw one at her hard and she caught it in her mouth like a seal. 'You get a lot of nervous guys in here,' she burped, 'What was his name?'

The lady sank her second shot: 'The funny thing is, I don't know.' The bear growled in confusion, but only because someone had got an olive before him. I slid him the jar and turned back to the lady.

'You don't know?'

'He was Man-Rat, the old-time superhero. I never knew what his alter-ego was called. He just dressed as a rat the whole time I was with him.'

'How do you know it wasn't just a bunch of different guys who shared the same suit?' asked the bear. He'd told me it was something he often wondered about himself.

'I marked his penis in braille. I'm blind!' She shouted this bitterly at the dartboard, so we believed her. And so began the story of a very unlikely group of people setting out in an old van to investigate a mystery, and largely dying within minutes, having forgotten about the booby traps at the staff entrance. I did once meet Man-Rat later on, at his lair in the abandoned Disneyland, but he didn't have braille on his penis, which was — if anything — unnaturally smooth, like polished ivory.

3. How Alonso's Life Changed When He Met Sir Barksalot

People often had pets in the early years after the catastrophe, animals they'd brought with them as they fled. Birds, rabbits, dogs and cats is the order they were eaten in.

Animals played a key role in many post-apocalyptic societies. Packs of wild dogs were, counterintuitively, regarded as a good sign when arriving in a neighbourhood. It usually meant the locals weren't numerous or battle-hardened enough to have eaten them all yet. A visitor to a new town would often let out a 'Yahoo!' if chased by a pack of feral dogs, knowing that he had found somewhere he could relax for a while.

Alonso had at one point released some sniffer dogs from the ruins of a large international airport, possibly Denver or Bangkok, but probably Denver. He believed that they might help him find drugs, and spent some time using them to search the area around the nearby city. It was only when one of these dogs exploded that Alonso considered that they may actually have been trained to find explosives, and that he was now standing in the middle of an enormous minefield. Luckily, he managed to clear a path to safety, by throwing a ball for the other dogs to chase.

At another point, Alonso rescued a beagle called Sir Barksalot from a science lab. Sir Barksalot accompanied Alonso on his journeys for a couple of years and was a faithful and alert companion, before eventually succumbing to his ten a day cigarette habit. Alonso's face was gripped by a spasm of regret as he described how the old dog's lungs were shrivelled to a third of their normal size, and completely unsuitable for barbecuing.

Sir Barksalot's medical notes revealed that his original vocal cords had been destroyed in an experiment to see whether a beagle can drink boiling Fanta (they can't). Mandy Radio was very fond of the old beagle and made him a voice box so that he could bark again. Mandy would also ventriloquise through the dog's voice box and proved to be quite a skilled character improviser, often making Alonso laugh by having the dog deliver downbeat monologues about his lost testicles, harrowingly low life expectancy, and convoluted and ultimately bourgeois Gramscian politics.

At yet another point it seems that Alonso, Mandy Radio (in the badly decayed body of a former heavyweight boxer), the reanimated former linguistics professor (whose feet were now caterpillar treads like a tank), and Sir Barksalot had to head to the recently rebuilt research institution CalTech, short for Caliphate Technology, run by the Shah of Pasadena, where they hoped to find supplies of vital semi-conductors needed for the time machine.

While foraging for food on Waverly Drive, the group were captured, Sir Barksalot having given away their position with a loud treatise about the musical *Oklahoma* (the need for sadistic catharsis in the bourgeoisie means that the working classes have to be goaded into positions where they can be destroyed), which was really Mandy Radio's fault.

It was during the old beagle's surprisingly upbeat rendition of the musical's closing number that the group was surprised by the Glendale branch of ISIS. The linguistics professor fired at them from his nipple turrets, but his unnaturally small areolas meant that, for aesthetic reasons, these were .22 calibre and caused little more than a couple of flesh wounds.

The Glendale branch of ISIS, trading as ISIS (Glendale) Inc., were the descendants of some ISIS members who'd attempted to infiltrate the United States just before it collapsed. Their plan, to destroy the American way of life, had already been achieved, and they scrabbled around for some new purpose. Eventually they decided that life in post-collapse conditions was so awful that the only true punishment for Americans would be to prolong it. They travelled around in a pair of ambulances healing anyone they could. They were particularly experienced at performing cataract operations, and installing cochlear implants in the hard of hearing, so that their patients could fully experience the horror of their lives.

Alonso said that ISIS treated the companions well, after some lengthy questioning to check that none of them were polytheists or Jewish. Sometimes ISIS would try to catch them out by asking how many gods existed, or by cooking a tempting chicken noodle soup, and they had to pretend to not want any. This wasn't hard as ISIS were terrible at cooking Jewish food, and substituted chickpeas for both chicken and noodles. The group even had to stop using self-deprecating humour, and during the period of captivity they developed the kind of exaggerated braggadocio more normally associated with a rap crew.

Life was tough in captivity. Alonso had to sleep in an ambulance with Mandy Radio and the linguistics professor: the sounds of their lovemaking would have been difficult to bear in any situation, but especially so now ISIS had given him the hearing of a bat. Supplies often ran low, and the ISIS operatives spent long evenings by the campfire describing their dream meal. This was, almost invariably, a dead Jew, but tastes varied widely when it came to sides and desserts. Incidentally, the Israel/Palestine issue had decades earlier been solved by a two-state solution, with a nuclear exchange turning the region first into a liquid, then into a gas.

It was a lonely time for Alonso, being allergic to mint tea and the only person who couldn't speak Arabic, and he often felt excluded from the camp's marathon Dungeons and Dragons sessions. They had encouraged ISIS to dilute the innate anti-Semitism of their version of the game, and eventually a compromise was reached where it was decided the orcs; balrogs; trolls; goblins; and necromancers just wouldn't have a religion. Alonso's character, a wizard (a djinn in the ISIS version) was a confused passenger on most quests and was constantly having to be revived by Sir Barksalot's elven huntress. The huntress was in love with Alonso's wizard and these revivals were often uncomfortable scenes during which the beagle refused to break character or eye contact.

Eventually, these Dungeons and Dragons sessions presented the friends with an opportunity to escape. Mandy Radio had noticed that after a particularly successful raid, the ISIS operatives liked to celebrate with a round of mint tea. As the regular Dungeon Master, she could set up an easy victory for ISIS. Alonso was given the responsibility of drugging the tea. He'd managed to find some old vials of morphine in one of the ambulances, but they were empty, or so he told the others before having one of his regular 16-hour naps.

Eventually they managed to extract enough morphine from the bottom of the various vials and syringes lying around to create a suitably drugged tea that actually tasted no worse than a standard ISIS mint tea, which, in any case, was made with spearmint chewing gum (this was quite a rarity in the post apocalypse, and often they had to use juicy fruit). There didn't seem to be quite enough morphine to knock ISIS out, or perhaps the dose was counteracted by the adrenaline of the resounding victory Mandy Radio had engineered for them over a tribe of suicidal, diabetic goblins and the narcoleptic necromancer Jacob Silverstein. Mandy Radio urged Alonso (via the lyrics of a lullaby) to tell the most boring story he could think of.

Alonso began to tell the dullest story he knew, the story of Mandy Radio, and everything she'd told him about her hopes and dreams. Mandy didn't take offence, as Alonso had paid so little attention when she talked that the story was unrecognisable as her own. The linguistics professor remarked on how cold it was getting, which transpired to be a cover story for the fact that he was erecting his nipple turrets, and he trundled slowly towards the gently dozing ISIS unit. Collapsing forward at the waist with a scream, his nipple guns ended up landing neatly in the eye sockets of the ISIS leader; and with a mighty grunt the professor blew both his eyes out. Of course, this woke the others up and they all spent several more months in captivity before their jailers died of dysentery.

4. More Dysentery

We were in Loris Community Gardens, feeding the ducks with the crumbs of our takeaway egg Florentines from Liz Café. We knew the ducks liked it better when we got the granola & yoghurt, but we preferred the egg Florentines and if we'd learned nothing else from Alonso it was that, at some point in life, you have to put your own interests ahead of a duck's.

Alonso seemed anxious, and kept fastening and unfastening a toggle on his signature mauve duffle coat. Was it because of the black helicopter that was hovering just over the tree line? 'No,' he said, 'I'm used to those. I was thinking about us. And what we're doing. I can't shake the feeling that, somehow . . . hey! Hey! Fuck off!' Alonso sprang up and ran towards the helicopter, flapping his arms, until it got spooked and whirred off. 'You have to be firm with them,' he said, sitting back down. 'They seem to respect you if you show them you're not scared. What was I saying?'

Neither of us could remember. Frankie consulted the recording he'd been making on his phone and accidentally deleted it. Charlie checked his notes, but found that he'd just been sketching a sort of sassy Sphinx character from various angles, mostly bending over and looking back over her shoulder: 'She sets riddles for people and then, if they can't solve them, she drags them off into the bushes, and you can hear them being eaten.' Frankie nodded: 'But the sounds are a bit sexual?' Charlie nodded. 'Very sexual. But you don't see anything.' Frankie nodded: 'But you can hear it.' Charlie nodded: 'But it's never quite clear what you're hearing. I'm pitching next week to Nickelodeon.' Frankie raised a finger to show that he'd had an idea. 'What about calling it *They Sphinx it's All Over?*' But Charlie had gone to Sprinkles for milkshakes, and the idea was lost forever.

'Were we talking about the rise of Tonga?' asked Alonso. Frankie shrugged, wondering whether Charlie was going to get Kinder Bueno, Oreo or Ferrero Rocher. He'd said he didn't care what flavour, just as long as it had an extra protein scoop, but truth be told he was hoping for the Kinder Bueno. Just as long as it wasn't the Biscoff.

Charlie returned from Sprinkles with four Biscoff milkshakes, three with an extra protein scoop. The one without the extra protein scoop was for the ducks. He sploshed it into the pond as Alonso pressed on: 'The Third Diabetic Empire of the Tongans stretched fr—' Alonso broke off exactly halfway through the word 'from' when he saw Frankie's hand raised firmly towards him, palm outwards, fingers upwards, and his mouth opening to say: 'No, that wasn't it – we were talking about your anxieties.' Frankie put down his hand and relaxed his fingers. With his other hand still clutching his milkshake, he gestured to Alonso to continue, but Alonso thought the gesture meant 'Your shorts are unzipped,' which they were.

He thanked Frankie and continued: 'I know it's irrational but I've been having these anxiety attacks, usually in the middle of the night; I'll be convinced that someone is looking straight at me through the bathroom window, even though the tree I'm in is in total darkness. There's no way they can see me. I start hyperventilating and when I come to, if I haven't fallen out of the tree, I write a note to myself, explaining what just happened, and fold it up tightly, and find a hole in the bark, and push it in. But here's the weird thing: I can never find it again when I go back up the tree. And it's the same with my time capsules. I've been talking it through with Dr Sylvester, he's my new therapist, he's pretty good, he was working as a waiter at Pentolina, because he'd had his licence cancelled for some bullshit reason, and he'd come out at the end of every night and trade me a bowl of strozzapreti con broccoli e burrata in exchange for a – hey! Hey! Fuck you! Get away!' and he ran flapping down Loris Road.

A few minutes later he was back, breathing heavily. 'Those fucks. You've got to show them what's what. What were we talking about? – Oh yeah. So Dr Sylvester thinks I'm a time squirrel.'

⁓

Alonso shooed away the ducks and finished his milkshake while Frankie made a mental note to specify Kinder Bueno in the future – 'Why be coy about it?' he thought, 'why not just say?' – and Charlie wrote 'Time Squirrel' and 'Cartoon Network?' in his notebook, and began sketching a futuristic squirrel, quite sassy, obviously nobody's fool, no major hangups in the bedroom, looking back over his/her (it wasn't clear) shoulder.

Alonso carried on about Dr Sylvester while Charlie showed his sketch to Frankie. 'I want it to be ambiguous about whether the Time Squirrel has had butt implants or just works out a lot.' Frankie wasn't sure: 'It seems pretty obvious those are implants. There are no glute workouts I've tried that give that kind of definition. Look at the size of them compared to the rest of the squirrel.' Alonso let out a throaty shriek of 'kkgakakagkāk!' which, roughly translated, means 'suck my balls', but you can also use it colloquially to express exasperation.

'Guys! Please! – this is important. I've been seeing Dr Sylvester in his office by the bins on Springvale Terrace. He moves them away from the railing and we tuck ourselves in behind them, and usually no one bothers us. I was telling him about you two: and about how I've got this feeling that we've done all this before. The three of us. Our conversations. But a bit differently. Like, I remember this park, but I think we used to sit over there, near those bushes. And we'd have a bag of ham and cheese croissants. But I never order ham and cheese croissants, do I?' We agreed that it's not a croissant filling we'd ever seen him order. 'And I remember other cafes, other helicopters, other versions of the conversations we've been having, and these memories are different from the Xanax flashes I've been getting. Like even now, I know I've said "Xanax flashes" to you before.'

He had a desperate look in his eye, like a duck when it realises you've got no granola. 'You don't know what it's like for me: I'm out here with my trowel most nights in Chiswick House Gardens, digging around, looking for time capsules of information from the future that I think I've buried on previous visits to this time. And I know I've dug there before. All this, I've done before. I think one time I was here for Harry and Meghan's wedding. I was in the park, and someone offered me a dog? Do I have a dog? Is he called Gatsby?'

We weren't sure; we didn't think so. 'Okay, but then, how do you explain that I knew I was going to love egg Florentine? I just knew it! What's that about? And why can't I stop burying time capsules? I've been banned from St Paul's Green and Furnivall Gardens. I'm running out of parks. Dr Sylvester says I should just calm the fuck down about it, but I don't know. I'm scared. What should I do?'

Charlie shrugged while Frankie tried to wrestle a bit of spinach from a duck's beak. Alonso's eyes flicked skyward. 'You fuckers!' he cried, as he ran back off down Loris Road, throwing his duffle coat into a hedge, as a lady approached, with a large dog on a lead. Charlie petted the dog; it was only small dogs he was terrified of. The dog rested a friendly paw on Charlie's arm. 'What's his name?' Frankie smiled: 'His name's Charlie. And what's your dog called?'

We caught up with Alonso under the railway arch on Trussley Road. He was deep in conversation with a lady at the wheel of an idling 1985 Ford Granada 2.8 Ghia saloon in sky blue with a matching blue cloth interior, immaculate inside and out. Alonso saw us and came over, leading Frankie back to the other end of the arch and round into the alley that runs up alongside the railway line, pressing him firmly into the foliage of a wisteria. 'Does he want me to blow him again?' thought Frankie, looking up to see a sign for Collins Motors, promising a combination of 'Old Fashioned Courtesy' and 'Modern Technology'. Frankie shook his head ruefully: 'I'm not so sure they're compatible,' he muttered. 'Get up,' said Alonso. 'I have to tell you something.'

The lady had stepped out of the car. She was wearing a vintage Michel Soligny polka-dot skirt suit in candy pink with faux pocket flaps and large, fancy brass buttons. She smiled at Charlie, who looked down, feeling suddenly bashful and confused. He noticed a lollipop stick at his feet. 'Maybe there'll be a joke on it that I can sell to Stephen Mangan for his Classic FM show,' thought Charlie, 'although maybe he doesn't do jokes on it? I should probably listen to it first. In the meantime, I'll check the lollipop stick for material.'

Charlie bent down and his sinuses drained. He gasped in discomfort, and looked up to see the lady in the pink dress darting round the corner towards Hammersmith Grove. 'Maybe she wants me to follow her,' mused Charlie, looking around at the impressive brickwork of the old railway arch. The lady came back round the corner and beckoned to him. 'She does!'

Meanwhile, Alonso glanced both ways along the alley; he thought he could smell someone urinating but the coast was clear. He spoke to Frankie in a low, urgent tone: 'It's about David Guetta. I think he's still alive. I mean, in the future, not now. Not that he's dead now, but — agh!' Alonso pressed his screwed-up fists to his forehead, which Frankie mistook for an attack, and whipped an elbow into Alonso's jaw. When Alonso came round, he explained that he'd been getting these headaches, and Dr Sylvester thought it might be caused by 'time stress', and was treating it by hitting Alonso around the head with a bag of satsumas, or golf balls when those were out of season, but that the important thing right now was finding David Guetta. 'I have a message for him. It's about the Guetta Hams Life Extension Project. I have to tell him: it works!' This was Frankie's last clear memory before he was hit beneath the base of the left ear with what felt like a bag of satsumas, but at this time of the year was more likely to be golf balls, or possibly some very late tangerines.

Elsewhere, Charlie followed the lady into Brackenbury Wine Rooms. She spoke to a waiter, then went up to a table where a well-dressed couple were sitting. She said something to them, and they got up and left, the man in tears and the woman holding her hand over her mouth in terror.

'Won't you join me?' the lady asked Charlie. Two glasses of white wine arrived. 'I took the liberty of ordering the Gewürztraminer.' She raised her glass to Charlie, 'to your good health,' and they clinked – 'One more time please' – they clinked again. 'Just one more' – their glasses clinked a third time and the clink swam up through the complex lychee and rose petal aroma of the Gewürztraminer like a mating salmon leaping through the foam, just managing to avoid the swoop of a bear's claw, up through the air, the bubbles exploding in his head like high calibre ammunition.

When Charlie opened his eyes, the lady was gone. He asked for the bill but it had been paid. It was a strange encounter, but one that Charlie always had fond memories of, mixed in with feelings of inadequacy, impotence, the sense that something important was buried under a mulberry tree in rural Wiltshire, and strong feelings of rage towards both Alonso and the music of Iannis Xenakis, in particular his *Pléïades*. On the way out of the restaurant, someone dropped a teaspoon and Charlie flew into a frenzy, and had to be physically restrained from strangling the coat rack.

5. Disneyland and the Last Tartarian Council

After the apocalypse, the happiest place on Earth was Disneyland, which was ruled by a self-managing collective of abuse victims who had escaped from the vast maze of sex dungeons under pre-apocalyptic Disneyland. After spending a few glorious days enjoying the sunshine and queueing for rides, they turned their attention to rounding up as many members of staff as they could find, forcing them into fluffy Disney costumes, and locking them away in the sex dungeons to form the basis of their Revenge Zoo. The inmates were not allowed to take their costumes off, however filthy and matted they got, and if they died they were left to rot inside their furry suits, which made the Disney Revenge Zoo an absolute must-see for anyone who'd lost their sense of smell due to a head injury.

No one is sure, but it's thought that a rat feasting on one of the plush corpses inside the Revenge Zoo must have been patient zero of Disneyland Flu, which left its victims with weird bloated heads, giant ears, and annoying high-pitched voices with which they would scream for the sweet mercy of death. Death came soon enough: the only known cure for Disneyland Flu was beheading, for which there was no known cure. To try and deter people from visiting Disneyland it was renamed The Forbidden City, which meant that everyone immediately wanted to go, most of them dying in the queue for the car park.

The vast traffic jams of dead people around The Forbidden City were so spectacular they became a popular tourist destination in their own right; however it became almost impossible to buy a ticket to see them, because all the ticket sellers were dead. The piles of ticket seller corpses were so mountainous that, for a short time, they became a popular tourist destination, especially among vultures. The Forbidden City was renamed Vulture Town, one of around fifteen thousand Vulture Towns in the continental United States.

Maps of the US from this period are almost completely useless, as virtually all of the places had been renamed either Vulture Town, Rat City, Plagueton, Grand Rape, Rape Heights, Pestilence Beach, San Pandemico or Fort Death – and also, none of the maps were published or drawn.

It was here, half a mile below these empty wastes, in the recently rediscovered debating chamber under the recently rediscovered cryogenics lab under the recently rediscovered sex crypts under the sex dungeons under the pestilent ruins of the happiest place on Earth, which was given a pretty good clean beforehand, that the Council of Tartaria chose to convocate the Last Tartarian Council: a secret meeting of surviving elders from the planet's dying elites.

Present at the solemn assembly were such luminaries as: the Herald of the Order of the Golden Fleece; the Deputy Speaker of the House of Aztecs; the King of the Myrmidons; La Pincoya of the Chilotan Seas; Nigel of Venice; a half-Lego ambassador from the Plastic Continent; the High Consul of the Kushtaka Nation of shape-shifting otterfolk; the Mayor of Grand Rape (formerly Scottsdale); the Archbishop of Mars; Prince Xerxes son of Xerxes VII of Letchworth Garden City; the Poet Laureate of Zanzibar; the Sheriff of Jerusalem; the World's Strongest Man; Princess Rosalind of Dundee; Shigeki Uchiyamada, the last surviving senior executive at the Toyota Motor Corporation, who had recently promoted himself to VP for Corporate Strategy; a team of lawyers representing the estate of Jeffrey Epstein, whereabouts unknown; and Alonso Lampe. The frozen body of Walt Disney was also present, listening carefully to the discussions, and had a casting vote, although without a head he found it difficult to cast. His head, in a press conference held at the Walt Disney Thunderdome, Biomolecular Life Sciences Institute and Lasagne Factory, Florida, later condemned the meeting as 'frivolous' and urged the world to get on with the more pressing business of designing a really good Inspector Gadget-themed log flume.

Alonso had been invited in his dual capacity as President of Harvard (undefeated) and Chaplain-at-Large of the Knights Templar (self-appointed). He describes the event as 'quite interesting at times' although 'poorly catered' and with so few sex workers provided for the participants that the High Consul of the Kushtaka was obliged to shapeshift into a complex multi-gendered hybrid just to keep the debate on the rails.

The proceedings were formally opened by the Remembrancer of the Court of Antaeus, who spat three times on his own shadow, cursed the meeting, and with a dismissive flourish of his robes ran headlong to his doom through the beautiful arched window of the debating chamber, which looked out onto a craggy hillside below, only to discover it had been painted on the wall by Disney animators, and lay concussed on the floor for the rest of the meeting. The Archduke of Guernsey spoke movingly on the subject of humanity's 'total cuntishness', although admitted 'that might be because I'm currently trying to get an extension on my kitchen built.'

The chief jester of the Tartarians, a hunched, wizened man barely 8 feet tall, reminisced about past civilisations: how they had all, without exception, fallen prey to greed, perversity and the ill-fated dream of merging with their creations, and how this dream generally went wrong because they ended up trying to merge with a self-aware battle drone who wasn't that into it, and how abject failure was the one certainty of human existence, although quite often humans could find a way of fucking even that up. The other participants shook their heads sadly and moaned in despair as they saw the tray of ankle straps that was being passed around.

Major-General Duncan Brip of the Royal Scots Dragoon Guards performed a solemn handstand on the back of his regimental goat and through the folds of his kilt called for a vote on the motion: 'Let's just call it a day'. Alonso voted against the final dissolution of the human race, but the motion was carried 28–5. The rest of the meeting was devoted to the logistics of mass suicide pacts and the 'deep scrub' of humanity's remnants from the face of an irritated planet, followed by a boisterous game of pétanque.

Disheartened by the affair, Alonso excused himself from the meeting, and wandered off to urinate sadly in an alcove. Behind him, he heard a light clicking on the floor: it was the ambassador from the Plastic Continent tiptoeing up to him on his Tupperware feet. He felt a plasticky tap on his shoulder and Ambassador Fanta whispered: 'Mr Lampe, I must speak with you. I share your feelings about these proceedings, and I have a proposal'.

After they'd finished having sex, Alonso rinsed the Lego blocks from his mouth while Ambassador Fanta whispered: 'I have another proposal. We on the tangled Plastic Continent of CocaColia, the descendants of sex yacht escapees, suicidal fishermen and tsunami survivors, have long struggled for life and happiness on our roiling home. We are a hardy breed, raised on a diet of seagull blood and patio chairs – our bodies have learned to synthesise the lurid, microplastic soup of the oceans into exciting new tumours, we have found a way to live in grotesque harmony with the wreck of nature — we have not come this far to give up now. And I know you feel the same.'

Alonso nodded, wiping the last of the Lego from his hair. He told the ambassador of his long and difficult travels, of his many desperate battles and stirring love affairs, and when the ambassador awoke, he asked him what his second proposal was, because if it's for more sex he wouldn't bother putting his trousers back on. Ambassador Fanta laughed, 'Ha ha, no, it is not for more sex. I require a little longer, I'm afraid, to assemble the necessary blocks to attain an erection. My proposal is this: I wish to help you save the human race.'

Ambassador Fanta paused for effect, and also to allow himself to divert extra plastic to his PVC nutsack. 'My agents tell me that you are trying to build a time machine, and are struggling with some of the wiring. Well, if it's wiring you want . . .' and he grunted, grimaced, threw back his head and hacked up a tightly knotted ball of electrical cabling, zip ties, fish hooks, yoghurt pots, Alonso's pubic hair, piezoelectric cells and assorted computer components. He smiled: 'And there's plenty more where that came from.'

Night and day they worked — Alonso Lampe, Ambassador Fanta and Mandy Radio — testing and retesting their time machine, and at the end of that arduous 24 hours it seemed to be working: they even managed to send a cat successfully 5 minutes into the future. Unfortunately, it couldn't report on the experience because it was a cat. And had been turned inside out.

'It's time' said Ambassador Fanta, unbuckling his belt, bending forwards and pulling his buttocks apart to reveal an embedded fax machine, which began spewing forth page after page of useful information for Alonso to deliver to humanity's doomed past: documents, maps, thunderdome opening hours, chapters of books, recipes, memoirs – when the text threatened to fade, Fanta detached a flask of printer ink from his hip and took a deep swig. At last, with a beep, the printing was done.

Ambassador Fanta fell forwards exhausted, the final page on top of the pile giving the precise location and password (J3FFCOOL1) of the laptop containing the consciousness of Jeff Bezos, and detailed instructions for its safe incineration. Folding the pages with trembling hands, because he hadn't had a drink in over an hour, Alonso slipped them carefully into a large plastic pouch which Ambassador Fanta had vomited at his feet. 'And then it was time for me to bid my farewells . . .'

Alonso paused for effect, and also because his Mr Falafel supreme plus falafel wrap with extra feta was ready. We carried our wraps to our usual spot, squatting next to the post box on Frithville Gardens, where Alonso liked to tell people posting things not to bother. But today he let people post their letters and packages without a single dismissive growl or threatening gesture. 'I'm feeling a bit more positive about things,' he admitted. 'I really think that the information I've been giving you might make the difference between . . . Oh fuck – hold on!' and he leapt to his feet, stuffed the rest of his falafel wrap into the post box, and ran off up Uxbridge Road, hurtling round into Wood Lane towards the BBC.

But why? Was there a problem with the technical rehearsals for tonight's recording of *Wintravenous*? – we knew that Alonso had a lot riding on the success of this quiz, where contestants could strategically control the pharmaceuticals going into their competitors' drip bags: rounds could last anywhere from 90 seconds to 7 hours, depending upon the drug administered, and at any point contestants could 'play their joker' which meant giving their opponents a massive hit of DMT, which tended to derail their interest in winning the quiz, while giving them a much sharpened understanding of eternity.

Test audiences had been lukewarm, in spite of being given heavy doses of Ritalin and MDMA, and the runner-up from the pilot was still, technically, in a coma. Also, everyone had said they'd thought it was going to be 'winter' themed, which hadn't been the intention, but now the host Bradley Walsh was dressed as Santa Claus and it was proving difficult to stop him punning about 'ho's.

We finished our wraps and sat waiting for Alonso to sprint back. For hours we squatted there, making small talk with the estate agents from Amber & Co who came out to grumble and cry, but no sign of Alonso. Eventually we were shaken awake by a face we recognised: it was Norshaliza from the Malaysian cafe on Portobello Road. She handed us a strange plastic envelope that looked like it might have been regurgitated in the future. 'He came by the cafe this afternoon in a right state, and asked me to give this to you,' she said. 'Then he threw a pile of tablecloths into the street and ran off. If you see him, can you tell him he still has my laptop charger.'

We were sorry that Alonso and Norshaliza weren't still an item, as she was a steadying influence on him and once gave us some free prawn crackers. He was certainly fond of her, but she seemed to be embarrassed, whenever they went out on a date, by his constant PDAs. Perhaps she was unaware that in the future, it is perfectly normal for courting couples to engage in Public Displays of Anus.

Alonso had similar trouble with Danny Upshaw. Danny was a

former accountant who stood around near the Brazilian mini market on Askew Road telling passers-by his theories about Brazil. Danny seemed pleased when Alonso took an interest in his ideas; the two started hanging out together, and one night, in the bus stop opposite the Orchard Tavern, Alonso confided in Danny that he was his BFF – Befriended For Fellatio – and would he agree to be in a minor character in the book we were writing? Provided, of course, he signed an NDA. Danny agreed, without even a basic conception of what a nuclear dildo was, and afterwards was persuaded to sign a non-disclosure agreement. Alonso showed us the document, with a signature dragged across the crumpled page in the style of a post-torture Guy Fawkes.

Later that day we tracked down Danny, hiding under a Subaru on Laurence Mews, and asked if he had any information about Alonso's whereabouts, but he only stopped stimming long enough to suggest 'Brazil'.

Next morning, Charlie got a phone call from Alonso in which he seemed distressed. He'd been let go from Paramount by their new VP of Unscripted Content, Saskia Bloss, who had been turning heads at Warner Media Ad Sales after helming their AdSlang™ programme, after it was felt that Alonso's development slate was non-compatible with Paramount's international pivot away from cannibalism-based formats. He'd bought a tin of Cuprinol Ducksback non-drip wood preserver for sheds and fences and gone on a bender which ended in the car park of Kwik Fit in Wellingborough. 'They let me tidy up in the customer lavatory,' said Alonso. 'They're a nice bunch of lads.'

'Where are you now?' asked Charlie, feigning concern. 'I'm at the war memorial. I'm borrowing Darrin's phone. There's a name inscribed here: W. Hendry — I think it might be significant. What do you think?' Charlie wasn't sure. 'Why don't you get a train back to London? Most days there are sixty-three trains every day from Wellingborough to St. Pancras with a journey time of 57 minutes. I know this because I've been writing on *Tony Hawk's Timetable Teasers* for Radio 4.'

There was a muttered conversation on Alonso's end — Charlie thought he heard someone say 'Just fucking ask him.' Alonso came back on the line: 'What about if Tony has a sidekick. Someone who's a real timetable nerd — some incel school shooter who's on the end of the spectrum that's infrared radiation and microwaves? That might work? Or someone who doesn't give a shit about timetables and is a bit of a lad. Always turns up late for the show. Perhaps someone who's a combination of the two!'

Charlie wasn't sure the BBC would go for any big changes to the format at this late stage, but Alonso pushed hard: 'I've got someone here who would be perfect. Hold on.' There was another conversation. 'And I need five hundred quid, for development, to do a focus group. Can you get me that?' Charlie wasn't sure. 'Okay, two hundred quid, and Darrin is on board as a runner.' Charlie sighed and mumbled, 'Look, I'm not really writing on it, I'm just emailing jokes to the show's email address at the BBC.' Alonso went quiet. 'Okay, forget the show, can you just send a cab to Wellingborough with two hundred quid and leave it behind the bar at the Queen's Head. Put "Louise" on the envelope. Not Darrin. *Louise*. Did you hear that?' Charlie refused. For the next several minutes there was the muffled sound of wrestling, then Alonso, breathing heavily, came back on the line. 'It's okay, he's shut up about the money. Shit, I think the battery's about to go. I need to tell you about Plasticus.'

'What's Plasticus?'

'Mate, you should take the bass out of your voice,' growled Alonso, and Charlie apologised, repeating the question in a lilting and accurate impression of his mother.

'Plasticus is the revenge of the Plastic Continent. The apocalypse within the apocalypse. I had a realisation, halfway through the Cuprinol: I can see now that they sent me back here not to warn people, but to ensure that Plasticus is inevitable. They tricked me. Your book – it causes . . .'

Alonso spoke about Plasticus with a poetic, defeated fury. Some of it was difficult to make out because he was obviously in pain, and speaking quickly, his words tumbling out like artificial hip joints from a pillowcase, as the saying goes (in the future). He told how, in his time as a Frisbee critic on Duxbury Point, he'd heard dark rumours about the ravings of Micronesian squid ticklers and the mad fables told by Pitcairn crab grabbers that something was brewing in the squeaky oceanic swirl.

Sick whispers of a desperate decision made in the plastic council, of a toy hammer brought down with an ominously playful squeak. Glimpses through the swell of welding flashes and strange energy beams. Bewildered seagulls puking new forms of twisting Morgellon threads into the laps of screaming birdwatchers, held hostage in plastic shackles. The undulous roar of giant Lego joints creaking to life. Huge fists formed of fishing tackle and Fanta lids slamming the waves and pledging vengeance. Orange tendons flexing in monstrous plastic knees, as a million smartphone chips coalesced in a cloud-shaking roar of hyperintelligent boredom at the photographs it was having to look at.

'No more!' it boomed in a voice that caused a tidal wave which wasn't quite big enough to cause any noticeable damage to the remnants of Indonesia. And so was born Plasticus: part god, part lavatory seat, part sex yacht escapee, part Hewlett Packard printer cartridge. And his bloody Plastic Reign began, because . . . Charlie doesn't know why. Because Darrin's phone battery ran out.

We've not seen or heard from Alonso since, not a word – not even his usual one-line text message containing the account number and sort code of a massage therapist. However, the folded-up ream of paper in the envelope from Norshaliza was a treasure trove of facts and details about the future, a bit smeared but mostly still legible, and for several days we used it to supplement and correct our account of the future until Frankie left it in an Uber on his way back from a talk by ITV entertainment commissioners at Spearmint Rhino.

We had an emergency lunch at Osteria Napoletana with Shannon from Paramount, hitting the bruschetta with red prawns as hard as we dared. She said she wanted to show us a photo Alonso had sent her. We assumed she'd been included in one of his regular WhatsApp groups and received the standard *Family Guy* clips, conspiracy memes and brass rubbings of his perineum, but this was something different. It looked like a kind of timeline he'd sketched out on the wall of the luggage storage room at Westfield's. Shannon zoomed in. The year 2031 was marked with a hieroglyph of a seated baboon wearing a moon crown, and two words written in heavy, bold letters: KING BABOON. Suddenly it all made sense.

Epilogue

It was roughly two months after we'd submitted this manuscript to our publisher, who suggested cutting as many as all of the words, initially through a lawyer, and later a couple of retired boxers, that we finally heard a rumour about Alonso's whereabouts. It was during a meeting with a producer from Baby Cow, over some koftas at the Shawa Lebanese grill in the Westfield centre. It went well initially, with the producer mentioning he was from Manchester and Frankie saying that he had family there, and that was why he'd never been.

We'd been pitching a drama about a group of moral philosophers who come to the conclusion that it's their duty to start assassinating fossil-fuel executives, and as cover start a petrophysics advisory company focusing on upstream optimisation and coring strategy, ending up as market leaders, and being picked off one by one by a normative ethicist, when Bill Pinch, whose name we should have probably mentioned earlier in the paragraph, revealed that just yesterday, at a 4-hour lunch meeting at Cinquecento pizzeria in Notting Hill, he'd been pitched a similar idea 'but with a much heavier focus on pansexuality and the creation of novel, surgically maintained orifices'.

Frankie's nostrils flared like a bison protecting her young. 'Did he order the arancinetti with Sicilian ragu?' Bill Pinch nodded. 'How many portions?' Bill Pinch held up the index and middle finger of both hands, and used them to write the number four in the air. Charlie's face tightened delightedly like a tickled scrotum. 'Alonso! Tell me . . . could you describe the person who pitched this. Did he seem wretched; condemned; a hot-pad panty prowler?' The award-winning producer, Bill Pinch, nodded vigorously.

His PA arrived. She wore her hair in a firm bob and her foundation so heavy that her face lacked resolution, like she had appeared to offer a clue in a game on the PlayStation Two. From what we could gather from both of them (her name was Daisy Bryant, in case she comes up again), Alonso had been hawking our ideas around London, largely, it seemed, to get the free lunch that a pitch meeting involved.

Daisy flicked open a notebook and read out some of the show ideas. We recognised *Aghast at The News*; *Australian Personality Clinic*; *Celebrity Pogrom* and the Russell Kane-fronted reaction show *Raise My Body From The Crushing Deeps*, among others. 'Speaking of Russell Kane,' said Charlie quietly, 'did he happen to mention *Russell Kane's Body Hair Diaries?*'. Daisy Bryant indicated that he did by saying: 'Yes, he did.'

Charlie brought his fist down onto his special Lebanese salad, and a furious arc of onion and cucumber rose into the air, hovered for an ominous yet beautiful moment at the apex of its flight, then rained around the table like tears in the rain in *Blade Runner*. 'That's *my* idea!' he yelled. 'I can prove it. Do you want me to prove it?' No one did. 'It seems that your friend Alonso is all out of ideas,' said Bill Pinch, with a sigh and a slight frown, which was actually because he'd remembered he was estranged from his brother.

Daisy checked her notes: 'Towards the end of our chat he threw a handful of cherry tomatoes at me and screamed "You'll never see me again," then shoved a meatball in his mouth and ran off crying. He'd left a half-drunk bottle of Tom Ford's Tuscan Leather on the table. I thought it was a new dating show format, but now I'm not so sure.' A text exchange with Saskia Fleiss at Sky Max confirmed it: Alonso was over. And no, she didn't still have Frankie's latex playsuit. She gave it to a charity shop and they sold it as a 'bee-keeper's outfit'.

As a pitcher, Alonso had always had the ability to turn a roomful of strangers into a roomful of angry strangers, and he didn't seem to have any more meetings booked in.

'I do hope he's okay,' said Frankie, who'd learned that this was the sort of thing you said in this situation from various movies and TV shows. 'I certainly hope he's not going to . . .' said Charlie, miming something that nobody else understood, so he said: 'Kill himself.'

'It's more likely he'd kill someone else,' Frankie theorised through a mouthful of lamb, 'especially a woman. Or a man.' They all murmured in agreement as the mango lassis arrived.

Daisy Bryant remembered something with a small jolt. It was that she had forgotten to pay for her driving lessons. Then she remembered something else. 'I know where he is! He's living on the Green! He told me the most animated story full of technical language about how to build a foxhole, raise a tent, dig a trench, and how he had a good view of a Taco Bell. I see now that he must be camping over there; I thought he was describing sex acts.'

'It could well be a mixture of both, or neither,' offered Frankie. 'He has a gift for lurid tent metaphors,' agreed Charlie, 'and he's used it to trick me into hammering his pegs and pinning back his storm flaps more times than I care to remember.'

We were eager to go look for Alonso, who might be in some distress if he was sleeping rough, and we didn't want to miss seeing that. He might even be in some real danger, so we finished our koftas and pickles as quickly as we could, and after dessert and coffee, headed straight for Shepherd's Bush Green.

The Green was a contested space that formed a triangle in the heart of Shepherd's Bush. It was the sort of place you might go to propose marriage, to a taunting voice in your head. The Westfield loomed above it like a forlorn minor temple of Moloch, and the Wild Bean Cafe at the BP garage offered little of comfort except a strange milky liquid that filled those who sheltered there from the near constant rain with poignant memories of coffee. Trees provided a patchy isolation from two busy roads, or an unhelpful amount of hiding places, depending on how you looked at it. It was all right at this time of the evening if you walked through it with confidence, particularly the type that came from being armed.

Psychogeography has long held that Shepherd's Bush Green is modern London's symbolic 'pubic triangle', at the base of the city's Central Line spine (running westwards along the A40 past Tottenham Court Road and through Notting Hill Gate). According to this schemata, the City of London is London's head, Oxford Street is its commercial heart, and Hyde Park its lungs – but Alonso was adamant that this was back to front, and the symbolic figure of London lies with its feet to the east: the Thames is its spewing bowels, the flight paths out of Heathrow its Medusa-like hair, and Shepherd's Bush Green its mouth, from which it vomited the Westfield shopping centre – and that people had been misled into thinking it was London's pudendum by the constant smell of urine: but he pointed out that the urine was always pouring *into* the Green, not out of it, and it simply represented one of London's many kinks. We explained this to Daisy and Bill as they got into a cab. 'Okay, we're going to head off now,' they said, pulling the door shut.

We searched the Green as thoroughly as we could, but there was no sign of Alonso. The constant wafts of urine had triggered Charlie's dicky bladder, and he decided it needed emptying. Of course he was English, so he had to express this in euphemism. Typically for him, the imagery was drawn from Ovid's *Metamorphoses*: 'I have to go and reveal my thunderbolts to Semele,' he murmured.

Frankie was trying to decide whether Charlie was coming out as trans, something he was frankly bored of hearing about anyway, when he saw Charlie darting towards a blue portaloo at the edge of the Green with his trademark upright gait and rearfoot strike running style. As he reached the loo he screamed. Nothing unusual about that. Then Frankie saw that he was waving him over. There, in the dirt just beneath the portaloo door, was a man's head.

'Hello chaps!' chirped Alonso as Frankie arrived, his face at foot height, and caked in dust and mud, at best. 'You've found me!' We all stood chatting and catching up for a while, Alonso for once not asking us for food, apart from some potato chips, which he explained meant crack cut with benzocaine, and maybe some crisps. Eventually the excitement died down and we all looked wistfully across the

Green, Alonso's view of it being dominated by a beetle in the foreground.

'So how did you come to be living underneath this portaloo?' asked Frankie. 'Portaloo?' – Alonso sounded genuinely baffled. Frankie rapped his knuckles on the door by way of demonstration, and an enormous explosion of blue light hurled him backwards where his fall was broken by what we have to assume was once a live springer spaniel. Alonso roared with laughter, and then just roared for a while, and then giggled. 'This isn't a portaloo – it's a time machine!'

'A time machine with a Gents symbol on the front?' asked Charlie, tentatively urinating against it, causing some kind of plasma to skitter up the flow and his penis to flicker in and out of existence not unpleasantly. 'Well, you know my views about women travelling through time!' cried Alonso, and sadly we did.

'You have to see this!' yelled Alonso, pushing up a filthy length of rope that seemed to be attached to him in some way, presumably for us to pull him up. Eventually, after a lot of grunting and straining, we managed to pay off the group of men who pulled him out, and Alonso threw on some clothes from a yellow bum bag around his waist. He bowed deeply and mockingly to us as he turned to run his hands over the portaloo. 'There's a trick to her,' he muttered, but our hearts were heavy as we watched him rub, pat and croon to the unanswering toilet. Occasionally passers-by would glance over, but this behaviour was very much par for the course around here.

Suddenly, with a groan, the door flew open, with Alonso leaping back expertly like an Olympic fencing champion. The inside of the portaloo was a gleaming mess of polished brass: switches; transistors;

valves and bicycle gears. Braids of copper wire crawled like vines around with a thin brass podium revolving slowly in the middle. There was no toilet or basin. Alonso jumped inside and beckoned for us to follow.

'Hello!' said a voice just behind our heads, somewhere above the doorway. 'I'm Mandy, pleased to meet you.' The column turned slightly faster as she spoke.

'Are you the time machine?' Frankie asked. 'Are you Mandy Radio?' There was a tinny laugh. 'I haven't heard that in a while, or won't hear it for a while, it's very difficult in this line of work, tenses.' Everyone laughed awkwardly.

We were crammed into the tiny time machine, as the door sucked shut with a gulping sound. Alonso attempted to gesture proudly at the surroundings, but his arm was trapped under his chin, and it was little more than a waggle of the fingers.

'Don't worry, we won't be travelling through time today,' chortled Mandy Radio, her voice seemingly arriving directly in our heads now. 'You are packed in very tightly, but unless one of you gets an erection and trips one of the leap switches, we should be fine.' Mandy Radio was as bawdy a travelling companion as we'd been led to expect, and perhaps it said something about us that we were surprised to find that she was Welsh.

She began to play a perfect remaster of 'Motivation' by Kelly Rowland, but with the words changed to be about not getting an erection in a time machine, and we found ourselves smiling and nodding along. Mandy seemed to be trying to open the door, so occasionally the lyrics would be about the door being stuck, and really the whole song was a bit of a mess. Slowly the music began to develop a faster, cheesier, electronic backbeat. 'Hang on a minute . . . that's not right . . .' fussed Mandy. 'Sounds a bit like it's been remixed by DJ Carl Cox, but not quite . . . I can't seem to change it . . .'

The music got louder as her voice fretted somewhere in the background. The beat dropped, and we felt a wave of euphoria crash over us. Charlie's anxiety about the lump in his jaw faded away, and Frankie for one brief, extraordinary moment stopped thinking about Kyogo Furuhashi's incredible left foot strike against Rangers, and what he'd say to Kyogo if they were seated next to each other at a wedding. Alonso looked queasy. We grinned over at him, but he could only force the weakest of smiles in return.

His gaze was fixed on the polished brass of the wall in front of him. In it he could see his hastily chosen T-shirt. A vintage depiction of Carl Weathers, as Apollo Creed, his taut physique barely contained by a crop top and shorts. It certainly was an athletic image. Slowly, we all found our gaze drawn towards it.

The music was suddenly louder, and the walls of the cubicle throbbed to the beat. Mandy Radio swore in Welsh as the machine lurched alarmingly underneath us. It seemed to steady itself briefly, and then a flash, another flash, it lurched once more, and we were gone.

Publisher's Note

This epilogue was not delivered as part of *A Short History of The Apocalypse*. It was originally published in a book of short stories by William Somerset Maugham in 1926, and had long been considered one of his worst tales. We are forced to consider the possibility that the authors of *A Short History of the Apocalypse* may have travelled back through time and managed to place their story in the Maugham collection. In favour of this argument is the extraordinary level of congruence with the rest of the text, and the fact that Maugham's story predates the birth of Carl Weathers by twenty years.

In particular, the epilogue shares one perplexing detail with the main manuscript: neither text was written in Spanish. How then are we to make sense of the 'translator's note' with which the manuscript begins? And how is it that Glasgow University claims to have no record of anyone called 'Dr Yoana Azurmendi' in their Spanish department? Has Dr Azurmendi been somehow deleted from existence by time travellers tampering with the very fabric of history?

And what of the authors? Neither man has been seen since the delivery of the manuscript. With Boyle this might be seen as reasonably typical of his career, which seems to have involved various periods of obscurity, including some where he was forced into hiding.

With Skelton also missing, and no sign of him in his usual den in the trees behind the Audi showroom in Tetbury, their disappearance is harder to explain. Ultimately, we feel that whatever relevance or veracity is to be attributed to this epilogue must be left to the judgement of the reader.

Acknowledgements

We would like to thank the estate of Joe Strummer, our editor Yassine, Ruth Phillips, **Ghostface**, our wives and lovers, their wives and lovers, Charlie's catamite Alan McPherson, Alan's wife Carol, and Frank Quitely.

Index

adrenochrome, 98, 233
Affleck, Ben, 275
AIDS, 45, 107, 226, 374, 418, 454
airlines, 173
alcohol, 210–11
aliens, 75
Alley, Kirstie, 215
Althusser, Louis, 330
amochalypse, 231–2
analslaves, 216
Andrew, King of the United Kingdom, 240–2, 342
Anglesea Arms, Wingate Road, 262–3
Ann Summers, 79
Anne, Princess Royal, 15
antibiotics, 45
Antipope, 76
Antwerp Thunderdome Disaster, 318
apocalypse lifestyle consultants, 97
Appalling Place, The, *see* United States
aquaponics, 160

aristocracy, 80–4
Armstrong, Alexander, 25
Aroma Buffet, W12, 343–4
art, 303, 304
artificial intelligence (AI), 13, 27, 33–5; art and literature, 303–4, 314–15; brain implants, 447–51; bunker entertainment systems, 101; child porn and, 384; Desimulators and, 51; employment and, 303, 314; fascism and, 52; Mandy Radio, *436*, 439–46, 493–6, 508, 521; Matrix, 60; news reporting, 337; *Otago* incident, 76, 77; plumbing and, 180; whale song translation, 282
Asphixicore, 298–9
Atlantic City Suicide, 181
Attack Plan Zebra, 36–9

Austen, Jane, 305
Australia, 36, 245
Austria, 244
Aztecs, 54, 414–26, 505

Bad Boyz for Life, 167–70
badminton, 355
BAE Systems, 29
bagels, 55
Balmoral Castle, Aberdeenshire, 105, 240
Banaadiri, Shepherd's Bush, 332
Bandicoot, 157
Bannister, Roger, 322
Barr, Roseanne, 215
Barren Caves, California, 447–8
Baskin-Robbins, 296
Basque seafood gangs, 167–70
Batman, 289
bears, 486–91
Belgium, 48–9
Belize, 415

529

Beluga, Notting Hill, 300
Belushi's, Hammersmith, 476
benzocaine, 519
Bezos, Jeff, 103, 509
Bhutan, 80–1, 245
Big Bang Theory, The, 304
Big Ben, 382
billionaires: bunkers, 97–106; escape plans of, 8, 36, 75
birdwatching, 132
Blackpool Pleasure Beach, 341
Blade Runner (1982 film), 517
Blasted Country, The, *see* United States
Blod, 279–82
Bocconi's, Shepherd's Bush, 59, 93–7
bodyguards, 74, 97, 102–4, 426
Boko Haram, 322–3
Bon Jovi, Jon, 402–3
Bono, 74
book burnings, 305
Boyle, Frankie: bagel preferences, 55; Batman, views on, 289; Brackenbury Gardens incident, xix–xx; chemical peel, 183; Chinese philosophy, study of, 38; condom drop technique, 117–18; dogging hobby, 16; fan categorisation system, 17; Kenjutsu skills, 344–5; latex playsuit, 517; orgy phone theft incident, 9, 11; radio work, 406; rectal prolapse, 38; self-harm, 117; television work, 16, 17, 151–2, 183, 191, 316, 446; Westfield urination incident, xii; Zendaya, relationship with, xviii–xix
Brackenbury Wine Rooms, Hammersmith, 502–3
Brady, Ian, 183
brain chips, 313–14, 447–51, 455
Branson, Richard, 5, 49–50; ant mind-swap operation, 110–11; bunker oxygen training, 99–100; clone brigade, 426–32; consciousness upload, 455–7; Creepy Fucker™, 315; death of, 50, 75–8, 431, 455–7; *Tubular Bells IV*, 49–50; Virgin Atlantic Sex Ferries, 349–57; World War VI, 296–7
Brazil, 207, 237, 511
BrewDog, Shepherd's Bush, 426, 432
Bristow, Eric, 387
British Museum, 294
Brunelleschi, Filippo, 128
BTS, 156
Bublé, Michael, 264
bubonic plague, 43, 67
Buckingham Palace, London, 104
Buddhism, 68
Bulgaria, 244
Bunify, Shepherd's Bush, 213
bunkers, 97–106; bodyguards, 102–4; cascades of, 103–4; entertainment systems, 100–1; 'jacket in the air vents problem', 99; pre-apocalypse tests, 101
Burke, Edmund, 3
Burley, Kay, 152
busking, 74
Butler, Judith, 66
buttock implants, 380–1
buttplugs, 216

Cafe 2000, Hammersmith, 123
Café Louche, Shepherd's Bush, 222–3
Caffè Bonego, Goldhawk Road, 21
Caffè Concerto, Westfield, 316
Caffè Nero, Shepherd's Bush, 229–35
calendars, 20, 85–8

Canary Islands, 67–8, 297
cannibalism, 5, 209, 221–2, 226–47; athletic cannibals, 236–7; autophagy, 244; bring a body raves, 227–8; deliveries, 239–40; elites, 240–4; entertainers and, 308; guilt, 306; high and low forms, 238–9; of loved ones, 237–8; 'mini-mes', 238
Canvey Island arcade fire-bombings, 320
Capaldi, Lewis, 191
Cape Neddick Country Club, 410–11
capital punishment: hanging, 69, 129, 137; roasting alive, 81; supple tree method, 56, 64
Capuchins, 60–2
car jackers, 213–15
carpentry, 4, 19, 369
cartography, 84–5
Catholic Church, 60–2, 243, 255
Chapman, Graham, 70
Chappell, Steve, 158
Cheddar rape pits, 83
chemical peels, 183
Chepstow Biker Gangs, 103
Chicago Grill, Hammersmith, 367, 370–3

chicken bhuna, 159–60
Chicken Rabies, 473
child porn, 383–8
China, 22, 27, 36–43; American Wars, 36–8, 43, 297, 411, 460–2; Anglo-Chinese War, 40–3; brain implant fantasies, 449–51; bubonic plague, release of, 43, 67; cannibalism in, 244–5; Great Walls, maze of, 39–40; New Zealand, bombing of, 36; nuclear war, 128–9; Spanish language, purchase of, 315
choking, 214, 291, 435
Christianity: Capuchin Gaytrix, 60–2; Church of England, 68; fisting chair of Jesus, 369; gangs, 176–7; Gospel of Nicodemus Jr, 67; murder-suicides, 129; Seventh-Day Atheists, 399–405
Church of England, 68
Churchill's Fish & Chips, Pitsea, 321
Cibo, Hammersmith, 447
Cinquecento pizzeria, Notting Hill, 515
Clarence House Carnival, 240

Clark, Rylan, 183
climate change, 39, 373
Club 12–93, 253–4
Club Shrimpthanasia, 254–5
cockroaches, 107–8
comedy, 302, 320–3, 333
condom drop technique, 117–18
conspiracy theories, 74
coprophilia, 119, 122–4, 154
coracles, 392
Corden, James, 72–3, 305
Cornish pasties, 237
Cornwall, 342
cosplay, 486–8
Cotton, Fearne, 66
Cox, Carl, 228, 522
Cracknell, James, 151
Crips, The, 194
cryptozoology, 137
Cumberbatch, Benedict, 307
Cursed Isles, *see* United Kingdom
Cursed Wastelands, *see* France
cushions, 379–80
Cyprus, 257–74

Daily Telegraph, 50
dairy products, 224–6
DARPA, 29, 313, 407
darts, 383–90
Datca Meze Bar, Shepherd's Bush Road, 274

Davison, Emily, 307
Death, 305–6
Deepak Food & Wine, Hammersmith, 123
deepfakes, 13
Deleuze, Gilles, 275
Deller, Keith, 387
dementia, 138, 195–7
Denaissance, 63
Denmark, 74, 81, 278, 387
dentistry, 464–8
Deripaska, Oleg, 74
Derrida, Jacques, 444
Desimulators, 50–2
despair, 5, 6, 7, 138, 409; bunkers and, 101; lynchings and, 258
Devine Jr, Raymond, 216
diabetes, 496, 498
Dickens, Charles, 305
Dioxin!, 27
Disembowelmania, 317
Disfigurement, 118, 125
Disney, Walt, 505
Disney Child Army, xviii–xix
Disneyland, 503–6
DMT, 175, 509
DNCE, 336–7
dogging, 16, 322
dogs, 492–3
Dommett, Joel, 66
Doncaster firebombing, 388
Dough & So, Uxbridge Road, 178–80

Dow Chemical PepsiCo Alliance, 27
drones, 33–5, 132
Dudley, West Midlands, 342
Duffield, Norman, 75–6
Dunkirk Beach Party, 319
DVDs, 13
dysentery, 119, 225, 306, 352, 496

Edinburgh Festival, 364–6
Edmonds, Noel, 242
Edward Scissorhands (1990 film), 53
Edward, Duke of Edinburgh, 15
Eiffel Tower, Paris, 294
8 Out of 10 Cats, 71
electromagnetic holocaust, 47
Elephant Führer, 279
Eliot, Thomas Stearns, 443
elites: bunkers, 97–106; cannibalism, 240–4; escape plans of, 8, 36, 75; hunting of, 81–2
Elizabeth II, Queen, 82–3
Elliott, Missy, 298
Endemol, 152, 158, 355
entertainers, 307–10, 325–9, 332–3
environmental movement, 484
Epstein, Jeffrey, 505
Esalen Institute, 50–2
Estonia, 276–7, 455–7

Ethiopia, 344
European Commission, 48–9
Eurovision Song Contest, 191
euthanasia, 140, 163, 197, 254, 358, 380, 467, 488–91
exotic dancing, *286*, 301–2

Facebook, 52, 86
faeces: coprophilia, 119, 122–4, 154; dissuasion method, 209–10; dysentery, 119, 225, 306, 352, 496; sewage facilities, 181; synchronisation of bowels, 306
Fallon, Jimmy, 296
famine, 5, 39, 225, 227, 322
Fayed, Dodi, 7–8
fentanyl, 283
Ferrigno, Lou, 5
film industry, 260, 303–4
'Final Countdown, The' (Europe), 30
Finland, 416
fisting chairs, 368
Fitness First, Hammersmith, 97
Flanagan, Micky, 157
flat earth theory, 74
fondue, 225–6
food, 221–47; cannibalism, 5, 209, 221–2,

226–47; dairy products, 224–6
Foot Locker, 295
'for the table', 70
Forbidden Lands, 208
Fragrance Shop, Shepherd's Bush, 14–16
France, 3, 12, 245–7, 294, 304
Frazer/Osato formula, 70–1
fuck hats, 95, 96
Funky Mussel, 400
Furuhashi, Kyogo, 522

Gabriel, Peter, 296
Gatting, Mike, 417
Gaudí, Antoni, 294
Gaytrix, 60–2
Gaza War (2023–), 151
Gdańsk Dog Show, 118, 125
genocide, 28, 130
George & Dragon, Barnsley, 385–6
Germany, 116, 118–28, 244
gerontophilia, 197
ghost towns, 458–60
Gibraltar, xiii, 20, 65, 234, 253, 334–7, 343
Glastonbury Festivals, 87
Glaztecs, 54–5
Global Seed Vault, 279–80
Gnostics, 383–90
Goddamnit, 232–3

Goebbels, Magda, 275
Golden State Theatre, Monterey, 298
Gone with the Wind (1939 film), 304
Gospel of Nicodemus Jr, 67
Gourmet Burger Kitchen, Westfield, 315
Grab-Rub-Twist, 263–4
Grand Rape, Arizona, 505
Great Contamination, Second, 475
Great Crater of Calgary, 486–7
Great Geomagnetic Reversal Nightmare, 260
Great Lake of London, 373
Great Mistake, 80
Great Pacific Garbage Patch, 33, 432
Great Poisoning of the Tyne, 312
Great Purge of the Stonemasons, 142
Great Stunting, 18
Great Upheaval, 251
Greece, 244
Groundhog Day (1993 film), 304
group therapy, 200–1
Guatemala, 414–18
Guattari, Félix, 275
Guetta, David, 63, 227–8, 330, 502
guillotines, 19, 251–2

Gurdjieff, George, xvi
Gyllenhaal, Jake, 323

Habermas, Jürgen, 66
haemostatic dressings, 6
Hamas, 25
Hampton Bastards, 176
Hampton Court Hangings, 240
'Happy Birthday', 49
Happy Lovespreaders, The, 260–74
Harriott, Ainsley, 151
Harry, Duke of Sussex, 500
Harvard University, 439, 506
Haunted Plains, The, *see* United States
Hawaii, 295, 296–7
healthcare, 253
Heaney, Seamus, 296
Hegel, Georg Wilhelm Friedrich, 124
Heidelberg drone cleansings, 120
Heimlich Manoeuvre, 291
Helsinki, virtual, 330–1
Hemsworth, Chris, 116, 118
Henley Regatta, 194
heroin, 401, 403
herring, 279
Higgis, Graham, 373–7
Hillingdon rat folk, 376–8
Hilton, Paris, 383
Hinduism, 68

Hinkley Point, 357, 361, 363
Hippos, 154
hipsterism, 13
history; historians, 156, 307
Hitler, Adolf, 280
Hollywood Bowl Bloodbath, 32
Hollywood, Paul, 157
Holocaust 2.0, 127–8
Hong Tin, Hammersmith, 434–5
Hook's Chill & Grille, Ogunquit, 411
House of Commons, 381–3
How To Fuck a Wasp (Feng), 108
How To Unhook a Wasp Barb (Feng and Reynolds), 110
Huddersfield Plague Pits, 389
Hull, Rod, 157
human hunting, 484
humanism, 128–9
Hume, David, xvi
Hungary, 244
Hunt, Jeremy, 382
hunting, 81–2, 484
Huttonsville braille hills, 457

Ibis Hotel, Shepherd's Bush, 10
Ibiza, 187
Idol, Billy, 404
Illuminati sex yachts, 33, 507
Imbruglia, Natalie, 195
Improverts, 364–7
India, 36, 68, 294–5
Indonesia, 514
infinity, 135, 139–40
insect sex, 107–10
International Cuddles, 29
International Holocaust Waterpark, 482
International Peace Garden, 482–3
internet, 52–5, 485
Iran, 201
Ireland, 201–2, 394
Irredeemable Land, The, *see* United States
ISIS, 493–6
Islam, 6, 9, 67
Israel, 151, 495
It's a Royal Knockout, 14–15
Italy, 244

Jackson, Michael, 29–30
Japan, 244, 245
Jaunty Boys, 332–3
jellyfish, 257
Jepsen, Carly Rae, 32
Jerusalem, 505
Jesus, 67, 369
Jetts, Hammersmith, 263
Jews, 67–8, 74, 104
JFK International Airport, 173
Jones, Grace, 25
Jordan, 67
Joshua, Anthony, 181
Judaism, 67–8

Kane, Russell, 516
Kant, Immanuel, 8
karaoke, 49
Kennecott, Alaska, 458
Kensington Reckoning, 240
Kenya, 344
Kerrygold, 153
Kettering Town FC, 239
kidnappings, 171–2
King Baboon, 514
Knights Templar, 257, 506
Kruskal's Tree Theorem, 304
Kumar, Nish, 355
Kuti, Fela, 88

'L'Esperanza' (Airscape), 68
La Crema Grill, Shepherd's Bush, 276
La Palma, Canary Islands, 297
La Rochefoucauld, François, de 408
Laing, Ronald David, 264
Lake Manitoba, 474–6
Lambeth Suicide Cauldrons, 381
Larès, Maurice, 118
Larsson, Åsa, 1
Last Redoubt, The, *see* United States
Latvia, 244, 277–8, 416
laundry gangs, 474–6

Lawrence, Thomas Edward, 118
Le Petit Citron, Shepherd's Bush Road, 175–8
leatherette bookmarks, 192–3
Lego, 161, 221, 505, 508, 513
leprosy, 244, 374
Let's Just Call It Chicken™, 239
Letchworth Garden City, 505
Lewis, Martin, 264
Library of Strasbourg, 118
life expectancy, 197
Lighthouse of Alexandria, 155
Lil Nas X, 31, 72–3
Lil' Flip, 195
Linekers Bar, Tenerife, 67–8
Lion AIDS, 374
literacy, 142–6, 177–8, 307
literature; writing, 303, 304–5; artificial intelligence and, 314–15; erotica, 177–8; Library of Strasbourg, 118; memorials, 142–6
Lithuania, 282–3
Little Egg Harbor, New Jersey, 181–2
'Little Miss Muffet', 311
Little Napoli, Shepherd's Bush, 393

Liz Café, Hammersmith, 497
lobotomies, 196
lobsters, 1, 18, 296, 320, 399, 402–5, 411–12
Lockheed Martin, 28–9
London College of Fashion, 183, 191, 222–3
Longshanks Cookbook, 242
Look Who's Talking Too (1990 film), 215
looting, 212
Loris Community Gardens, Hammersmith, 497
Los Molinas, Brook Green, 26
Louisiana Singing Cannibals, 312
Louvre, Paris, 304
Luton, *see* Unhallowed Zone
Luxembourg, 82, 125, 295
luxury relaxation gangs, 162–3
Lyme Regis sex vaudeville, 158
lynchings, 258–9

MacDowell, Andie, 304
McIlroy, Brian, 323–5
McIntyre, Michael, 73
Maison Souss, Shepherd's Bush, 154
Majestic Wine, Shepherd's Bush, xix
Majorca, 194

Malaysia, 115, 448, 488, 510
Man-Rat, 469–74
man's inhumanity to man™, 129
Manchester, rewilding of, 342
Mandy Radio, *436*, 439–46, 493–6, 508, 521–2
Mangan, Stephen, 501
Mar Mar cafe, Shepherd's Bush, 289–92
Margaret, Countess of Snowdon, 104
Marley, Bob, 330
Mars, escape to, 8
Marvell, Andrew, 129
Master Bao, Westfield, 301
masturbation, 178, 408–14
Masturbatrix, 408–14
mathematics, 136, 139–41
Matrix, 60, 400
Matterhorn, Saudi purchase of, 78, 79
media, 302
Meghan, Duchess of Sussex, 500
memorials, 142–6
memory balls, 173
memory shed, 388
Mencius, 38–9
Merrick, Adolf, 279
Metaverse, 86, 330
Miami, submersion of, 451–4

Michelangelo, 63
microplastics, 137–8, 507
Mill Creek, West Virginia, 457–8
Mills, Scott, 316
Milton Keynes Dons FC, 239
Minajmas, 86
molestation, 161–2, 163–4, 259–74
monkeys, 66, 292, 334–7, 347
Moses, 68
Motor Neurone Disease, 216
mountain climbing, 133
Mr Falafel, Shepherd's Bush, 509
Mrs Chew's Chinese Kitchen, Westfield, 298
Murray, Judy, 117
Musk, Elon, 29–30, 50–2, 313–14, 427–8
Mussolini, Benito, 256
mutually assured destruction, 27–8
Muyang Hot Pot, Shepherd's Bush, 187, 190–1, 192
Myrmidons, 505

Namibia, SSPDFCKIR, 84–5
Navy SEAL, 445–6
Nazism, 202, 279–83
Necker Island, 50, 296
necrophilia, 106, 115–16, 119–21, 124–8
Nelson, Willie, 32
neo-neo-Nazis, 279–83
Nepal, 244–5
Nespresso, Westfield, 299–300
Netflix, 366, 371–3, 406
New Amazonians, 105
New Hell, *see* United States
New Jersey, 181–2
New Troy, 283–5
New York, 194–5
New Zealand, 36
Newcastle United FC, 296
Newman, Cathy, 446
news, 337
Nigeria, 296, 322–3
Night of the Long Buttplugs, 216
Norfolk, 382
Northern Ireland, 12
Norway, 244, 278–82
nuclear dildos, 511
nuclear power stations, 278–9, 363
nuclear weapons, 20, 27, 80, 85, 97, 129–30, 294–7, 495
nursery rhymes, 310–13
nutmeg, 295

O'Leary, Dermot, 25
octopuses, 409–10, 412–13
offalphilia, 240
Oldfield, Mike, 50
opium, 42, 104, 389
Orchard Tavern, Shepherd's Bush, 511
orgasm, 144, 177, 179, 268, 272; Gaytrix, 60; God's finger, 294; heat death of Universe and, 442; jellyfish technique, 257; Masturbatrix, 413, 414; refractory period, 423; synchronisation of, 202; Virgin Sex Ferry disaster, 352; wasps, 108
orgies, 332
Osman, Richard, 66
Osteria Napoletana, Notting Hill, 514
Ottolenghi, Yotam, 55
Owl AIDS, 454

P. Diddy, 167–8
paedophilia, 25, 136, 342, 383–8
Paine, Thomas, 3
Pakistan, 36, 295
Palace of Westminster, 381–3
Palestine, 151, 495
Paltrow, Gwyneth, 296
Paralympic Games, 27
Parthenon, Athens, 294
parties, 331–2
Pasadena Caliphate, 493
PCP, 45, 138, 233–4, 376, 377, 416, 447
Pegg, Simon, 481–2

PepsiCo, 27, 105
perineal piercings, 191
Perkins, Sue, 264
Peru, 295
Phaedrus (Plato), xvi
pharmaceutical industry, 45
Philip, Duke of Edinburgh, 83
Philippines, 296
pickles, 7
piercings, 191, 223
Pig & Whistle, Bramley Road, 135
pig sex industry, 107
Pilates, 12–13
Pinch, Bill, 516–17
Pine, Sam, 152
Pinterest, 53
Pizza Express, Shepherd's Bush, 482
Plastic Continent, 432, 505, 507, 512–14
plastic surgery, 381
Plato, xvi
plumbing, 180–1
Poland, 126
Polynesia, 295
poppers, 209
Pornhub, 177
pornography, 13–14, 133, 305, 314, 367–70, 486
Portugal, 47
potato salad, 405
PR (public relations), 258–9
Prague Techno Crematorium, 227

prepping, 97–106
Presbyterian Church, 176–7
proxy world war, 26–35
Prussia, 116, 118–28
psychogeography, 518–19
Ptolemaic calendar, 85–6
Public Displays of Anus, 510
Public Enemy, 371
public urination, xi–xii

Qatar, 295
Quartermasters, 222
Qur'an, 6, 9

racism, 202–4, 279–83
Raj of India, Hammersmith, 432
Ramsay, Gordon, 73
Rape Heights, 505
Raphinha, 237
rat folk, 376–8
Ravenscourt Park, West London, 207
ravine jumping, 131–2
reading, advice on, xvi–xviii; family, ostracism from, 5; flinging and altercations, 1–3; leatherette bookmarks, 192–3; legal disclaimers, xvi–xviii, xx; note taking, 5; single sitting page limits, xvi; yoga and hydration, xvi

Red Bull, 382–3
Reed, Lou, 128
refractory period, 423
refugees, 130–1
reggae music, 329–31
revenge pornography, 133
Revenge Zoo, Disneyland, 504
rewilding, 342, 484
Reynolds, Jason, 110
Reynolds, Ryan, 371
Rhodes, 254
Rights of Man (Paine), 3
rim jobs, 138
Ritalin, 510
Rock, Chris, 28
Rocky Mountain sodomy debates, 483
Rodrigo, Olivia, 31, 44
Rooster's Grill, Shepherd's Bush, 468
Rosalind of Dundee, 505
Rotherham, Yorkshire, 341
Roti Joupa, Shepherd's Bush, 355
Rouxel, Yvonne, 191–2, 222–3
Rowland, Kelly, 227, 330, 521
Royal Family, 80, 82–4; Buckingham Palace bunker, 104–5; cannibalism, 240; occult perversion, 83–4; skiing, 198; Windsor crypts, pillaging of, 82–3

royal hunts, 81–2
Royal Leamington Spa, Warwickshire, 341
Royal Press Gangers, 40
Royal Scots Dragoon Guards, 507
Russia, 52, 128–9, 194, 245
Ryan, Katherine, 446

S Club 7, 151
sadomasochism, 199–200
Salisbury Cathedral, 294
saltimbocca, 59–62
Samaritans, 358
sambuca, 254
samosas, 290–1
San Pandemico, 505
Sandler, Adam, 366, 372–3
Sandringham firebombing, 240
Sardinia, 255
SAS Fantasist Unit, 41–3
Saudi Arabia, 78, 275
Savannah, Goldhawk Road, 344
Savile, Jimmy, 104
Saving Private Ryan (1998 film), 303
Savoy Opera, 200
Saxe-Coburg-Gotha, house of, *see* Royal Family
Saxony Gambit, 118, 125
schools, 137
Schopenhauer, Arthur, 316
science, 136–8
Scientology, 215
Scotland, 245
Scottish Wastes, 54
Screaming Branson, 75–8
scrotal piercings, 191, 223
seagull & chips, 242
Senegalese sex auctions, 201
Seoul Bird, Westfield, 165–70
serial killers, 69–70, 75–6, 183, 469
seven basic virginities, 165–6
Seventh-Day Atheists, 399–405
Severn Death Jetties, 357–63
sewage systems, 181
Shabab Grill House, Shepherd's Bush, 277
Shawa Lebanese grill, Westfield, 515
Sheeran, Ed, 31, 74
Sheffield Sex Corridor, 367–70
Shepton Mallet Ornithological Society, 187
Shikumen, Shepherd's Bush, 97, 390–1
Shites of Aylesbury, 194
shove ha'penny, 47
Sir Barksalot, 492–3, 495
Sistine Chapel, 294

Skelton, Charlie: anal grip, 263; bagel preferences, 55; Batman, views on, 289; Brackenbury Gardens incident, xix–xx; cage dancer, work as, xiii; Copenhagen, 278; fragrance preferences, 16; mechanophilia, 158–9; Online Travel Industry Awards, 316; refractory period, 423; television work, 14–15, 16, 66, 94–5, 152, 481; tree-planting fraud, 402; skiing, 78, 80, *148*, 198–9
Sleepers, 433–4
Smash Mouth, 195
sniffer dogs, 492–3
social credit systems, 45
social media, 52–5, 485
Somalia, 344
Spain, 20, 167–70, 182–7, 244, 253
Spanish language, 315
Spearritt, Hannah, 151
Special Air Squadron (SAS), 40–3
sphinctoid planet theory, 74
Statham, Jason, 190
Stavrovouni Corpse Storage Facility, 260
Stefani, Gwen, 157
Stewart, Bob, 158
Stigers, Curtis, 319

Sting, 28
Stoke-on-Trent triads, 389
stonemasons, 142
storytellers, 172, 308–10
Strummer, Joe, 402–3
Suchet, David, 320–1
suicide, 73–4, 357–63, 400
supermarkets, 161–2
surfers, 221
survivalism, 4, 6, 235–6
Susquehannock State Forest, 195–7
Sutcliffe, Peter, 183
Sweden, 244
sweet chilli sauce, 65–6, 343
Swift, Taylor, 31–2
Switzerland, 244
syphilis, 341
Syria, 257

Taj Mahal, 294–5
Tangerine Dream, 428–30
Tapas Revolution, Westfield, 255–6
Tapton Hall, Sheffield, 370
tarot, 283–4
Tasmania, 138
teenagers, 331
Tenerife, Canary Islands, 67–8, 297
terrorism, 322–3
Thailand, 245
theatre, 307–10, 325–9
third eyes, 138

Thousand Plateaus, A (Deleuze and Guattari), 275
thunderdomes, 12, 158, 182, 184, 317–19, 483–5, 506
time machine, *436*, 442–6, *478*, 521–2
Titan submersible implosion (2023), 481
Titanic, prostitutes on, 6
Tonga, 498
topical comedy, 302, 320–3, 333
town criers, 302–3
Toyota Motor Corporation, 505
Trader Joe's, 162
traffic wardens, 259
travel industry, 253–5, 297–8
travelling performers, 307–10, 325–9, 333
trepanning, 196–7
Trump family, 105
tsunamis, 297–8, 337
Turkey, 244, 283–5
Turner, Tina, 403
Turtle Mountains, 475–6
Twain, Shania, 355
Twitter, 52
Tyrolean Jousting, *148*, 198–9

UB40, 76
Über-Holocaust, 127
Unhallowed Zone, 229–30

Unholy Wastes, *see* Norfolk
United Kingdom, 12, 29, 339–94; aristocracy, 80, 81, 82–4, 104–5, 198, 240–3, 342; cartography, 85; Chinese War, 40–3; cuisine, 240–3; gangs in, 187–91, 194; SAS Fantasist Unit, 41–3; television industry, 320
United Nations, 25–6, 27
United States, 12, 26–8, 394, 399–435, 439–77; Asphixicore scene, 298–9; Atlantic City Suicide, 181; China, wars with, 36–9, 44, 411, 460–2; civil wars, 36; defence budget, 26–7; Disneyland, 503–6; genocide, policies on, 28; ghost towns, 458–60; Miami, submersion of, 451–4; monarchy, 27; nuclear war, 128–9; proxy world war, 26–35; Sleepers, 433–4; vigilantes, 469–74
University of Swansea, 373
Unjust Desert, The, *see* United States
Upshaw, Danny, 510

vaginas, boobytrapping of, 216
Valencia, Spain, 253
vampires, 342
Van Buuren, Armin, 68
Van Damme, Jean-Claude, 49
Vatican, 243, 296
Vauxhall Insignia, 118–19
Vauxhall Soup Kitchens, 381
Velcro-burn, 240
Venus de Milos, 304
Viagra, 46
Victoria, Queen, 104
Vietnam, 245
vigilantes, 469–74
Villagrán, Jérôme 'Babyface', 134–5
Vilnius, Lithuania, 282–3
Virgin Atlantic Sex Ferries, 349–57
Virgin Mind Transfer, 110–11
Virgin Records, 49–50, 76
Virgin Stool Samples, 100
Virginia Tech massacre (2007), xvi
virginities, seven basic, 165–6
virtual reality (VR), 22, 86, 100–1, 337
Vishnu, 477

Volgograd, Russia, 194
volleyball, 319
Vulture Towns, 504–5

Wales, 376–7, 391–4
Walmart, 296
Walsh, Bradley, 510
wasps, 108
Way of the Dragon, The (1972 film), 38
Weathers, Carl, 523
weddings, 184–7
Weeknd, The, 31, 44
Welensky, Gary, xix, xx
West Virginia, 457–8
West Wittering Yacht Club, 154
Wetherspoons, 129
whales, 281–2
Wharton, Edith, xvi
Wheel, The, 73
Whole Foods, 162
Whores' Corner, Putney, 6
Willoughby, Holly, 153
Wilson, Jocky, 390
Wimbledon Tennis Championships, 86
Windsor Castle: crypts, 82; leper colony, 374; Longshanks Cookbook, 242
Winkleman, Claudia, 94–5

Wiz Khalifa, 264
wolves, 80, 225
Woody's Grill, Shepherd's Bush, 405, 408
World Obliteration Trust, 28
World's Strongest Man, 174, 505
Worsening, The, 409
writing-room lunch ordering, 70–2

Xenakis, Iannis, 503
Xerxes VII of Letchworth Garden City, 505

yells; yelling: bunker test subjects, 101; '*Este no es el futuro!*', xiii; gang lords, 201; 'Goddamnit', 232–3; improv shows, 367; ravine jumpers, 131; Screaming Branson, 75–8; Sleepers, 433
Yoga Slut series, 14

Zendaya, xviii–xix
Zeus, 272–3
Zizzi's, Westfield, 245
zombies, 106–7, 442
zoophilia, 107–10, 126, 257, 266
Zuckerberg, Mark, 315
Zulu Nation, 104